Carol Ericson is a bests[eller] [autho...writt...]re than forty books. S[he has an eerie] fascination for [tru]e-crime stories, a love of film noir and a weakness [for] reality TV, all of which fuel her imagination to create [her] own tales of murder, mayhem and mystery. To find [out] more about Carol and her current projects, please [visi]t her website at www.carolericson.com, 'where [rom]ance flirts with danger.'

[USA] TODAY bestselling author **Barb Han** lives in north [Tex]as with her very own hero-worthy husband, three [bea]utiful children, a spunky golden retriever/standard [poo]dle mix and too many books in her to-read pile. In [her] downtime, she plays video games and spends much [of h]er time on or around a basketball court. She loves [inte]racting with readers and is grateful for their support. [Yo]u can reach her at barbhan.com

Discover more at millsandboon.co.uk

ROOKIE INSTINCTS

CAROL ERICSON

TEXAS TARGET

BARB HAN

MILLS & BOON

First Published in Great Britain 2020
by Mills & Boon, an imprint of HarperCollins*Publishers*
1 London Bridge Street, London, SE1 9GF

Rookie Instincts © 2020 Harlequin Books S.A.
Texas Target © 2020 Barb Han

Special thanks and acknowledgement are given to Carol Ericson for her contribution to the *Tactical Crime Division: Traverse City* series.

ISBN: 978-0-263-28053-1

1120

ROOKIE INSTINCTS

CAROL ERICSON

Prologue

The wind whipped off the lake, its chilly tentacles snaking into his thin black jacket, which he gathered at the neck with one raw hand, stiff with the cold. His other hand dipped into his pocket, his fingers curling around the handle of the gun.

His eyes darted toward the dark, glassy water and the rowboat bobbing against the shore before he stepped onto the road...and behind his prey.

She hobbled ahead of him, her shoes crunching the gravel, her body tilted to one side as she gripped her heavy cargo, which swung back and forth, occasionally banging against her leg.

A baby. *Nobody said nothing about a baby.*

He took a few steps after her and the sound of his boots grinding into the gravel seemed to echo through the still night. He froze.

When her footsteps faltered, he veered back into the reeds and sand bordering the lake. He couldn't have her spotting him and running off. What would she do with the baby? She couldn't run carrying a car seat. He'd hauled one of those things before with his niece inside and it wasn't no picnic, even though Mindy was just a little thing.

He crept on silent feet, covering three or four steps to her one until he was almost parallel with her. Close enough to hear her singing some Christmas lullaby. Close enough to hear that baby gurgle a response.

The chill in the air stung his nose and he wiped the back of his hand across it. He licked his chapped lips.

Nobody said nothing about a baby.

The girl stopped, her pretty voice dying out, the car seat swinging next to her, the toys hooked onto the handle swaying and clacking. She turned on the toes of her low-heeled boots and peered at the road behind her, the whites of her eyes visible in the dark.

But he wasn't on the road no more.

He stepped onto the gravel from the brush that had been concealing him. Her head jerked in his direction. Her mouth formed a surprised *O*, but her eyes knew.

When he leveled his weapon at her, she didn't even try to run. Her knees dipped as she placed the car seat on the ground next to her feet.

She huffed out a sigh that carried two words. "My baby."

He growled. "I ain't gonna hurt the baby."

Then he shot her through the chest.

The sound of the shot buffeted his eardrums, and a few birds screeched and took flight, but there was nobody here to help her or her baby…just him.

The girl had crumpled to the ground, her knees drawn up, her hand flung out to the side, inches from the car seat. If her lullaby had put the baby to sleep, the gunshot had awakened him and he wailed as if he knew his momma was gone.

He shuffled forward and hovered over the body. Brushing aside the brown hair that had swept across her neck, he placed a finger at her throat. Her pulse had stopped. Her song had ended.

With the sound of the gunshot dead in the night, the baby's howls faded into squishy, blubbery sobs.

"Shh. Don't cry, little buddy." All babies looked the same to him, but this one had a blue beanie on his head and a blue blanket dotted with panda bears tucked around his body. His sister always dressed her daughter in pink just so everyone would know she was a girl.

The baby hiccupped and put a knuckle in his mouth, his blue watery eyes wide.

"That's it, little buddy. I ain't gonna leave you out here for long." He retrieved a crumpled tissue from the front pocket of his jeans and dabbed the baby's damp cheeks and runny nose. He didn't bother to blot the blood spots on the blanket.

Then he shoved his hand into his cheap jacket and withdrew a plastic bag, whispery smooth between his fingers. He wiped off his fingerprints with the edge of his shirt and, still pinching the bag with fingers poked into his shirt, leaned over the dead girl and tucked the bag of Dance Fever in her purse. The bullet hadn't touched the strap. It remained crossed over her body, soaked with the blood still oozing from her chest.

"Just a few more minutes, little buddy." He dipped into his pocket once more and pulled out the burner phone they'd given him. They should've said something about the baby at the same time.

He flipped up the phone and called 9-1-1. When the operator answered, he pitched his voice low and scratchy. "Yeah, there's a baby in a car seat down by the lake all by himself. Looks abandoned."

"Where are you sir? Is the baby hurt?"

He gave the operator directions to the gravel road snaking beside the lake, flipped the phone shut and walked back to his boat, whistling the lullaby.

Chapter One

Humming off-key, Aria punched the elevator button with her knuckle and then wiped her clammy palms on the thighs of her black slacks. When the doors whispered open, she stepped inside the car and released a breath as she stared at her mottled reflection on the elevator doors.

She slid her finger beneath the elastic band that held her hair back and pulled it out. She shook her head to loosen the strands over her shoulders. The ponytail begged, *Take me seriously.* She didn't need props to get that message across to her coworkers.

She shrugged out of her black wool coat, leaving the purple scarf twined around her neck. Squaring her shoulders, she said aloud, "Oh, the scarf? Too busy to notice I still had it on."

She snorted and unwound the scarf, leaving two purple-fringed ends hanging to her waist. The elevator dinged and she stood at attention until the doors opened on the seventh floor.

Hiking her laptop case on her shoulder, she strode down the hallway to the conference room, the heels of her black boots clicking on the floor in a steady, confident beat.

The door to the conference room yawned open on a large space with a gleaming, oval table in the center and two large video screens on either side of the room. A smaller desk hunched in the corner, overflowing with a laptop, an abundance of cords and a variety of AV equipment. The only other person in the room, a curvaceous bottled-blonde with a colorful clip in her hair, hovered over the computer. With a flash of red lipstick, she gave Aria a quick smile and a wink and returned to her work.

Director Alana Suzuki, smart in a navy pantsuit with a snowy-white blouse, barreled through the door. "You made it." She thrust out her hand to Aria, her eyes gleaming behind translucent-framed glasses. "Welcome aboard. I'll do the introductions when everyone gets here. Take any seat around the table."

"Director Suzuki." Aria gripped the older woman's hand, giving as good as she got. "Glad to be here."

"Alana, please." She ran a hand through her short black hair, unapologetically peppered with gray. "We're an informal bunch here."

The woman tapping away at the computer called out. "Uh, you might want to revise the invitation to take any seat. There's no assigned seating, but everyone always claims the same spot. Habit or security."

Alana waved her hand at the other woman. "Don't pay any attention to Opaline. She's our tech guru and her mind works in mysterious ways. Opaline, this is our new team member, Aria Calletti. Aria, Opaline Lopez."

Opaline raised her hand and wiggled her fingers, her long nails matching the red of her lips.

Aria cleared her throat. "Nice to meet you."

With Opaline's words about the seating hanging in the air, Aria folded her arms across her bag and wedged a shoulder against the wall. She didn't want to ruffle anyone's feathers on her first day.

As long as you played by the rules, went by the book,

you'd fit in. She'd discovered that as a beat cop on the mean streets of Detroit. Go along, get along and do your job.

The other team members started to filter into the room, a few in pairs, a few on their own. As Aria glanced at each person, his or her name flashed into her brain. She'd done her research on the Tactical Crime Division team when Director Suzuki—Alana—had invited her to apply for it. And apply she did.

She'd given up her job with the Detroit PD and hit the ground running at the FBI Academy in Quantico. Five months later, she'd taken the assignment with the TCD and was ready to hit the ground running again.

A few of the team members nodded at her as they grabbed seats. Aria had pretended to be looking through her bag to explain her delay in taking her place at the table—with the big boys and girls. When everyone seemed settled in, she slid into a seat next to Supervisory Special Agent Axel Morrow, his large frame dwarfing the chair.

His blue eyes assessed her as she scooted her chair forward, making her glad she'd opted for slacks and a jacket but regretting the loss of her ponytail.

Alana stood at one end of the table and commanded the room. At just over five feet tall, her physical stature was not responsible for the snap to attention, all eyes on her, conversations dying out. The woman had a presence—an erect, military bearing that radiated confidence and demanded respect.

She had Aria folding her hands on the table in front of her like a schoolgirl.

"Welcome back, everyone. I want to congratulate you on the successful completion of Operation Lollipop. A job well done."

The room erupted in applause and Aria joined in. She'd

read the files on the human trafficking case and couldn't wait to be part of this team that did so much good.

"Okay, okay." Alana held up her hand. "Don't get too carried away. We have the next case on our plate. Before I get into that…we have a new team member I'd like to introduce Aria Calletti. She can say a few words about herself and then we can go around the room and you can tell her who you are. Try to keep it under a minute, Opaline."

The other team members chuckled, as Opaline tapped a finger to her chest, her heavily mascaraed eyes wide.

As she took her seat, Alana nodded in Aria's direction. "Tell us a little something about yourself, Aria."

Aria cleared her throat. "I grew up in Holland, Michigan, and joined the PD in Detroit. Due to my age, I did a lot of undercover work in narcotics, especially at the schools, and worked dope as a beat cop. While working as a cop, I put myself through Wayne State, criminal justice major. Got lucky on a big case and helped bring down a drug kingpin. That's when Director Suzuki invited me to apply to the FBI with this division as my goal."

Axel, Alana's second-in-command, held up a finger. "That's 'Alana' to you. We're not into formalities."

Selena Lopez, the K-9 handler, her dark hair in a sleek chignon, nudged Axel in the shoulder. "And don't you dare call Axel 'Supervisory Special Agent Morrow.' He hates that."

"She's right. We're on a first-name basis around here." Axel rubbed his arm. "Impressive stuff, Aria."

Alana took off her glasses and hunched over the table. "Yeah, that was a little more than luck, Aria. Her investigative work was instrumental in bringing down that dirtbag. That's why she's a perfect fit for this team. Anything else you want to tell us?"

Anything else…such as how she felt as if her entire career hinged on her ability to pull her own weight on this team? Such as how she felt like an imposter? That her real self was that distorted image in the elevator door?

"That's it." Aria pressed her lips together and eked out a small smile.

"You, go." Alana leveled a finger at Opaline in the corner.

"We met earlier because I was the first person here, as usual." Opaline wiggled her fingers in the air. "I'm the tech support for this motley crew. They'd fail miserably without me. Oh, and I heard you had a bunch of brothers who are firefighters, so if any of them are single I'm willing and able...and that was well under a minute."

Aria shot a quick glance at the K-9 handler, Selena Lopez. She'd read in the bios that these two were sisters. Selena's tight smile and clenched hands in front of her told Aria nothing...well, almost nothing.

"I'll go next." The tall, cool blonde sitting across from Aria held her up hand. "I'm Carly Welsh. I've been on TCD for three years, and before that, I was with the FBI in Detroit. So, we have that in common, Aria. Welcome to the squad."

Selena spoke up, her low voice vibrating. "That's *Dr.* Carly Welsh. She's got a Ph.D. in biological warfare."

Aria's gaze darted back to Carly, a rosy hue washing over the blonde's pale cheeks. The knots in Aria's gut twisted a little more.

The brooding man at the end of the table ran a hand over the top of his head. "I guess I'll go next. I'm Max McRay. Explosives. Did a stint in the Army. Looking forward to working with you, Aria."

Axel put a hand over his mouth and coughed. "War hero."

Aria nodded at Max. He hadn't mentioned the fact that

he'd lost the lower half of his left leg to a bomb in Afghanistan. Although he'd had a slight hitch in his step when he'd walked into the conference room, if Aria hadn't read his bio, she wouldn't have known about his leg.

"I'm Selena Lopez." Selena put her long, slender fingers in the air and wiggled them, just as Opaline had done. "My *raison d'être* on this team is surveillance and tracking. My partner's a white shepherd named Blanca, and if she doesn't like you… I don't know, Aria."

"Blanca's a good judge of character." Axel tugged on the lapels of his jacket. "She happens to love me."

Max shot back. "That's because you give her treats when Selena's back is turned."

"Busted." Carly flicked a rolled-up piece of paper at Axel, who caught it easily in one hand.

Aria's lips stretched into a smile. The relaxed camaraderie of the team tightened those knots in her belly even more. Would she ever be able to engage in this friendly back-and-forth?

She'd never been one of the boys on the PD; had always felt like she had her nose pressed against the glass. As the only girl in a family of five siblings, she was accustomed to that feeling. Her brothers loved her, of course, but were overly protective and, like Rudolph, she'd never joined in their reindeer games.

Axel bobbled the ball of paper Carly had fired at him between his palms, his blue eyes alight. "I'm Supervisory Special Agent Axel Morrow. You can call me Axel or Axe. I would say that I'm Alana's right hand, but we all know that honor belongs to Amanda over there, furiously taking notes on her laptop."

The cute redhead seated next to Alana peered over the top of her computer and grinned. "You got that right."

Aria studied Axel as he reeled off his background—

his work background. His gift of gab must be one of the reasons for his top skills as a hostage negotiator. He could probably get anyone to do anything. At the FBI Academy, they'd studied some of Axel's criminal profiles for their insight and accuracy.

Now, Aria narrowed her eyes at the good-looking blond and practiced a little profiling of her own. Did he use his charming manner to mask the tragedy of his young life?

"That's me in a nutshell, but feel free to ask any of us anything anytime. We're here to help you." He flattened a hand over his heart. "Great to have you on board, Aria."

"Now, for my true right hand, last but certainly not least, Amanda Orton." Alana tapped the redhead on the shoulder.

Amanda stopped typing. "I'm Amanda Orton. I'm Alana's assistant. If you want to reach Alana or schedule a meeting with her, you come through me."

"And if you want to get to Amanda, you have to go through that massive security guard downstairs, who happens to be her husband." Axel raised his eyebrows. "You see him? He looks like a linebacker for the Lions."

"You do not need to go through him to see me." Amanda's lips and eyes turned up at the corners. "You can reach me anytime, Aria, and I'm the keeper of the birthday club so I need to get that from you at some point."

Carly rolled her eyes. "As if we need to be reminded of our birthdays every year."

"Let me know when you want it, and I'll give it to you." Aria tucked her hair behind one ear. "Thanks for introducing yourselves. I'm so impressed with your work, and I can't wait to be a contributing member of this team."

Silence. Ugh, had she laid it on too thick?

"The only one missing is Rihanna Clark. She's our PR person. She interacts with the media, the local PDs and crime victims. She had a meeting today," Alana said, rapping on the table and pushing to her feet. "Now that the niceties are out of the way, we have work to do. Opaline?"

Opaline clicked her keyboard and the oversize TV screens on either side of the room came to life—only to show death. Two young women, both on their backs, sprawled on the ground, a gaping gunshot wound in their chests.

Alana aimed a pointer at the split-screen, the red laser hovering over the bodies. "Two victims in Port Huron. Both near the lake, different roads. Single gunshot to the chest, point-blank. The Port Huron police don't have any leads yet but…"

The next slide jumped onto to the screen and Amanda gasped. "I-is that a baby?"

"It is." Alana clenched her jaw. "A baby in a car seat was next to the most recent victim. Child Protective Services has the baby now, and the PD ordered DNA tests to determine if the baby belongs with the dead woman."

Max growled. "Was the baby hurt?"

"The baby is fine, which is how the second body was discovered. Someone called in an abandoned baby. Didn't mention the dead body next to the baby, but reported the baby."

"Was it the killer?" Axel hunched forward, the veins popping out of his forearms, hands clenched.

Alana shook her head. "We don't know. He didn't leave a name or contact info, but could just be a scared bystander."

Selena asked, "Did they trace the call?"

"Cell phone. No info on that phone yet."

Opaline looked up, shoving her glasses higher on her nose. "I'm looking into the phone now."

"Has the PD identified the victims? Do they have any similarities?" Carly scribbled on a notepad in front of her.

"The first victim had opioids in her system, too soon for toxicology on the second victim, and both had a small amount of fentanyl on them—packaged to sell."

Alana tipped her head at Aria, and Aria squared her shoulders. Fentanyl she knew, along with all its street names: China Girl, Dance Fever, Apache, Goodfella, and on and on.

Alana continued. "Both women were about the same age, brown hair, brown eyes, not sex workers—at least, not known to the PD—and they were dressed conservatively. They did both have ID on them."

Selena slumped in her seat. "That makes things a little easier."

"Not quite." Alana took a big breath. "The IDs they had were identical."

Aria blurted out, "Identical?"

"That's right. These women not only look alike, they were carrying IDs that have the same name, same address, same height, same weight. For all intents and purposes? The same girl died twice."

Chapter Two

Aria hunched her shoulders as a chill shot up her spine. "Someone's going through a lot of trouble to give these women the same ID only to kill them."

Max scratched his jaw. "Maybe their deaths are part of a plan nobody told them about, but what kind of plan calls for two identical women?"

"I'm assuming the PD already checked that person and address?" Selena's short nails clicked on the mahogany surface of the table as she drummed her fingers. "Is she a real person?"

"The name on the ID is Maddie Johnson. Fake. Everything fake down to the Port Huron address, which doesn't exist." Alana pressed a button on the remote in her hand and gestured toward the screen now displaying two fraudulent IDs side by side. They were identical except for the pictures of the dead women.

"If that was the killer on the phone—" Axel pushed back from the table and crossed his ankle over his knee "—why'd he make the call? Why'd he spare the baby?"

"Thank God, he did," Max replied. "So, we're not dealing with a total monster."

"Maybe he likes puppies, too." Carly's brown eyes darkened to two chips of coal. "The guy murdered two women…a woman with a baby."

Max held up his hands. "I'm not saying he should win the Nobel Peace Prize, but leaving the baby untouched tells us something about him. Something we can use."

Aria had pulled out her laptop during the discussion and had been taking her own notes, although she figured they'd all get a copy of Amanda's. Without looking up from her keyboard, she asked, "Do we know the grade of fentanyl they were carrying?"

Dead air hung over the room and Aria glanced up to find several pairs of eyes on her.

Max broke the silence. "Is that important? Should we know that?"

Her gaze traveled across the different expressions—curious, piqued, encouraging—and she said, "Yes. Sometimes we can trace the packaging and the purity to a specific dealer."

"Didn't know that." Selena formed her fingers into a gun and pointed at Aria. "That would definitely help. Good call, Aria."

Aria held up one finger. "Another thing about the location of the bodies and the drugs... Port Huron is a border town on the water. It's a prime location for smuggling. The packets of Dance Fever those women had could be part of a larger ring moving drugs across the border."

As Alana clicked through the rest of the slides and the team bandied about more ideas, the tension that had been gripping Aria's shoulders, tension she hadn't even realized she had, began slipping away. She could do this.

An hour later, Alana put up the last slide—the baby in the car seat, a set of oversize plastic keys in primary colors and a little fuzzy sheep clipped to the handle. "Good start, people. Remember why we're doing this. This little guy lost his mother. Someone lost a daughter, a sister, maybe a wife. Go home, get your affairs in order and we'll meet at the airport. Private plane will take us to Port Huron at four o'clock sharp."

Opaline ended the slide show, Amanda put the finishing touches on the meeting notes, and the team members began gathering their laptops, notepads, pens and coffee cups.

Axel's voice rose above the rest. "Good hire, boss. Aria has a lot to offer."

Max reached across the table, extending his hand. "I'm excited about what you can bring to the team, Aria."

She smiled and nodded, giddiness bubbling in her veins.

They all seemed confident she could do the job. Now she just had to convince herself.

As THE SUN SET, the TCD's private plane touched down in Mount Clemens. Port Huron didn't have an airport, so the Selfridge Air National Guard allowed them to fly onto the base, which was about forty-five minutes from Port Huron.

The descent provided Aria with a bird's-eye view of the area, near two lakes and not far from the Canadian border. The proximity to water and the border confirmed her suspicions about drug smuggling. But why kill the smugglers? Why kill the young women willing to do your bidding?

Dealers exacted rough justice on the street sellers, the runners and the smugglers whenever they started bucking the system or tried to circumvent it. If a smuggler decided to go into business by herself, started using the product instead of shipping it, or got cold feet, or worse, turned informant, she would most likely end up meeting the business end of a gun.

Carly leaned across the aisle of the plane, her blond hair spilling like sunshine over her shoulder. "At least we get our own rooms at the hotel this time. Sometimes we have to share. That means Selena and I usually bunk together, the guys pair up, and Amanda and Rihanna share.

Alana always has her own room. She claims it's because she snores."

"Opaline doesn't come along?" Aria cranked her head over her shoulder. She'd noticed the tech specialist's absence when she'd boarded.

"Usually she stays in Traverse City, and sometimes Rihanna goes where she's needed. Rihanna's already in Port Huron. She came out here yesterday to take charge of the baby and make sure he's placed with a foster family while the police ID his mom." Carly blinked her golden lashes rapidly. "Poor little thing."

Pressing a hand to her heart, Aria said, "I just keep thinking how terrified his mom must've been when the killer pointed that gun at her. Her last thoughts must've been for the safety of her baby."

Carly stretched one long denim-clad leg into the aisle, the heel of her suede boot digging into the thin carpet. "She probably thought her killer was going to shoot her baby, too. I can't even imagine."

"Why didn't he?" The plane finished taxiing, its wheels squealing to a stop, the engines cutting out. "Why'd a cold-blooded killer spare a baby?"

"Maybe he knew the victim. Port Huron isn't exactly a big city, is it? Perhaps he didn't know the identity of his target until he faced her."

"So, you're saying someone ordered a hit." Aria reached down and pulled her purse from beneath the seat in front of her.

"Based on the duplicate IDs and the drugs, it has to be. Wouldn't it?" Raising her eyebrows, Carly tilted her head.

"Unless the killer is a fellow smuggler and got jealous or made it personal." Aria released her seat belt. "Just trying to look at all angles here."

"No, that's good. Keep it coming, Aria. That's what

makes this team so great—everyone coming from different places, everyone contributing their own ideas. Your theory also gives another reason why that killer had a soft spot for the baby." Carly stood and pulled her designer luggage from the overhead compartment, setting it in front of her.

Aria blew out a breath. The theory had made sense to her, but she was glad it made sense to Dr. Welsh, too.

Aria shuffled off the plane with the rest of the team and headed down the steps to the tarmac where a black van awaited them. After the driver loaded their luggage and equipment, Blanca, Selena's K-9, jumped in the back.

The brisk air carried the scent of fish and brine, and Aria's fingertips buzzed with impatience. She'd have to sit through a dinner tonight and actually try to get some sleep, but the investigation started tomorrow.

They were still awaiting ballistics from this most recent murder, to see if it matched the first victim, and on toxicology reports for the second victim and the baby. The DNA would take longer.

They piled into the van and Aria scooted into the very back, next to the window.

Alana took the seat next to Aria and patted her knee. "We'll spare the tall people the trouble of crawling back here, but I'm not going to be very good company. The ride to Port Huron is long enough for me to pull out my laptop and get in a little work."

"Go ahead." Aria dropped her voice. "We shouldn't be discussing the case in front of the driver, anyway, right?"

"No, but I'm not all business all the time. I'd like to get to know you better on a personal level, Aria. I make a point to learn as much about my agents as I can." Alana winked. "Figure out what makes them all tick."

From the seat in front of them, Carly twisted her head

around. "Watch out for Alana. She has a knack for getting to our deepest, darkest secrets. She should be the one interrogating all our suspects. She'd give Axe a run for his money."

Alana pulled her computer out of her bag and positioned it on her lap. "The better I get to know you, the more smoothly the team runs."

The van stopped at the gate on the way off the base and then hit the highway north to Port Huron. Max sat in the front seat and chatted with the driver, who was retired Army. Axel and Selena sat behind them, their heads together, exchanging whispers, probably work-related, and Carly and Amanda had claimed the middle row, each glued to her phone.

As Alana tapped away on her keyboard, Aria stuffed some earbuds in her ears and listened to classical music. She leaned her head against the cool glass and watched the scenery pass by. She couldn't see much in the darkness, but occasionally a freeway sign would pop up with the miles remaining to Canada, reminding her just how close they were to the border.

Almost forty minutes later, the van took the turnoff toward downtown Port Huron. As they rolled past the lake, Aria cupped her hand over the glass and gazed at the gleaming water, boats bobbing in the docks, a few decked out with colorful Christmas lights that reflected off the lake's dark surface.

Aria squinted so that the lights blurred in a rainbow pattern. Somewhere out there, another brown-haired, brown-eyed young woman with dreams of financial security in her eyes and packets of Dance Fever in her pocket, faced potential danger.

And unsuspecting families sat on a precipice of the most devastating news of their lives.

THE WIND GUSTED and the halyards on the docked boats clanged against the masts, chiming out quittin' time. Grayson grabbed the rope attached to the last pallet he'd loaded for the day. The rough hemp dug into his palms, already toughened from a few days' work on the docks.

He dragged the pallet to the warehouse and hoisted it on top of a stack, ready for tomorrow morning.

Chuck smacked him on the back, the contact from the former hockey player and now his coworker reverberating in his chest. "Good work today, Gary. Some of the boys are going for a beer. Wanna come along?"

"Thanks, Chuck. Maybe next time." Grayson rolled down the sleeves of his denim work shirt, the cold air finally soaking into his skin now that the heavy lifting had come to a backbreaking end. "I'm still dealing with stuff from my landlord in the new place. He's supposed to fix the toilet tonight."

"Yeah, you gotta watch these landlords. They'll try to skip out on paying for anything." Chuck spit on the ground. "Rich bastards."

"I got my eye on this guy, and I plan to hold his feet to the fire." Grayson thrust out his fist for a bump. "Hit me up next time for a brewski."

Chuck plowed his raw, reddened knuckles into Grayson's. "You got it, man. We'll hoist one for you tonight."

Grayson held up his hand to a few of the other guys as he headed for the used truck he'd bought yesterday. He climbed in and gripped the steering wheel, his own knuckles abraded, staring at the docks over the rim.

Despite his reason for being on the docks in Port Huron, the work invigorated him. The soreness of his muscles when he ran a marathon or worked out at the gym didn't equate to the ache that permeated his bones after a few days loading and unloading cargo. This pain felt righteous.

He snorted. He'd better not utter that sentiment to the men, and the woman, he worked with on the dock. They'd kick his ass for that…rich bastard.

He cranked on the engine and blasted the heat. Reaching under the front seat, he retrieved his cell phone. He didn't carry it on the job. Didn't want anyone getting a look at his texts or photos.

With a knot in his gut, he checked his calls and texts. After thumbing through a few work-related issues and listening to his assistant, Patrick, whine in not one but two voice mails, he slumped in his seat.

Nothing from the police yet. Not that he expected anything. The guy at the front desk of the Port Huron PD could barely keep his eyes open when Grayson had gone in to file the missing persons report. There'd been one unidentified dead woman, but she hadn't matched the description Grayson had given the officer…in more ways than one.

He slammed his hands against the steering wheel. Where the hell was she? If the police didn't give a damn, he'd have to do his own searching.

He hadn't heard anything on the docks yet, but he hadn't been there that long. He still had hope of gleaning some information from the guys as they started to loosen up more, accept him as one of their own. That beer tonight would've gone a long way toward that end, but he had his own mission after work—and it didn't include a broken toilet.

By the time he pulled out of the parking lot, the other workers' vehicles had disappeared. Who wanted to hang around the commercial end of the dock once you punched your time card?

Grayson eyed the lake as it curved around to the noncommercial side of the dock where pleasure boats, fishing boats and a few small rowboats clustered, some already decorated with Christmas lights. Already? Thanksgiving was last week with Christmas right around the corner. The realization punched him in the gut. Thanksgiving should've been a joyous holiday, a prelude to Christmas.

He cruised along the street that bordered the shoreline and turned into the parking lot for the noncommercial harbor. Boats, all this water—it would be easy for someone to disappear.

He clambered out of the truck and trudged down to the wooden dock, the cold air biting at his cheeks. Shoving his hands into his pockets, he stooped his shoulders and gazed at the nodding boats, talking to each other in creaks and sighs.

Lights emanated from inside a couple of the larger sailboats. He knew that a few hardy souls lived on their boats full-time, but he'd already identified and dismissed them as possible sources of information.

His head jerked sideways as the sound of clicking heels came from the other side of one of the bigger boats. He squinted into the distance and his heart skipped a beat when he saw a young woman in a dark coat, dark jeans and what had to be boots, not deck shoes, to make that noise.

He took a step in her direction, a name on his lips, which he choked back when he saw the girl flip her dark hair over one shoulder. As she drew closer, passing beneath the glow from a light, Grayson released a long breath.

When she spotted him, her steps faltered, but she grabbed the strap of her purse and soldiered on toward the gate. She pushed through without giving him a second look.

She could be someone else's sister. "Hey, you should be careful walking around on your own out here at night."

Without turning her head, she gave him a one-fingered salute and yelled, "Mind your own damn business."

So much for being a good Samaritan. He twisted his

head to the side and watched her cross the parking lot and walk up to the street, her stride purposeful, her shoulders back and the knit cap on her head bobbing up and down. At least she didn't look like a victim.

He watched the boats and the water for another fifteen minutes, not knowing what to expect. But instinct buzzing in his ear that this area held a clue to Chloe's disappearance, kept him rooted to the same spot.

The tip of his nose numb and his eyes stinging, he pushed away from the post he'd been clinging to with stiff fingers and returned to his truck.

If he hurried, he might catch the guys for a beer, but right now he couldn't carry off the jovial dockworker whose only care in the world was the Lions' dismal record.

Right now, all he cared about was finding his sister... and her seven-month-old baby.

Chapter Three

Rihanna Clark chucked the baby under the chin and jiggled the set of plastic keys in front of his face. "Hello, there, Baby Doe. You sure are cute."

The baby reached out with his chubby fist and curled his fingers, wet with drool, around the yellow key. He shoved the end into his mouth and gnawed on it with his gums.

Rihanna leaned forward and tapped Shereen North, the CPS social worker on the shoulder. "Is that okay? He has that key in his mouth."

Shereen looked in her rearview mirror and smiled. "That's fine. He's teething. I'm guessing his age is around six or seven months. He might be older if he has drugs in his system and some delayed development, but he looks healthy. You don't have children?"

Rihanna shrugged her shoulders and shook her head. After being attacked and held captive by a homicidal maniac a few years ago, she couldn't fathom the idea of bringing any children into this world.

Alana had assured her that she'd get over those fears one day, but she'd actually have to find a man she could trust. For now, she preferred admiring from afar and going goo-goo-gaga over someone else's baby.

"I hope he doesn't have drugs in his system." She reached over to the baby next to her in the back seat and stroked his cheek with her knuckle. "He seems too calm to have NAS."

"At seven months, he might be too old to display many of the characteristics of neonatal abstinence syndrome, but he'll be tested. If he's positive, we can work with that."

"If we don't find next of kin soon, is this foster family prepared to deal with that?"

"Rick and Sarah are among our best, and they have experience dealing with NAS babies. Rick works as a firefighter—in fact, that's how they started as foster parents. Rich was called out to a terrible fire that killed the parents of a baby. He and Sarah cared for that baby for a short time, and they were hooked. Sarah's a retired teacher. They have two grown sons, no grandchildren yet, and love these babies."

"They sound perfect. Let's just hope this is another short-term assignment." Rihanna pinched Baby Doe's toes through his soft suede moccasins. "This little guy needs his family…if they want him."

Ten minutes later, Shereen turned down a street of neatly groomed homes, smug in their middle-class comfort. She pulled in next to a red truck in the driveway of a home that had an actual white-picket fence.

Baby Doe dropped the key and the keychain slid down the handle of the car seat.

"Don't worry, baby boy. You're going to be in good hands." She smoothed a finger over his silky blond hair, and he rewarded her with a look from his blue eyes. Given Mom's looks with the brown hair and brown eyes, Dad must be blond-haired and blue-eyed.

Shereen cut the engine and they both got out of the car. Rihanna lifted the latch of the gate to the walkway as Shereen circled around to get the baby.

Hearing their approach, Rick and Sarah emerged from

the house and stood on the porch. Rick's arm curled around Sarah's shoulder, while Sarah clasped her hands in front of her, a smile lighting up her face. She had to have been a kindergarten teacher.

Rihanna's boots clipped on the pavers as she walked up to the porch. "Mr. and Mrs. Colby? I'm Rihanna Clark, the FBI's liaison on the murder case of the baby's mother—or, at least, we think she's his mother."

Sarah reached out and clasped Rihanna's hand, tugging her in for a hug that smelled like warm apples and cinnamon. "Thank you for bringing him to us. We'll cherish him as one of our own, until his people can be found and notified."

Rihanna inhaled the woman's homey scent and blinked back tears. Maybe Rick and Sarah could adopt her, too?

Just when Sarah released her, leaving her out in the cold, Rick dove in for a bear hug that almost swept Rihanna from her feet. He kept hold of Rihanna's hand and said, "I hope you Feds catch the SOB who did this to his mother."

"Rick, shh." Sarah patted his muscular arm. "Not in front of the baby."

Shereen had followed her to the porch, Baby Doe's car seat swinging from her hand, the keyring and fuzzy sheep dancing in the air.

Rick squeezed between the two women and lunged toward Shereen. "That looks heavy, Shereen. Let me take him."

Rick brought the baby into the house and set the car seat on the floor. Crouching, he released the straps, scooped Baby Doe out of the seat, and tucked him in the crook of his arm. "He's a big boy. Six months old? What do you think, Sarah?"

"I think he's a little angel."

As the two foster parents cooed over their new charge,

Rihanna glanced around the room, her gaze lighting on a playpen outfitted with colorful toys, a battery-operated swing, a mat on the floor with an arched mobile and a spinning, rocking baby walker—a cornucopia of fun times for baby.

Although Rihanna knew all too well looks could be deceiving, CPS had solid, favorable reports of this couple, and Baby Doe couldn't be in better hands.

Rihanna cleared her throat. "We'll keep you posted on any information we have about the baby's identity and his family, including whether or not they'll be making a move for custody."

"Thank you, Rihanna." Sarah rested her cheek against the baby's head. "I'm sure Shereen told you, we're old hands at this. The baby is ours until he isn't."

Shereen withdrew a folder from the bag hanging over her shoulder. "You know the drill. I have some forms for you to sign before we leave."

"Kitchen table." Sarah turned to Rihanna with the baby in her arms. "Do you want to hold him for a few minutes while we take care of this, Rihanna?"

"Of course." Rihanna stepped forward, holding out her arms, and Baby Doe went willingly to her. This personable little guy must be accustomed to strangers. He hadn't let out one peep, except for happy babbles, ever since she and Shereen had picked him up from the hospital—the same hospital where his mother lay on a cold slab in the morgue.

Rihanna cuddled him close and then dipped her head, putting her lips next to the downy curve of his ear. "Don't worry, baby. Like Rick said, we're going to catch the SOB who took your momma away from you."

THE DINNER THE night before had been just what Aria needed. The rest of the special agents on the team had seemed almost human as they'd consumed actual food and drink instead of manna from heaven.

She'd gotten to know them a little better as individuals, especially Max, who'd been seated next to her. He'd lifted up his pant leg and showed her his artificial limb, explaining how the high-tech prosthesis worked. He also talked about his toddler son, which explained why he'd been one of the first agents in the meeting to show concern about the baby left with his dead mother, presumably.

The DNA on mother and child hadn't come back yet. They hadn't even received the autopsy report on the second victim, although cause of death was obvious—gunshot to the chest.

As Aria eyed the scoop of congealed oatmeal she'd plopped in her bowl from the hotel's complimentary breakfast bar, wondering if she'd made a mistake, Axel poked at her bowl with a spoon. "That looks disgusting."

"That doesn't look much better." With her fork, she tapped his plate, heaped with clumpy, orangey-yellow scrambled eggs and greasy sausage links.

"Breakfast of champions. And, speaking of disgusting—" he jerked his thumb over his shoulder at Carly, decked out in lululemon tights and a sleek running jacket, her blond hair scooped into a high ponytail "—get a load of her. She makes the rest of us look like slugs."

Aria flicked a glance at Axel's broad chest and biceps visible beneath his shirt. Not a very likely slug.

"How's the breakfast?" Carly grabbed a plate and joined them, her cheeks still flushed from her run. Even the sweat glowing from her forehead had a chic sheen to it.

"No green smoothies, or anything like that. Plain old bacon and eggs and whatever Aria's got going on in that bowl."

"I think we can make that palatable with some brown

sugar, banana, nuts." Carly grabbed a glass and shoved it beneath the juice dispenser.

When they were all seated around a table near the window, Axel said, "Alana's working on getting that autopsy report for us and pulling some strings to accelerate the toxicology test on Mom and the DNA test on Mom and baby. The more we know about these women, outside of their fake IDs, the faster we're going to solve this case."

Carly looked up from slicing her banana into her oatmeal. "I'm going to be looking at the first victim's toxicology report today. If I have any questions about the opioids in her system, I'll hit you up, Aria."

"Sounds good. Axel and I are going to Jane Doe number two's crime site today, just to get a lay of the land." Aria dipped her spoon into the oatmeal and swirled the brown sugar into a ribbon through the sludge.

"I'm not late for breakfast, am I?" A tall woman who looked more like the supermodel Iman than an FBI liaison strode into the breakfast room, her dark curls bouncing at her shoulders. "I'm starving."

"Don't skip out on a team dinner next time," Axel scolded. "Come over here and meet our newest agent."

Rihanna Clark put her plate down and floated toward the table like a ballerina in *Swan Lake*.

"Oh, get your breakfast first." Aria flicked her fingers at Rihanna.

"The breakfast will still be there in two minutes. I feel bad about missing your first meeting." Rihanna flashed a smile at Aria that made her feel like her best friend in the world. "First things first. I'm Rihanna Clark."

Aria grabbed her extended hand and then loosened her grip on the delicate bones of Rihanna's fingers. "Aria Calletti. Nice to finally meet you."

"I know." Rihanna pouted, her lips turning down at the

corners. "I missed the big meeting yesterday because I was settling the baby, and I missed the team dinner, as Axel called it, because I had to do some follow-up with CPS after we dropped the baby off with the family."

"How *is* the baby?" Aria curled her fingers around her spoon so hard, it almost sprang from her grasp. The thought of him outside next to his dead mother squashed her appetite even more than her lumpy oatmeal.

"He seems healthy. Doesn't seem like he has drugs in his system, but the toxicology will tell. His foster parents are topnotch. No worries there. Poor little guy." Rihanna's dark eyes shimmered with tears.

"Go get breakfast. We're not going anywhere." Aria plunged her spoon into her untouched bowl of oatmeal.

"Speak for yourself." Axel stuffed the remainder of his eggs into his mouth, leaving the sausage on his plate, proving his choice wasn't much better than her own. "I have to sign for our rental car, which is being delivered to the hotel in a few minutes. Meet me out front when you're done with breakfast—no rush."

As he walked away, Carly said, "Axe is just like Alana. Even though he's the supervisor, he sees himself as one of us."

"He seems very…charming, personable. Those qualities must be invaluable as a negotiator and interrogator."

"He amazes me, given his…past." Carly shot Aria a look from the side of her eye.

"I know." Aria's knees bounced beneath the table. "We read about his background in the Academy, about the murder of his parents and brother when Axel was a child. How awful. I can't even imagine."

"Most people can't." Carly picked up her coffee cup, pinky in the air, and took a dainty sip.

"Oh, now I have to sit with the healthy oatmeal girls."

Rihanna clicked down her plate, overflowing with eggs, bacon, sausage and hash browns. "And I put ketchup on everything."

Aria widened her eyes. "Doesn't everyone?"

"I knew I liked you." Rihanna jabbed her fork in the air at Aria.

Aria chatted with the two women while they finished breakfast. She then excused herself to meet Axel, with a detour to her hotel room to grab her bag and make sure she didn't have oatmeal stuck to her teeth.

When she exited the hotel, she spotted him behind the steering wheel of a dark blue sedan, nodding his head. Was he on speaker phone? Should she interrupt?

She approached the vehicle and peered through the glass, which was practically vibrating with the loud, thrashing rock music blaring from the car's speakers. She tapped on the window as she pulled open the passenger-side door.

Axel's head shot up and he cranked down the noise. "Sorry about that. Just getting into the mood. Do you like heavy metal?"

"Mmm, I'm more of a pop girl, top forty stuff, but I've been getting into classical lately. I find it soothing."

"I do, too. If you're just learning about classical, I can steer you to a couple of composers and forms—sonatas, concertos and symphonies. I have an extensive collection."

"But you like headbanger music, too."

"Yeah, there's a time to relax and a time to…not relax." His jaw formed a hard line as he pressed the ignition button on the rental.

Axel drove to the location of the second murder and parked on the street above the gravel walkway along the lake. Aria followed Axel out, stumbling down a dirt pathway through the marshy land and tall grasses.

Her nose twitched at the scent of dark, dank peat. "Why would she be walking down here when there's that perfectly good Blue Water River Walk?"

"You're the drug czar. If she were selling, would she be doing that in a more populated area or out here in no-man's-land?"

"That depends." When they reached gravel road next to the water, Aria brushed off the wet grass clinging to her low-heeled boots. She threw her arm out to the side. "Plenty of places to hide. If the killer stalked her, he'd have cover."

"*If* he stalked her?"

"I mean, if he wasn't with her. She could've known him, been with him, come out here with him. Again, that would explain why he didn't harm the baby and how he got close enough to take that shot without any defensive moves on the victim's part." She sucked in her bottom lip. "She dropped where she stood, right? No evidence that she fought back or turned to run."

"Kind of hard to run carrying one of those car seats with a six-month-old baby inside. That's gotta add another twenty, thirty pounds to the load, right?" Axel spread his hands, as if he didn't have one clue about babies.

He probably didn't.

"Closer to twenty than thirty pounds, maybe a little less." She shrugged. "I'm no expert, but I do have nieces and nephews."

"That's more than I got."

Aria sealed her lips. She had a wealth of siblings while Axel had lost his only brother in the most tragic way imaginable.

The gravel crunched beneath Axel's feet and he stopped and closed his eyes. "If he took her by surprise, he wouldn't have followed her on this road—too noisy."

"Over here, close to the water." Aria trailed her hand along the tall grasses that bordered the lake's edge.

Still rooted to the ground, Axel pointed ahead. "Right there. That's where it happened."

Aria jerked up her head and narrowed her eyes at a piece of yellow crime scene tape with a jagged end dangling from a bush. Then her gaze tracked to the dark stain soaked into the dirt. "No rain yet to wash that away."

His mouth grim, Axel strode toward the site and circled the bloodstain. "The shot spattered the baby with blood, you know. Little red droplets interspersed with the pandas on his blue blanket."

Curling a hand around her throat, Aria swallowed. "I saw that picture."

"So, she knew him, came here with him, or he snuck up on her through the reeds and grasses. Bam! Shot her point-blank. Left the scene and called 9-1-1 in a fit of conscience or to show off his handiwork."

"Not a serial killer, though, not with the exact same IDs and the drugs." She cocked her head, and the ponytail she'd decided on today slipped over her shoulder. "Why do you think he left the scene before calling 9-1-1?"

"Give himself some time to hightail it out of here." Axel stuffed his hands inside his pockets. "What are you thinking, Aria?"

"Water all around this area. He could've had a boat. She could've had a boat. I keep coming back to the boats. He could've called from here and hopped in his boat. Maybe he even laid low and made sure the first responders showed up in the right place—for the sake of the baby."

"A real prince," Axel growled low in his throat.

Aria sidled up next to the bloodstain and pivoted toward the water. She glanced at the ground and the trampled grasses. Could've been the killer. Could've been the cops on the scene. A white scrap of paper had been caught on the side of one of reeds and she ducked through the grass to take a closer look.

"Axel, there's a tissue caught on a plant. The cops scanned the area for cigarette butts and all the rest, right?"

"They did." Axel hovered over her shoulder. "It could've tumbled in here after."

"Or they missed it. That tissue is awfully white and unsullied for being debris from the lake or the road above." She cranked her head over her shoulder. "Do you have an evidence bag on you?"

He patted the leather satchel strapped across his body. "I have a few in here. I even have some tweezers."

After scrambling through his bag, he handed her a plastic baggie and a pair of tweezers.

Aria crouched, used the tweezers to pluck the tissue from the reed and then dropped it into the baggie. She handed it to Axel. "We should drop that off at the PD. Detective Massey in the Major Crimes Unit, right?"

"Yeah, he's the lead. Good find, Aria."

They spent another thirty minutes at the site without any more aha moments, and then Axel drove to the Port Huron Police Department with their find.

Massey brought them back to his office and folded his tall, spare frame into the chair behind his desk. Aria wondered where he crammed his storklike legs. He toyed with the plastic-bagged tissue in his long, bony fingers. "I'm not trying to cover for my guys, but I don't think this was out there."

"It's breezy. It could've blown in after the fact."

Axel had enough experience to know, as FBI, you didn't ruffle the PD's feathers. You'd never get their cooperation when you needed it, if you did. Aria had been on the other end of that relationship with the FBI coming in and taking charge of cases. In some departments, there was no love lost between the PD and the Feds.

"Could be from our killer." Massey tapped the bag with his fingers. "We'll send it over to check for DNA. Did you find anything else out there?"

"No, just trying to get a sense of things. I'm going to go through the autopsy reports with Director Suzuki today. Did she get those?"

"She did. Delivered to the hotel this morning." Massey shuffled through a stack of papers at his elbow. "I do have something you might be interested in, something for you to check out when you have the time."

"We'll take anything and everything you have, Detective." Aria squared her shoulders. "I used to work as a beat cop in Detroit, and I know the leads can get overwhelming, especially as so many of them go nowhere."

"Detroit, huh?" Massey raised his gray eyebrows, which seemed to stick out at odd angles, giving him a surprised look. "Do you know Smitty? Lieutenant Gerald Smith?"

"I do know Lieutenant Smith. He was something of a mentor of mine."

Massey nodded, a smile cracking his lean face. "He always liked to take cops with promise under his wing."

"Great cop." Aria reveled in the warm glow of the room, comfortable knowing she was appreciated. Not only had she won the approval of Massey, Axel had bumped her knee.

The detective shook out a piece of paper he'd slid from the stack and pushed it across the desk toward her. "We took a missing persons report a few days ago about a young woman."

Aria glanced at the first few lines on the page for the missing woman—a Chloe Larsen. "This woman is about the right age as our victims, but she has blond hair and blue eyes."

"That's why we didn't connect it to the first victim and overlooked it for the second, but read a little farther down the report."

Axel leaned into her space as Aria ran her finger through the words. She sucked in a breath. "A baby. This is a missing persons report for a young woman and a seven-month-old baby, and CPS is telling us that the baby found with Jane Doe number two is between six and eight months. Despite the dissimilar physical descriptions, it's a big coincidence."

Axel jabbed his finger at the paper. "Too big to ignore. Who reported the woman missing?"

"A Gary Rhodes. He's working at the docks. You might be able to catch him on his lunch break, but give him a call first at the number on the report. He said something about not being disturbed at work."

Aria held up the report. "Can I take this?"

"Take it. We have a copy in our computer system."

Axel asked, "What is Gary Rhodes's relationship to the missing woman and baby?"

Massey steepled his fingers and stared at them over the tips. "Brother and uncle."

Chapter Four

When they pulled up at the hotel, Axel left the car running and scrambled out of the front seat. "It's all yours, Aria. Don't crash it."

"Too funny." She slid out of the car and walked around to the driver's side. "Let me know if you and Alana discover anything in the autopsies I should know. If this could be a match to Jane Doe number two, can I bring this Rhodes guy to the medical examiner's office to ID the vic?"

"Do it." Axel saluted, two fingers to his forehead that ended in a bow. "Good luck."

When Aria got in behind the wheel of the sedan, she adjusted the seat then squealed away from the hotel, laughing at Axel's raised fist in her rearview mirror.

Axel had put the address of the commercial dock in the car's GPS, and Aria followed the voice now. As she turned down the street that led to the parking lot, she slowed and entered the number from the report into her phone. It rang three times before flipping over to voice mail with a recorded robotic greeting.

At the beep, she said, "Mr. Rhodes, this is Special Agent Calletti with the FBI. I'm calling about your missing persons report for a Chloe Larsen. I'm heading to the dock, so if you have a minute to talk to me on your lunch break, give me a call back."

She left her cell number and continued toward the dock. Instead of pulling into the parking lot, she rolled to a stop across the street.

She slumped in her seat and scanned through the photos she'd taken of the crime scene this morning. That was a lot of blood for one person to lose.

The phone rang in her hand and she checked the display before answering. He'd gotten back to her as soon as he could. "Special Agent Calletti."

"This is Gray... Gary Rhodes returning your call, Agent Calletti. Do you have news about my sister?" His voice, pitched low, had an urgent quality to it.

"Maybe. I'd like to ask you a few questions. Can I meet you at the dock?"

"Not a good idea, but I'm suddenly feeling ill. There's a diner on the other end of the docks, a marina where the pleasure boats are moored. Can you meet me there in half an hour?"

She didn't know why it wasn't a good idea to talk to him at work and didn't understand how he thought he was the one calling the shots, but she found herself agreeing to his proposal. "I'll find it. I have dark hair and I'm wearing a black coat with a purple scarf."

"Thanks." He ended the call before she could dictate any terms of her own.

She pulled away from the curb and curved around the dock to the end where people kept their boats and where there was a rental office. Would that office have a record of any boats rented out the night of the second victim's murder?

The diner sat back from the marina, a blue-and-white awning flapping over the front door and large windows eyeing the bay. She parked the rental on one side and entered the restaurant.

A hostess with shocking pink hair and a jewel gleaming in the side of her nose looked up from her phone. "One?"

"Two. The other person isn't here yet."

She swept her arm toward a couple of empty booths. "Sit anywhere."

Aria waited until a busboy finished clearing off a table by the window and then slid into the blue-vinyl banquette, which had definitely seen better days. The window gave her a view of the boats bobbing in their slips—and the little cottage that housed the rental office.

When the waiter moseyed by, Aria had to ask for two of everything. As she sipped her water, she glanced up from her phone every time the door to the diner opened with a jingle.

Finally, a single man strode through the door, running a hand through his collar-length, blond hair, his eyes scanning the room. When he settled on her, a little frisson of—recognition? Prescience? Pleasure?—tickled the back of her neck.

She had to cross her legs and grip the edge of the table to keep from jumping up to greet him. Apparently, Gary Rhodes's commanding presence affected other women in the diner in the same manner; quite a few pairs of eyes followed his progress across the room.

He reached her table and stuck out his hand. "Special Agent Calletti?"

"Yes." She placed her hand in his, the rough skin on his palm abrading hers. "Have a seat."

"Gary Rhodes." Scooting onto the bench seat across from her, he said, "Thanks for meeting me like this. I have my reasons."

She waited for those reasons but, instead of explaining

himself, Rhodes grabbed the glass of water in front of him and downed half of it. "Sorry, busy morning at work."

"You must be hungry, too. Feel free to order lunch."

"I can't eat anything until I know what you have on Chloe." He hunkered forward, his strong, corded forearms braced on the Formica, his blue eyes, which matched the vinyl, sparking. The vitality of the man took over the table...and Aria. "Did you find a woman matching her description?"

"Not exactly. Chloe is your sister?"

His leg bounced beneath the table. "Yeah. My half sister."

That would explain the different last names, or maybe not. "Is Chloe married?"

"No." He took a deep breath, which expanded his chest beneath his blue work shirt, which also matched his eyes. "Why does this matter?"

"Just gathering information, Mr. Rhodes." She pulled a notepad and pen from her purse, so she could actually take notes instead of ogling Mr. Rhodes's physical assets. "You described your sister as five foot five, slim build, blond hair and blue eyes, correct?"

"That's right." He waved away the approaching waiter and he pivoted and left them alone. "Did you find her?"

"We didn't find a woman with that hair and eye color, but she did match your description in another way."

"She has a baby with her." He spread his hands on the table and drummed all ten of his fingers. "That's it, isn't it? You found a woman with a baby, a baby boy."

"We did. That's why the Port Huron Police Department turned your missing persons report over to us." Aria sipped her water to avoid meeting his intense gaze. She'd had to deliver bad news to victims' families before, and it never got easier, but for some reason she couldn't stand to look into this man's eyes, full of hope and cautious optimism.

"To us." Dragging his nails on the tabletop, he curled his hands into fists. "You're the FBI. I-is it drugs? Did you arrest her for drugs?"

Aria almost choked on her water. *His* Chloe was into drugs, too? She dabbed her lips with a napkin and raised her gaze to meet his. "We didn't arrest this woman, Mr. Rhodes. She's a murder victim."

The knuckles of his fists blanched and a muscle ticked at the corner of his mouth. "She's dead?"

"She is. Her body was found two nights ago, on a deserted gravel path next to the lake…"

"The baby?"

"He's safe. He's currently with Child Protective Services, although I think they've found him a foster home for now, until we can identify him…and the woman found next to his car seat."

Rhodes rolled his broad shoulders and cranked his head back and forth, as if resetting his course, or maybe preparing for the worst. "Did the car seat have toys attached to it? Some keys? A sheep?"

Did it? Were there keys? She was not going to devastate or give false hope to Mr. Rhodes on the basis of a set of plastic keys and a sheep. "I'm not sure. You asked about an arrest for drugs. Was Chloe involved with drugs?"

"Yeah, she was." With the tip of his finger, he traced a bead of water down the outside of his sweating glass. "She was addicted to opioids. Every time I read about an unintended overdose due to opioids, my heart stops. Are you sure this woman was murdered? Could it have been a drug overdose?"

"The victim was shot through the chest—and she's not the only one. There was another murder victim a few weeks ago in the same area, same scenario." She didn't have to tell him about the IDs or the drugs...not yet. "Was Chloe just a user or did she deal?"

"God, I don't know." He dug his fingers into his thick hair, ruffling the ends. "I think she may have sold some small quantities to finance her habit. She couldn't get money from me...for that. Anything she needed for herself or Danny, I bought. I didn't give her money because she'd spend it all on drugs."

Danny, the baby's name was Danny—if the victim was Chloe. Jane Doe number two had brown hair and brown eyes—but then, so did the other woman. The IDs indicated brown/brown.

"When did you realize Chloe was missing?"

"Just last week—Thanksgiving. She was supposed to come to my place for the holiday, told me specifically she'd be there, and then didn't show up."

"She's an addict."

"I know. That's why she usually blows off my invitations. If she has no intention of following through, she tells me flat-out." He ran his knuckles over the sexy reddish-blond stubble on his chin. "She told me she was coming for Thanksgiving, had a little money."

"She said that?" Aria scribbled in her notebook. She could've been dealing.

"Uh-huh."

The waiter crept up to the table again. "Are you going to order something?"

"Yeah, I'm sorry." Mr. Rhodes—Gary—picked up the laminated menu and ordered a cup of coffee.

Feeling sorry for the guy, Aria ordered a turkey sandwich on wheat, to go.

"How am I going to find out if this murder victim and

baby are my sister and nephew?" His Adam's apple bobbed in his throat when he swallowed. "Do you have pictures?"

Aria didn't plan to whip out pictures of a dead body in the middle of a diner—even if she had them on her, which she didn't. "The victim's body is at the St. Clair County Medical Examiner's Office. I can take you there to ID the body."

The line of his jaw hardened, as if he were clenching his teeth. He gave one brisk nod. "I'll do that."

The waiter returned with Gary's coffee and a caddy of cream, sugar and fake sugar, placing everything on the table in front of him.

When the waiter left, Gary shoved the cup and saucer toward Aria and the dark liquid sloshed over the rim. "I don't want the coffee. I just felt like we should order something for taking up a table. Do you want it?"

"I felt the same way." She dumped some cream into the cup and swirled it through with a spoon. She didn't want it to go to waste, so she took a sip, wrinkling her nose.

Gary cocked his head. "You don't have to drink it if you don't want to."

"We never wasted anything in our house. If I don't drink at least half of this coffee, I'll have it put in a to-go cup." She brought the mug to her lips to hide her warm cheeks. She never got personal on the job. She had no idea what had made her spill embarrassing family habits.

"Frugality is not a bad quality to have." He drew shapes on the table with the tip of his finger. "Sometimes I think… never mind."

"Oh, come on. I revealed my family's extreme cheapness."

"I think if my family had had more qualities like prudence and self-awareness, maybe Chloe would've never gotten hooked on drugs. Having the best of everything without working for it, never denying yourself one single, thing—" he shrugged "—it's not a healthy way to live."

Aria sucked in the coffee too fast and it burned the roof of her mouth. She fanned her face as her gaze tracked over Gary's work clothes. The best of everything? Didn't this guy work at the docks?

She took a sip of water and rolled the glass between her palms. "Why'd we meet here instead of on the job? Your boss wouldn't have given you a few minutes to talk to the FBI about your missing sister?"

"I didn't want anyone to know I had a missing sister." He spread his hands, which had calluses but not the ground-in grit around his fingernails that most longshoremen accumulated after years on the docks.

Aria narrowed her eyes. "Why not?"

He lifted one shoulder. "I'm new on the job. I don't want the attention. I don't want my boss to think I'm not focused on my work."

Those were three reasons he gave her. Why did they all sound rehearsed? "So, you told your boss you weren't feeling well today."

"A little white lie." He leaned in close over the table. So close, she could smell his masculine scent, a mixture of soap and sweat. "Can you keep my secret, Agent Calletti?"

When he looked at her like that, like they shared a secret, special to just the two of them, she'd not only keep his secret, she'd swallow the key.

"We don't need to tell your boss." She ducked her head and reached for the coffee she didn't want, just to break away from his blue gaze that seemed to hold sway over her. "But if I'm going to be keeping your secrets, you'd better dispense with the agent business and call me Aria."

"Like a song from an Italian opera." He planted his

elbow on the table and propped his chin on his fist. "I appreciate your...discretion."

Her heart fluttered in her chest like she had a crush on the high school football captain, who'd actually known better than to even look her way with her brothers standing guard. "If your sister does turn out to be this victim, you might not be able to keep your boss in the dark. You do have different last names, though."

"Chloe is my half sister. Same mother, different fathers and different last names." As the waiter dropped off her bagged sandwich, Gary said, "Anyway, thanks for meeting me here instead of barging onto the dock."

"No problem." She flipped open her wallet, pulled out a ten and three ones and anchored a bottle of ketchup on top of the bills.

Gary reached for his wallet. "I'll pay for the coffee."

"Taken care of. I'm not *that* cheap."

"Good to know." He pinched her bag of food between his fingers. "Can we get going now?"

Why was that good to know? It would only be good to know if they planned to see each other again, and they'd only see each other again if this Jane Doe turned out to be Chloe. She hoped fervently that wasn't the case and that she never saw Gary Rhodes again.

"You can follow me over." She slid from the booth and he followed suit, the bag dangling from his fingers.

He reached the door before she did and held it open for her. They walked side by side to the parking lot. He pointed to a beat-up white truck. "That's me."

"I'm in the black sedan on the next row. I have the address to the medical examiner's office, so you can follow me over," she repeated. She stood in front of him awkwardly, tilting her head back, waiting for her sandwich. "You can keep that if you want."

"Oh." He blinked lashes way too long for a longshore-man, and placed the bag in her hands as if it were precious cargo instead of a turkey sandwich. "I'll see you over there."

As she reached her own car, Aria mumbled to herself, "Don't turn around, don't turn around."

She did anyway and caught Gary next to his truck, looking after her.

He raised his hand and she did the same, as if just verifying with him that he knew which car belonged to her, instead of wanting to get one last look at him—before his world was possibly wrecked.

When she got in her car, she placed a call to the medical examiner's office to give them a heads-up. She recited the case number and let them know a possible family member was coming in for an ID.

With this knowledge, the morgue attendant would get the body out of the cooler. Nobody wanted to see his or her loved one being pulled from a drawer. They'd also cover the body with a sheet and just fold back the cover from the face.

As soon as she ended the call, another one came in from Axel. "Hi, Axel. I'm on my way to the ME's office with the brother tailing me. He confirmed his sister was into drugs and her baby is seven months old, but she is a blond-blue."

"Yeah, about that, Aria…" Axel cleared his throat. "I was looking over the autopsy reports with Alana, and Jane Doe number two doesn't actually have brown eyes."

Aria's gaze darted to the rearview mirror with Gary's beater on her tail, a sick churning in her gut.

"What does that mean, Axel? White female with brown hair and brown eyes—that's what we got."

"Jane Doe number two was wearing contacts—brown contacts."

Chapter Five

Grayson tried to keep up with the sedan in his rumbling truck. Didn't FBI agents have to be good drivers?

He ran his tongue along his teeth in his sandpaper mouth. That eight-ounce glass at the diner hadn't cut it. He needed about a gallon of water. He released his tight grip on the steering wheel and flexed his stiff fingers. Despite the chill outside, a bead of sweat ran down his back beneath his clothing.

This victim had brown hair and brown eyes. Chloe had blond hair, lighter than his own, and big blue eyes that used to sparkle when she was a little girl—before the bad choices and the drugs.

When Dad had died in a private plane crash and Mom had married Gunnar Larsen—too soon after Dad's death for Grayson's liking—he'd resented it. Had resented the stepfather who'd tried to replace Dad, who'd lived high on the hog on the money Dad had earned. But he never resented his little sister. He'd always protected her. But he'd gotten busy expanding Dad's business and Chloe had gotten wild after her own father had died on a drink-and-drug-fueled binge.

Maybe Grayson hadn't done enough, but he'd make it up to Danny. If this poor woman, with brown hair and brown eyes, didn't turn out to be Chloe, once he found his sister, he'd do better for both her and her son.

How could this be Chloe, unless Agent Calletti was mistaken about the victim's description? Agent Calletti—Aria—didn't strike him as someone who made mistakes. Except when she drove.

Did she just roll through that stop sign? He tapped the brake pedal and accelerated after her. She put on her turn signal and he followed her into the parking lot of McLaren Port Huron hospital.

He was out of the truck before she exited her vehicle and waiting by her open car door as she collected her bag and purse from the back seat.

She seemed surprised to see him next to her car, as if she'd forgotten the purpose of this visit. He couldn't, and he shoved his unsteady hands into his pockets.

"Are they expecting us?"

"I called on the way over. I'll let hospital reception know we're here and on our way to the medical examiner's office, which is located in the hospital." Her coffee-colored eyes shimmered when she looked at him. Then she dropped her dark lashes to shutter them.

A feather of apprehension brushed the back of his neck. Did she realize she'd made a mistake about the coloring of the victim? He didn't want to put her on the spot in the middle of the parking lot, so he stiffened his spine and said, "I'm ready."

The hospital doors whispered open and Aria strode up to the reception desk and stated their business.

The receptionist, her lip-sticked mouth pinched into an *O*, slid a glance his way. He must look as bad as he felt. He licked his lips. It couldn't be Chloe. She had blue eyes.

"They're ready for us." Aria's low heels clicked on the linoleum as she walked to the elevator.

When the doors opened, a few people spilled out and Grayson smacked his hand against the door to hold it open for Aria.

As a man jogged up to squeeze in before the doors closed, Aria said, "We're going down."

"Oops." The man backed up and the doors trundled to close the two of them in the dark interior of the elevator.

Of course, the morgue would be in the basement. Cold, dim, isolated. Chloe didn't belong in a place like that.

The doors opened into a long hallway, one fluorescent light at the end flickering, giving the place a ghoulish atmosphere. He rolled his shoulders back. His imagination was working overtime down here.

Aria walked ahead of him, hardly moving fast, but his own footsteps trailed behind hers as if he had lead boots on his feet.

She stopped at a door with a window in the top, safety glass with embedded wire mesh. Aria was too short to see through the glass, but Grayson could make out a metal table with a body covered by a sheet on top of it. Pain stabbed his temple.

Aria touched his arm. "Do you want me to come in with you or wait here at first?"

He cranked his head toward her, widening his eyes. It never occurred to him that he'd have to do this alone. As the only person who knew about his fears except for the blasé police, Aria had to be with him in this. He had no one else.

Her hand still on his arm, she squeezed it. "I'll come in with you."

She rapped on the door with one knuckle and a man in blue scrubs and a blue tinge to his skin opened the door.

He nodded as he widened the door, his face grim, to match the company he kept in here.

The chill in the room didn't faze Grayson. His muscles had seized up as soon as they'd left the elevator, and his jaw ached from the clenching.

The attendant stood at the head of the metal gurney and Grayson looked at the form beneath the sheet for the first time. Chloe had more substance than that draped figure. She'd never been that tiny, had she?

"Are you ready, sir?"

Grayson swallowed the lump in his throat and nodded.

The attendant gingerly lifted the white sheet like a groom lifting his bride's wedding veil.

Grayson began shaking his head as he took in the white face with the brown hair scooped back from the forehead. It couldn't be Chloe…and then he saw the tiny mole, about a half an inch above the corner of her mouth. She used to call it her Marilyn Monroe mole to match her hair. Her hair. Brown hair. Chloe with brown hair.

"Gary?" Aria whispered his fake name, as if afraid to wake the sleeping girl on the ice-cold slab. "Is this Chloe?"

His nose stung and he sniffed. "Yes, that's her. That's my sister Chloe Larsen."

"I'm sorry for your loss, sir." The attendant flicked the sheet back over Chloe's face…and her mole.

Grayson's feet were rooted to the floor and the three of them stood around Chloe's body in a frozen tableau. He realized Aria and the morgue attendant were waiting for him—to scream, yell, cry, collapse? Probably just waiting for him to move so the guy could shove her back into that drawer.

Aria's hand brushed his; it was the only thing that felt warm and alive in here. "Do you want to leave, Gary?"

He peeled his tongue from the roof of his mouth and managed a sound in the back of his throat. He turned for the door with a stumble in his step and Aria caught his arm.

She yanked the door open and practically shoved him into the hallway.

He walked toward the elevator and then did a half turn and fell against the wall. He covered his face with one hand and uttered the one thing that had been keeping him going since the moment Aria had called him. "I didn't see her eyes. Her eyes were closed. Chloe has blue eyes."

"Gary—" Aria touched his shoulder "—Chloe was wearing brown contacts. And, as you saw, her hair was dyed brown."

His hand slipped from his face. "Why? The hair, maybe, but why go through the trouble of wearing contact lenses to change your eye color?"

"There are a few things I didn't tell you about the case." She glanced over her shoulder at the door to the morgue. "Let's get out of here."

They didn't say a word to each other until they walked out of the hospital. Grayson filled his lungs with fresh air, taking several deep breaths. Chloe was dead. Murdered. He'd have to tell Mom…if he could find her. At this time of the year, she'd probably be in the Caribbean with her latest European *royal* boy toy.

Aria dragged some keys from her purse. "Let's sit in my car for a minute. Do you need some water? I can run back inside and get you something to drink from the vending machine."

Grayson grabbed the back of his neck and dug his fingers into his flesh. "I have some water in my truck. We can sit there. Do you need to let someone know I ID'd the…victim?"

"I'll send a text. You need to sit down."

Did he look like he was about to unravel? He needed

to stay strong. He may not have always been there for Chloe in the past, but he planned to be there for her now. "I'm all right."

He led her to his truck and opened the passenger door for her. He placed a hand on her elbow as she stepped onto the running board and helped her inside the vehicle.

He went around to the other side and got in behind the wheel, reaching into the back for his lunch pail. He unzipped it and pulled out a bottle of water and a sandwich. Holding the food out to Aria, he said, "You didn't get a chance to eat. Have this."

"I'm not hungry. Are you all right? I'm so sorry for your loss. I know you never believed this woman was your sister until you looked at her face."

Closing his eyes, he chugged down the water. "It didn't even look like her, not really, not with the brown hair, and her face looked so…but I recognized the mole above her mouth. And once I saw that, I saw Chloe. But why the contacts? Why the hair color? What the hell is going on?"

"I mentioned the other victim to you—also brown hair and eyes. She and your sister looked very similar."

"Was that victim wearing contacts, too?"

"No, and her hair was naturally brown."

"What does it mean?"

"Both women were carrying identical IDs—same name, same physical description, same address."

Grayson squeezed the bottle of water with one hand, denting it. "What was the name on the ID?"

"Maddie Johnson. Does that mean anything to you?"

"No. Is she a real person?"

"Nothing about those IDs was real. The address was fake, too."

"Chloe wore brown contacts and dyed her hair to match

this ID for some reason. Is there any other connection between my sister and the other woman?"

Aria pinned her hands between her knees, and her chest rose and fell quickly. "They both had packets of fentanyl on them—packaged to sell. The first victim also had opioids in her system, but the toxicology report on your sister hasn't come back yet."

Grayson slammed his hand against the steering wheel. "I knew it. This has something to do with drugs. She was using. She was selling. And she put Danny in danger. Where is he? Who has Danny? I need to see him."

"I told you before, Gary, Danny's with a foster family right now for his protection."

"Protection from me?" He jabbed his thumb against his chest as his blood heated. The shock and sadness that had hit him in the morgue were quickly morphing into anger—anger at Chloe, anger at her killer, their mother, himself. With the water bottle still gripped in his hand, he slammed it into the cup holder. "I'm his uncle. He doesn't need protection from me. I'm the one who's going to protect him from now on."

Aria watched him steadily, her dark eyes liquid pools of sympathy. "Look at it from the viewpoint of CPS. This baby escaped an encounter with death. CPS doesn't even know who his mother is right now. They don't know his father, and they don't know who you are. They can't allow some random guy to show up and claim the baby. You understand that, right?"

Her measured tone sounded like she was talking to some wild man who had to be talked off the ledge. His chest heated with shame. Aria didn't deserve his anger.

He tilted his head back against the headrest and drew in a long breath. "I'm sorry, Aria. I didn't mean to go off on you."

"Look, you don't have to apologize to me." She swept her ponytail off her shoulder with one hand. "This has been a shock. I understand you're upset. You have every right to be upset, angry, howling at the moon."

"Not quite there yet." He ran a hand through his hair. "What do I need to do to prove I'm Danny's uncle? How can I get him back?"

"Our FBI liaison is working with CPS. I'll get in touch with her and let her know I've located the baby's uncle. The Port Huron PD already ordered a DNA test for Chloe and Danny to make sure they were mother and child. Once CPS has Danny's DNA, you'll probably be asked to submit yours for a match. Will there be a father involved?"

"I have no idea who Danny's father is. Chloe never told me—if she even knew." He crumpled his hand into a fist and pounded his chest. "I'm all he has now. Our mother is not interested in being a grandmother. I don't think she's even seen Danny once."

"Are…are you married?"

"No. Why do you ask? You don't think a single man can take care of a baby?" He folded his arms and glanced at her from the corner of his eye.

"I think it's difficult for a single man or woman to care for a baby, especially without experience…unless you have children." Her knee bounced up and down, and he almost placed a hand on her leg to stop it.

He dug his fingers into his biceps. "I don't have children, and you're right, I don't have any experience with babies. But I can take care of Danny."

"You'll need help." She held up her hand, flashing him a peace sign. "No offense, but I know what it's like to work long hours. As a longshoreman, you probably work long and physical hours. It's a lot to expect you to deal with a baby when you get home from work."

"I'm not a longshoreman, Aria. I'm here in Port Huron under false pretenses, and my name's not Gary. It's Grayson, Grayson Rhodes, and I'm going to find out who killed my sister."

Chapter Six

Aria whipped her head around to face him. That explained some things about the mysterious Mr. Rhodes, but not all. For all his outrage, was he mixed up in his sister's death?

"Whoa, back up. You've been lying to me?" She pressed her lips together in a hard line.

"Not about the important stuff. Chloe is my sister and Danny is my nephew." He plucked the misshapen plastic bottle from the cup holder and took a sip of water.

"How'd you wind up in Port Huron working at the docks under an assumed name—half assumed name?"

"When Chloe and Danny went missing and the cops didn't seem to give a rip, I figured I might be able to do some snooping around on my own. Chloe had mentioned hanging out around here, so I figured it was a good location to start. What better place to glean some information about a missing person near the border than at a dock, around boats?"

"So, you're undercover? That's why you don't want your boss to know about Chloe." Civilians working undercover never turned out well—even when the civilian was the very capable-looking Gary—Grayson. No longshoreman in the history of mankind was ever named Grayson.

She clicked the window button. "I need some air."

Grayson turned the key in the ignition and she buzzed

down the window a few inches. The cold air that blasted into the truck hit her like a slap to the face—a second slap to the face. She was FBI now. Shouldn't she have figured out he really wasn't a longshoreman? The signs had been there. Axel would've made Grayson in about two minutes.

"That's right. I'm hoping to pick up some information. The ice there is just beginning to thaw."

She narrowed her eyes. "How'd you get that position so fast? Work at the docks is a prime job around here."

"I'm not taking a job away from anyone." He raised his right hand. "I swear. I know someone who knows someone in high places, and the opening was created for me—and I earn my keep. I'm no slacker."

Her gaze traveled across his wide shoulders and got caught on his solid biceps beneath his shirt. "Didn't say you were. Have you heard anything, yet?"

"No, but now that I know more details about the murders of Chloe and the other woman, I'll have a better idea of what to look out for." His blue eyes, as he stared over the top of the steering wheel, were chips of ice. "Are you going to rat me out to the cops or your FBI buddies?"

"The cops? No. My FBI *buddies*? Maybe. I'm the new kid on the block, and I don't want to start out my career by keeping secrets from my coworkers."

"I understand that, and I don't want to put you in a compromising position." He touched the back of her hand and drew back as if he'd received an electrical shock. "I want to thank you again for coming in there with me."

His touch acted like a prod and she almost jumped in her seat. "I—I had to be in there with you for the purposes of the identification."

"Not that. I know that." He held on to the steering wheel again with both hands, as if to anchor himself. "Having you there softened the blow. You knew it was Chloe before we walked in there, didn't you?"

"I had received a phone call from my supervisory agent, who'd been going over the autopsy reports, and he told me the victim had been wearing brown contacts. So, I knew her eyes were blue. Yes, I knew. I'm so sorry."

"It's still so unreal right now." He rubbed his knuckles across his scruff. "But I'm not giving up on finding Chloe's killer. I'm keeping that job on the docks."

"I'm not going to encourage you to investigate on your own, but I'm not going to stop you." She pulled her purse into her lap and inserted her fingers in a side pocket to pull out her business card. "I didn't even give you my card yet."

"I have your number in my phone from when you called me."

She dug in her purse for a pen and scribbled on the back of the card. Pinching the card between two fingers, she held it out to him. "My personal cell phone number… just in case."

As he reached for it, she yanked it away. "Are you going to tell me who you are? What made you come to Port Huron to look for Chloe? You're not from here."

"I live in Detroit. When my father died, he had left the majority of his business in trust for me. I was only eight when he passed away. My mother remarried a few years later and she and her new husband had Chloe. Chloe's dad died when she was a teen and then she spiraled out of control. My mother couldn't handle her, and I was busy building up my father's business." He pinched the bridge of his nose and squeezed his eyes closed.

She wanted to reach for him again, run her hand down his arm, soothe away his guilt, but that wasn't her job. The best way she could serve Grayson and Chloe was by catching her killer. "Chloe moved to Port Huron?"

"Chloe didn't move anywhere—she just moved around. Sometimes she'd tell me where she was and sometimes I didn't hear from her for months at a time. I knew about Danny, tried to send her things for the baby, things she couldn't hock for drugs." He twisted his head toward her when she'd made a sound in the back of her throat. "Yeah, it was that bad."

"How'd you know she was in Port Huron?"

"I invited her to my place for Thanksgiving, just like I always did, only this time she accepted. She rarely took me up on my invitations, but this time she agreed to come over. Told me she was in Port Huron for a job." He snorted, the nostrils of his patrician nose flaring. "I should've known what kind of job."

"Was Chloe ever involved in…sex work?" Aria bit her bottom lip.

"I don't know. I wondered if that's where the baby came from." His mouth tightened. "I hate to admit it, but it wouldn't surprise me if she was hooking. She had an expensive habit."

"So, she'd do anything for money, including sell drugs?"

"I think so. You found fentanyl on her, right? Enough to sell?"

"That, or she'd just made a buy."

"Question for you." Grayson braced his hands against the steering wheel. "Why didn't the person who killed her take the drugs off her? Why not take it to use or to sell or to point the finger in a different direction?"

"You're thinking like a cop. We're not sure, unless the drugs were left on the victims to make a point." Her cell phone rang and she held up her finger to Grayson. "I need to take this."

When she answered, and before she could even say hello, Rihanna started breathlessly talking into the phone.

"I heard from Axel that you identified Jane Doe number two. Good work, Aria."

"I did." Aria's gaze slid to Grayson, staring out the window, a muscle twitching next to his eye. "She's Chloe Larsen, and her baby's name is Danny. I'm with her brother and the baby's uncle right now. He wants custody of the baby. The grandmother is out of the picture, and he's the nearest living relative."

Grayson nodded.

"That's great. Danny's a little love. His foster parents got him last night and adore him already." Rihanna lowered her voice as if Grayson could hear her over the phone. "Is the uncle prepared to give his DNA? We can't go handing this baby off to a random stranger. What's the uncle's name?"

"His name is Grayson Rhodes, and he's more than willing to have his DNA checked. He's anxious to get custody of Danny."

Grayson nodded again, more aggressively this time.

"Grayson Rhodes." Rihanna whistled. "I know that name."

"You do?" Aria's gaze darted to Grayson once more, now glancing through his phone.

"He's a hotshot developer in Detroit. His company is coming in and gentrifying whole blocks. The dead girl is Grayson Rhodes's sister?"

"I'll tell you about it later. When do you want Mr. Rhodes to submit his DNA and to whom?"

"I'll take charge of him—and if he looks anything like his pictures, I'll be more than happy to do so."

Two spots of heat flamed in Aria's cheeks. "I'll have him contact you. Thanks, Rihanna."

"Thank *you*, superstar."

Aria ended the call and cleared her throat. "I'm going

to give you the number of our liaison with CPS. Her name is Rihanna Clark and she'll walk you through the DNA submission. The sooner they can verify you, the faster you'll get Danny."

"I just want him home for Christmas. Do you think that's possible?"

"You'll have to ask Rihanna, but I don't see why not." She checked the time on her phone. "You should probably see if you can get that done while you're off work. I assume you're going back tomorrow."

"I know so much more now, thanks to you. I know what to listen for. I know what questions to ask."

"Don't show too much interest or you'll give yourself away."

He raised one eyebrow. "Thanks for the tip. You do much undercover work?"

"Believe it or not, I was a narc working in high schools." She smoothed her hands over her professional slacks.

"I can believe it—I mean the looks, not the attitude—unless you were the quiet girl who kept her mouth shut."

"That's exactly what I was, and I advise you to be the same type. Keep your eyes and ears open, but don't snoop around. You'll give yourself away." She dipped down to reach into her laptop case, feeling for Rihanna's cards. They all kept Rihanna's cards along with their own for moments like this. She snapped the card onto the console. "This is Rihanna Clark's info. I'll let you go now so you can take care of the DNA and not have to miss out on work."

"Thanks, Aria. I don't think I could've gotten through this without you today." He pointed to his smooshed sandwich on the console. "You can have that, if you want."

"I've got my own sandwich from the diner, remember?"

Sitting across from him in the diner seemed like it happened a million years ago. "You eat it. You've had a shock."

"I don't feel like eating anything." He picked up the sandwich and let it drop. "Is food supposed to cure shock?"

"I'm Italian. Food cures everything." She smiled at him and her heart hurt for the pain in his blue eyes.

"Maybe later." He picked up Rihanna's card and held it up to the window, framing it with his fingers. "Is she expecting my call today?"

"If you explain your work situation and she's free, I'm sure she'd be happy to take you over this afternoon before the office closes."

"My work situation." He flicked the corner of the card. "I didn't hear you tell her I was here under false pretenses."

Aria coughed. "She recognized your name. She knows who you are."

"And you didn't?" He flattened out the card on his knee.

"Rihanna deals with the media all the time, so it makes sense that she'd know your name and company."

"Is she going to be willing to keep my name out of the news in regard to Chloe's murder? Once my cover is blown at the docks, I won't be able to sniff around there."

"I think she'll oblige you. We don't want too much getting out about these two murders just yet." She pulled the door handle and the door of the truck creaked as it swung open. "Are you okay?"

"No, but I'll do what I need to do now." One corner of his mouth lifted. "Thanks again for your help, Aria."

"You're welcome, of course. I didn't really do anything except bring you bad news, though."

"Bad news I needed to know."

She swung her legs from the truck and placed one booted foot on the runner, the other hanging in the air. "Call me if you do hear anything…and be careful."

"I will."

Hanging on to the truck, she slid to the ground and hiked her purse and laptop case on each shoulder as she walked to her car. This time she didn't turn around, but when she pulled out of the hospital parking lot she waved at Grayson sitting in his truck, his phone to his ear.

She drove back the hotel, her stomach rumbling with hunger. She parked in the hotel lot and ripped into the bag on the seat next to her. As she took a big bite of the turkey sandwich, she thumbed through her text messages. Apparently, Grayson's name hadn't rung any bells with Axel.

She also checked her personal cell phone and squeezed out a small breath when she saw a few texts from her family and no voice mails. Not that she expected Grayson to contact her immediately after talking to Rihanna.

She shouldn't expect Grayson to contact her at all, unless he had some information about the case. Rich guy slumming to catch his sister's killer. Did he think he was in some cheesy TV show?

She swallowed the last bite of the sandwich and dragged a napkin across her mouth. Then she bunched the paper bag in her fist and exited the car.

She made her way up to Alana's suite where the director had set up a temporary office. The Port Huron PD was in the process of clearing out one of its conference rooms for them, and Opaline was over there directing installation of the equipment they'd need for the case.

She brushed crumbs from her navy-blue slacks and tugged on her matching jacket. She'd taken note that the others had dressed down a little, so she'd play it by ear.

She knocked on the door and Alana swept it open. "Good work on ID'ing Jane Doe number two, Aria. Come on in here."

Aria ducked her head and lifted her hand at Axel and

Selena. "I really didn't do anything except meet with Mr. Rhodes, who'd reported his sister missing. Until Axel let me know Chloe was wearing brown contacts, I wasn't even sure we had the right person, except for the baby— matched the age and sex of little Danny."

"Did he give you any information about his sister?" Axel wedged his foot on the edge of the coffee table, littered with soda cans, coffee cups and water bottles. "We'll have him come in for further questioning."

"I'm sure he's eager to give us any info we need, but he just started a new job and can't get away that easily."

"Even after the murder of his sister?" Selena reached across Axel's leg and grabbed a can.

"H-he doesn't want his work to know that was his sister."

"I get that." Selena blinked her dark lashes and gulped down some soda. "We can make other arrangements for him. What's he going to do about his nephew?"

"Oh, he wants custody. I already put him in touch with Rihanna for a DNA sample. Says he wants him home for Christmas."

"That's sweet." Axel drilled a finger in the side of his cheek. "Is he a suspect?"

Aria's mouth dropped open. "A suspect? Wait. What? In the murder of his sister?"

"He's the closest one to her. We work outward." He drew ever-widening circles in the air. "We need to eliminate him."

"He reported her missing." Aria felt her voice rise in indignation and sealed her lips. Axel was right. They should look at close family as suspects. She'd been blinded by her sympathy for Grayson. Still, her gut told her he wasn't involved and she'd been right to trust him.

Axel didn't seem to notice her passion as he replied,

"Killers report their victims missing all the time to pretend they didn't know they were already dead. What was his demeanor?"

"In denial when I told him the Jane Doe had brown hair and eyes. Couldn't believe it was her, but thought the baby with her was too much of a coincidence. When he saw her in the morgue, he was shocked, upset, got angry later. Just what you'd expect. I doubt he has a motive to kill his sister *and* some other woman who happens to have the same phony ID. He did say Chloe had an addiction and it wouldn't be out of character for her to sell drugs or turn tricks to indulge her habit."

Selena raised her eyebrows. "You spent a lot of time with this guy, huh?"

"I—we met in a diner to discuss his missing persons report, and then we drove to the morgue at the hospital... separately, to ID the body. I couldn't just leave him after that. He was upset and he had questions about Danny."

Alana looked up from her laptop. "You handled it perfectly, Aria, and I agree with you. He doesn't seem like a suspect, but Axel will perform his due diligence to rule him out."

Axel winked at her. "Still waiting on the toxicology tests for Chloe Larsen, but I'm not expecting a different result from the first victim's if the brother told you she was using."

"Obviously, Chloe was wearing brown contacts and dyed her hair brown to fit the description on the ID. The first victim already had brown eyes—no contacts—and maybe brown hair." Selena stood and walked across the room. She snagged a plastic bag and waved it in the air. "Who wants to help me clean up this mess? I'm looking at you, Axel."

"I will absolutely help, but now I know why Max high-tailed it out of here."

"I'm going to shoo all of you out of here in a minute. I'm having dinner in my room, and I'm going to turn in early." Alana removed her glasses and rubbed her eyes. "We should have our command center set up by tomorrow at the PD, so report there in the morning after breakfast unless you have somewhere else to be."

Dinner alone and an early bed sounded good, but Aria didn't want to miss out on any team time. "Is anyone else planning anything for dinner?"

Axel held up his fingers and ticked them off with each name. "Opaline's going to be busy setting us up for tomorrow, and Amanda just went over before you got here to help her. Rihanna is meeting a friend for dinner after she takes care of Rhodes's DNA test. Max is out for a marathon workout. Carly's running down some leads on the fentanyl found on the victims. Who'd I miss?"

"Me." Selena swung a full bag of trash from her fingertips. "I'm hanging out with Blanca. We have some training to do, and Axel's helping me. You're welcome to join us, Aria."

"You know, I think I'll head back to my room, order room service and put my notes in my laptop." Aria patted the side of her bag. "Do you need help with the cleanup in here?"

"You didn't even contribute to the mess." Selena flicked her fingers at the door. "Go—and take a can of soda with you." She pressed a cold, wet can into Aria's hand.

When she got back to her room, Aria realized she hadn't had anything to drink since that horrible coffee at the diner. She popped the tab on the soda and downed half of it before coming up for air, her nose tingling with the carbonation.

After transferring her notes from her meeting with Grayson into a file on her computer, she ordered fish and chips, coleslaw and a small bottle of chardonnay from room service and changed into a pair of sweats and an FBI T-shirt.

While finishing off her meal, Aria's personal cell buzzed. She licked the ketchup off her fingers, squished a napkin in her hand and tapped the display to read the text.

Her heart stuttered when she saw Grayson's name. She pushed away the tray and picked up the phone between her palms. She read the text: Gave my DNA. Couldn't see Danny.

She wiped her hands thoroughly and texted back, You will. Be patient.

She watched the blinking cursor in the text field for several seconds and then took a swig of wine. Maybe she shouldn't have responded so quickly.

When the words blurred before her eyes, she set the phone on the nightstand and hoisted her tray from the bed. She placed it outside the door of her room.

Grabbing her half glass of wine, she settled on the bed and turned on the TV. Another glance at her phone told her Grayson hadn't responded to her eager reply.

The wine or the TV must've lulled Aria to sleep because she woke with a start, her heart pounding. Then she bolted upright at the sharp knock on the door.

"Aria, are you awake?" Carly's voice on the other side of the door, low and urgent, had Aria scrambling from the bed. She pressed her eye to the peephole and pulled the door open.

Carly, in a pair of leopard-print PJs, her face as pale as her hair, folded her arms and said, "Alana got the call. We have another one."

"Another one?" Aria shook her head, dislodging the wisps of sleep clinging to her sluggish brain.

"Another murder of a brown-haired, brown-eyed girl."

Chapter Seven

Alana shoved her gloved hands into her coat pockets and puffed out a breath, watching it form in the cold air. Her boots crunched the gravel as she moved toward the bright lights illuminating the crime scene, the body crumpled on the ground, little numbered cones scattered around the victim, a young cop unfurling a roll of crime scene tape.

With the Port Huron PD already out here, Alana had sent just Aria, Carly and Axel from the team—Axel to interface with Detective Massey from the Major Crimes Unit, Aria and Carly to remind the PD who was really in charge.

Aria didn't want to step on any toes, though. An FBI agent could get a lot more information if the PD felt it was working with you, not in competition with you. She'd seen it enough on the other side.

She approached Massey with her hand outstretched. "Detective Massey. We hit pay dirt with that missing person's report from Mr. Rhodes. Good instincts there. At least we've identified one of these victims, and maybe your department can help us ID this one, as well."

Running a hand over his thinning gray hair, trying to adjust it over his bald spot, a move he probably did subconsciously, Massey nodded at her. "Damn shame. I have two daughters around the same age. Makes me sick. Don't ever get used to it, Agent Calletti. If it still tortures you every night, you haven't lost your humanity."

Axel took a step in their direction, stopped and pivoted, leaving Massey to her.

"That's what Smitty used to tell me, sir." She circled the body, her finger ringing the air. "This looks a little different from the other two, doesn't it? The first two victims were flat on their backs, probably blown back from the blast of the gun. This one is on her side, scuff and drag marks in the gravel around her body."

Massey's shaggy gray eyebrows furrowed over his nose. "Like there was some kind of struggle."

"He either surprised the other two or they knew him. This time it looks like there was a tussle."

"Thank God, no baby with this one." Massey, grabbed one of the uniformed officers by the sleeve. "Pressler, make sure the victim's hands are bagged before the medical examiner gets here."

"Who found the body? No mysterious call this time?" Aria crouched beside the victim and eyed her dark roots. Another dye job?

"It was a jogger. Everything else the same, though. Same ID as the other two, and a quantity of fentanyl tucked in her purse, ready for sale." Massey cupped a hand over his mouth and yelled, "Make sure you do a thorough search this time. Agent Calletti found a tissue near victim two's crime site that we missed. Don't miss anything."

After several more minutes with Massey, Aria stepped away from him in case Max wanted an opportunity to talk to the PHPD detective. "Thanks for your help, Detective Massey."

She wandered over to where Carly was examining an evidence bag containing the baggie of fentanyl found on the latest victim.

Carly said, "Thanks to you, Aria, I'm having all the fentanyl tested for its purity and makeup. Maybe we can track where it's coming from."

Axel sidled up and wedged himself between them, ducking his head. "And thanks to Aria, we have a great relationship with the PHPD. She has gruff old Detective Massey over there eating out of her hand."

Aria opened her mouth to protest that it was just because they both knew Smitty, but she snapped it shut when Carly squeezed her arm. Why not take a little credit? She couldn't be the starstruck fan-girl her entire career with the FBI.

Instead she allowed a tiny smile to curl her lips—until she caught sight of the victim lying on the ground, a dark pool of blood at her back.

She wasn't here to score points. She was here to find a killer—and as Massey said, you never wanted to lose your humanity.

That woman was someone's daughter, wife…sister.

GRAYSON STUFFED A sandwich into his lunch pail and grabbed a bottle of water from the fridge. His current abode was one of those pay-by-the-week motels a few blocks from the lake—only the finest.

He'd spit into a tube yesterday to prove he was related to Danny. He'd do a lot more than that for the little guy if he could. He wanted that baby home for Christmas, wanted to give him the kind of life Chloe couldn't.

He'd tried to reach Mom last night, but she hadn't picked up. Probably didn't even have international calling on her phone in Mustique or wherever she was this time.

He'd almost texted Aria back after their exchange last night. Some need had driven him to let her know he'd supplied his DNA to CPS, but when she'd responded by advising him to be patient regarding seeing Danny, he felt like he'd whined enough to her.

Aria was typically the kind of woman he wined and dined and spoiled—at least in the looks department. But her demeanor couldn't be more different from the women he usually dated. He had a feeling Aria wouldn't be impressed by expensive bottles of champagne, a weekend in Paris or a Tiffany bracelet as a lovely parting gift.

He snorted and slammed the lid of his lunch pail. Why was he thinking about dating the serious FBI agent, anyway? She probably had a hard-nosed, no-nonsense cop husband or something and two kids. The fact that she didn't wear a wedding ring meant nothing.

As he unhitched his coat from the hook by the door, his phone buzzed. He glanced at the display, and his pulse picked up speed. Agent Calletti's ears must've been ringing.

"Hello?"

"Grayson, it's Special Agent Calletti... Aria. How are you doing this morning?"

"What are those stages of grief? I'm through the shock and denial, still feeling the guilt, and now I'm on the verge of white-hot anger—and I'm going to stay there until Chloe's killer is brought to justice."

"I—I have some news for you. Maybe you've seen it on TV already."

"Have you arrested someone? Did you find more evidence?"

"Another young woman was murdered last night." She rushed her next words as he absorbed this new shock. "Same MO—one shot to the chest, brunette carrying fentanyl and with the same ID as Chloe and the other woman."

Grayson gritted his teeth. "Another one. What the hell is going on, Aria?"

"We don't know yet, Grayson, but we're going to figure it out. The drugs and the IDs link these women, and being this close to the border, I'm betting the murders are connected to the drug trade."

He heard voices in the background as she said, "I have to get going, but I wanted to let you know about this murder."

"Thanks for keeping me informed. It means a lot."

They ended the call and Grayson charged out the door of his room, stuffing his arms into his jacket. The cops and the FBI agents weren't the only ones who were going to get to the bottom of this.

He needed to start making some friends on the dock.

AT THE END of the workday, Grayson punched his card in the time clock with the cracked face and jammed it into the slot on the wall. He said to everyone and no one in particular, "Helluva day. That one load nearly broke my back."

"C'mon, Gary. You're a big boy. You can handle it." Will, a beefy redhead with freckled arms, cackled.

"Yeah, seemed to me Gary was handling most of that load, Will, while you were sitting on your backside." Chuck punched his own timecard and winked at Grayson. "We're heading to The Tavern tonight for some beers. Wanna come this time? Did your landlord fix that toilet?"

"Yeah, he did, but it was kinda like Will here. He sat on his ass while I did most of the work." Grayson smacked Will on the back and the redhead let out his annoying laugh again. "The Tavern's the place near the noncommercial dock side?"

"That's it. They do a happy hour with half-price beers and some decent bar food." Will slung his jacket over his shoulder. "Just don't drink and drive in this town. I already got one deuce. The cops are real jerks about it."

"Got it. My place isn't that far if I have to walk."

Will elbowed Grayson in the ribs. "I'm hoping to get lucky with one of those pretty young things that flutter around the boats."

Grayson's breath hitched in his throat. "Oh, yeah? Do they hang out at The Tavern?"

"That, they do, my man. That, they do."

One of the younger guys yelled back, "Yeah, Will's been trying to hook one of them for years."

"Never give up." Will held up his index finger and then swapped it for his middle finger as he trudged to his truck.

Grayson headed for his own truck with his blood fizzing. Could the young women who hung around the pleasure boat dock and The Tavern be the ones involved in the drug trade?

Like a caravan, the work trucks pulled out of the parking lot and wended their way around the marina on the other side. Grayson followed along, glancing at the diner where he'd met Aria yesterday. He hadn't heard anything from her today but hoped the third victim had provided more evidence.

As his coworkers pulled their vehicles to the front of the bar, Grayson parked at the edge of the parking lot—better for a quick getaway. He dropped his phone into his pocket, leaving it on vibrate, and slid from the truck.

As he entered The Tavern, classic rock music thumped in his chest and several TVs silently broadcast sports channels, giving a blue glow to the dim interior. Grayson squinted toward the bar and didn't have to guess at the drink of choice as the place reeked of beer. The smell of it seemed to emanate from the walls, the wood floor and the pores of the clientele.

The dockworkers occupied most of the seats at the bar and a couple of them had wandered to the back room where the crack of pool balls dominated. Grayson made his way to Chuck and Will, bellied up to the bar, two longnecks in front of them.

Grayson ordered a round for the three of them and knocked back half the brew before wiping his mouth on his sleeve and grabbing a menu from between two napkin holders. "What's good?"

Chuck lifted one big shoulder. "The nachos. The wings."

Two young guys from the dock pushed their way to the edge of the bar and the dark-haired one smacked his hand on the sticky surface. "Chili cheese fries, Trevor."

The bartender flicked a white towel over his shoulder and wedged his hands on the bar, his tattoos snaking up one pumped-up arm in a multicolored sleeve. "Wait your turn, dude. Your uncle hasn't ordered yet."

Grayson's gaze flickered over the dark-haired, olive-skinned, twenty-something who'd demanded the fries—Tony something—and Chuck's ruddy face.

Chuck twisted his mouth. "My sister's kid, Tony Balducci. Pain in my big hairy backside. He works with us, although if you blinked, you'd miss it."

Tony laughed, his dark eyes turning into slits. "C'mon, Uncle Chuck. That job's just a temporary for me. I got me some bigger, better plans."

Chuck rolled his eyes. "Kid thinks he's gonna be a rap star. Anyway, bring us some wings and nachos, Trevor, and hell, bring out the chili cheese fries for Tony and Zane."

Grayson had seen Zane around the docks, too. With his pimply neck and skinny arms, the kid didn't do any heavy lifting.

Zane held out his fist, a different letter on each finger before the first joint, for a bump with Chuck's. "You're the man, Uncle Chuck."

With a quick glance at the letters, Grayson could make

out B-A-L-E-R. Was that supposed to spell baller? Clearly, Zane was a genius.

"Bring on the hotties." Will tipped his bottle toward the door at two young women sashaying into the bar, their heads together, both brunettes—or, one brunette and the other a raven-black.

Grayson's heart thumped in his chest. Could these two be involved in whatever was going down at the lake? A lot of women had brown hair, but he held up his phone anyway, peering at it and aiming it at the women. He snapped a few pictures.

As Will leaned in to see his view, Grayson switched to text. "Damn, ex-wife is texting me again."

"Put that number on ignore, dude." Will rapped his knuckles on top of the bar.

Grayson slid the phone into his pocket and finished his beer. "Who's ready for another round?"

"You got the last one." Chuck waved at Trevor. "It's my turn."

Two other guys from work joined them and they all proceeded to buy rounds of drinks until Grayson had three bottles lined up in front of him. He couldn't refuse. He also couldn't drink all that beer and expect to do any digging.

To Grayson's advantage, The Tavern got more and more crowded, filling up with the after-work and boating crowds. The number of people gathered around tables and standing at the bar afforded him some cover.

When he saw the two dark-haired women make a bee-line for the poolroom, he pushed away from the bar with a full bottle of beer in his hand. Might as well try to leave this somewhere. "I gotta hit the head."

As soon as he peeled away from the bar, another guy filled his place. Clutching his bottle by the neck, Grayson squeezed through clutches of people on his way to the poolroom.

He stepped just inside, propping up the wall with his shoulder, pretending to watch the action at the tables.

The two women he'd spotted earlier seemed to be waiting for the table where Tony and Zane were making ineffectual stabs at the stripes and solids, their beer bottles balanced on the edge of the felt.

Grayson narrowed his eyes as one of the women, dressed in a short denim skirt with knee-high boots, tugged on Tony's sleeve. He shook her off and wiped his nose with the back of his hand.

She backed off and leaned against the wall, her arms folded, her hands picking at the sleeves of her fringed jacket, the toe of her boot tapping.

Grayson had seen that same restlessness on his sister when she'd been jonesing for a high.

The game ended and the black-haired woman in jeans shrugged off her purple, fake-fur jacket and dropped it on a chair as she took the cue stick from Tony.

Tony then turned his attention to the nervous woman in the skirt. He grabbed her upper arm and yanked her in his wake as he stalked across the poolroom.

Grayson turned to the sign-up sheet next to the door and bent over it.

When Tony and the woman spilled into the bar, Grayson straightened and poked his head out of the room. Tony was charging toward the back hallway of the bar, pushing the woman in front of him.

Grayson, keeping his head down, followed them. Were they going into one of the bathrooms? Maybe this was nothing more than a quick hookup.

Then Tony continued past the restrooms, toward the red

exit sign glowing at the end of the hallway, and pushed the silver release handle, shoving the back door open.

Grayson flattened himself against the wall and inched his way down the hall. He couldn't charge out the back door without Tony noticing…but he could go outside from the front door and make his way around back. He drilled his bottle into the dirt of a potted plant where the hallway opened to the bar and weaved through the crowd to get to the front.

As he stepped outside, he turned to two women several feet away from the entrance, huddled into their jackets, puffing on cigarettes.

He asked one of the women, her red lips puckered as she blew out a stream of smoke, "Can I bum a smoke and a light?"

Her black-lined eyes widened. "Sure, handsome. Can I bum your phone number?"

Grayson chuckled. "Got a girlfriend."

"I bet she doesn't let you smoke." She shook a cigarette from her pack and pressed a book of matches from The Tavern into his palm. "I'd let you smoke. I'd let you do whatever you wanted."

"Thanks, ladies. Have a good night."

He cupped the cigarette and matchbook in his hand as he veered around the corner of the building. He slowed when he got to the back and hugged the clapboard as he crept toward a Dumpster behind the bar, his ears perking up at the sound of voices—one low, one high.

He crouched, pressing himself against the cold metal of the trash bin. The woman's voice floated toward him first.

"But what happened to them? Why were they killed?"

Grayson's heart thundered in his chest so hard, he was afraid it would pound against the metal and give him away.

Tony's voice, gruff like a wannabe gangster's, answered

her. "You don't have to worry about that, Brandy. You don't get greedy. They got greedy."

"What do you mean? They just did what they were told to do."

"They didn't."

Brandy gave a squeak of pain, and Grayson balled his fists. *Coward.*

"What about the rest of us? What about me? I'm scared."

"You don't got nothin' to be scared of."

"Wh-what does that mean? How do you know that, Tony?" She gasped. "You didn't…"

"Shut your damn mouth. Those blah boaties got what was comin' to 'em. You keep your mouth shut and you take care of business, or you'll get what's comin' to you."

Brandy sobbed. "But the other girls, the baby…"

"Shut it!" A slap resounded in the crisp air. "That baby didn't get hurt 'cuz he didn't do nothin'. And if you don't do nothin', you won't get hurt, either."

Chapter Eight

Grayson clamped his teeth together against the sour bile rising from his gut. Tony killed Chloe. He knew it. He could take the bastard out right now and the world would be a better place.

A swell of music filled the alleyway and a rectangle of yellow light spilled onto the ground as someone opened the back door of The Tavern.

"What the hell? You two makin' out, out here?"

"Shut up, Zane. This is business."

"All right, all right, man. Rita's lookin' for Brandy, that's all."

"I'm coming." Brandy sniffed and the heels of her boots clicked on the asphalt.

Grayson bent forward and slipped around the corner of the building. He braced his hand against the wall for several seconds as he took deep breaths, calming his rage. "Blah boaties"? That's what they called these young women? His sister?

He'd tell Aria, but he had no proof. He couldn't have recorded that conversation from so far away. But he could get a picture of that animal.

With unsteady hands, he lit the cigarette and took a long drag. Better have a reason for stepping outside. He continued to smoke the cigarette as he returned to the front of the bar.

After a few more puffs, he ground out the smoke in the ashtray and returned inside. The noise level had increased a few more decibels since he'd left, and he wended his way back to Chuck and Will at the bar.

"Where'd you go?" Chuck shoved a beer at Grayson. "You have some catching up to do."

Grayson held out the matches between his two fingers. "Fell off the wagon and had to go out for a smoke."

Will waved a hand in front of his face. "You smell like an ashtray, dude. You'll never get the ladies that way."

"Unless the ladies are smokers." Grayson tilted back his head and poured some beer down his throat.

Chuck yelled across the room, "Hey, your chili cheese fries were getting soggy. We had to eat half of them."

Grayson's head snapped around and his adrenaline coursed through his veins as he watched Tony saunter across the bar, his arm casually slung around the shoulders of the woman he'd just assaulted and threatened in the alley.

Brandy, her eyes wide and her hair a tangled mess, wriggled away from Tony and turned back toward the restrooms.

Tony sidled up next to his uncle and dug his fingers into the sloppy fries, scooping up a handful. He shoved them into his mouth, congealed cheese hanging off the edge of his chin.

Tony plucked several napkins from the dispenser and wiped his face. He leaned over the bar, balled up the napkins and tossed them into the trash. He then grabbed another napkin and blew his nose.

Grayson traced his fingers around the edge of the phone in his pocket, barely breathing.

Tony stuffed the napkin he'd used on his nose into his pocket and picked up his beer. He gulped it down and placed the half-full bottle back on the bar, tilting his head to watch the TV above the bar.

"This better not be the ex, again." Grayson pulled his phone out, held it in front of him as if reading a text, and snapped two quick pics of Tony.

"I told you, man. You need to block that number." Will smacked him on the back. "Ready for another round?"

Grayson held up his bottle. "I'm good."

Zane stumbled up to Tony. "You ready to bounce? I wanna go home and play Fortnite."

"Yeah, I'm done with this place." Tony dug into his pocket and pulled out several bunched-up bills. He smashed them in front of Chuck. "Here's for the fries, Uncle Chuck, and a few of those beers. Gotta take care of family."

Grabbing a fistful of Zane's jacket, he hustled him out of the bar.

Chuck flattened the bills, ironing them with the side of his thumb. "Good kid. Always takes care of his family."

Yeah, you just have to worry if you're not in his family.

"That's good to see." Grayson corralled several bottles, including Tony's latest, and nudged them toward the inside edge of the bar. Then he grabbed a napkin and picked up Tony's bottle by the neck.

"I'm gonna hit the road." He tipped the bottle toward his group of coworkers. "Catch you tomorrow."

"Don't let the cops see you with that open container in your car." Chuck pinged the bottle with his dirt-encrusted fingernail.

"I'll finish it off before I get in the truck. Don't wanna waste it."

The bottle hanging from his fingers at his side, Grayson turned and almost bumped into Brandy, her makeup and hair repaired. She started to back away from him and he cupped her elbow, leaning close. "Are you okay? Do you need help?"

Her dark eyes widened for a second and she shook her head. Then she pivoted and scurried to her raven-haired friend.

Stepping outside, Grayson took a couple of deep breaths. What the hell was a blah boatie? "Blah" because they all looked alike? The cash, the threat to Brandy, the knowledge about Danny—if Tony Balducci wasn't the killer, he was involved up to his eyeballs.

When Grayson reached his truck, he tipped the bottle, pouring the beer onto the asphalt of the parking lot. He ducked inside his truck and tucked the bottle into his lunch pail.

He had Tony's fingerprints, DNA and picture. Even if the FBI had only his word that Tony threatened Brandy and talked about dead blah boaties, they could still check this guy out. They must have some evidence at the crime scenes that could link the killer to his victims—Chloe.

He withdrew his phone and, cupping it in his hand, tapped his photos. Brandy, her long brown hair hanging over one shoulder, her arm through her friend's as they walked into the bar, could pass for Chloe. Grayson half closed his eyes and, through the blur, either woman could pass for Chloe, except for the darker hair of Brandy's friend.

Was the other young woman… Rita…was she a blah boatie, too? If she was, she didn't seem as worried about the murders as Brandy—if she knew about them. Maybe she was Chloe's replacement and was just waiting for her dye job.

He swiped his finger to the left to study the next picture. Tony didn't look like a monster. He had a soft spot for family. Is that why he'd spared Danny?

Grayson switched to his contacts and stared at Aria's number for a good ten seconds before tapping her initials, AC. He had information and he needed to give it to her.

She picked up after two rings. "Hello?"

"It's Grayson Rhodes. Sorry to disturb you this late, but I heard something I think you need to know."

"Okay."

"Are you busy?"

"I—I'm not. Just finished a working dinner." She paused. "Can you tell me what you heard?"

"Not over the phone." He rushed on. "I have something to give you, also."

"Can you come to my hotel?"

"I don't want to be seen there, just in case. I'm sure there are hotel employees who know who you are and why you're there. Those employees might know someone at the docks. I might be paranoid…"

"Not at all. You've put yourself in a precarious position. Where should I meet you?"

"I'm staying at a motel off the 25. The St. Clair Motel, room sixteen on the first floor."

"Got it. I'll be right over."

Aria ended the call and Grayson cranked on the truck. After a few sputters, the engine rumbled and Grayson pulled out of The Tavern's parking lot.

Could this information have waited for tomorrow? He gripped the wheel and punched the accelerator. Maybe the information could, but he didn't want to wait one more day to see Aria Calletti.

ARIA SPOTTED GRAYSON'S truck in the parking lot of the St. Clair Motel or the "St. lair Moel," according the partially burned-out sign. As she got out of the rental, the smell of fish choked the air and a brisk breeze off the lake stung her cheeks.

She pulled up her purple scarf and nestled her chin in the fuzzy folds. What could Grayson have discovered about the case? At least he was definitely off their suspect list. Axel had looked into his background and his whereabouts when Chloe had been murdered. Grayson was in the clear.

Still, was it guilt driving him? He didn't have to feel guilty about Chloe. He should know by now an addict couldn't be forced into recovery unless she was good and ready.

When Dad had gotten laid off at the auto plant, he'd hit the bottle pretty hard. There was nothing Mom, or any of them, could have done to make him stop. He'd had to go down that road himself. His DUI had finally woken him up; he'd started attending AA meetings. His younger sister had been killed by a drunk driver and his arrest for drunk driving had been the slap in the face he'd needed— his own rock bottom.

A couple of figures huddled in the shadows near the motel's office, and Aria rested her hand on her purse where her 9mm SIG-Sauer nestled. Grayson couldn't have found a better area? He probably could've purchased an entire motel out here.

She'd done a little internet searching and the guy was loaded. He'd expanded and solidified the real-estate development company he'd taken over from his father's partner. No wonder he was confident he could take care of his nephew. Men like Grayson had all the confidence in the world.

She made a wide berth around the two men, who were passing a paper-bag-wrapped bottle between them, and strode along the rooms bordering the gravel parking lot until she found sixteen, lights glowing from the front windows.

Leaning in close, she tapped on the door with one knuckle. She jumped back when Grayson swung open the door.

"Thanks for coming." He ushered her into the room with a sweep of his arm. "Sorry for the meeting place. Did those guys sharing the bottle bother you?"

She patted her purse. "They didn't, but I could handle them."

"Yeah, of course." He snapped the door closed behind them and slid the chain into place.

"What did you discover and how did you discover it?" Might as well make it perfectly clear she'd rushed out here to see him in the middle of the night for any light he could shed on the case—not because she'd been thinking about him on and off all day.

He wiped his hands on the thighs of his faded jeans. "I think I know who killed Chloe and the other women."

Aria felt her eyes bugging out of her head, not her most attractive look, but purely authentic. "You found out the killer? How? Who is it?"

"Can I start from the beginning? I want to lay this all out for you." He patted the back cushion of a worn sofa. "Have a seat."

She placed her purse next to Grayson's cell phone on the coffee table, scars crisscrossing the wood. As she sat on the sofa, she got a peek of the bedroom, the bed neatly made. This must be one of the weekly rentals, as it also boasted a small kitchen. Her gaze swept past the beer bottle on the counter. Had Grayson been drinking tonight?

As he took a seat next to her, the smell of tobacco wafted in her direction. She wrinkled her nose. One of her brothers smoked, and she couldn't stand it. One black mark against the perfect Grayson Rhodes.

"You're a smoker?"

His eyebrows shot up to single lock of blond hair on his forehead. "What? No, that was part of my disguise."

Remove the black mark. He *was* perfect.

"I'm sorry. Go ahead. What do you have?"

"I accepted an invitation to go out drinking with the crew after work at The Tavern. It's down by the pleasure boat side of the dock, near that diner."

She nodded. "I saw it."

"While I was there, two young women came into the bar, both with brown hair, about the same age as Chloe. I followed them into a back room with pool tables, and one of the dockworkers, nephew of my buddy, marched one of the girls out back."

"They didn't see you skulking around?"

"The Tavern is a hot spot, crowded, noisy. They didn't notice me. I couldn't follow them out the back exit, so I went out the front and circled around."

"You had cover?"

"Dumpster. Their voices carried in the alley. Bottom line—the nephew, a Tony Balducci, was threatening this girl Brandy to keep quiet. She was worried about the murders."

As Grayson recounted the conversation between Tony Balducci and Brandy, Aria's fingernails curled into the thin material covering the arm of the sofa. "'Blah boatie'? That's what he called them?"

"I figured 'blah' because they all look alike and 'boatie' because they must be doing something on a boat."

"Oh, my God. That makes me sick." She sat forward on the edge of the sofa cushion. "He knew the baby was okay, but more importantly, he said the baby didn't get hurt because he was innocent. How would he come to that conclusion unless he was the killer?"

"My thoughts exactly."

"Grayson, this is huge. I suppose you didn't get a recording of them."

He reached for his phone on the table, his gray T-shirt stretching across his back muscles. "I didn't record the conversation—too far away and I didn't want any light or noises coming from my phone. But I took pictures of the women and I took a picture of Tony."

Scooting next to her, he held out his phone in front of her. "These are the two women. Brandy is the one on the right in the skirt."

"May I?" She covered his roughened hand with her own, moving the phone closer to her face. She studied the pretty girls. Both brunettes, the one on the left smiling and Brandy, on the right, wide-eyed with stiff posture. "She looks nervous."

"That's nothing compared to what she looked like after her meeting with Tony in the alley." Grayson swiped to the next picture. "Tony Balducci."

Grayson had caught Tony in profile, his dark hair swept back from a high forehead, long, dark lashes framing his eyes. She'd met hundreds of young, Italian men like Tony, working-class boys looking for a brighter future. Where had this one gone wrong?

"This is great. It's more than luck that led you to this discovery. You had an instinct about the docks, didn't you?"

"Just made sense."

"I'm sure I can make a case for bringing him in for questioning. You overheard a conversation that sounded suspicious." She rubbed her thumb across her chin. "But unless he confesses, I'm not sure we'll have anything to hold him. Not to say we can't keep an eye on him."

"There's more." Grayson put the phone in her lap as he bounded from the sofa. He gripped a beer bottle on the counter by the neck and lifted it. "I got Tony's DNA."

Aria's mouth dropped open. If Grayson ever got tired of making bundles of money, he could have a new career with the FBI. "How did you get that?"

"His uncle, Chuck O'Leary, is my buddy at work. We were all sitting together at the bar, so when Tony came back inside, he had a beer next to us. I just snagged the bottle when he left. Nobody noticed that it wasn't my beer. Like I said, lots of action in The Tavern."

"Do you have a bag for that bottle? We don't have any fingerprints from the crime scenes, but the fewer prints on that bottle, the better. I'm assuming we'll have the bartender's prints, yours."

"On the neck only. Tony had the bottle by the base." He ducked to slide open a drawer in the kitchen and popped up, waving a plastic grocery bag. "Will this work?"

"Perfect. Can you send these pictures to me, too?"

As Grayson carefully placed the bottle in the bag, he said, "You can do that. You're in my phone as AC."

She warranted a name in his phone?

Aria brought up his texts, found herself and attached the pictures of Brandy and Tony. "Are you sure you weren't a detective in another life?"

"This is personal, Aria. When I heard that dirtbag threaten Brandy and slap her, I wanted to wring his neck with my bare hands. My sister made a lot of mistakes in her life, but she didn't deserve this ending. None of them did."

"The work you did tonight is going to go a long way to help solve your sister's murder." She drummed her fingers against his phone. "This doesn't end with Tony, though. He's just a grunt. We need to get to the top dog."

"I figured as much. That's why I didn't take down the little weasel where he stood." Grayson punched his fist into his palm, and all sorts of muscles rippled beneath his T-shirt.

Either his body had responded to the hard labor on the docks in spectacular fashion, or developing properties and making oodles of money was more strenuous than she'd imagined.

Her phone buzzed and she pulled it out to check that she'd received the text with the picture attachments. She pushed to her feet and sauntered into the kitchen, which could barely accommodate the two of them side by side.

"Thanks for turning this information over to me." She placed her phone on the counter next to the bagged bottle.

"Who else?" He shrugged.

"You could've given it to the PHPD or my director or supervisor, Rihanna. Thanks for trusting me with it."

He turned to face her, his blue eyes kindling. "You're the only one I trust right now, Aria. You're the only one... I wanted to see."

His low voice vibrated, touching a chord deep within her. She swallowed and ran her tongue along her bottom lip. Bad move.

His gaze followed the sweep of her tongue and instead of sealing her lips like any professional FBI agent would do, she lodged the tip of her tongue in the corner of her mouth and met his eyes.

He tilted his head and brushed his knuckle across her cheek, a question in his eyes.

Her knees weakened along with her resolve, and she swayed toward him, pinching the material of his shirt between her fingertips. Was that a yes? She wanted it to be a yes.

His hand slid to the back of her head, cupping it in his palm, his fingers entangled in her hair.

Her lashes fluttered as she parted her lips, her heart thundering in her chest.

When he pressed his mouth against hers, it soothed an ache in her core she hadn't even realized she'd had until this moment. His tongue slid into her willing mouth, and she melted against him as he wound an arm around her waist to pull her closer to his body.

Their kiss deepened. Her arm encircled his neck. His pulse throbbed against the pads of her fingers as she skimmed them along the warm flesh of his throat.

Her phone buzzed on the countertop.

Grayson jerked away from her, leaving a blast of cold in his absence. "I'm so sorry. I…"

She dove for her phone, heat washing into her cheeks. In her confusion and haste, she didn't even check the display. "Hello?"

Axel's voice, clipped and professional, greeted her. "Where are you? You're not in your room."

She stuttered some inanity and Axel cut her off. "Never mind. I'm not your daddy, but I thought you'd be interested in this piece of news, superstar."

Superstar? She felt anything but right now. She wiped her hand across her mouth, rubbing away Grayson's kiss.

"What news?"

"We got the rapid DNA van out here and you know that tissue you picked up at the Chloe Larsen murder site?"

"Yeah." Aria's gaze darted to Grayson, making a big deal out of washing a few dishes in the sink.

"It contains DNA."

"I figured it would. It's a tissue."

"Ah, let me finish." Axel paused for drama and a drum-roll if he could have it. "We also collected DNA from beneath the fingernails of the third victim, and guess what?"

Aria sucked in a breath. "They're a match?"

"They are a match, which means we have the killer's DNA. Now we just have to find someone whose DNA is a match to the tissue and the skin, and we've got our guy."

Aria pressed her hand against her heart and grabbed the back of Grayson's T-shirt. "I've got news for you, too, Axel. We found our guy and, with the DNA at the crime sites, we've got him dead to rights."

Chapter Nine

Aria touched her tender lower lip, still feeling Grayson's mouth against hers. She'd literally been saved by the bell… or the buzz. No telling how far she would've gone last night under that man's spell.

"Coffee." Max set a mug in front of her with a clunk. "You looked like you needed it."

"Thanks, Max." She picked up one of the little thimbles of creamer he'd dumped next to her cup. "Do I look that out of it?"

"You look like someone who's been working her tail off. Way to make a splash on this team." He put down his own cup and plopped into the chair next to hers at the table set up in their war room at the PD.

At least Max didn't think she looked like an agent who was mooning over a victim's brother. Let him think her exhaustion was all about the case—not that the murders hadn't robbed her of sleep, too.

Opaline had set up her computer at one end of the table and was clicking furiously on her keyboard with her long nails. She sighed. "Not exactly like home, but it'll do, and I wholly approve of the new scenery. I rate the Port Huron boys in blue a solid seven."

Max rolled his eyes. "Do these poor guys know they're

being ranked and judged? There's a name for that when men do the same thing to women."

"It's called standard operating procedure." Opaline straightened the flowered clip in her hair, the ends blue this week.

Alana entered the room, closely followed by Amanda, and she took a seat next to Opaline. "Did you get all the pictures and graphics Amanda sent you?"

"Yes, ma'am. Created a slide show and everything." Opaline wiggled her fingers in the air. "Good morning, Carly, Rihanna, Axe."

Opaline's voice trailed off as her sister Selena followed Max into the room. Then she ducked her head and checked some cables going to the projector.

Aria took in the mask that had dropped over Selena's face. What was it with those two? Having four brothers, Aria would kill to have had a sister growing up.

Alana rapped on the table. "Axel, the door, please."

Axel tipped his chair back on its legs and reached across with his long arm to push the door closed.

"I'm sure you've all heard the exciting news by now." Alana folded her hands and practically beamed at them. "We have DNA from murders two and three, connecting those crimes—a discarded tissue from the Chloe Larsen scene and skin under the fingernails of the third victim."

Opaline brought up the first slide with a picture of the baggie containing the used tissue Aria had picked up at the second crime scene. Next to it was a close-up picture of the third victim's violet-polished nails, blood and tissue beneath them.

"Even more exciting, because this particular DNA is not in CODIS, we have a suspect along with the suspect's DNA. That suspect's DNA has been delivered to the rapid DNA van and we should have the results shortly. If the suspect's DNA matches that on the tissue and the skin from the fingernails, we have our guy."

Rihanna clapped and then looked around. "For being the media liaison, it seems I'm the only one out of the loop. Who is this guy and how'd we get a line on him?"

"Sorry, you were with CPS this morning, Rihanna, not that we want any of this getting out to the media yet." Alana touched Opaline's shoulder. "Show them what we have."

Tony Balducci's picture appeared on the screen, and Alana ID'd him. "This is Tony Balducci. He works at the docks, and he has no criminal record except for a few minor infractions as a juvenile. Someone working at the docks overheard him talking about the murders and threatening another young woman. We got his DNA from a beer bottle that he discarded."

"Sweet." Rihanna smoothed her thumb over her eyebrow. "Wait, isn't Chloe Larsen's brother, Grayson Rhodes, working undercover at the docks right now? Did we get this from him? Did you get this from him, Aria?"

"I did." Aria dropped her chin to her chest and relaxed all her muscles in the hopes that she could keep her blush at bay.

Alana came to her rescue. "Like I said, we're waiting on the DNA results to come back and then Max, Carly and Aria are going to bring him in. Do it without fanfare, but I'll let you decide how."

The next slide showed the two young women walking into The Tavern. Alana used her red penlight to circle Brandy's face. "This young woman may be in the same line of business as the other three. Her name is Brandy, and that's all we have. Max and Selena are going to track her down. Her friend's name is Rita, and we don't know whether or not she's involved. Find Rita, maybe you find Brandy."

Opaline clicked through more slides, showing the ballistics that matched the weapon for all three murders. She commented, "Max got the ballistics reports this morning and it confirmed the same gun was used in all three murders, a .22 caliber, small but deadly."

"I'm going to let Aria talk about motive. Our contact at the docks overheard some conversation between Balducci and Brandy, which led him to take that picture." Alana sat. "Take it away, Aria."

Aria stood and circled the table to take Alana's place next to Opaline. "When Balducci was talking to a very upset Brandy, he told her she had nothing to worry about if she followed the rules. He mentioned that the other women had gotten greedy and had to be dealt with."

Max whistled. "So, drug smugglers dipping into the product?"

"That's what it sounds like. Balducci also mentioned a name for the women."

Selena asked, "You mean Maddie Johnson—the name on the other vics' IDs?"

Aria braced her fingertips on the tabletop. "No. He called the women 'blah boaties.'"

Carly made a sound in the back of her throat and wrinkled her nose. "That makes me sick. Are you thinking what I'm thinking? 'Blah' because all the women looked alike? Nondescript brunettes with brown eyes?"

"And 'boaties' because they must be smuggling the drugs across the water." Max flattened his hands on the table, the whites of his nails standing out against his dark, brown skin, his two thumbs touching. "That hints at something big. This Balducci character is small-time. He's a cog in the wheel. We need to find the person spinning that wheel."

"When Axel and I are on the hunt for Brandy and Rita

today, we'll check out the boat rentals at the pleasure dock. See if a Maddie Johnson has rented any boats recently."

Axel said, "While we're out there, if we have time, we'll take a boat to Canada ourselves. I think the most common trip from Port Huron is across the St. Clair River to Point Edward. Might be a good idea to see what's over there."

"Anything else, Aria?" Alana stood beside her.

"That's it."

"We all know what to do. Aria, Carly, Max, decide how you're going to bring in Balducci without making waves. Axel, Selena, find those young women so we don't have another victim on our hands." She tipped her head at the last slide, a picture of all three dead women. "Remember why we're doing this."

Chairs scraped and voices murmured as the meeting ended. Aria traipsed around to the other side of the table and pulled out the chair next to Rihanna. "Can I talk to you about something?"

"Absolutely. You're the hero of the hour." Rihanna pushed back from the table and crossed her legs, her knee-high boots squeaking as she swung one long leg over the other.

"Is there any way we can use rapid DNA for Danny and his uncle, Grayson Rhodes?" Aria held her breath.

Rihanna blinked her dark lashes. "We can't request it for a standard DNA test."

"If CPS can't ask for quicker results, can they just use what they have? Grayson showed you his pictures of him and his sister with Danny, right? He described the toys attached to Danny's car seat because he bought them for him. Isn't that enough to prove he's family?"

"I don't doubt he is, Aria, and neither does CPS, but there's protocol to follow." She tilted her head, wrapping one of her curls around her finger. "He really got to you, didn't he?"

Rihanna had no idea.

"It's just that I want to do something for him after he did all this for us. He brought us Tony Balducci. Even with Balducci's DNA from the crime scenes, we wouldn't have been able to ID him because he wasn't in the Combined DNA Index System. We'd still be flailing around if Grayson hadn't stalked Balducci at the bar and eavesdropped on his conversation—at great danger to himself, I might add." Aria flushed as her final words rang out, louder than she'd planned, turning a few heads.

"I'll tell you what." Rihanna patted Aria's hand. "I'll talk to CPS and see if Grayson can visit Danny with the foster family. The evidence he showed us is compelling enough that we all believe he's Danny's uncle. Danny even has those same impossibly blue eyes…but then, you probably know all about those eyes, don't you?"

Aria's mouth gaped open until Rihanna cracked a smile and said, "I don't blame you, sister."

"Thanks, Rihanna."

Max pounded his fist on the table. "Everyone out, except Carly, Aria and me. We got a bad guy to take down."

Aria scooted closer to the table, folding her hands to make up for her previous outburst. She shouldn't be getting so personally involved in her first case, should she? But Grayson deserved a break.

"I verified Balducci's working today. We can pick him up at lunch, but we don't want to alarm his coworkers—just in case any of them are involved. Carly, you approach him first." Max held up his hands. "Sorry, ladies, Balducci is the type of guy who's not going to expect a female cop coming at him. He'll probably feel more comfortable with one of you."

"A lot of the guys bring their lunches and eat at some tables on the dock when it's not raining or snowing. Even Carly can't go marching in there without arousing some suspicion." Aria tapped on her laptop as she entered notes. "There is a lunch truck that comes in, but there's no guarantee Balducci will get his lunch there."

"We have to make sure he does. You have a connection at the docks—use him." Max raised his brows at Aria.

"I—I could ask Grayson if he can get Balducci out to the food truck." Aria sucked in her bottom lip. Were they exploiting Grayson's hunger to nail Chloe's killer?

Carly tucked a strand of blond hair behind her ear. "That would work. I can approach him there and tell him we have a few questions, get him away from the truck, and go in for the arrest."

"I hope his DNA comes back as a match, because we can't hold him based on an overheard conversation and, once he's out—" Max flicked his fingers "—he'll be gone like a cool breeze off the lake."

They discussed their plan for another thirty minutes and then Max leveled a finger at Aria. "Can you make that call now?"

"Grayson really does work when he's there, so it's better if I text him." Aria pulled out her phone and sent a text to Grayson asking him to try to get Tony out to the food truck at lunch. She had faith he could get the job done.

Carly rose first. "I think it's a good idea if we stick around the station. I'm going to get something to drink and work on those drug reports. Anyone want anything?"

Max held up his phone. "My ex-wife's been trying to reach me about our son. I'm going to step out and call her."

"I'm fine, Carly. I'm going to nurse this lukewarm coffee Max brought me earlier and do some work in here, if nobody minds."

"I think it's ours for the time being." Carly held the door open for Max, and they both slipped out of the war room.

Aria continued with her notes, taking surreptitious glances at her phone. She and Grayson hadn't spoken much after that kiss last night.

After Axel's call, she'd told Grayson about the DNA matches at the crime scenes, but they'd avoided the elephant in the room...and had avoided any additional contact with each other. He'd acted as if she'd had a repellent bubble around her, keeping him a good five feet out of her aura—and that's the only way she could've operated around him.

He'd apologized again when he'd walked her out to her car in the seedy motel's parking lot, as if he'd pounced on her in a moment of weakness when she'd been a willing participant the whole way.

Something Max had said stuck in her throat. He'd called Grayson a contact and had advised Aria to use him. Would Grayson feel that way when he received her text asking for his help? Would he think that's why she'd allowed the kiss last night?

Carly had pulled out the chair across from Aria before she even realized she'd returned to the room. "You snuck in here like a cat."

"No, I didn't. You were just concentrating so hard on your work, you didn't hear me." Carly planted one elbow on the table and cupped her chin with the palm. "You know, I have to tell you, we're all really impressed with you. You're a great asset and you fit in like you've been on the team for years. Alana is so good at spotting people and recognizing just who we need."

"Thanks. I have to admit you all intimidated me that first day. All so accomplished." Aria picked up her phone. "Text from Grayson Rhodes."

He'd texted just three little words. Count on me.

She didn't need any more than that from him. She knew she could.

"Good news?" Carly peered at her over the rim of her soda can. "That smile makes you look like the cat who swallowed the canary, or the cream, or whatever."

Aria tapped her phone and folded her arms. What had happened to her poker face, the one she'd used to lure dozens of drug dealers into a false sense of security? She'd become an open book—a silly, smitten, open book.

"Grayson indicated he'd take care of getting Balducci out to the lunch truck. I'm not going to ask how, but after his feats last night at that bar, I'm not worried."

"Attractive guy, isn't he?" Carly ran her fingertip around the rim of her can. "Rich, angsty."

"Angsty?" A laugh bubbled to Aria's lips despite her best effort. "Whatever that means."

"Oh, come on. He lost his sister, he's trying to reclaim his nephew, he's bound and determined to see justice done."

"Are you telling me I'm getting sucked into an image?"

"I'm telling you to be careful. This job—" she circled her finger in the air to encompass the room with the bulletin board of pictures and lines of string connecting those pictures, Opaline's laptop with the gruesome slideshow of murder victims and their crime scenes, the discarded coffee cups and empty bags of potato chips "—doesn't lend itself well to a personal life, marriage, kids."

Aria scooped in a deep breath, ready to protest that marriage with Grayson Rhodes had never occurred to her. Max's entrance and his fist pump saved her from protesting too much.

"We got him. The DNA from the beer bottle matches the DNA from the tissue and the skin beneath Jane Doe number three's fingernails. It's enough to arrest, charge and hold him."

Carly met Aria's eyes and, with a lilt to her voice, said, "Perfect. Aria's guy is going to get Balducci out to the truck. We're golden."

Max rolled his wrist inward and checked his watch. "We have just about an hour until go time. Anyone need to change clothes, pick up a different weapon, stash their stuff back at the hotel? I'm going to grab a sandwich at that place across the street from the hotel."

"I'd like to drop off my bag." Aria snapped her laptop closed. "And maybe we should clean up this room, so the cops don't think we're all a bunch of slobs."

"Way ahead of you." Max dangled a plastic garbage bag from his fingers. "Alana and Amanda are coming back in a few, so they can start messing it up again."

Carly picked up a half-full chip bag and swung it back and forth. "I don't think it's Alana and Amanda we have to worry about."

They spent a few minutes picking up, locked the room behind them and piled into Carly's rental for the ride back to the hotel. Max peeled off to get his sandwich, and Aria and Carly ducked into their rooms.

Aria put her bag with the laptop on the desk and downed the rest of the water left in the bottle by the nightstand. Standing in front of the full-length mirror, she secured her holstered SIG-Sauer and yanked her sweater over it.

This morning she didn't know she'd be in on the arrest, but she'd dressed more casually in jeans and low-heeled boots, as the other team members seemed to dress down away from the office in Traverse City. Tipping her foot onto her toe, she studied the heel of her boot. Could she run in these if she had to?

The crepe-soled shoes she wore on patrol gave her fleet

feet, but running shoes would be even better and she could actually get away with wearing them with jeans. She sat on the edge of the bed and traded her boots for a pair of sneakers. Then she grabbed her jacket and went downstairs to meet the others.

When Max saw her from the lobby, he stuffed the rest of his sandwich in his mouth and brushed his hands over the yellow paper on the table in front of him. "Carly's waiting for us out front in the car. You ready?"

"I used to work patrol, remember? This stuff is second nature to me."

"I know. My buddy took a job with the LAPD when we got back from deployment. He said working patrol on the streets of L.A. was more dangerous than being in Iraq."

"Detroit's no picnic, either." She gave Max a wide berth as he pushed up from the soft lobby sofa.

"Relax. I'm not going to fall over on you." He cracked a smile and tapped his leg below the knee. "Like you said, second nature."

Aria put a hand to her throat. "I'm sorry. Is that how I looked?"

"Don't worry about it. It's the typical reaction when people first find out about my leg, but they get used to it."

"If I hadn't read your bio, I don't think I would've even realized you had a prosthetic."

"That's due to the ingenious stuff the engineers keep coming up with." He stepped aside and allowed her to exit the automatic doors ahead of him.

As they reached the car, Max bent his head toward the driver's-side window. "Remember? You're letting Aria drive. That way we have a driver behind the wheel in case we need to take off while you're talking to the suspect."

"Oops, forgot already." Carly slid out of the car and jogged around the back, while Aria took her place.

She moved the seat up a bit and waited until both Max and Carly were in place before taking off. As planned, she dropped off Max a block from the docks and left Carly next to the food truck. She parked farther down the street with a view of the docks and the truck.

As the digital clock in the car ticked over to twelve o'clock, the activity at the docks seemed to shift away from the boats and the water and surge toward the office buildings up front and the parking lot.

Although Carly had seen the picture of Tony, when Aria spotted him swaggering through the parking lot, she shot Carly a quick text that he was on his way. She knew she could count on Grayson.

Max had moved within striking distance of the food truck, and Aria swallowed as the players moved into position like pieces on a chessboard—with Tony Balducci as the pawn. But who was the king?

Looking both ways, Tony jogged across the street. When he reached the lunch truck, he shoved his hands into his pockets and studied the menu board out front.

Carly made her move. She pivoted toward Tony and began talking to him. Tony's posture changed. The hands came out of the pockets and his spine straightened.

As Carly reached into her pocket for her badge and ID, Tony's head twisted to one side and then the other. Aria clutched the door handle. She recognized the signs of a runner, and Tony was displaying Usain Bolt level ones.

His legs bicycled backward a few steps and then he pivoted and took off—right toward Max. Max was ready. As Tony ran past him, Max's arm shot out and he grabbed him, slowing his pace.

Tony twisted away from him and ran into the street, toward the boats, with both Max and Carly on his tail.

Aria jumped from the car and joined the chase, her

sneakers giving her lightning speed. Tony's work boots slowed him as they pounded against the metal decking of the marina dock. Aria reached him as he turned onto a gangway of a boat bobbing in its slip.

She grabbed the back of his jacket but couldn't hold him. Then Max came out of nowhere and tackled Tony to the ground.

"I didn't do nothing. I didn't do nothing." Tony squirmed beneath Max's knee planted firmly on his back.

When Max slapped on the cuffs, Tony slackened like a rag doll. Max hauled him to his feet.

"Why'd you run if you didn't do anything?" Carly wedged a hand on her side, panting. "We just want to talk to you."

Her own breath heaving, Aria said, "That's right, Tony. We just want to talk to you about the dead blah boaties."

Chapter Ten

Tony cooled his heels at the Port Huron jail while Amanda ran down Axel. Alana wanted him to lead the interrogation of Tony, and she wanted Aria to sit in and watch the master.

Tony had clammed up on them on the drive over, but they'd expected that. He didn't know what they had on him, but once they told him, he might rethink his silence. If he called his uncle and got himself an attorney, they could be facing a longer process, but they had his DNA at both scenes. Science didn't lie.

Alana had contacted the shift supervisor at the docks and told him they had Tony Balducci in custody but wanted to keep it quiet. The supervisor agreed and when Aria had sent Grayson a quick text, he'd confirmed that not even Tony's uncle was aware of what had gone down.

Most of the team converged in the war room to wait for Axel.

Amanda held up her phone. "That was Selena. They're on their way. They didn't have any luck finding Brandy, but they might have a line on her friend, Rita."

Alana praised the arrest team. "Good job bringing him in. Max, you okay after that tackle?"

He gave them a thumbs-up while he dug into another sandwich from the order Amanda had placed for the team.

"Rihanna is preparing a press release, letting the media

know we have an arrest in the cases, but she's not going live with it yet. We don't want to scare anyone off—or put anyone in danger."

Aria pointed to a sandwich near Carly and then pointed to herself. "Is that turkey?"

"Yep." Carly shot the sandwich across the smooth table, and Aria snagged it before it launched onto the floor. "Chips?"

"Barbecue."

Alana removed her glasses. "I'm sorry. Am I interrupting your lunch?"

"Actually, you are." Carly popped a chip in her mouth.

"Okay, eat. We'll wait for Axel, and then I want to review with him what we want out of Balducci—and Axel will get it, eventually."

As they were eating, Amanda answered her phone. When she hung up, she said, "Axel wants the cops to move Tony Balducci into the interrogation room now. He said, give him time to stew."

Alana looked up from her computer. "Max, could you go down and make sure they bring him over from his cell to the interrogation room?"

A few minutes later, Max returned. "That's taken care of. Small room, no windows, stationary chair for him— just the way we like it."

Another thirty minutes passed before Axel arrived. "I wanted to give Tony some time alone, so I dropped Selena off at the hotel. She's training with Blanca." He rubbed his hands together. "Are you ready, Aria?"

"I am." She balled up her sandwich paper and chip bag and tossed them into the wastebasket. "Anything for Tony?"

"We'll give him his choice from the vending machines.

He's our guest here—for a little while." Axel ran a hand through his messy blond hair.

In fact, Aria had never seen Axel so…casual before. His jeans, basic Wrangler, were faded at the knees and he wore his waffle-print Henley untucked and rolled up at the sleeves. He looked ready to meet Tony on an even playing field.

As they took the stairs down to the interrogation room, Axel cocked his head toward hers. "Feel free to chime in at any time with questions of your own, and don't be surprised if I bring you into the conversation with Tony. He's been isolated long enough, and we're going to go right in and build rapport with him. We don't want him to ask for an attorney. We don't want him to know what we have on him right away. Let's make him comfortable."

Axel's steady stream of instructions ended when they reached the interrogation room at the end of the hall.

As she followed Axel into the room, Aria glanced at the claustrophobic four walls. Max hadn't been kidding about the size.

Tony glanced up from his seat in the corner, a table to his right and two chairs across from him, his ankle resting on his alternate knee, his foot jiggling up and down.

"Hey, Tony." Axel turned on the megawatt smile and thrust out his hand. "I'm Supervisory Agent Axel Morrow, and this is Special Agent Aria Calletti. Are you comfortable?"

Axel didn't wait for an answer because, of course, Tony wasn't comfortable in that hard metal chair. "Do you want something to drink? Coffee? Soda? Wish we could offer you a beer, but that's not on the menu."

Tony swallowed and he gripped the edge of the table. "Yeah, a Coke, please."

"Aria?"

"Sure, I'll be right back with that. Anything else? Chips? Cookies?"

Tony's gaze bounced from her face to Axel's as if he couldn't believe his good fortune. "Yeah, chips *and* cookies. I never got my lunch."

A little bit of belligerence was okay. Showed he thought he was in control.

"I'll be right back." She snapped the door behind her and jogged down the hallway to the vending machines. She pulled some bills out of her pocket and fed them in the slot with shaky fingers. She didn't want to miss anything.

Hugging the chips and cookies to her chest and clutching the soda in her hand, she scurried back to the room. She tapped on the door once and Axel invited her in.

"Here you go." She dumped the bags in front of Tony and placed the can next to the snacks. "Hope those are okay."

"I was just asking Tony how he liked working on the docks, and you know what he told me?"

"What?" Aria took her seat and gave Tony an encouraging smile.

"It's just a temporary gig for him. He wants to be a rapper."

Aria widened her eyes. "Really? There's a guy from my hometown who just cut his first demo."

They let Tony ramble on about his nonexistent rap career for a few minutes and then Axel smacked the table, making both Aria and Tony jump.

"Hey, you know Aria here is from an Italian family, too. Maybe you know some of the same people."

Aria laughed and met Tony's eyes, which had lost some of the deer-in-the-headlights look. "Agent Morrow thinks all Italian families in Michigan know each other."

Tony gave a nervous titter like a schoolgirl trying to fit in with the cool kids but not understanding their jokes.

Axel continued to use his charm to disarm Tony, who'd started to explain to Axel who the Lions needed in their next draft.

They talked for a good long time and, as every minute passed, it was clear Tony moved from wary to relaxed to nervous again. Axel was wearing him down with the mere passage of time, and the skillful agent seemed to have the instincts to tell when the precise moment was to strike to get what they needed.

With a smile still on his handsome face, Axel asked, "Who's using drugs in Port Huron, Tony?"

Tony blinked and his Adam's apple bobbed. "N-nobody. I don't use no drugs."

Axel spread his hands. "Oh, we know *you* don't use drugs, but there's a drug culture here for sure. Lotta chicks use? Put out for a little weed?"

Aria's stomach churned, but she kept her face impassive.

Tony's bottom lip jutted forward. "Yeah, there are a few of those girls around."

"Brandy one of those? Maddie? Rita?"

A red stain stood out on Tony's neck. "I dunno. I don't know them girls."

Lie number one.

"You don't?" Axel's brows shot up. "Those girls are involved in the drug trade. Maybe they got what they deserved, maybe not."

Tony nodded and then stopped himself, covering his mouth with his hand.

"How do you think those drugs are getting across to Canada, Tony?"

"Smuggling drugs to Canada? I don't know nothing about that."

"When was the last time you were in Canada? Right across the river, you must go there a lot."

"I—" Tony rolled his eyes upward, searching for his answer on the ceiling "—not sure. I don't remember. I didn't…"

"Sure, you did." Axel cut off Tony with a slicing motion of his hand.

Tony's gaze slid to Aria, confusion wrinkling his brow. "I was gonna say I didn't have nothing to do with the murder of those girls."

"I know what you were going to say." Axel patted the file folder. "C'mon, Tony. We know you did *that*. We're just trying to figure out if you're the guy in charge."

Tony's wild eyes skimmed across the bulging folder on the table and then flew to Aria's face. "Is he kidding?"

"Oh, I don't know. You seem like a bright guy. It's not so far-fetched that you're the kingpin of this operation." Aria folded her hands in her lap.

"Kingpin? I ain't no kingpin. What the hell?"

"But you know who is." Axel leaned back in his chair, crossing his hands behind his head.

"I don't know who the kingpin is. I just do what I'm told."

Aria sipped in a small breath. If Tony realized he'd just admitted to there being a smuggling ring in Port Huron and that he worked in that ring, he didn't seem to realize it.

She hunched forward, elbows on her knees. "You did a good thing, Tony. You spared that little baby. That tells us something about your character."

Tony slumped. His chin dropped to his chest and his shoulders rolled forward. The classic posture of surrender.

"I—I couldn't hurt the baby. They didn't tell me nothing about a baby."

A muscle at the side of Axel's mouth jumped. "You even reported the baby to 9-1-1, so he wouldn't have to stay out there by himself all night. We knew we were dealing with someone...special, someone with a conscience."

"I couldn't just leave the baby there. My sister has a kid. My niece is around the same age as that baby. No way was I gonna leave that baby there. He wasn't gonna be no witness, anyway." He lifted his chin. "Is he all right?"

Aria answered. "The baby is fine—thanks to you."

Of course, he has no mother, thanks to you.

"How'd you find me?"

"DNA." Axel shook his head. "Almost nobody gets away with murder these days, Tony. Your bosses should've told you that, too. They don't care about you. They didn't even tell you one of your targets was going to have a baby with her, did they?"

Tony's dark eyes got darker, and a mulish look played about his mouth. "Nobody told me nothing about that baby."

"That's right." Axel's voice soothed, dripped with understanding. "Those are some bad people who don't have your best interests at heart. They're not like family, Tony."

"No, they're not." Tony thumped his chest with his fist. "Family is everything."

"Who are they? Give me some names." Axel whipped out a sheet of paper and held a pen, poised at the top, as if he expected all the names right now.

Tony's mouth formed a stubborn line. "I got nothing for you, man. I don't know the names. I follow orders."

"All right." Axel rotated the piece of paper 180 degrees with the tip of his finger so that it faced Tony. "We need you to write down everything you know, everything about those three murders you committed."

Tony licked his lips and wiped the back of his grimy hand across his nose, leaving a streak of dirt on his face.

"And the baby you saved." Aria leaned forward and put a hand on his arm.

His arm twitched beneath her touch, but he picked up the pen and started writing. He talked as he wrote, filling in more details about the killings, including the third victim and how she'd lunged at him before he got off his shot, scratching the side of his neck.

As he pulled down the collar of his jacket to show them the scratch, still red, the knots in Aria's gut tightened.

He continued to write, and Aria asked, "Who's this Maddie Johnson? Is she a real person?"

His pen stopped moving, drilling an inky hole in the paper. "Nah, that's just the fake name they came up with. They gave all the girls the Maddie Johnson ID, made them dye their hair the same color brown and even wear contact lenses if they didn't have brown eyes."

An image of Grayson's blue eyes flashed across her mind. Chloe's must've been the same color.

"Why?" Axel asked. "Why the same look for them all?"

"IDs. Like I said. We had the Maddie Johnson ID for women who looked like that."

Axel flipped open the file and shuffled some papers. "How'd they get into Canada with the drugs?"

Aria held her breath. Tony hadn't actually admitted to knowing about the smuggling scheme yet, but he'd just admitted to killing three women and he seemed in a loquacious mood.

"Oh, they had Maddie Johnson passports, too." Tony waved his hand in the air. "They all used the same boat, a motorboat for a pleasure cruise across the river. Some pleasure cruise—it was loaded up with Dance Fever and Blues."

Axel interjected. "Blues?"

Aria supplied the answer. "Oxy."

"Go on." Axel crossed his arms. "Where'd the Maddie Johnsons get the drugs?"

"Tunnels by the docks, man. I think they're stored there, and the blah boaties pick 'em up and ferry 'em across the river. The sellers are on the pleasure cruise with the drugs."

Axel peppered Tony with more questions before he could have time to pause and think. "Pleasure cruise goes into Point Edward in Canada? How do they get the drugs in? Are there more tunnels on the other side?"

Tony tugged on his earlobe. "Yeah, Point Edward. I don't know how they hide the drugs, and I don't know about no other tunnels. Just the ones on this side."

"Where are those tunnels?" To stop her hands from fidgeting on the table, Aria shoved them beneath her thighs. They were getting more info out of Tony than she'd ever expected...but they needed the top dog.

"I don't know that, either." Tony shook his head back and forth. "I'm gonna keep writing. I can't talk and write at the same time."

When Tony finished scribbling out his confession, Axel cocked his head. "You sure you don't want to tell us who gave you the orders?"

Tony dropped the pen and held up his hands, a little drop of blue ink staining his thumb. "I don't know. Like I wrote in here, someone left me the burner phone and the .22. Hey, do you think I can get a special deal for helping that baby?"

Axel screwed up his mouth. "Maybe, but if you could give us those names of the people at the top, that might go down easier."

Tony's jaw hardened. "I dunno."

After almost three hours, Tony was clearly done and they'd gotten his confession for the murders, so at least other young women would be safe.

Axel wrapped up the interview with Tony, promising him they'd visit again, and then they left him in the interrogation room for the cops to return him to his cell.

When they got clear of the interrogation room, Axel gave her a fist bump. "Good work in there, Aria."

"Tony really thought we were his best friends—until we weren't."

"He still thinks we're his best friends, and we're going to keep it that way until we get the name of the person running the show."

"Do you think he knows?" She placed one foot on the first step of the staircase leading to the war room and turned toward Axel.

"Oh, he knows. He's afraid to tell us. He wants to make sure he doesn't get whacked in prison. But he'll figure out soon enough that, even if he keeps his mouth shut, he has a lot to worry about inside, especially without our protection." He shrugged. "He'll come around."

"We'll have to play up the fact that he didn't kill little Danny, and we know he's not all bad."

"Yeah, we'll play that up." Axel stepped past her and jogged up the steps, calling over his shoulder, "But he's still a killer."

Chapter Eleven

Grayson didn't want to raise any alarms, so after work he met the boys for a few beers at The Tavern. Nobody seemed to know what had happened to Tony Balducci, not even his uncle Chuck, and Grayson wanted to keep it that way.

The FBI must've contacted the supervisor, Bud Ellison, because Bud told someone Tony had left for the day feeling sick.

Grayson had gotten a text from Aria that Tony had confessed to the murders, but nothing else. He'd kept his lips zipped on the mastermind.

He'd waited for another text from her, but she'd gone radio silent—probably regretted that kiss. Probably didn't want to see him again. Why would she? She figured his part in this drama was over. But she didn't know him… yet. He wouldn't give up until the person responsible for Chloe's murder was behind bars—or dead.

When he and his coworkers bellied up to the bar, Grayson bought the first round and then took his beer to the back room to play some pool. One game, be visible, and then he had to get out of there.

Will got a table first and invited Grayson to play with him. As Grayson chalked up his stick, he caught sight of Rita, giggling on the arm of some buffed-up dude.

Grayson moved around the table, taking shots, bantering with Will and a few women looking on. Out of the corner of his eye, he noticed Rita edging closer and closer to the pool table, her beefy friend nowhere to be seen.

When Will stopped to talk strategy with one of the young women who'd been dogging him, Rita touched Grayson's elbow and, through her smile, whispered, "That girl I was with last night—Brandy? She wants to meet with you later."

Grayson grinned and nodded. Pointing to an angle on the table, he answered, "Why me?"

"I don't know. She said you were nice. She's in trouble."

He hoped nobody else in the bar had noticed his concern for the frightened woman. He rapped his knuckles on the edge of the table. "C'mon, Will. The shot's not going to get any easier unless you let Becca take it for you."

As Will guffawed and bent over Becca, his arms wrapped around her in the guise of helping her with the cue, Grayson took a step closer to Rita. "Why not call the cops?"

"She's scared. Look, I don't know what she's mixed up in, but she's in real trouble here. Can you meet her or not?"

Grayson kept his voice low. "Yeah, yeah. I'll meet her. Where and when?"

Rita stuck two fingers in the back pocket of his jeans and whistled. "Atta girl, Becca." Then she spun around and met the pumped-up dude as he returned with her glass of wine.

Grayson blew out a long breath. He had no intention of meeting Brandy on his own. The FBI would want to talk to this woman. She must've heard somehow that Tony was off the streets.

Grayson finished the game with Will, intentionally losing to speed things up, and said his goodbyes to his coworkers. He sauntered outside and dove into his back pocket for the slip of paper Rita had put there.

She'd written "9:00 p.m. on the *Fun Times*, slip 128." Grayson glanced toward the marina, the colored lights on display for Christmas, and wondered where slip 128 was located. Was she there now? She must be scared to reach out to a stranger.

He hesitated for two seconds before pulling out his phone and calling Aria. He had a perfectly legitimate reason for calling her, but he still let out a sigh when she picked up after two rings.

"Grayson?"

He got straight to the point, so she wouldn't misconstrue his call as anything other than business. "Brandy contacted me through her friend Rita and wants to meet me in less than an hour at the marina."

"You're kidding. We've had two agents looking for Rita and Brandy all morning. Why you?"

"I guess Brandy trusts me because I asked after her last night, probably a stupid thing to do, drawing attention to myself, but I thought about Chloe when I saw her after Tony threatened her, and I couldn't stop myself."

"No, that looks like a good move on your part. I wonder why she doesn't call the cops."

"Scared."

"Are you supposed to come alone and all that?"

"The note I got didn't say, but I figured Brandy wouldn't be spooked to see me with a woman—might even make her feel better, but I think just you. We don't want to scare her off."

"No, of course not. I do have to give my director a heads-up, but it's important for us to talk to Brandy. She might be able to tell us something about the tunnels."

"Tunnels?"

"Some info we got from Tony. I'll tell you later. I have some other news for you…good news."

"About Danny?" Grayson gripped the phone so hard, it dug into his palm.

"Rihanna talked to the foster family, and they're willing to let you visit Danny. Even though the DNA isn't back yet, they saw your pictures and know that you accurately described his car seat."

A rush of emotion made him unable to speak for a few seconds and then he managed to strangle out a few words. "That's great. Thanks, Aria."

"It was all Rihanna." She cleared her throat. "Where do you want me to meet you?"

"Behind the boat rental shack. I'm outside The Tavern right now, and it's quiet along the marina."

"I'll be there in about thirty minutes." She ended the call and he stood tapping the edge of the phone against his chin.

Even though she'd minimized her role, Aria had gone to bat for him with Rihanna and CPS. His getting to see Danny wouldn't have an impact on the case, wouldn't benefit Aria in any way. She'd helped him out because she had a big heart.

With time to kill, Grayson wandered toward the diner, turning up his collar against the wind. He scanned the interior through the windows first, to make sure nobody from the docks was there. They were more likely to be at The Tavern. But there were plenty of family men on the job who might be eating out.

He didn't recognize a soul, so he ducked inside and stationed himself at the counter. He ordered a piece of warm apple pie and a coffee.

He'd let Aria do the talking when they met with Brandy. She'd obviously gotten a lot of information from Tony Balducci today and had a better understanding of what they were dealing with now. Brandy just might be able to steer them to the person calling the shots.

He finished his pie and ordered two coffees to go. As the waitress behind the counter reached for the second to-go cup, Grayson, said, "Wait. Can you make that second cup a hot tea?"

"Sure, hon. What kind of tea?" She rattled off a bunch of catchy names until he held up his hands.

"Maybe one of those herb teas you mentioned. You pick."

She filled up the cup with hot water and then dredged a tea bag in it before capping it.

With a cup in each hand, Grayson pushed open the door with his foot. The cold hit his face like an icy rag and his eyes watered. He arched his shoulders and made his way to the boat rental office, decked out in holiday cheer, a red-nosed Santa in the window. He slipped behind the office, leaning his back against the faded wood, and placing one cup on the window ledge.

On the edge of the darkness, beyond the lights of the parking lot, a lone figure zigzagged between the cars. He could tell from her quick, light gait that it was Aria, although she kept to the shadows.

He squinted into the night, making sure nobody was following or watching her. His brain understood she was a special agent with the FBI and she was packing heat, but his instinct reacted to a petite woman, walking on her own in a deserted area at night. He couldn't turn off that part of him, so he watched her with eagle eyes, his muscles coiled, his hand hovering over the weapon he had in his jacket pocket.

The black beanie on her head, pulled over her loose hair, and her flushed cheeks somehow made her look even more defenseless. He knew better than to remark on this or to coddle her. Aria took her professionalism very seriously…and he did, too.

When she reached him, she smacked her gloved hands together. "It's chilly out here, and it's not even December."

"I hope that means a white Christmas—Danny's first." He handed her the cup with the paper end of the tea bag fluttering in the breeze. "I got you some tea. You mentioned you didn't like to drink coffee late."

Her dark eyes widened as she took the cup from him. "Thank you."

"It's herb tea. I have some packets of sugar in my pocket if you drink it like that."

"Plain is fine." She popped the lid and walked to the trash can at the corner of the building. She plucked up the string on the tea bag, held the dripping bag over her cup for a few seconds then tossed the bag into the garbage.

She pivoted and returned to his side. "Rita gave you a note?"

He pulled it from his pocket and shook it out for her. "Short and sweet."

Leaning in, she read the note. "I wonder what she thinks she's going to get from you. Protection?"

"We'll find out in about ten minutes." He wedged a shoulder against the wooden structure. "Tell me about Tony."

"He confessed to the murders." Aria reached out and touched the hand he'd bunched into a fist at his side. "I'm sorry. He confessed to all three. They were hits. He was ordered to take out those women."

"Why?" He'd known Tony was the killer, had barely been able to look the guy in the face this morning at work, but the news still hit him like a sledgehammer to the chest.

"The women, including your sister, had been hired to run drugs across the river to Canada, and they started skimming." She blew the steam from her tea and took a sip. "It's an old story, Grayson. As long as there have been drug dealers and drug runners, there has been skimming, stealing, sampling, you name it—and it usually doesn't end well for the skimmers."

"Dammit. Why would Chloe play with fire like that? She knew she could ask me for money at any time." He squeezed his eyes closed and tossed his coffee onto the ground with a splash. "Who am I kidding? As long as she was using, I wouldn't give her money."

"Why would you? Give her money to kill herself? She took a chance, just like the other women. Even if they hadn't been double-crossing the boss, they were living a precarious existence. We don't even know if Tony is telling the truth or if he knew the truth. Maybe the kingpin just wanted to get rid of these particular dealers. We don't know enough yet, Grayson."

"Do you think he'll tell you who's in charge?"

"The other agent I'm working with is a great interrogator, so I'm sure he'll get it out of him. If not?" As they passed the trashcan, she dropped her cup inside, and he followed with his empty cup. "Maybe Brandy will tell us."

They walked to the boats together, their shoulders bumping occasionally, Grayson's instincts on high alert. When he'd been here on his own, he hadn't sensed the same level of danger that now pricked the back of his neck, giving him the urge to grab on to Aria's hand and keep her safe.

The circumstances and the scene, the masts of the boats jutting into the sky, the ballasts creaking and whining, were shifting his imagination into overdrive. If anything, Aria could not only look after herself, she could probably protect him, too.

But he'd failed to guard one woman from evil, he had no intention of falling short again.

Aria brushed her fingers against his hand. "Slips 110 to 130 up ahead. We should find *Fun Times* at the end of this row. I—I mean, *Fun Times*, the boat."

"Got it." He entwined his fingers with hers. "Somehow I don't think there are fun times ahead."

She nodded at a big powerboat sporting colored lights, an American and a French flag flapping in the breeze. "That's a nice one."

"Beautiful Place."

"Port Huron? It's nice, but I wouldn't call it beautiful."

He pointed back at the big boat they'd just passed. "The name of the boat—*Beautiful Place*."

"Oh, I guess that would be their beautiful place."

He kept hold of her hand until they reached slip 128, and then she disentangled her fingers from his.

His boots made more noise on the metal walkway than her sneakers, so he tried to lighten his step. When they drew closer to the boat, a twenty-five-foot bow rider, its outer railings decorated with Christmas lights, Grayson peered at the deck. "Brandy?"

When silence met his tentative overture, Aria called out, "Brandy? We're here to help you."

Grayson kept his breath shallow, as if by breathing deeply, he'd scare away the already-frightened woman. "I'm coming on board. I brought my friend. You can trust her."

His boots clomped along the gangplank, no need for silence now. He reached the bow of the boat where a step-ladder nestled against the fiberglass. Planting one foot on the step, he peeked over the side. "Brandy?"

The empty cushions and bolted-down tables rocked

back and forth with the sway of the boat. "Maybe she's not here yet. Maybe she changed her mind."

Aria materialized behind him and he jumped when she touched his back. "This must be the boat the blah—the women were using to smuggle the drugs into Canada. I can see it. Festively decorated for the holidays, eight to ten people heading over for the day or longer. How'd they get the drugs into Point Edward?"

Grayson grabbed onto the railings and pulled himself into the boat. He kicked the side of a refrigerator with the toe of his work boot. "Refreshments and everything."

Aria pranced up the steps, as lithe as a cat, and squeezed past him to the fridge. She flipped up the lid. "Drinks, snacks. They had a whole operation to cover their…operation."

"Do you hear that?" Grayson cocked his head to take in the sound of rhythmic tapping, something hard against the fiberglass of the boat. The noise kept time with the undulations of the boat.

"What is that?" Aria let the lid of the fridge fall and stood with her chin lifted. "It's coming from the side of the boat in the water."

Aria shuffled to the starboard of the boat and peered over the edge. "Grayson."

Her stark tone had him lunging to her side. As he gazed into the water, Brandy's white face, looking like a reflection of the moon, stared back at him. The zipper on her jacket kept hitting the side of the boat saying, *I'm here, I'm here, I'm here.*

Chapter Twelve

Aria glanced in her rearview mirror to make sure nobody from the TCD team was following her—not that they would be. After she'd called 9-1-1, she'd called Alana, and most of the team had converged on the marina a few minutes after the PHPD first responders.

The local cops deferred to the FBI to process the crime scene once Alana had convinced them the murder was tied to their Blah Boatie case. Aria hated that they'd chosen "Blah Boatie" for the nickname, hated it for Grayson and all the other families of the dead women, but it fit and so it stayed.

Alana had cited case confidentiality when the lead PHPD cop on the scene asked Aria how she'd happened to be at the marina and found the dead woman. Aria had told Alana about how Brandy had contacted Grayson and why.

She had also shooed Grayson away from the scene before the PHPD arrived. He was proving too valuable at the docks to have the cops blow his cover. Alana had approved of her decision.

Alana probably wouldn't approve of this decision, though.

At this point, Aria had to trust her gut. Grayson needed to know what they'd found on the boat, and just maybe he needed her.

The look on his face when he'd realized Brandy was dead in the water had bruised her heart. He'd just had to identify his own sister, and another dead woman was staring him in the face—literally staring him in the face with her dead, brown eyes. Another woman who'd trusted him.

Her foot heavy on the accelerator, she made the next turn faster than she'd intended, the tires squealing to hurry her on. The car bounced as she pulled into the parking lot of Grayson's motel and wheeled into a space.

She scrambled from the car and half jogged to his room. The door flew open before she could knock, and he pulled her inside.

"Should you be here?" A pair of dark blue sweats hung low on his hips and droplets of water glistened in the hair sprinkled across his bare chest.

"Maybe not, but I had to see you after what happened." She crossed her arms, hugging herself when she really wanted to hug him.

He ran a hand through his hair, the wet ends flipping up. "I don't get it. Was she another blah boatie? Tony's in jail. Did they order another hit man to pick up where he left off?"

"She wasn't killed like the others. This is something else." Aria perched on the arm of the threadbare sofa. "Brandy didn't have any ID on her, wasn't carrying any drugs. She didn't die from a bullet wound to the chest. This was meant to look like an accidental drowning."

"Oh, my God." Grayson dug two fingers into his temple. "They knew she was going to squeal, didn't they?"

"They must have. If they'd suspected her of stealing drugs or money, she would've died like the others."

"Do you think they know she went there to meet me? Do you think someone was watching us as we boarded the boat and found her?" He paced to the window and cracked the blinds, which hung down on one side.

"I don't know. Did you see or hear anyone around before I got there?" She yanked a damp towel draped across the back of the sofa and walked toward him slowly, holding it out. "I interrupted your shower. You're still wet."

"I was just getting out when I heard a car drive into the parking lot. In case it was Brandy's killer coming for me, I didn't want to meet him naked and unprepared." He pulled a Glock from the pocket of his baggy sweats. "Don't worry, Special Agent Calletti, it's registered and I have a permit to carry."

"I don't care at this point. If the killer saw you at the marina, you'll need protection." She bunched up the towel and pushed it against his chest. "And you need to dry off. You'll get a chill."

He set his gun down on the table by the front door and took the towel from her. He wiped it across his chest and cranked up the heater underneath the window, giving it a kick with the side of his foot at the same time. "Were you able to convince the rest of your team to keep my name out of this?"

"It didn't take much convincing. My director understands the importance of maintaining your cover. We told the PHPD that we had an informant who led me to that boat…and wait until I tell you about that boat."

"You mean *Fun Times* doesn't live up to its name?" He hung the towel around his neck and two-stepped past her. "Let me get a sweatshirt."

He disappeared into the other room and emerged, yanking a white T-shirt over his head. "That heater is surprisingly efficient."

He didn't have to tell her that. In the short time she'd been standing with her back to it, her body temperature had risen several degrees…unless she could attribute that to watching Grayson saunter across the room, his sweats slipping a little lower with each step.

He patted the back of the sofa. "Sit down and tell me what happened. Take off your jacket. You look like you're about to keel over from heat exhaustion."

She shrugged out of her maroon jacket with the fur-lined hood, the gun in her pocket banging against her leg. She hung it on the back of a chair with a cigarette burn in its blue-plaid cushion.

She lowered herself to the sofa, next to Grayson, sitting on the edge. "You know those drinks we saw in that fridge?"

"Yeah, first-class all the way."

"They were fake. All the containers were faked with false bottoms or hollowed out."

Grayson whistled. "For drugs?"

"That's what we think. The Maddie Johnsons picked up drugs somewhere on the US side, perhaps already packed in these containers, or they did that themselves when they got on board the *Fun Times*. Then the sellers hopped on for their pleasure cruise across the river to Canada, got served refreshments, disembarked in Point Edward, carrying their fake snacks, and distributed the drugs there. The women then came back to this side, ready for another shipment and another cruise."

"Except some of them got greedy, including Chloe."

"We don't know that for sure. We only have Tony's word."

Grayson shifted on the sofa and she dipped toward him, her shoulder bumping his. "To think I was working alongside Tony, and all this time he was a stone-cold killer. His uncle's a good guy. Tony's arrest is going to hit him hard. Do they know yet? Does Tony's family know?"

"We're not releasing his arrest yet. We don't want to tip anyone off, and Tony isn't all that anxious for word to get out that he's in custody. We need to convince him the only way he's going to keep safe is if he gives up the name of the kingpin in exchange for our protection. We're not going to protect him otherwise. We have his confession and, once the guys at the top realize we have their hit man, Tony's in trouble whether he tells us anything or not."

"You're going to make it in his best interest to cough up the name."

"Or as much as he knows. But at least we've grounded *Fun Times*, putting a crimp in their smuggling business for now. They'll have to look for another way to get their drugs to Canada."

"What about those tunnels? They stashing the drugs there?"

"That's what we think."

"If they're near the docks, I can do a little digging—not literally—and see what I can find out." Grayson wedged a bare foot on the rickety table in front of them.

"You don't have to do anything else, Grayson. You've done enough. You lost your sister and still you identified the killer for us, and then you managed to discover the smuggling boat." She folded her hands around one knee, her fingers fidgety. "You can hang up your career in law enforcement and go back to Detroit…wait for Danny to come to you and give him the kind of life Chloe never could."

"Is that what you want?" His warm hand covered hers, stilling her agitated fingers. "Do you want me to go back to Detroit? Leave Port Huron? Leave you?"

His words hung in the air between them and she took little sips of air, afraid to disturb the words, preferring to let them float just within her grasp, preferring to believe in dreams.

"Do you want me to leave you, Aria?" He slid his hand upward and circled her wrist with his fingers. "Because I don't want to leave you."

Her lashes fluttered as she swallowed, afraid to meet his eyes. She spoke to the strong fingers that had her in a light clasp that felt like vise around her heart. "I…you… I've been here for you, that's all this is. You're caught up in this moment. You just lost your sister. Your life will return to normal soon, although you'll always mourn your sister, but this is my life, Grayson. I'll go on to the next case, the next victims, the next victims' families."

He released her and jumped up from the sofa, turning his back on her. "Is that what I am to you? Another grieving family member? Someone to pity, humor, maybe use?"

His accusation twisted a knife in her heart and she sprang up from the sofa and grabbed the back of his T-shirt, her fingers skimming his smooth back. "Absolutely not. If you could've heard me at war with myself on the drive over here, excoriating myself for being unprofessional and then letting those warnings fly out the window as my heart took over."

Grayson turned slowly and she was sucked into the depths of his blue eyes, as dark as Lake Huron on a stormy day. "You're here. Your heart won."

She parted her lips to protest, to object, to regain her stature as an officer of the law. Instead, her mouth invited his kiss and he pulled her into his arms and sealed his lips over hers.

Her body molded to his, as if their parts fit together like some well-oiled piece of machinery. But his hands on her back, beneath her shirt, sliding over her skin, felt purely human.

In danger of melting into a puddle at his feet, she curled one arm around his neck and the other around his waist, pulling him closer.

As his pelvis thrust against her, he prodded her with his erection, hard and unrestrained beneath his loose sweats. She slipped her hand beneath the elastic waistband, her palm skimming the solid muscle of his backside.

Without breaking their kiss, Grayson reached up and released the clasp of her bra. He then stepped back to create a whisper of space between them and his hand traveled to her breast, cupping it with one roughened palm. He circled her tingling nipple with the pad of his thumb as he deepened their kiss even more to the point where she couldn't tell where the outline of her body left off and his began.

She moved her hips against his in a slow, sensuous dance, and he rocked with her, the wordless song playing in both of their heads, new to them but oddly familiar.

His lips left hers and continued their path of discovery across her face to her ear. He flicked her lobe with his tongue and then planted a new trail of kisses down her throat, his teeth grazing her collarbone.

She wanted him more than she'd ever wanted anything in her life. Wanted him to take a piece of her, as surely as she wanted a piece of him.

But right now that logic she'd thrown out the window on her rush over here had seeped beneath the door of the motel room, had started curling around her heart, causing a chill between them.

Touching his forehead to hers, Grayson cupped her face in his hands. "I'm sorry."

His gruff voice, ragged with passion, pricked her with shame.

"You don't have to apologize. I wanted you...still want you, but..."

He put a finger to her lips. "You don't have to explain anything. I got carried away—we both did. There's this thing between us. At least tell me you feel that."

"I do." She turned her head and pressed her throbbing lips against his palm. "Why do you think I flew over here?"

"To tell me about the boat?" He stepped back from her and the space between them felt like an ocean. He smiled and kissed her forehead. "You'd better put yourself together and get going. You still have a lot of work to do on this case, but I'm not going anywhere, Aria."

"I don't want you to." She twisted her arms behind her to clasp her bra, giving it about three tries before Grayson said, "Turn around."

She presented her back to him and he pulled up her top and hooked her bra. He even ran his fingers through her tangled hair.

"There, you're Special Agent Aria Calletti again."

She twirled around and, with a catch in her voice, said, "And I always will be."

ALANA CRACKED OPEN the car door of her rental and dropped the half-smoked cigarette on the ground. She stuck one leg out of the car and ground the butt with the toe of her boot. Then she leaned over, pinched it between two fingers and dropped it in a plastic bag.

When she shut the door, she waved the fumes out the window before rolling it up against the chill. Two and a half cigarettes this week—not bad, considering this case.

The motel door she'd been watching for the past half hour opened and two figures stood in silhouette within the frame. The taller one bent toward the shorter one, their shadows merging for a second in a good-night kiss.

Alana narrowed her eyes as she watched Aria float through the parking lot toward the blue sedan. Grayson

Rhodes stood at the door of his room, also focused on Aria until she got into her car. The guy had a protective streak a mile long. Too bad he hadn't been able to save his sister.

But then his sister was an addict. You couldn't save an addict. Isn't that what they always told you?

Alana sniffed and wiped her nose with a tissue. Damned smoke. She'd almost given up the filthy habit completely but some days, some cases… She shrugged.

If Steve ever caught her, he'd read her the riot act. They'd quit smoking together and, as far as she knew, her husband had stayed nicotine-free. But you couldn't force people to give up their vices. Isn't that also what they always told you?

Sneak smoking was the only secret she had kept from Steve. She'd confessed her biggest one to him before they'd married. When she'd told Steve about the child she'd had at eighteen and given up for adoption, he hadn't blinked an eye. He told her he'd support her in whatever way she needed, even if she wanted to reach out to Tania—at least, that's what her adoptive parents had named her. To Alana, she'd always be Miko.

With open adoptions, she'd always hoped Miko would try to find her. Alana and Steve had never had children together. He had two sons from a previous marriage; high-school-age boys when she and Steve had gotten married. Neither she nor Steve had the career to accommodate a baby, maintaining a marriage was hard enough.

She'd accepted it…because she'd always believed one day Miko would find her. But her daughter had never made the effort. Alana knew all about Miko though, tracked her, followed her through social media, relished in her successes, agonized over her failures—all her failures.

Alana blinked and blew her nose. She cranked on the engine, although Aria was long gone from the parking lot.

So, the new agent was falling for a victim's brother on a case. Should she warn her? Reprimand her?

Alana pulled out another cigarette and rolled down the window. Who was she to give personal advice?

Chapter Thirteen

Aria shivered, teeth chattering, as she watched Max pull up his wetsuit and squeeze his arms into the sleeves. He reached over his head, grabbed the cord on the zipper and secured himself inside the neoprene, which couldn't really be airtight enough to keep out the cold waters of Lake Huron.

A few of the dockworkers had gathered on the next pier over to watch the FBI's activity, but they couldn't possibly know what was going on. Rihanna had released nothing to the media regarding tunnels under the water, near the docks.

Now Rihanna stood near the roped-off entrance to the dock, sharp and elegant in a belted raincoat, her appearance deceiving the few members of the press craning their necks toward the action, trying to get a story. If they thought Rihanna would let anything slip about this procedure on the docks, they had the wrong woman.

Once Tony had mentioned tunnels, Opaline and Max had delved into old plans for Port Huron and the docks. They'd discovered some blueprints for underwater tunnels supposedly created during World War II.

So far, what Tony had revealed to her and Axel during the interrogation was panning out. They just needed one more vital piece of evidence from him.

Aria twisted her head around, pretending to brush off a few raindrops from the shoulder of her FBI jacket, but really sneaking a peek at the dockworkers. Was Grayson among them?

She'd almost succumbed to her desires last night. What would Alana think of her if she knew she'd gotten entangled with a victim's brother on her first case?

As if conjured from her thoughts, Alana appeared at Aria's side and rubbed her back. "Are you doing okay? Better Max than us, right?"

"I can't even fathom what it's going to feel like for him once he slips into that icy water. And I'm fine. You?" Aria raised her brows at her boss, the question not altogether idle.

The dark circles beneath Alana's eyes had added a few years to the otherwise ageless director's appearance, her brisk step a little slower this morning.

"I never sleep well in hotel rooms. Although my husband and I spend a lot of time apart, I do miss his company at night when I'm on the road." Alana squeezed her arm. "In this job, it's good to have someone to come home to, Aria."

"Alana!" Max waved his arms over his head. "I'm ready."

Aria sucked in her bottom lip as she watched Alana stride toward Max at the water's edge, squaring her shoulders, putting back on her military strut as if it were a jacket she'd momentarily shrugged off.

Then she caught up with her just as Alana clipped an underwater camera to Max's weight belt. "If you see anything of interest down there, take some pictures."

Two members of the PHPD dive team were accompanying him under water—not that Max would do anything as foolish as paddling into a tunnel on his own, but he was an experienced diver and experienced divers never went solo.

As Aria watched the three divers slide into the dark water, her phone buzzed. She pulled it out of her pocket and glanced at it.

Alana asked, "Any news?"

"It's a text from Rihanna."

"The Rihanna standing right over there, keeping the press at bay?" Alana pointed at Rihanna, who was giving Aria a thumbs-up sign.

Aria cupped the phone in her hand and reread Rihanna's message as her heart soared, a smile curving her lips.

"Ah, good news." Alana crossed her arms and wedged one foot against a wooden stump.

"CPS is allowing Grayson Rhodes to visit his nephew, and the foster parents have agreed and invited him over tonight." Despite the frosty bite in the air, Aria felt her cheeks warm.

If she'd known Alana was going to question her about the text, she never would've been so transparently happy. Who was she actually kidding? She wouldn't have been able to control herself one way or the other. If Rihanna had walked over here and told her in person, she probably would've hugged her.

Alana dipped her head once. "You should go with him."

"M-me?" Aria clasped the phone between her two hands like an ecstatic schoolgirl, and then dropped the phone back in her pocket. "Shouldn't Rihanna go with him? She's already met the foster parents."

"Rhodes trusts you. You've been his contact through all this. You were there when he ID'd his sister. The two of you discovered Brandy's body last night." Alana crossed her fingers. "There's a connection between you."

"Okay, I'll call him later and set it up."

A squad car pulled up and Opaline emerged from the back seat, pulling the fur-lined hood of her pink jacket over her head. She bent forward, leaning her head in the passenger window and chatting with the officer before spinning around and picking her way across the wooden planks of the dock in her high-heeled boots with fur at the top to match her hood.

"It's freezing out here." Opaline pulled on a pair of mittens.

"You don't have to be out here. You did enough work finding the plans for the tunnels." Alana peered around Opaline's shoulder at the cop car. "Special delivery service?"

"Oh, that's Gordon. He was coming this way and offered me a lift." Leaning forward, Opaline cupped her mouth and whispered, "He likes cats."

"So did your ex." Alana chuckled and wandered toward the water.

Opaline stared after Alana for a few seconds and said, "Is she okay?"

"She looks tired, doesn't she?"

"She does, but I hope you didn't tell her that." Opaline jerked her thumb over her shoulder. "How long have Max and the other divers been below?"

"Just about ten minutes. They're going to need hot coffee and warm showers when they get out." Aria hunched her shoulders. "I hope they find something. Do you know why the government built those tunnels?"

"Munitions. Maybe they thought the Germans were going to attack the US via the Great Lakes. Unfortunately for us, the plans we saw didn't have the land endpoints— just the construction of the tunnels beneath the water. I think we were missing some maps or plans."

"Maybe Max can find those points and those will lead

us to the drug storage area. All three bodies were discovered near the lake. When the hit on them was put out, their locations weren't a secret. The women weren't killed in their apartments or their cars. They were alone on those roads near the lake, for some reason. One even had her baby with her." Aria pressed a hand to her heart.

"Picking up their stash for the trip to Canada. I think we can shut this down, but we need to get the person at the top because he'll just set up shop somewhere else, using other resources, other people, to get his product across the border." Opaline pushed her hood back from her face, the blue ends of her hair clinging to the fur. "Do you think Tony Balducci will give up the top dog?"

"Axel seems to think so, and I have faith in him."

"Uh-oh." Opaline peered over Aria's shoulder. "Looks like it's lunchtime for the boys on the dock. I hope they don't come nosing around here. Maybe Gordon can ward them off while Rihanna keeps the press at bay."

"They've been eyeballing us all morning, but the PHPD has us cordoned off." Aria's phone buzzed in her pocket and she pulled it out. She read Grayson's text, asking if she could talk.

She tipped her phone back and forth at Opaline. "I need to make a call. Excuse me for a sec."

"Go ahead. I'm going to see what Alana knows…or at least see if she needs any coffee."

Aria moved away from the staging area for the divers and called Grayson. He barely let one ring finish before he answered.

"What's happening over there?"

"We have divers looking for those underwater tunnels. We think the drugs might be hidden there."

"I hope you find them, get them off the streets."

"What's the talk at the docks?"

"Everything from you guys found another body to it actually being Tony's body."

Aria drew in a breath. "Tony hasn't reached out to his family yet?"

"Nope, or Chuck's not telling me. Is that good or bad?"

"It's good. It means Tony's afraid of reprisals and we can use that to get him to talk. Without our protection on the inside, he's toast." With the back of her hand, Aria dashed away a raindrop that had hit her cheek. "I have some other news for you—good news."

"I could use some about now."

Aria gripped the phone in her hand as butterflies swirled in her stomach. Was he referring to the way she'd shut him down last night?

She rushed to fill the expectant silence. "If you're free tonight, you can visit Danny."

His excited words burst over the phone. "Are you serious? I can see my nephew?"

"DCS approved it and the foster parents agreed—six o'clock tonight, and I'm going with you."

"I'm glad it's you." Grayson had lowered his voice and the tone sent a delicious thrill curling through her body. "Look, last night…"

She held up her hand, as if he could see her. "Don't. It's all right."

"Okay, good. I'm going to eat my lunch. Do you want to pick me up tonight at my luxurious motel? I get off at five, and I'll head back, shower and change."

"I can do that. Can you be ready by around five forty?"

"I can. And… Aria?"

"Yes?" She couldn't control the breathlessness of her voice or the fluttering of her heart when Grayson said her name.

"I'm glad we didn't make love last night in that dump. When we come together, it's going to be something special."

He ended the call before she could reply to his outrageous statement. So, that's why he'd said it was all right that they hadn't continued down the path their touching and kissing would've surely led them. He'd figured their union was inevitable anyway, and he could bide his time for the right moment.

Was he wrong?

Alana whooped. "They're coming up."

Stashing her phone, Aria rushed to the water's edge where the rope that had followed the divers down was now taut and vibrating.

Her heart lodged in her throat until the first diver's mask broke the surface. As Max clambered out of the brackish lake, water sluicing off his prosthetic, he ran a finger across his throat.

Aria grabbed Alana's elbow. "They didn't find anything?"

"Let's wait and see."

As the divers sat on the wooden stumps that littered the dock, removing their fins and masks, Opaline scurried up with a cardboard drink holder containing three cups of coffee.

When Max emerged from his mask and accepted a coffee from Opaline, Aria followed Alana to his side.

He brushed a hand over his head. "Damn, that's cold."

"What did you see, Max?"

He unhooked the camera from his belt and dangled it from his fingers. "It's all on here. We did find the entrance to one tunnel, so they still exist, but the door is either locked or rusted shut. There's no way we can get in there."

Alana smacked a fist in her palm. "But we know they exist and Tony's story isn't a lie. The exits on the land must be somewhere, and I'm guessing they're near where the bodies were found. What else were those women doing there by themselves?"

"We searched those sites for evidence. Now we need to search the surrounding locations for possible hidey-holes for the drugs." Max slipped a fin off his prosthetic.

Turning to Aria, Alana said, "I'm going to get Selena and Blanca on that, and I want you to go with her, Aria, so you can see how the K-9 tracker works."

"I'd like that."

"I got some more good news for Mr. Rhodes. Carly called me with the toxicology and DNA results on mother and baby. Danny is Chloe Larsen's child, which we knew, anyway, but he didn't have any drugs in his system at all. Chloe, on the other hand..." Alana stopped and turned her head to the side. She dragged a tissue from her pocket, dabbed her eyes and wiped it across her nose. "Sorry, damn cold. Chloe, on the other hand, had a small quantity of opioids in her system."

Max peeled down the top of his wetsuit. "Damn, that girl was on the highway to hell."

Aria put her hand on Alana's stiff back. "It's been a raw morning out here, and it's starting to rain. Why don't you go back to the hotel and put your feet up for a few hours? We all know what we're doing."

"Nonsense." Alana flipped up the hood on her FBI jacket. "I'm going back to the war room, and Opaline's going to blow up these underwater pictures Max took. I suggest you and Selena join us. You too, Max."

"As soon as I get some warm clothes and a hot lunch." He raised a hand to the other divers. "Thanks, guys. I'll buy you some chili."

Alana had hurried away and hopped into her rental, taking off after a few words with the PD.

Aria tapped Opaline's shoulder. "Hey, Opaline. Do you think your hot cop can give me a lift back to the station in his squad car? Alana must've forgotten she was my ride."

"Yeah, she sure was in a big hurry to get out of here."

Aria stared after Alana's rental as it zipped around the corner and out of sight. It didn't take any investigative skills to know Alana didn't have a cold. Those had been tears in the usually stoic director's eyes.

WHEN GRAYSON GOT off work, he rushed to a store, where he bought a stuffed tiger and a saucer-shaped contraption for the baby to sit in and entertain himself with the little gadgets and dials along the tray that encircled the seat. He hoped the foster parents didn't mind, but every time he'd seen Danny in the past, he'd come bearing gifts—and diapers, and diaper wipes, and clothes, and even big-ticket items like that car seat Danny had been found in next to his mother's dead body.

By the time Aria drove up to his motel, he'd showered and changed into a pair of jeans and a flannel shirt and was standing outside his room with the tiger under one arm and the saucer at his feet.

Her eyes widened when she saw him. She parked and then slid from behind the wheel. "You come prepared."

"I always bring Danny something when I see him." He picked up the saucer by the edge. "Do you have room for this?"

"You can wedge it in the back seat." She yanked open the door for him and he turned the saucer seat on its side and shoved it into the back.

He climbed in next to her in her car, clutching the tiger in his lap. "The foster parents are okay with this?"

"Rihanna said they were thrilled that Danny had an uncle who wanted him. She said they're incredible people."

"They must be." Unlike Danny's mother. He stroked the tiger's ear with his thumb.

"Don't get too attached to that tiger." Aria tugged on the toy's tail before she pulled out of the motel's parking lot. "You're going to have to fight Danny for it."

He stretched his lips into a smile. He didn't know why his nerves were jangling. Either he was afraid Danny would reject him…or that Aria would.

He tossed the tiger into the back seat. "Nothing came from the search for the tunnels today?"

"Max found an underwater tunnel, but the entrance was locked. We have no way of knowing where it pops up on land."

"Probably where the women were murdered. Why else would they be walking in those areas at night by themselves?"

"Exactly. I'm going out with our K-9 agent and her dog tomorrow. The handler will give the dog something belonging to the victims to sniff and see if she can track them."

Aria's GPS spit out some directions and she joined the highway traffic. "It's not far, maybe ten minutes."

"Did Rihanna indicate when the DNA results would be in?"

"Shouldn't be much longer because…" She lodged the tip of her tongue in the corner of her mouth and flicked on her turn signal.

"Because what?"

"We got other test results back, which confirmed that Chloe and Danny were mother and son, and that Danny didn't have any drugs in his system."

Grayson blew out a breath. "Yeah, I could've told you that. I grilled Chloe on that score and, while she didn't always answer my questions, when she did, she told the truth. You're leaving something out."

Aria's hands tightened on the steering wheel and she shot him a glance from the corner of her eye. "Toxicology came back on Chloe, too."

"Let me guess." His eye twitched. "She had drugs in her system."

"Opioids."

Grayson's hands curled into fists, despite himself. "I could've told you that, too."

He stared out the window at the scenery rushing past, draped in gray, thinking about all the times he'd tried to get Chloe to stop using. The last time had been before her pregnancy when he'd sent her to a high-end, live-in treatment center. She'd lasted two weeks before running off with some musician. That guy could even be Danny's father, but if Chloe hadn't mentioned it to her fellow escapee, Grayson had no intention of suggesting to this guy that he might be a dad. Grayson wanted Danny to have a good life. From here on out, sunshine and…tigers.

"We're on the street." Aria tapped the window. "Nice homes."

She pulled up in front of a house that had a midsize SUV and a red truck parked in the driveway. "Ready?"

"Oh, yeah." He had the door open before she cut the engine. Ducking into the back seat, he grabbed the toys and marched up to the porch, Aria tailing behind him.

The door swung open before he had a chance to knock, and a man whose shoulders practically spanned the doorway stuck out his hand. "Rich Colby. You must be Danny's uncle. Same blue eyes, same expression when someone tries to take one of his toys away."

I must look ready to do battle or something. Grayson puffed out a breath and, with the tiger under his arm, shook the man's hand. "Grayson Rhodes, and I can't tell you how much it means to me that you took in Danny."

A woman with fluffy blond hair peeped over her husband's shoulder. "You do look like Danny. I'm Sarah Colby. C'mon in."

"I'm sorry." Grayson turned to Aria. "This is Special Agent Aria Calletti with the FBI."

While Aria shook hands with the Colbys as they stood in the entryway, Grayson dropped the toys on the floor and made a beeline for his nephew, standing in the playpen across the room, his hands curled on the side, swaying back and forth.

"Hey, buddy. Do you remember your uncle Grayson?" He swept the boy up and pressed his nose against Danny's soft hair, a towhead, just like Chloe was as a baby.

Danny's legs wrapped around Grayson's waist and he patted his face with sticky hands.

Grayson's nose stung and he bounced Danny in his arms for a few seconds before turning around and facing Aria and the Colbys. "I think he remembers me."

"Of course, he does." Sarah beamed. "He's totally comfortable with you. That DNA test is just a formality. DCS has to be sure before they release a baby. My guess is you'll have him by Christmas."

Danny seemed to approve as he squealed and kicked his legs against Grayson's hip.

Aria rescued the stuffed animal from the floor and waved him in the air. "Did you see the tiger Uncle Grayson brought you?"

Danny chuckled and reached out for the toy.

Grayson squatted on the floor near the play mat. "He's crawling, isn't he? I—I haven't seen him for a few months, but the last time I talked to my sister, she said he'd started crawling."

"Crawling, rolling, pulling himself up to standing and almost cruising." Sarah put her head to one side, looking like a feathered bird. "You're going to have your hands full, Grayson. Are you married?"

"I'm not, but I'm my own boss and I can work from home. And I'll be hiring a nanny."

Rich snorted. "I don't have to tell you, Sarah already looked you up online, so we know you're in a good financial position to care for the boy."

"I am, but it's more than that. I want to make up for... everything he lost."

"I'm sure you will." Sarah sniffled and dabbed the corner of her eye with her fingertip. "Do either of you want anything to drink?"

"No, thanks." Grayson had put Danny on the play mat and handed him the tiger, which he was now squishing between his arms.

"Just some water for me." Aria sat beside Grayson, tucking her legs beneath her and waving at Danny.

Danny dropped the tiger and reached out for Aria. She pulled him into her lap, facing him toward Grayson, wrapping one arm around his belly and bouncing him, while he giggled.

Sarah returned with a glass of water for Aria, which she placed on the coffee table next to her. "You look like you can handle a baby."

"I have four brothers, and they all have children. I have a plethora of nieces and nephews, and I've filled in as a babysitter more times than I can count."

"You should find a nanny like Aria, Grayson." Sarah's gaze darted back and forth between them. "We'll give you some time alone with Danny, and then it's bedtime for this little guy."

Sarah wasn't wrong. Aria was a natural with Danny.

Maybe she reminded his nephew of his mother. She made Danny laugh, and Grayson caught himself more than once with a big, goofy grin on his own face. Aria obviously had the gift to charm the Rhodes men.

Grayson watched Aria holding Danny's hands as he stood, rocking back and forth. She'd make a great mother someday.

"What?" She tilted her head and Danny made a grab for her hair. "You're looking at me like you're trying to figure me out."

Could he be more obvious?

"Four brothers, huh? That must've been a challenge for you."

"In a way. They're very protective—all firefighters."

What a gauntlet for any man to walk who wanted to date Aria. "Your father, too?"

"My dad was an autoworker for a while—got laid off."

"Familiar story."

"My mother was a police officer before she had my oldest brother. When Dad got laid off, Mom wanted to go back to work, but he wouldn't allow it." Her jawline hardened and her eyes narrowed. "Can you believe that? Stubborn, macho nonsense."

"That's...yeah, doesn't make much sense."

His inadequate response got lost in Danny's giggles as he plopped onto his bottom. He'd have to thank his nephew for that bit of intervention later.

After about thirty minutes, the Colbys crept back into the room discreetly. "Is he starting to get a little fussy?"

"Maybe a little wound up." Aria pushed to her feet, leaving Danny clinging to Grayson's arm as he tried out his sea legs. "Say good-night to your uncle, Danny. Your new daddy."

Grayson pulled Danny against his chest and stood

with him wrapped around his body like a baby chimp, as Aria chatted with the Colbys by the front door. He kissed the side of Danny's head and whispered, "Be a good boy for Rich and Sarah, and then I'm coming back for you, Danny... I'm coming back for you for your mom's sake."

As Aria pulled away from the Colby house, Grayson said, "Wow, they're just about perfect, aren't they?"

"Danny couldn't ask for a better set of foster parents." She patted his thigh and his knee jerked. "But Danny is obviously taken with his uncle. You'll do fine."

"He was obviously taken with you, too." *Like uncle, like nephew.*

He kept that thought to himself. He'd already come on too strong over the phone today, telling her how and when he planned to make love to her. He always got what he wanted, and he'd never wanted anything more in his life than Aria Calletti. But she was not his for the tak-ing—no matter how soft her lips looked when she talked to him or how her dark brown eyes turned to liquid when they met his.

"Well, yeah, I do have all those nieces and nephews, and I'm not kidding when I say my brothers use me as a babysitting service." She snapped her fingers. "Speaking of which, you should start looking for a nanny...or a wife."

He raised one eyebrow at her. Did she really want him to find a wife? He remembered her saying how she'd move on to the next case, the next victim, after this. He'd hoped she was convincing herself, but maybe he was the one who needed convincing that she just didn't see any future for them beyond this investigation. It stung.

He ignored her suggestion and gazed out the window as she fiddled with the radio, turning it up to fill the now awkward silence between them. She even sang along, mak-ing things even more awkward.

Grayson actually blew out a sigh of relief when she pulled into the motel parking lot and turned down the radio. She laughed. "Home sweet home."

"That it is." He opened his door and turned toward her before she could cut the engine. "Thanks, Aria. Thanks for coming with me and thanks for pushing for the meeting."

"I..."

"I know it was you, and I appreciate it." He got out of the car and leaned back in. "I'll keep my eyes and ears open on the dock."

He shut the door and walked to his room, listening for her car to take off, not wanting to turn around. They couldn't have a repeat of what happened last night. Maybe she didn't even want a repeat if she was suggesting he find himself a wife. He had misread her, had thought she felt something she didn't feel.

Instead of driving away, she turned off the ignition. He kept trudging to his door, hoping she'd think better of it.

He pulled out his key, but he didn't have to use it. The door had been kicked in. He pushed it open and a knot formed in his gut as he surveyed the room.

Shoving his hand in his pocket, he curled his fingers around the handle of his gun.

When Aria's boots tapped against the concrete walkway, he turned to her. "Stay back."

Her eyes popped open. "What's wrong?"

"Someone broke into my room and tossed the place. I've been made."

Chapter Fourteen

A sharp spike of adrenaline made Aria dizzy and she licked her dry lips. Why was Grayson telling her to stay back? He was the civilian here.

He held out his hand to her and withdrew his weapon from his pocket. "Let me make sure he's gone."

She pulled her own gun out of her purse and spun around toward the parking lot. Was the intruder still there? Watching them?

A minute later, Grayson poked his head out the door. "All clear. All clear out there, too?"

"I didn't see anyone, and nobody started a car, but that doesn't mean he's not still there, watching."

"We won't give him anything to watch. Come on in."

She shoved her gun into the side pocket of her purse, dropped it by the door and brushed past him into the room. She widened her eyes and gulped. "You're not kidding. Someone did a number on this room."

Her gaze traveled from the upended sofa cushions to the gaping drawers in the compact kitchen, spilling their guts to the books and papers on the floor. She didn't even want to look in the bedroom.

"Closets in the bedroom? Clothes? Suitcase?"

"Same." He grabbed a cushion from the floor and tossed it onto the sofa.

"Did you have anything in here to tie you to Chloe or Danny? Anything with your real name on it?"

He patted his pockets. "I have my phone on me, my wallet. I didn't bring a laptop. Any pictures I have are on my phone. I didn't keep any receipts from the motel or anywhere else. But even if they don't know what my connection is to this case, someone has figured out I'm not the new dockworker hoping to make a home in Port Huron... unless this is some random break-in."

"While this isn't the best area in town, there are no coincidences. You were targeted. Someone saw us together."

"Or it could be that someone knew Brandy reached out to me. Maybe this drug ring thinks Brandy told me something."

Aria balled a fist against her stomach, which had started churning. That notion worried her even more than if someone just thought Grayson was working with the FBI or was some kind of informant.

She swallowed, which was more like a gulp. "If the drug dealer running the show thinks you know something about the operation, know something about him, your life is in danger."

"If he thought Brandy already spilled her guts to me, they wouldn't have killed her. Or they would've waited at the marina and killed us both."

"We don't know that, Grayson." She pressed her folded hands against her chin. "You should leave Port Huron. Quit the job and leave. When Danny is released to you, you can come back and pick him up, but it's time for you to stop this game you're playing."

"I'm not going anywhere." He took her by the shoulders. "And you don't have to worry about me. I haven't had anyone worry about me since my dad died."

"You're not going back to work, are you? You don't

have to pretend anymore. You can move out of this dump, at least." He was in danger now, and she worried that he didn't understand the breadth of the risk. These drug dealers didn't fool around.

"This dump?" He released her and spread his arms. "I'm getting kind of used to it, and I'm not quitting the job. I'm going to carry on as if nothing happened. Let them wonder about me. Let them wonder what I'm doing here."

"Grayson! They won't wonder. That's the problem. They'll act. And we've both seen what that looks like." She ducked and shoved a cushion into place on the sofa, trying to keep her emotions under control by not looking at him. "Do you always get what you want?"

"Almost always."

The low, sultry tone of his voice made her heart flutter just a little, and she was afraid to turn around. She patted the cushion and picked up the next one.

"Why did you follow me inside?" He righted a table and stacked his books on top of it. "I thought you left after you dropped me off."

She smoothed her hand over the threadbare couch, letting her hair fall around her face like a curtain. She'd run after him because she'd felt empty inside when he'd left her. She'd run after him to tell him not to find a mother for Danny. She'd run after him because, after pushing him away, she wanted him close again.

"You know, in all the excitement, I forgot what I was going to tell you."

"You don't have to help me clean up." He snatched up her purse from the floor by the door where she'd dropped it and swung it next to her. "You have another busy day tomorrow, and I have to work."

She took the purse from him and hitched it over her

shoulder. "I can't convince you to give this pretense up, can I?"

He smiled. "No."

She stared at him, thinking how different he was. He was wealthy enough to have hired a private detective to look into his sister's disappearance, but he'd taken on the task himself, unafraid of where that might lead him. Now that he knew Chloe was dead, he still wouldn't let go until her killers were all rounded up. It was futile to try to convince him otherwise.

"Let me know if you discover anything missing," she said, resigned to his insistence on staying involved.

"Yes, ma'am, and I'll walk you out to your car—just in case."

Crossing her arms, she said, "You do understand that I'm an armed FBI agent, right?"

"Oh, I know that, ma'am. You never let me forget it." He walked to the door and swept it open. "Almost never."

She brushed a hand across her cheek, as if trying to brush away the warmth creeping across her skin. "I'm just saying, if I don't have to worry about you, you certainly don't have to worry about me."

"I know I don't have to." He flicked the broken wood in the doorjamb. "I'm going to have to visit Bernie in the management office to see if he can put a lock on tonight and fix this tomorrow."

Grayson walked her to the car and stood in the parking lot, watching her drive away. When he no longer appeared in her rearview mirror, she slumped behind the wheel.

How had she fallen so fast and so hard for Grayson Rhodes? The man wasn't even her type—gorgeous, successful, sexy and sensitive?

Looked like she just found a new type.

THE FOLLOWING MORNING Aria returned to the scene of Chloe's murder with Selena and Blanca. The white shepherd sensed it was time to work, and her restlessness permeated the car. Aria bounced her leg in response to the tension, but Selena seemed unfazed. If both dog and handler were excited, they'd be pinging off the interior of the car and Blanca probably wouldn't be able to work.

They had the shirt Chloe had been wearing the night of her murder. Selena would let Blanca sniff it, and see if she could track Chloe's progress on that road. With any luck, Chloe's scent would lead them to the endpoint of that tunnel and the drug storage area.

Aria parked on the road above the gravel path next to the water. She led the way down the trail, with Selena keeping Blanca on a tight leash behind her. The scrap of yellow crime scene tape, still stuck to a bush, waved at them.

Blanca whined and her ears perked up as Selena told her to sit, using the German word. Selena pulled Chloe's top from the bag and held it to Blanca's nose, which twitched and quivered.

Selena then unclipped Blanca's leash and said, *"Track."*

Blanca put her snout in the air and sniffed. She trotted a few steps forward and then dropped her nose to the ground and snuffled along the gravel. The dog alternated between sniffing the air and the ground. When she reached the dark stain, somewhat diluted by the recent rain, where Chloe had lost her life, Blanca sat and barked sharply two times.

"Good dog." Selena stood in front of Blanca and offered her the shirt again. She pointed in the other direction. *"Keep going. Track!"*

Blanca followed her path back to where they started and kept going in the other direction.

Every time the K-9 paused, Aria would hold her breath as Selena shouted more commands.

As the marshy ground got more uneven, Blanca began veering toward the water's edge.

Aria whispered to Selena, "Will it be harder for her to track the scent in the soft reeds as opposed to the ground?"

"That rain didn't help, but she should be okay—if there's anything there."

Finally, Blanca made a decision and sat next to a pile of muck, barking twice.

"She may have found something." Selena hustled toward her dog. *"Good dog."*

Before Selena reached Blanca, the K-9 was on the move again, pacing and circling the area by the water. Occasionally, she'd stop and sit and give out two barks, which Selena had explained was her "alert" signal, telling them she'd noticed something.

Aria said, "She seems to like that spot."

"But she can't seem to alert to just one." Selena gave a sharp whistle between her teeth and ordered Blanca out with an *"out"* command.

Blanca retreated and returned to her handler's side, tongue lolling out of the side of her mouth. Selena withdrew a bottle of water and tipped it. Blanca lapped at the stream of water.

Selena pointed to the spot. "Do you want to have a look?"

Aria didn't have to be asked twice. She slogged through the reeds and wet grasses toward the water seeping onto the land. "This place would make perfect sense for the endpoint of a tunnel under the lake."

She scanned the space, kicking at rises with the toe of her shoe, getting on her knees and scrabbling against the dirt with her fingers.

Selena called out to her. "Let the CSI team have a crack at it. We'll make our report to Alana and Max."

Aria waded out of the mire, pulling her sneakers from the glop beneath her feet, brushing the wet knees of her jeans. "Hey, do we know if Chloe had grass and mud stuck to her boots? That might tell us something."

"Unless she cleaned them off." Selena leashed Blanca again and patted her head. "I hope this is it."

"Blanca could be our hero." Ara knew enough from the police academy and the K-9 units at Detroit PD to understand that she couldn't wrap her arms around Blanca and bury her face in the dog's thick fur. So instead, she said, *"Good dog."*

They returned to the car, and Selena called Alana to tell her about Blanca's alerts and to send Max and a CSI team from the PHPD.

When she ended the call, she pulled a pack of hand sanitizer wipes from her bag and held it out to Aria. "We might as well eat lunch while we're waiting."

"Is Blanca going to go back to the scene?" Aria plucked a wipe from the package and cleaned off her hands. Nothing much she could do for her jeans.

"No, we'll stay behind when CSI gets here. I don't want her to get confused with all the different scents." Selena tugged a plastic bag from her backpack and plunged her hand inside. "Did you get a ham on rye, too?"

"Pastrami."

Selena handed her one of the wrapped sandwiches they'd picked up on the way in case Blanca kept them out here all day.

"Napkins?" Aria held out her hand and Selena slapped a handful into her palm.

She dangled a bag of chips from her fingertips for a second, reading the print, and then tossed them into Aria's lap. "Pastrami and jalapeño chips. I hope you're not meeting Grayson Rhodes after this."

Aria had been in the process of ripping open her bag of chips. Her hands jerked and the chips spilled all over her napkin-covered lap. "What does that mean?"

"It means your breath is going to be…spicy." Selena carefully unwrapped her ham sandwich.

"And why should I care if Grayson Rhodes thinks I have…spicy breath?" Aria collected the chips and dropped them back into the bag, popping one into her mouth.

"He's a good-looking guy, and you're spending a lot of time with him." Selena waved her sandwich at Aria. "Not that I'm saying it's not all legit."

Selena bit into her sandwich and then wiped her mouth.

"Alana's the one who sent me with him to visit his nephew last night."

"What's up with her, anyway? Although, I shouldn't be asking the new kid on the block." Selena shook out a little packet of mustard. "But take it from me, Alana hasn't been her usual energetic self."

"Even I noticed she's looking tired—doesn't stop her from working ten times harder than the rest of us, though." Aria wiped the spicy jalapeño seasoning on the napkin in her lap. "I swear she had tears in her eyes yesterday."

"Maybe the work just gets to her sometimes. Nice to know she's human like the rest of us."

Aria nodded and took a big bite of her sandwich, just happy the subject of the conversation had switched from her and Grayson to Alana.

"How *did* it go with the baby last night?"

Aria dabbed her lips. Grayson hadn't wanted her to tell anyone about his room getting tossed. "It went well. Little Danny obviously remembered his uncle, and Grayson was impressed with the foster parents, who are right out of the guide for foster parents."

"Here they come." Selena adjusted her rearview mirror,

Blanca stirring in the back. "Don't you worry, girl. Your work is done for the day, and I'll give you a big meal."

"Selena, you and Blanca don't have to wait for me. Once you tell Alana what happened with Blanca, you can take off. I'll get a ride back with someone else."

"Sounds good."

They finished off their lunches in a hurry and then took Alana and Max down to the water's edge where Selena explained what had happened with Blanca.

When Selena left, Aria stood with Alana as Max and the CSI team searched the area, digging, collecting, thrashing through the reeds.

After more than an hour, Max popped up and shook his head. Aria's stomach dropped. "Nothing? There has to be something there. Why would Chloe be near the water's edge?"

"Maybe she took a boat to this spot." Alana kicked a small rock and it skipped and bounced on the ground. "Damn. I thought this was it. You and Axel are going to have to have another go at Tony Balducci. Really put the screws to him this time. The kid's not too bright. Use that."

Alana waved her arm in the air and called out to Max, "Keep it up for a while longer to make sure you're not missing anything. I'm going back." She spun around and made a beeline for the trail leading up to the main road.

"Alana." Aria had to jog to keep up with the director. "Can you give me a ride back to the station? I'm going to try to get together with Axel to plot out our next move against Tony."

Without turning around, Alana called over her shoulder, "Sure."

Aria scrambled up the path in Alana's wake, and they both climbed into her rental car. The director sat behind the wheel, her finger resting on the ignition button.

Snapping her seat belt, Aria glanced at Alana's frozen profile. "Um, where's Amanda? I haven't seen her around."

"She's spending a lot of time in the war room. I couldn't function without her, especially—" Alana broke off and clutched the steering wheel with both hands, resting her forehead on the top.

Aria's breath hitched in her throat, wishing one of the other team members was there instead of her. She reached out tentatively and put her hand on Alana's arm. "Do you want to tell me what's wrong, Alana?"

With her head still on the steering wheel, Alana turned to her and Aria's heart jumped as the director's professional mask slipped away. Her dark eyes shimmered with tears and her mouth trembled.

"Alana, what's wrong?"

Alana lifted her head and took a deep, shuddering breath. "It's this Blah Boatie case."

"Th-the dead women? The baby?" Aria's mind sifted through the cases the TCD handled with Alana at the helm—child trafficking, kidnapping, serial murders, bombings—Alana had seen it all.

"When I was eighteen, before I enlisted in the Army, I had a baby, a daughter." Alana gazed into space and time through the windshield. "My father was old school, a colonel in the Army. I gave the baby up for adoption."

"I'm sorry. I didn't know."

"Nobody knows, except my husband." Alana blinked. "It was an open adoption, and I always figured my daughter would get curious and find me. She never did. But I found her, and I followed her life from afar. When Miko became addicted to opioids, I knew about that, too."

Aria covered her mouth with her hand. "I'm so sorry. No wonder this case is getting under your skin."

"I wanted to step in, help her, make her better, like I'm

sure Grayson Rhodes wanted to do with his sister, but you can't make a user stop using. Ask your Mr. Rhodes about that."

Aria let the implication pass and retrieved a tissue from her bag. She handed it to Alana, who crushed it in her fist.

"I'm assuming Miko's adoptive parents know about her addiction. Have they tried to intervene? Maybe under the circumstances, it's time for you to step forward."

Alana lifted one shoulder and the corner of her mouth twitched. "It's too late for all that. Miko died of an overdose six years ago."

Chapter Fifteen

Aria clutched the base of her throat with one hand, her pulse thudding beneath her fingertips. "I'm sorry."

The words sounded small and inadequate. No wonder Alana had been on edge. Every time she saw one of those dead blah boaties, misguided, lost, opioids in their systems, she must've been thinking about her own daughter.

Alana continued, almost as if Aria wasn't beside her in the car. "The day I found out she died, I'd been working a kidnapping case, helping other families find their children when I'd just lost my only daughter forever. I attended her funeral—a stranger in the back, on the outside, an observer, just as I'd been her entire life."

Aria kept her lips sealed under Alana's need to unburden herself. Another "sorry" wasn't going to ease this woman's pain.

Her eyes dry now, Alana shredded the tissue in her lap. "At the funeral, I watched Miko's parents—they'd named her Tania—bent, broken, their faces ravaged by grief. I felt the same way inside, beneath the clenched jaw, the rigid muscles. I wanted to scream and cry and beat my breast for the world to see, but I'd given up that right."

Aria clasped Alana's hand. "You were still her mother. You had every right…and you still do."

"Maybe I should've stepped forward, inserted myself

into her life. Maybe I could've gotten her to turn her life around. Or maybe I was the reason she started using in the first place."

"Stop." Aria smacked her hand against the dashboard. "You, of all people, with the work we do, understand that nobody can make an addict stop using. And thousands of children are adopted every year. It isn't a precursor for addiction."

"I know that. You're right." Alana pressed the mangled tissue to her nose. "You're so vehement, so passionate. No wonder Grayson Rhodes turns to you."

Aria's mouth dropped open as she struggled to find the words to respond.

But then Alana squared her shoulders, pinning them back against the seat, and punched the starter on the car with her knuckle. "Let's get back to work. We have a drug dealer to catch. And please don't bring this up to anyone else on the team. Nobody needs to know my personal weaknesses. I'm sorry I dumped this on you. I'll be fine."

"Of course." Aria folded her hands in her lap.

Talk about personal weaknesses. She was falling for someone intricately tied to her first case on the Tactical Crime Division…and everyone knew it.

ARIA SPENT THE rest of the afternoon in the TCD's war room at the PHPD, reviewing the underwater photos Max had taken of the tunnel entrance and meeting up with Axel to review their strategy for questioning Tony the next day.

A few surreptitious glances at Alana assured Aria that the director had bounced back with a vengeance after her confession in the car. She was all business as she dictated to Amanda and jetted between Max and Opaline, comparing the maps to the photos, and Selena reviewing the area where Blanca had alerted. Was she regretting it now?

Aria felt honored that Alana trusted her with her confidence, but she didn't have a choice. The story probably never would've come out if Aria hadn't hit up Alana for a ride. She'd caught the director in a weak moment, but if Alana feared the revelation about her daughter and her death from opioids would tarnish her authority, she had nothing to worry about. Alana's disclosure had only solidified Aria's respect for the woman, and made Aria feel as if she could trust her boss with anything.

Axel took a seat across from her, straddling it and crossing his arms over the back. "You look tired. We're all good on our technique for interrogating Balducci tomorrow, so why don't you head back to the hotel, get something to eat and relax."

"When everyone's still here, working?"

"Nobody will think that. You've more than pulled your load on this case." He cranked his head back and forth. "Besides, look around. Carly's not here, and I'd bet she'd like some company for dinner. You two can even work through dinner, if you insist. I know she has some results for the drugs the women were carrying, and she'd probably like to run those by you."

Stretching her arms over her head, Aria yawned and said, "You convinced me."

"Good, bright and early tomorrow morning, then. We're going to nail Balducci to the wall."

Aria approached Alana, hovering over Amanda as she entered text in a spreadsheet, and touched her shoulder. "I'm going back to the hotel. I'm going to see if Carly has some info on those drugs."

Alana twisted her head over her shoulder and smiled. "You do that. Get a little rest while you're at it."

Aria hesitated, raising her eyebrows. Alana straightened to her full height, which was a few inches shorter than Aria's, and took her by the shoulders. She lowered her voice. "I'm fine. Thanks for listening, but there's nothing for you to worry about. Nothing."

Aria smiled and gave Alana a quick, one-armed hug—and didn't care what any of the team members thought about her gesture.

Blinking back tears, Aria left the conference room and took one of the rental cars back to the hotel. If Carly wanted to discuss her findings with Aria, it must not be that urgent because she hadn't answered her texts. Axel had probably just wanted to give her an excuse to leave.

And no wonder—Aria leaned in close to the full-length mirror on the hotel closet's door and ran her fingers through her messy hair. The damp spots on her knees from searching the swampy area next to the lake today had dried into dirty, stiff stains.

When she'd joined the team for the first time several days ago, which now seemed like a lifetime ago, she'd been worried about a ponytail. Now, look at her.

She called room service to order some soup and then hopped in the shower. By the time she'd changed into some sweats and dragged out her FBI binder on interrogations, her food arrived.

She slurped her soup from a spoon as she flipped through the pages of the binder, reading transcripts of interrogations—some of which had been conducted by Axel Morrow. She'd follow his lead tomorrow, and hopefully they could trap Tony into revealing the head honcho. He had to know something. He'd been the hit man. The guy at the top had to have some level of trust in him.

The presence of Danny had unraveled Tony. In addition to Tony's DNA on that tissue she'd found at the murder scene, Danny's DNA was also present. Tony had used his own tissue to wipe Danny's nose or tears. Danny had led them to his mother's killer.

Aria pushed the binder off her lap to grab her buzzing phone. Selena had sent a text, along with a picture of Blanca, thanking her for coming out today with her and her K-9. Aria replied with a smiling doggie face.

Blanca had been circling the same area by the water but hadn't taken them any farther. Could Chloe have come from the water? No boat was found, but Tony could've taken care of that. Maybe the tunnel had been in a different area.

Checking the time on her phone, Aria scooted off the bed and grabbed her grimy jeans from the top of her suitcase. She still had the keys to one of the rental cars and a flashlight. It couldn't hurt to take a quick trip back out there, not that she believed she'd find the tunnel entrance, but she was restless anyway.

She pulled on her jeans and layered a few shirts under her jacket before stuffing her feet into a pair of sneakers. She crept down the hallway, not wanting to raise an alarm and convince her teammates she'd lost her mind.

Ten minutes later, she pulled onto the side of the road above the lake access and exited the car, flashlight in hand. She followed the beam down the path to the gravel road that snaked beside the lake.

She located the place where Blanca had alerted, marked by the trampled grasses and slashed bushes. She slogged into the marshy soil, sweeping aside the long reeds with her arms, like a windmill.

The rain had never materialized today and the wind blew just enough to lift the ends of her hair from her shoulders, so the faint sound of splashing water had her freezing in place, her feet sinking into the muck.

She hunched over as the sound grew louder—plop,

splash, plop, splash. She pulled her gun from the pocket of her jacket and killed her light.

A dark shape appeared on the water and her muscles twitched as it drew closer. A man's body rocked back and forth, the oars in his hands dipping in the water and sluicing it back, propelling him closer and closer to the shore... and her hiding place.

Several feet away, he pulled the boat onto the shore, securing it. As he unfolded to his full height, the hood of his sweatshirt fell back and the moonlight caught the gleaming strands of his blond hair.

She gasped and loosened her hold on her weapon. "Grayson?"

His head jerked toward her as his hand dipped into his pocket, where she knew he had his Glock. "Who's there?"

"It's Aria." She turned on her flashlight and held the beam to her face.

"I was ready to shoot you."

"Great." She slipped her SIG-Sauer into her pocket. "What are you doing out here?"

"This isn't my first time." He kicked the boat with the toe of his boot and trudged over the grass to stand beside her. "I figured since you didn't text me, you didn't find anything today with the K-9."

"Yeah, well, the dog alerted, but nothing turned up." It had taken a lot of willpower for her to resist contacting him today. "How'd it go at work today after the break-in last night? No more trouble?"

"I pretended nothing happened. When I told the motel manager about the door, I said a drunken friend had kicked it in and I didn't want to report it to the police. He was cool with that. Nobody knew about it at work, and nobody was acting suspiciously. If someone there does know my true identity or suspects me of being a plant, he's not saying."

"But somebody knows something, or your motel room wouldn't have been targeted." She rubbed her hands against the thighs of her jeans, suddenly cold.

"You should have some gloves." He took her arm. "At least get out of this muck."

She stamped her feet when they hit the gravel.

Grayson cocked his head. "If you didn't find anything out here, what are you doing? And why are you by yourself?"

The reproachful tone in his voice had her grinding her teeth. "I'm a special agent with the FBI. I don't need an escort. I don't need a bodyguard and, unlike Danny, I don't need a nanny."

"Whoa." He held up his hands. "I hit a nerve. I'm sorry."

She flipped her hair over her shoulder. "Sometimes I think you forget who I am. I know I haven't acted in the most professional manner on this case..."

"I think you're a kickass FBI agent. You're smart, fearless and professional when it matters." He caught her hand. "But you're right. I forget because I'm falling hard for you, Aria. Hard and fast. I know myself. I don't usually do this. I'm careful, especially with my heart. You're different. Special. I don't want this to end..."

She dropped her lashes because, if she met his eyes, she'd invite his kisses again. "I—I don't know what to say, Grayson."

"You don't have to say anything at all." He squeezed her hand and released it. "I just lost my sister. You're right. My behavior toward you is over the top and unreasonable, but I can't handle another loss. This thing you do...terrifies me."

She flexed and then curled her fingers, missing his touch already. He'd told her in the space of a minute he was falling in love with her but couldn't handle her job. They couldn't be together. She always knew that.

She brushed her hand against his, selfishly craving the comfort of his arms.

His fingers tangled with hers and he ducked his head toward her.

Then a shot rang out in the night and Aria dropped to the ground.

Chapter Sixteen

Grayson's body jerked at the loud report and a soft whizzing sound behind his head.

At his feet, Aria wrapped her arms around his legs and hissed. "Get down. Someone just took a shot at us."

Grayson dove to the ground next to her at the same time another crack split the air above him. The damp earth absorbed his fall as he frantically scrambled for the gun in his pocket. "Did you see where it came from?"

Aria, crouching behind a bush, clutching her 9mm, held a finger to her lips. She whispered. "Must have come from the road above."

Rising to his knees, Grayson turned toward the road but Aria kicked out her leg, her shoe landing against his thigh.

"Keep low and still. The shooter has the advantage. You're never going to get a shot at him from down here. He'll kill you on your way up." Her voice caught in her throat. "Call 9-1-1."

Grayson fished his phone from his pocket. "We can't just be sitting ducks."

"We're not. We have cover where we are now—as long as you stay down. Keep your head below the reeds, and he won't be able to see you." She swung her gun in front of her. "If he tries to come down that path to get a better shot, we have the advantage."

"We have the jump on him if he tries to come by water, too." Grayson nodded at his boat, its prow wedged against the shore. He called 9-1-1 from his cell and referenced the sight of Chloe Larsen's murder. "Anyone else?"

With her gaze pinned to the path leading to the road, she reached into her pocket and tossed her phone to him. "Call my director, Alana Suzuki. She's listed as TCD on my phone."

Grayson made the call. A woman answered after the second ring. Didn't these people ever sleep?

"Suzuki."

"Director Suzuki, this is Grayson Rhodes, Chloe Larsen's broth—" He barely finished his intro as she spoke over his last word.

"Is Aria all right?"

"Aria's fine, but we're under fire at the site of my sister's murder. We're by the lake, and someone's taking shots at us from the road. We already called 9-1-1, and Aria asked me to call you, too."

The director sighed on the other end of the line. "You'll be fine with Aria, and the PHPD first responders will scare away the shooter. Tell her I'm on the way."

She ended the call and Grayson was left with his mouth hanging open. Director Suzuki had been worried about Aria at first because he'd been the one to make the call, but then she'd flipped the script and told him *he'd* be safe with Aria.

Since the shots were first fired, Grayson had felt the weight of taking care of and protecting Aria, but she'd been the one in control of the situation. Even realizing a bullet had just whizzed by his head, he'd been too shocked to drop to the ground. And then he'd added dumb to dumber by thinking he could get into a shoot-out with a gunman with a vantage point.

"What did she say?"

"She's on the way." He put Aria's phone in his pocket. He didn't want to distract her in case the gunman came at them. Grayson needed her professionalism now to get them out of this mess.

His heart pounded as he watched the water for movement. When the first wail of the sirens reached his ears, he blew out a breath. "They're on the way."

"Just keep down until they get here with the lights and sirens and weapons. The shooter could still be in the area."

Two minutes later, the scene was awash with cops, lights and voices. Grayson waited for Aria to make the first move. She holstered her gun and signaled him to do the same. Then she rose slowly with her hands in the air, her badge pinched between her fingers.

She shouted, "FBI. We're the ones who made the call."

Grayson followed suit, rising from the muck as if being reborn, raising his hands.

The first cop on the scene swept his light across their faces. "I know, Special Agent Calletti. What happened out here?"

As the cops canvassed the area and looked for the two bullets that had missed, Grayson and Aria spoke to a sergeant. Aria did the talking. She had the expertise to describe what had happened, and the sergeant didn't even blink when she explained what Grayson had been doing there.

A dog barked and as Grayson followed the sound to the path leading to the lakeside road, he spied several of Aria's teammates with the director in the lead. He hoped she wasn't going to be reprimanded for being here…with him.

When the PHPD sergeant finished his questioning, Director Suzuki approached them. "I suppose you didn't get a look at the shooter?"

"Not at all." Aria shook her head. "I think he was hiding on the road. Any shell casings recovered?"

"No. No evidence at all up there."

"We must be onto something. Blanca wasn't wrong. The drug organization doesn't want anyone snooping around this area."

"Or they were after him." The director leveled a finger at Grayson. "They probably know your relationship to Chloe, and they know you're not some random dockworker. Did you two come together?"

"No." Aria jerked her thumb over her shoulder. "Mr. Rhodes paddled here by boat—and it's not the first time, he told me. I just couldn't relax. I kept thinking about Blanca today, and thought I'd have another look. We just… ran into each other."

"That's good." Director Suzuki rubbed her gloved hands together. "At least nobody followed the two of you together. Even if they know he's Chloe's brother, they still might think that Mr. Rhodes is a grieving family member returning to the sight of his sister's murder, and is not working with the FBI, but someone obviously thinks you're getting too close or too nosy."

"Technically, I'm not working with the FBI, ma'am. I'm happy to give you information when I hear it, but it's not like I'm on the payroll. I'm going to continue showing up on the docks. I don't believe anyone there knows my true purpose—even the supervisor who was ordered to hire me with no questions asked doesn't know why."

"The good news is, the shooter didn't kill you…or Aria."

Grayson chuckled despite the gravity of the situation. "Yeah, I'd say that's good news for both of us."

Aria tapped her chin. "What Alana means is maybe the gunman didn't intend to kill us, just warn us off."

"That had the opposite effect." Grayson swept his arm to the side to encompass the lights and activity.

Almost an hour later, the search started to wind down. The shooter hadn't left behind any evidence, but Aria's Tactical Crime Division decided to search the area again tomorrow.

Grayson pulled Aria aside and put his lips close to her ear. "Thanks for saving my life tonight."

Her dark eyes widened. "Do you mean because the bullet missed you as you bent down to kiss me?"

"I guess that shot would've come a lot closer if I hadn't had the sudden urge to kiss you." His lips twisted into a smile. "But that's not what I meant."

"No?"

"Under fire, I had no clue what to do, even with a gun in my hand. I could've put us both at risk." He rubbed his chin. "You didn't need my protection, did you?"

"In that instance, no, I didn't." She broke their eye contact by leaning to brush off her filthy jeans. "I'm not your sister, Grayson."

"You made that abundantly clear...and I'm not your father."

Still bent over, she turned her head and looked at him, her eyes deep and unfathomable. "These jeans are hopeless, aren't they?"

"About as bad as mine." He pointed up to the place where someone had just been shooting at them. "Can I walk you back to your car, or are you going to stick around and wrap this up?"

"I think I can leave." She waved one hand over her head. "Alana, I'm heading back."

He followed her up the path to the road, now flooded with cars and a news van. "Are they blocking you in?"

"I don't think so." She strode to her car and tripped to a stop. "Looks like the cops missed this."

Grayson whistled and kicked her slashed tire. "Guess you're not going anywhere, unless you want to hop in my boat."

"Not a good idea." Her gaze flicked to her teammates still working below. "I can get a ride back by land."

"Then I'm going to hit the road...um, the water. I have a full day of work ahead of me tomorrow."

As he turned, Aria called after him. "Be careful. Someone knows who you are."

"I know who *you* are, Aria Calletti." He kept walking, his sodden boots crunching the gravel as he started down the path to the lake.

And he wanted her now more than ever.

ARIA FLICKED THE loose hair from her eyes and brushed on some black mascara with a heavy hand. She was still Tony's friend, someone he could trust. She was the Italian girl next door, not the hardcore FBI agent interrogating a criminal.

She added a little lipstick and smacked her lips together. Maybe that almost-kiss had saved Grayson's life last night. What had he meant when he'd said he knew her? What had he meant when he'd said he was falling in love with her?

She sighed, dropped her lipstick into her makeup bag and stuffed the bag into her purse. Time to shift her focus to Tony and the interrogation. She'd finally heard back from Carly through a text, and though they'd tracked down the kind of drugs on Chloe, it hadn't yielded as much information as she'd hoped. At least, nothing to help them with questioning Tony more.

Axel tapped on the bathroom door. "You ready to roll?"

"All done." She pushed open the door and patted her face. "Did I overdo it?"

"Not at all. You look like a woman Tony might hit up at The Tavern."

"Thanks." She fluffed up the ends of her hair. "I think."

They entered the interrogation room together, and Tony sat straighter in his chair, his smile a little less cocky, his chest a little less puffed up. "Are you gonna move me out of here soon?"

Aria perched on the edge of her chair, while Axel swung out a chair and sat, facing Tony across the metal table secured to the floor, just like Tony's chair. "You like it here, huh? Safer than prison, for sure."

"If anyone thinks I talked, I'm in trouble. But I didn't tell you nothing you didn't already know, right? You knew I killed them girls." Tony licked his lips. "Right? One of the other prisoners here told me cops sometimes lie just to get you to say things."

"We know you killed those women." Axel patted the thick folder at his elbow. "We know they were smuggling drugs. We just need to know who they were working for. Who you were working for."

Tony's gaze darted from Axel's face to Aria's. "I—I don't really know that."

Aria leaned forward, her elbow planted on the table, her chin in her palm. "C'mon, Tony. We don't want his full name, address, marital status and social security number. We just need something—even talk on the street. Anyone ever meet him? Have a beef with him? Everyone bitches about the boss, right, Axel?"

Axel smirked. "I know you do."

Tony's head tilted to the right and his gaze dropped to the V-neck of Aria's red sweater. "Yeah, there was some talk."

"And what was the word on the street?" Axel tapped

his pen on the folder. "Cross him and you're dead? I mean, that's what happened to the blah boaties, right? They went into a little business on the side, the boss found out and ordered the hits."

"That's why I'm not saying nothing." Tony crossed his arms. "I confessed to killing those bitches, and that's it."

Aria slid one hand beneath her thigh to stop herself from slapping Tony's face. Instead she smiled. "But your boss doesn't know that. We haven't released any information about your arrest. As far as your boss knows, you're in here singin' like a freakin' bird."

"And that's—" Axel drilled his finger into the tabletop "—what we're gonna put out there. Furthermore, if you don't start coughing up some information, we'll ship you off to prison with absolutely no protection."

Tony's Adam's apple bobbed and a bead of sweat formed on his brow. "What kind of protection can I get?"

"We can do whatever we want." Axel swept a hand in the air. "We can give you what amounts to witness protection in the prison—different name, anonymity for your specific crimes, maybe even a few creature comforts."

Aria held her breath. So far, they'd managed Tony without any lawyers present. She was impressed with how far Axel could take him without his insisting on legal representation, but Tony trusted them now.

Tony slicked back his hair. "Can we start with a haircut? And maybe something besides these slippers on my feet? My feet are always cold, man."

Not as cold as those women. Aria ground her teeth together but managed to squeeze out a few words. "I think those things can be arranged. Axel?"

"We can iron out those details…when you start talking. All we've heard from you so far is 'I don't know, I don't know,' and *we* know that's BS, Tony. What's the word on the street about the guy at the top?"

Tony dropped his chin to his chest and watched his fidgeting fingers. "Lives in Port Huron—at least, right now. Been running the ring for a few years, always using different girls to run the cruise to Canada, different girls but the same—you know, blah boaties."

Aria swallowed and relaxed her tense muscles. "Does he swap out the girls by killing them and finding new ones?"

Tony's head shot up. "Nah. I mean I don't think so. These girls were skimming something off the top—a little Apache for themselves or money."

Aria said quietly, "Brandy wasn't."

"What do you mean?" Tony's body stiffened and he gripped the edge of the table.

They'd kept Brandy's murder from Tony on purpose. Now seemed the right time to drop the news.

"Aww, you didn't know about that, Tony?" Axel tipped his chair onto the back legs, folding his hands behind his head. "Someone killed Brandy—strangled her and threw her over the side of a boat—*the* boat, *Fun Times*."

Tony swore and buried his head in his folded arms on the table. With a muffled voice, he said, "I told her to keep quiet and calm down. They must've known she was getting nervous, close to talking."

Close to talking to Grayson. Is that why someone took a shot at him last night?

"Seems to me this kingpin is ruthless—punishes his enemies. You can help us get him off the street. Protect yourself, Tony."

The chain on the table jingled as Tony bounced his knee up and down. He raised his head, his eyes bright with tears over Brandy.

Aria reached out and laid a hand on his arm. "Think

about Brandy, Tony. Think about your friend. Think about that baby, the same age as your niece. What would your niece do if she lost her mother?"

Tony swiped a hand across his nose. "I don't know his full name…like you said. It's just an initial."

Aria exchanged a glance with Axel. It was better than nothing.

She increased the pressure on Tony's arm. "What initial?"

"V."

Axel let his chair drop forward with a bang and hunched over the table. "V? Just V? That's all you got? I don't know if that's enough for fuzzy slippers. What do you think, Aria?"

Tony's arm vibrated beneath her touch and she withdrew her hand. "What do you think the V stands for? First name? Last name?"

"Not sure." Tony glanced at her but his gaze kept sliding back to Axel, now looming in front of him and seemingly not going anywhere.

"Let's play a game." Axel pulled back and steepled his fingers, tapping them together. "What do you think V could stand for? Aria, you go."

She lifted her shoulders. "Vincent, Victor, Vance, Vernon."

"Your turn, Tony." Axel banged his fist on the metal table.

Tony jumped. "I dunno. Victoria, Vanessa, Veronica, Vivian…"

Tony trailed off, his face blanching as Axel propped his chin on top of his now clasped hands and whispered. "The drug kingpin is a woman."

Chapter Seventeen

"A woman with a first, last or nickname that starts with *V.*" Alana gave a nod to Max as the whole team crowded into the war room. "Max has been cultivating some local informants since we arrived. The drug scene is alive and well in Port Huron."

Aria studied Alana's face as she stood at the front of the room. Confession must've been good for Alana's soul because the pep was back in her step, the verve back in her voice. Aria wasn't taking any credit for the director getting back on firm footing on this case. She'd just been in the right place at the right time for Alana to spill her guts. Maybe she'd take a little credit. Alana may have felt more comfortable revealing her secret to Aria, the newest agent. Everyone had secrets.

Carly held up a small, plastic bag containing two blue pills and shook it in the air. "With Aria's help, we've identified the fentanyl the blah boaties were carrying as Blue Apache. That's its street name here, and any junkie worth his or her salt knows where to score Blue Apache."

Including the guys on the docks. The stuff was all over the place, and it would be hard to trace any particular lot. Aria stroked the phone in her pocket. After the interview with Tony and the explosive information she and Axel had extracted from him, Alana had called an emergency meeting at the station and herded them all in here.

Alana and the team hadn't wanted to use Grayson as an official informant for a variety of reasons, including his safety, but Aria knew Grayson had no immediate plans to step away from his undercover job at the docks. Why not make use of that? The man could more than take care of himself. The good news was that he'd finally realized last night that he didn't have to take care of her, too. Aria hadn't had one second to text the news to Grayson—but she had every intention of doing so.

And what had she realized? She cared for him. The thought of leaving him behind after this case was over hurt and distracted her.

"...and Aria."

Feeling several pairs of eyes drilling into her, Aria jerked her head up. "I'm sorry. What?"

"I said—" Alana shot her a stern look from the head of the table "—you will stand by with Axel in case Max and Carly turn up any information on V. The two of you can move on it right away."

"Yes, ma'am." A few of the team members snickered. "Uh, Alana."

Alana's lips twitched. "After the shots fired at Aria and... Mr. Rhodes last night. Selena and Blanca are at the first murder sight today to see if there are any similarities in the layout of the land. Anything else?"

Rihanna raised a finger with a perfectly polished fingernail at the tip. "You may have seen the news. Tony Balducci's name has been released as a suspect in the murder of the three women. So far, there is no connection to the drug trade, and we want to keep it that way. If Carly and Max are going out looking for this V, we don't want her to take flight."

"I also have something." Opaline flicked her purple-edged locks out of her face. "I've been working with Customs on the Canadian side of the river, and they have records of the *Fun Times* cruises. They're working now to get the passenger names. Those are most likely our dealers in Canada."

Alana brought her hands together. "Good work, people. We just need to bring in V, so she doesn't set up shop in some other unsuspecting border community."

"I have a question." Max scooted up to the table. "Do we know for a fact that a hit was put out on those women because they were skimming money or drugs? Or was that V taking care of business before she packed up and moved somewhere else?"

Axel answered. "We don't know for sure. That's what Balducci told us."

Amanda popped her head up from behind her computer screen. "If she were doing cleanup, that's hardly a ringing endorsement for the next set of employees."

"If the next batch of blah boaties even hears about it or connects the dots…" Aria shrugged. "As long as there are addicts, V will have an endless supply of employees."

Biting her bottom lip, Aria slid a gaze to Alana's impassive face.

"Aria's not wrong about that." Alana clapped her hands. "Let's get on this. I'm ready to wrap this up and leave Port Huron—no disrespect to PH."

As Axel rose, Aria tugged on his sleeve. "I'll be here at the station if you need me. I'm going to grab some lunch and have a look at any photos coming from Selena of the first murder sight."

"Good to know. I'll be in and out." He held out his fist for a bump. "Great job in that interview room, Aria. Balducci had no intention of revealing V's moniker...until he did."

"Learning from the master."

Axel lifted one shoulder, too humble to acknowledge the truth, and followed Max out the door.

As the only other person left in the room, Amanda glanced up from finishing her notes. "Never got your birthday, Aria."

"June 3."

Amanda tapped on her keyboard. "Makes you a Gemini—two personalities. I guess you're in the right job for that."

"You're right. I think I do have two personalities." One the professional and one falling hopelessly in love with Grayson Rhodes.

GRAYSON CUPPED HIS phone in his hand and read the text from Aria on his way to the lunch truck. The person at the head of this drug organization, the person who'd ordered his sister's death, was a woman. Damn.

As he waited for his lunch, he texted Aria that he'd call her in a few minutes. After he picked up his greasy burger from the truck's window and squirted ketchup on his equally greasy fries, Grayson carried his lunch to the end of the docks, where the FBI had been diving for those tunnels. As he usually ate lunch alone, nobody questioned him—too busy talking about Tony's arrest.

He straddled one of the wooden stumps left there for some unknown reason and called Aria.

She answered breathlessly as if she'd just run a 10K. "Can you talk?"

"I'm eating lunch by myself. Are you all right after last night?" He snapped his mouth shut. He shouldn't be asking her questions like that.

Her low voice caressed his ear. "I'm fine. Are you all right? I'm so glad you were there last night. Two is better than one."

Grayson got so excited, he almost dropped his phone in the ketchup. "Yeah, we made a good team. The drug kingpin is a woman, huh?"

"Kind of sickening when you think about how she's putting young women at risk."

"Well, I wouldn't exactly hold her up as a role model for young women." He popped two fries into his mouth. "What do you need from me?"

"You don't have to do anything, Grayson. Two of my team members are out there right now, leaning on PHPD informants for information about this V and the fentanyl she sells. Something will turn up. I know from experience, drug dealers don't work in a vacuum. Tony had heard the name V and others may know more than just the nickname."

"I know I don't *have* to do anything, Aria, but I'm still working at the docks. Nobody is the wiser where I'm concerned. Nobody knows I fingered Tony Balducci. I'm still just the new guy. Maybe they're a little freer in their conversation around me because I don't know the lay of the land. Whoever shot at me—at us—last night is not connected to the docks. Whoever broke into my place is not connected to the docks."

"But if V targeted you, she might have contacts at the dock. She'd warn those contacts about you."

Grayson squinted at his coworkers eating their lunch, the younger ones horsing around, the older ones bone-weary and busy shoveling food into their mouths. "Hasn't happened yet. Hey, I have some good news."

"Would love to hear it."

"My assistant, Patrick, has started the hunt for a nanny.

He's going to use a service he and his partner used. They do all the vetting and they will send over the ones that meet my criteria. All I need to do is interview them."

"That's fantastic news. I'm sure you'll find someone perfect for Danny."

"I have a favor to ask." Grayson held his breath.

"Anything. After all the help you've given us, putting yourself in danger, we can't make you an honorary FBI agent, but we'll do whatever we can to assist you."

"I don't want everyone's help…just yours. Can you be there when I interview for nannies?"

"I…" She sniffed, cleared her throat and coughed. "Are you sure? None of my siblings has a nanny."

"Yeah, because they use you. Because of all your nieces and nephews, you have a better idea of what babies need and want, and the important qualities for a good caregiver." He curled his hand around the phone. "I'd really appreciate your help. You know, obviously when this case is all over and you have some time."

"I'd be happy to help, if I can swing it timewise."

"You've taken a big weight off my shoulders. Patrick will be glad to hear I have someone else involved in the decision-making process, too." A distant whistle blew and Grayson shifted his gaze to the work area. "Lunchtime is over. I'll see what I can find out about V."

He cut off the call before Aria could protest. He dumped his unfinished lunch into a bag and tossed it in a garbage can.

When he returned to work, Grayson managed to grab a pallet alongside Chuck and linger as the older man stopped to rest.

Grayson nudged Chuck's shoulder. "I forgot to ask you earlier, Chuck, how's your sister taking the news about Tony?"

"As you'd expect. Hit her hard. I think she's been at church ever since she found out." Chuck rubbed the back of his neck. "I just don't get it. Maybe there's some mistake."

"Did he know any of those women? Did he have a girl-friend?"

"Not that I know of. Those girls were strangers around here. He'd hook up with girls he met at The Tavern some-times. That's the thing. He liked that girl, Brandy. Why would he want to kill her?"

The story going around must be that Tony killed all the women, including Brandy. Chuck would be relieved to find out later that at least Tony wasn't responsible for Brandy's death, but Grayson wasn't the one to tell him.

"Was Brandy his girlfriend?" Grayson rubbed his palms on the thighs of his jeans.

"Nah, just friends, I think. What do the kids call it these days? Friends with benefits? Something like that." Chuck nodded toward Zane at the end of the dock, clipboard in hand. "If you ask me, there's trouble right there."

"Zane? What do you mean? Do you think he had any-thing to do with the murders?"

"If he did, the cops would've arrested him, too. But Zane was into drugs and hung out with a shady crowd. Tony started running with the same bunch once he met Zane here at work. Maybe it was my fault for getting Tony a job on the docks."

Grayson smacked Chuck on the back. "Don't blame yourself for anything. If it did go down like they're say-ing, Tony's the only one to blame."

About an hour later, after Chuck left early to support his sister, Grayson wandered over to Zane, who was clutching his clipboard with one hand and his phone with the other.

Grayson tipped up his chin. "Did you record that last pallet? Chuck left early, but Bruce stepped in."

"Got it." Zane drummed his pencil on his clipboard in a staccato beat.

"Hey—" Grayson glanced over his shoulder "—did you know what Tony was doing in his spare time?"

Zane dropped his pencil and stooped to pick it up, his face reddening to the roots of his hair. "Hell, no. Why does everyone keep asking me that? We were buds and hung out. I never knew he was a serial killer."

"Serial killer?" Grayson cocked his head. "I never heard that. I thought it was some drug thing. You know, the girls were working for him and stole some money. Something like that."

"Tony?" Zane's eyes rounded and bulged from their sockets. "You think Tony was running the show?"

Grayson spread his hands. "Someone's gotta run the show, right? You know, in my day, before weed was legal in Michigan, we always kind of knew who was in charge."

"It sure as hell wasn't Tony." Zane narrowed his eyes. "You have any weed on you now?"

"On the job? Are you kidding? Anyway, I thought maybe Tony was second-in-command." Grayson got close enough to Zane to see the red veins in his eyes. "Even I know the top dog around these parts for dance fever is V… or should I say the top bitch?"

Zane dug his uneven teeth into his bottom lip. "Damn, you know about V?"

"I think it's common knowledge if you hang with the right people. Do you hang with the right people, Zane?"

He puffed out his scrawny chest. "I know everyone."

"I thought you did." The adrenaline was racing through Grayson's body and he clenched his hands in his pockets. "I heard V's got it goin' on, too. Heard she's a dime piece."

Zane wrinkled his nose. "Yeah, she might be okay for old dudes like you, but her sister? She's a smoke show."

"Her sister?" Grayson's heart thudded in his chest. "She's in town?"

"Just moved here. You probably seen her at The Tavern. Rita. Rita Beaulieu."

MAX SLIPPED HEAVILY into a chair at the conference table and chugged down half a can of soda. He dragged a tissue across his nose and balled it in his fist. "Carly and I hit up every informant known to PHPD—at least, those we could reach. The good news is we have a first name for V. The bad news is it's a pretty common first name—Victoria."

Carly shrugged off her coat where it pooled around her in the chair. "We hit up PHPD vice, and they combed through their files. No Victoria, very few women drug dealers at all, and none currently operating in this area."

Aria tapped a pen against her chin. "Victoria is even a name Tony came up with when he was brainstorming, but I don't think it had any significance to him."

"It's something." Alana folded her hands on the table. "More than one informant gave you the name?"

Max held up two fingers. "Two, and while a few more claimed not to know her name, they did verify that a dealer known as V was working the area. So, we did get some confirmation. Our boy Tony came through."

Axel pointed at Aria. "Furry slippers on order."

"Then we concentrate on finding Victoria. Before we get out of here and break for some dinner, Selena and Blanca found a similar pattern at the other murder sights. Selena?" Alana nodded at the K-9 handler.

Selena coughed. "Opaline, do you have those photos I sent you ready?"

"Of course, I *do* know my job." The TV screen on the wall came to life, displaying the same type of gravel walkway next to the lake where Chloe's body had been found.

"This is Jane Doe number one's murder site." Selena aimed a red laser pointer at the screen and circled an area in the reeds by the water. "Blanca alerted next to the lake, as she did at Chloe Larsen's crime scene. And the same for Jane Doe number three's… Opaline?"

"On it." Opaline brushed cracker crumbs from the table into her palm and brought up the next slide.

Aria's gaze darted between the two sisters. She'd hate to spend Christmas with the Lopez family.

Her phone buzzed on the table in front of her and she swept it off. Resting it in her lap, she glanced at Grayson's text. Her gasp nearly choked her and drew all eyes in the room.

Alana raised her eyebrows. "Something you need to share with us, Aria?"

She lifted her head and met Alana's eyes. "I know Victoria's real name…and where we can find her."

Chapter Eighteen

On Grayson's information, Max and Carly headed down to PHPD vice to run the name "Victoria Beaulieu" past them, and Opaline got to work on several databases to check for both Victoria and Rita Beaulieu.

"Amanda, order some pizza for us. It's going to be a long night." Alana took a seat across from Aria and Axel. "If I'd known how valuable having someone at the docks would've been, we could've put one of our own in there. But picking up on his sister's reference to the docks, Mr. Rhodes has worked out quite nicely."

"He has." Aria picked up a bottle and gulped back some water. Why did her cheeks have to heat up like a sixteen-year-old girl's every time someone on the team mentioned Grayson?

"Uh—" Axel picked up the half-empty bottle of water and shook it "—this was my water."

"Oops, sorry. I'm not sick or anything, I promise." Aria made a cross over her heart.

"Axel, I'd like you and Aria to track down Rita Beaulieu while Carly and Max continue working with the informants to get to her sister, Victoria." Alana called over her shoulder to Opaline, "You have an address on Rita yet?"

"Coming up. I'll be sending it to Axel's and Aria's phones." Opaline's long nails clicked on the keyboard.

"Nothing on Victoria, but that's to be expected. Rita hasn't been associated with this address for very long, so maybe it's actually her sister's. We can hope."

Aria tapped her phone to receive the address Opaline had sent, an address not far from Grayson's motel. "What I don't get is that Rita is the one who carried a note to Grayson for Brandy. Why would she jeopardize her sister's smuggling ring?"

"You're assuming Rita knows what her sister does for a living. She may have been completely in the dark." Axel held up his phone to Opaline. "Got it, thanks. Let's enlighten Rita."

Axel drove to Rita's last-known address in a sketchy area of Port Huron. He tapped on his window, toward the building. "You'd think her sister would've warned Rita what areas to avoid in town."

"Unless Victoria lives with her and can protect her. It makes a good cover for V."

"Don't get your hopes up. Even if she does live with her sister, V may know we're onto her. I hardly think she'll be reclining on the sofa, watching TV, waiting for our arrival." He pulled up across the street from an apartment building with a set of stairs on the outside and an overflowing Dumpster, not quite hidden at the side of the building.

Aria released her seat belt. "Not quite what I expected from a drug lord."

As they jogged across the street, Axel said, "Number four."

They reached the base of the stairs and Aria ducked her head beneath it. "The odds are downstairs—one and three down here, so two and four must be upstairs."

"I'll go first. Stay behind me. Don't draw your weapon, but be ready."

Aria followed Axel up the stairs, her hand hovering

over her gun tucked into the holster on her hip, beneath her jacket. A low light burned inside number four, and Axel stood to the side and rapped on the door with his knuckle.

No noise or voice responded.

Axel knocked again, this time calling out, "Rita? Rita, are you there?"

The door to number two cracked open and Aria stepped back to get a clear view, her hand resting on the butt of her mm.

A man poked his head through the space. "You looking for Rita?"

Axel stepped away from Rita's door. "Is she home? Do you know where she is?"

"Gone. Who are you?"

Aria stepped in front of his door. "Gone, gone? Or gone, out for the evening?"

"She's gone, gone. Who are you?"

Axel flicked open his badge. "FBI. We have a few questions for Rita. She's not in trouble or anything."

"Yeah, that's what you think." The man shook his gray head.

"Sir, can you please step outside? Show yourself?" Aria held out her own badge to the crack of the door.

The crack widened to reveal an old man with faded blue eyes and gray scruff on his chin that could pass for a beard in a certain light—not this one.

"My name's Hal Bernard. What do you wanna question Rita about?"

"Mr. Bernard, what did you mean when you said Rita was in trouble?"

"She came back here last night in a big hurry, tires squealing and everything. Ran right upstairs, and I heard a bunch of banging around, so I knocked on her door to see what was going on, and she was packing up. Said she had to leave 'toot sweet.'" Hal winked. "That's 'very fast' in French."

"Thanks for the translation." Aria was close enough to Hal to smell the booze on his breath, but then she could also be downstairs for that. "Did she say why she was leaving?"

"People come." Hal shrugged his narrow, sloped shoulders. "People go."

"What makes you think she left because she was in trouble?" Axel folded his arms and took a deep breath that expanded his chest, making himself look larger than he was. Her brothers always pulled the same trick on her.

It worked on Hal, as he seemed to snap to attention. "It was what happened after."

Aria asked, "Happened after she packed up?"

"That's right. She dragged her bags down the stairs—" Hal lifted his chin "—I helped her. After she loaded her car, another car came tearing up. The woman that got out of the car tried to talk to Rita, but Rita wasn't having any. She screamed and yelled at the woman…had flashbacks to my ex-wife."

Axel shot her a look from the corner of his eye. "What were they arguing about?"

"I dunno, tried to tune it out and get the hell away from them." He bunched his shoulders and faked a shiver in memory.

"You didn't hear anything they said, even though Rita was yelling?" Aria tapped the toe of her boot.

"Something about a warehouse. Rita was screaming that she saw the warehouse, and I don't know." Hal scratched his grizzled whiskers. "Maybe there was booze in the warehouse."

"Booze?" Axel braced a hand on the stucco wall. "What makes you say that?"

"Because Rita was screaming something about brandy—that's it. Brandy, warehouse, and that she was leaving town. Don't call her. Don't find her."

Aria's pulse jumped in her throat. "Did you hear the other woman's name?"

"No, but I seen her before."

Axel asked, "Where?"

"Right here. She visited Rita before—and they might be related."

"Why do you think that?" Aria ran her tongue along her bottom lip.

"They both had that black hair, both lookers." Hal nudged Axel. "If you know what I mean."

"I know exactly what you mean, Hal."

They tried to get more information out of Hal about the other woman's car, what she looked like, specifically, her other visits to Rita, but Hal had reached his limit—and his limit was pretty good.

They both handed Hal their cards and walked back to the car—in Aria's case, more like bounced. When Axel got behind the wheel, she turned to him and grabbed his arm. "That was V. Rita must've discovered her sister's side gig and freaked out, knowing Victoria was responsible for Brandy's murder."

"And there's a warehouse." Axel pulled out his phone. "That's clearly where and how Rita found out about her sister."

Aria listened, her legs bouncing up and down as Axel got on the phone to Alana, putting her on Speaker.

He described their meeting with Hal. "We need info on a warehouse, Alana. Get Opaline on it right now. Maybe she rented it in Rita's name. My guess is it's by the docks. V needs to be close to the water."

"Don't come back in, yet. You're on speaker phone,

and Opaline has already started searching Port Huron for warehouses near the water. Max and Carly didn't get any hits on Victoria Beaulieu from PHPD vice. She's not on their radar."

Aria said to Axel, "While we're waiting, I'm going to see if the manager can let me into Rita's apartment. I saw a manager sign on number one. Maybe she left something behind."

"Do you want me to go with you?"

"No, I'm good. You wait on the phone with Alana. I'm just going to take a quick look around." Aria reached into the back seat and grabbed an FBI jacket. She slid from the passenger seat and stuffed her arms into the windbreaker, pulling it over her leather jacket. Ducking her head into the car, she said, "Just in case he needs some convincing."

"You look convincing to me. Go get 'em."

Aria crossed the street again and knocked on apartment number one, the gold Manager sign nailed to the wall next to the door.

A woman's smoke-roughened voice came from the other side of the door. "Who is it?"

"FBI, ma'am. I'm wondering if I can have a look in Rita Beaulieu's apartment, number four upstairs?" Aria flipped out her badge and held it up to the peephole.

The manager swung open the door and straightened her red wig. "You don't have to tell me which apartment it is. That girl hightailed it out of here, breaking her lease."

"Did you hear the argument she had with the woman in the parking lot before she left, Mrs…?"

"Hammond." She cracked her gum on the left side of her mouth. "Got a blow-by-blow from Hal upstairs. She do something wrong, that girl? Besides run out on her lease?"

"We just wanted to talk to her, but it might be helpful

if I can have a look around her place. Did she leave any-thing behind?"

"A few odds and ends." Mrs. Hammond was already pulling a set of keys from her pocket. She plucked one from the ring, the rest dangling from her fingers in front of Aria. "Here's the master. You're welcome to look around and then drop these in my box when you're done."

"Thank you, Mrs. Hammond." As Aria clomped up the stairs, she glanced at Axel still in the car across the street. She passed Hal's apartment, wondering if he had his eye to the peephole or his ear to the wall.

She let herself into the apartment, the light from a lamp in the corner casting shadows in the corners. The place must've come furnished because a sofa, one chair, a table and a small dinette set remained.

Aria started with the bedroom, but Rita had emptied the closet and drawers. Even the sheets had been ripped off the queen bed.

She returned to the living room, but Rita had cleared out this room, as well. Four long steps took Aria right into the small kitchen and she opened the fridge. A few beer bottles rattled and a couple of condiments fell over in the door. Rita was not much of a cook.

Aria pulled open some drawers and thumbed through some paper receipts and take-out menus. Some circular cardboard coasters fanned out in the drawer, and Aria began collecting and stacking them.

She jumped when the front door burst open.

Axel called into the room. "It's go time. We have a warehouse listed under Rita's name."

Aria shoved the coasters into the pocket of her leather jacket and exited the apartment, locking the door behind her. When they reached the foot of the stairs, she veered toward Mrs. Hammond's door and dropped the keys in the box.

When they got to the car, Axel took off before she even closed the door. "Is it near the docks?"

"Not too far from where Max found one of those tunnels." Axel took the next turn at high speed and Aria gripped the edge of the seat.

They made it from Rita's apartment to the docks in just under fifteen minutes and were the first ones on the scene. Axel squealed to a stop. As he got out of the car, he pointed to a row of gray warehouses away from the loading zone and on the other side of the water from the marina with the pleasure boats.

Axel took off running, his long legs putting him far ahead of Aria. He disappeared around the corner of a building. As she scrambled to keep up with him, gunshots echoed over the water. She pulled her gun from its holster, her legs pumping, her feet pounding against the asphalt almost as much as her heart.

She reached the building and skidded to a stop. With her gun raised to her chest, gripped in both hands, she yelled, "Axel!"

"I'm okay. Stay down. They got away, but they have to be in the area."

Panting, Aria crouched and poked her head around the corner of the building. Her heart stuttered for a second as she spotted Axel flat on the ground. "You all right?"

"They didn't hit me, and I don't think I hit them. The two of them took off out of that warehouse at the end."

Engines roared and tires squealed behind Aria. She cranked her head over her shoulder. "The cavalry's here. If you wanna give chase, I got you covered."

Axel rose to his haunches and Aria's muscles twitched

with tension as he propelled himself forward and behind a wall. No more shots rang out.

When the other agents crowded behind her, Aria gave a quick account of the situation. "Axel saw two people leave the warehouse at the end. One of them exchanged fire with Axel. Nobody hit. They took off in the other direction."

Alana ordered Max, Carly and Selena, Blanca primed and ready at her side, to fan out around the back side of the warehouses. "Go through the loading docks if you have to. We didn't see any cars pull away. They have to still be on foot."

Axel continued his approach toward the warehouse, jumping from cover to cover, and Aria kept after him. When he reached the warehouse, he yanked up the overhead door, which had been left ajar.

Aria joined him as the door rolled up, both agents with their guns pointed in front of them. The squeaking ended and Aria took a breath as her gaze darted around the mostly empty warehouse. "Looks like Rita's place. Someone left in a hurry."

"And with guns blazing." Axel's blue eyes had their own fire. "It was her, Aria. I had V in my sights, and she got away."

Chapter Nineteen

The disappointment socked Aria in the gut. To be so close and have her slip through their fingers. If they'd come here before Rita's place, they would've caught V in the act. But they wouldn't have known about the warehouse without going to Rita's and talking to chatty Hal.

Aria blew out a breath. "Maybe she won't get away. The others are here, and they're hot on her tail."

Alana strode toward them, her gun primed and ready. "Nothing?"

"I wouldn't say 'nothing.'" Aria stepped into the warehouse, her boots ringing on the cement floor. "They didn't have time to clear out everything."

"Was it V, Axel?" Alana asked.

"A tall woman with black hair. She had a gun, but it was her henchman doing the shooting. They just seemed to disappear into thin air." Axel shook his head.

Max circled around from the other side and lifted his arms, shrugging. "Poof. Gone."

"I saw nothing, but I heard the engine of a boat." Carly jogged up to them and ducked into the warehouse. "But what do we have here? Looks like packaging."

"V probably made a last stop here to collect whatever she has left to start somewhere fresh." Axel banged against the wall of the warehouse with his fist.

Selena was the last to join them, Blanca trotting by her side. "Water. They left by water. Blanca tracked them to a small jetty where they could've easily had a boat waiting."

"That's it. She's gone." Axel holstered his gun, which he'd been holding as if expecting V to saunter back into his sight.

"I'm counting on those tunnels. If V still has product in this area, she's not going anywhere without it. She may be the big fish around Port Huron and Point Edward, but she answers to a bigger fish—and that shark is not going to allow product to be left behind." Alana clapped her hands. "I know it's late, people, and you're tired and disappointed, but we have a warehouse to search."

THE FOLLOWING NIGHT, Aria sat with her team after dinner, discussing their next move with V. Alana was convinced their prey was still in the Port Huron area, taking care of last-minute business, but they had a small window.

"Not that we can't follow V to her next location." Alana dropped her napkin on the table. "She doesn't know us if she thinks we're going to give up that easily."

"Hi, all. Sorry I missed dinner." Rihanna strutted across the dining-room floor looking like a model on a runway. "But you all dumped a lot of work in my lap with that raid on the warehouse last night, and I have another dinner to go to in a less than an hour."

"News is out there, but nobody knows V, huh?" Carly stretched her long arms over her head, catlike, and yawned.

Opaline answered. "We don't have her official picture, but we do have a sketch artist working on a composite. If she's lurking around Port Huron, she'll be spotted."

"Although V does seem to be partial to hair dye, like someone I know." Selena flicked her fingers at her sister's lavender locks. "She could dye that black hair blond or brown, cut it, change her makeup. She could completely disguise herself."

Axel pushed away his plate. "Or just send her minions out to collect what's left in the tunnels and tie up any loose ends."

"Ugh, so morose." Rihanna snatched a fry from Max's plate. "I do have good news, though."

Rihanna held up the French fry, waiting for all eyes on her. Then she turned her gaze toward Aria. "The DNA results came in, and Grayson Rhodes and little Danny are definitely related. He can take custody of his nephew as early as tomorrow."

A smile tugged at Aria's lips even as pain tugged at her heart, knowing this meant Grayson would be returning to Detroit. He'd probably forget that he'd even asked her to help vet his nanny.

"That is great news, Rihanna. Does he know?" Aria's hand felt for her phone in her pocket. Grayson hadn't texted her at all today—not that she hadn't been busy processing evidence from the warehouse.

"I called him when I received the news, right before I got here." Rihanna picked up her phone in its jeweled case and glanced at the display. "Which means he should be calling you in five, four, three…"

Aria laughed along with the others. What did she have to lose now? The case in Port Huron was probably finished. Grayson would be taking Danny back to Detroit. Aria had already lost everything.

Team members began to wander away from the table. Max had a video date with his son over the phone. Opaline had an actual date with Gordon the PHPD cop. Axel and Selena were heading off to spend some time with Blanca. Carly planned to go for a run and Rihanna had a dinner meeting. Alana and Amanda were going to spend another hour in Alana's room to finish some reports.

Feeling as low as the others looked, Aria shuffled back to her room and fell across her bed. A minute later, her cell phone rang. The name on the display made her heart flutter—still.

"Grayson, I heard the good news."

"That's right. I can pick up Danny from the Colbys tomorrow. My mother actually got back to me, and was heartbroken over Chloe, despite everything. She's promised to visit her grandson the next time she sets foot on American soil."

"That's good to hear." Aria curled up into a ball. "Does this mean you're leaving your job? Port Huron?"

"I've already told the supervisor, Bud. He's going to make up a story for the other guys, but yeah, today was my last day."

"Again, we can't thank you enough for the part you played in solving this case. Your presence at the docks was invaluable to us and a great personal risk to you."

"That all sounds so formal. I called because I want to see you before I leave. You haven't forgotten your promise, have you?"

Aria closed her eyes and swallowed the lump in her throat. "I haven't forgotten. Do you want to come here this time?"

If he thought his own motel was too crummy for making love, would this one work?

"Actually, I'd like to meet at the marina. It's a cold night, but clear. Maybe we can have a piece of pie at that diner where we first met."

Aria bounded from the bed. "I'd love that. Forty-five minutes?"

Grayson agreed, and Aria ended the call and darted

around the hotel room to get ready. She shimmied out of her grungy jeans and slipped into a pair of skinny black jeans. She pulled on a soft, coral sweater, a pair of black boots with a heel and grabbed her leather jacket.

She met Carly in the hallway, coming back from her run. Carly paused at her door. "Are you okay?"

"Couldn't be better. I'm heading to the marina to see Grayson." Aria waved a hand in the air as she got into the elevator.

She drove more carefully than she ever had before. It wouldn't do to get into an accident on her way to what might be her last time seeing Grayson.

As she pulled into the parking lot of the diner, Grayson waved from where he stood, leaning against his beat-up truck. He'd already told her he planned to give that truck to Will when he left.

When she reached him, he pulled her into his arms, wrapping them snugly around her, and kissed her. He murmured against her mouth, "I missed you. Do you really think I can return to Detroit without you?"

"How is that going to work, Grayson?" She placed her hands against his chest, and his heart thundered beneath her palm. She curled her fingers around the collar of his flannel shirt. "I want to be with you, but I have this job."

"Let's walk." He draped his arm around her shoulders, and led her toward the boats in all their multicolored splendor.

She rested her head against his upper arm. "I like the tradition of decorating boats for Christmas. They're beautiful, aren't they?"

"You're beautiful." He stroked her hair. "We can figure this out, Aria. I can pretty much run my business from home. I'll be there with Danny and the nanny you're going to help me select."

The clanking halyards almost sounded like church bells pealing. Maybe it was some kind of sign.

She sighed and shoved her hands into her pockets. Her fingers traced the rounded edge of hard cardboard, and she pulled it out. She held it in front of her and squinted in the dark.

"What's that?" Grayson flicked the edge of the cardboard with his finger.

"Oh, yeah. I picked them up in Rita's apartment. They're coasters from a restaurant or something." She turned on her phone's flashlight and illuminated a coaster, turning it over in her hand.

"Beautiful Place?" Grayson's brow furrowed. "That sounds familiar."

"It does, doesn't it? A restaurant near your motel?"

"A beautiful place near *my* motel? I don't think so." He snapped his fingers. "I remember. It's the name of a boat down here. We walked past it on our way to *Fun Times* to meet Brandy. What do you think Rita was doing with coasters from a big boat like that? Party?"

Aria dropped the coaster and grabbed Grayson's arm. "Beautiful place... Beaulieu."

"Huh? You lost me. What does beautiful place have to do with Victoria Beaulieu?"

Her fingers dug into the arm of his jacket. "*Beaulieu* means beautiful place. That's V's boat. I know it. That's how she's been able to come and go at that warehouse. That's how she's been able to stay below the radar in Port Huron. She's on that boat."

The adrenaline pumped through Aria's system and she spun around on the marina, the Christmas lights blurring in her vision. "Where was it? Where were those slips?"

The FBI had already towed away *Fun Times* for additional processing, and Aria's excitement was adding to her confusion.

"*Fun Times* was in slip 128. *Beautiful Place* is in the same row." Grayson seemed to have better bearings than she did at this moment, and he grabbed her hand and tugged her in the other direction. "It's one over."

Aria's hands trembled as she tapped her phone for Alana's number. "I'm calling the team, but we can't wait. We missed V once already at the warehouse. We can't afford to miss her again, or she'll be gone."

Amanda answered and Aria spit out directions, sounding incoherent to herself, but Amanda must've understood.

Aria cursed her heels as she and Grayson ran across the marina and turned toward the slip that housed *Beautiful Place*. In the still night, an engine rumbled to life.

Grayson cursed. "It must be her. She has someone looking out. The minute anyone comes her way, the boat sets out on the lake."

"They're gonna have company this time." She scanned the other boats in the slips. "Do you know how to drive a boat?"

"You're kidding, right?" He swept past her and jumped onto the first boat in line. "And I know where most boaters hide their keys."

Twisting her fingers in front of her, Aria called out, "Hurry, they're getting away."

Grayson jumped into the next boat with no better luck. The third boat he dismissed as too small. From inside the fourth boat, he shouted, "Got 'em."

Aria climbed into the boat just has Grayson started the engine. She clung to the edge. "Can you cut the lights?"

"Not if you don't want to crash into something in the marina. They'll have to know we're coming after them, but V's boat is made for comfort. This baby—" he patted the steering wheel "—she's made for speed."

To emphasize his point, Grayson revved the engine and then zipped out of the marina onto the lake. He pointed. "I see them."

"Do they see us?"

"If not, they soon will." Grayson pushed the stolen powerboat to its limits as he followed in the bigger boat's wake. The choppy, frigid water sprayed into the boat, hitting Aria's face, but she never took her eyes off the *Beautiful Place*.

V's boat sped up, but was no match for the power beneath her and Grayson. As they drew closer to the big boat, the lights went out, sending a chill through Aria's body.

They tagged along behind *Beautiful Place* and then Grayson made a move to pull up beside it. That's when the bullets started flying.

"They're shooting. Get down."

Aria crouched, her gun leveled at the deck of *Beautiful Place*. When a bullet pinged off their boat's fiberglass, Aria squeezed off several shots. She didn't know how much longer they'd be able to hold off V, but hoped it was long enough for the rest of the team or the Coast Guard to get out here.

Grayson gunned the boat and yelled. "Stay down and hold on, Aria. I'm gonna try something crazy."

She sank to the deck, clutching the edge. Grayson fired a few times from his own gun, which she didn't even realize he had with him.

When the explosion hit, it lifted their boat off the lake and a fireball rolled across the water in front of them. Intense heat scorched the air, and Aria held her breath.

Grayson cut the engine and swung the boat around toward the *Beautiful Place*, now engulfed by flames, black smoke belching from the masts that looked like matchsticks ready to topple over.

A woman screamed, and Aria hung over the side of the boat, dragging a lifesaver to the edge.

V and a man paddled frantically away from the inferno, both clinging to debris from the wreckage.

Grayson jumped down beside Aria and waved ash away from her face. "Are you all right? I hit the gas tank. I figured that was the best way to stop them."

Aria clambered to her knees, aiming her gun over the side of the boat, V in her bull's-eye. "Of course, I'm fine. Haven't I told you? I'm a special agent for the FBI."

Epilogue

Amanda studied the décor, her head tilted, her red hair sweeping over one shoulder. "Is it too much? Tell me the truth."

Aria blinked at all the Christmas lights, the little individual Christmas trees at every table and the Santa in the corner, keeping up a steady stream of ho, ho, ho's.

"It's pretty, but maybe the Santa…"

"The Santa is hideous and annoying." Opaline crowded in next to them, a plate of crab rolls, wontons and mini *taquitos* balanced on one hand. "Get rid of him."

Amanda laughed. "I knew I could depend on you for the truth, Opaline."

Max walked up and put his hand on Amanda's shoulder. "I'm going to the bar. Drink orders?"

"I'm going to get rid of Santa first before he drives everyone crazy." Amanda scurried away.

"White wine for me, please." Opaline examined a crab roll. "Do you think these have a lot of calories, Aria?"

"If it's fried, it has a lot of calories." Carly held up a stick of celery.

Opaline turned up her nose. "I wasn't asking you, Carly. Aria?"

"Yeah, I'm afraid Carly's right." Aria tapped her chest. "I'll have a white wine, too."

"Oh, are you taking drink orders?" Carly raised her eyebrows at Max. "You owe me after dragging me around the underbelly of Port Huron for three hours talking to lowlifes."

Max crooked his finger at Carly. "You're coming with me because I'm pretty sure I'm not gonna get your drink order right."

"Good call." Carly followed Max to the bartender set up in the corner.

Selena held out a plate to Aria. "Take something. The *taquitos* are good. Gringo food, but good."

Aria picked up the appetizer and blew on it. "This is nice. Do you always have a party at the end of a case, or is this for Christmas?"

"It's both—definitely doubling as our Christmas bash and a celebration of the closing of the case, thanks to you." Selena waved as Axel entered the room. He pointed to the bottle of beer in his hand and Selena nodded.

"And thanks to Blanca for finally discovering those tunnels." Aria crunched into the *taquito*.

"With a little help from V—once she recovered from her burns and near drowning."

Alana and Rihanna finally finished their conversation at one of the tables and walked over to the group, drinks in hand.

Rihanna spun around in place. "Amanda outdid herself this time. I'm ready to break into a Christmas carol—and I'm glad she got rid of that Santa."

"Someone had to tell her." Opaline pushed back her green-tinted ends.

Rihanna flicked Opaline's hair. "You disappoint, Opaline. I would've expected green on one side and red on the other for Christmas."

Max returned, carrying a beer and one glass of wine,

which he handed to Aria. Carly followed him with Opaline's wine and a martini glass with an onion and an olive hanging off the side.

Axel joined them with beers for him and Selena. "With this setup, you must've invited more than just us."

"Some members of the PHPD are joining us—the guys from the dive team, some members of Vice. Detective Massey is coming, and a few others."

"Gordon." Opaline held up her wineglass and Alana tapped it with hers.

"Gordon, of course." Alana asked Axel, "Is Tony Balducci all settled in his new home?"

"He is, but I think he's safe from V for now. She wasn't high enough in the organization to warrant any retaliation on her behalf. The cartel has dismissed her. She's the one who'd better watch her back in prison."

Selena put down her plate of food and wiped her hands. "Did V ever confirm that the murdered blah boaties were stealing from her?"

"She claimed they were, but she was paranoid." Axel tipped some beer down his throat. "We may never know the truth, but she felt she had to get rid of those women and she wanted to set them up as being involved in the drug trade, never imagining it would lead straight back to her."

The noise level of the room increased as some of the invited guests began arriving for the party. Before they lost this moment, before they got back to their normal professional roles, Aria touched Alana's shoulder. "How are you doing?"

Alana smiled, a little mistily. "I'm fine. It was a tough case for me. I'm not going to lie, but I appreciate your listening to me and your discretion."

"Of course. Always."

Rihanna squealed from across the room. "It's our boy!"

Aria jerked her head toward the door and a warm feeling encased her heart as she saw Grayson holding Danny.

Rihanna held out her arms and Grayson poured Danny into them.

Cuddling the baby against her chest, Rihanna danced across the room. "Look who I have. My favorite little man."

Carly dipped her head toward Aria's. "And yours—only Grayson isn't so little."

Aria opened her mouth to protest and then snapped it shut as her gaze traveled from Carly's face to Selena's to Opaline's, and rested on Alana's.

Selena snorted. "You don't think it was a secret, do you? The fact that you were falling for Grayson Rhodes?"

"I… I just thought. I mean…"

Alana squeezed her hand. "Go to him, Aria. It's all right."

With her eyes stinging, Aria crossed the room slowly, all the noise, the people, the music, the singing, even Santa now silent and stuffed in the corner, fading from her senses. She only saw the man in front of her.

As she drew closer, he reached out for her and pulled her outside the banquet room, away from the party. He led her to a dark corner by the window where the lights of the boats in the marina blinked.

They sat on a red-velvet love seat, her hands still in his. "H-how is Danny?"

"He's going to be fine. I have that list of nannies whenever you're ready."

She pulled his hands against her chest. "Can we really do this? Does it make sense?"

"I love you, Aria. I know I never want to be without you by my side—and I don't mean that literally. If we're together, in each other's corners, in each other's hearts, it'll all make sense in the end."

"I…" She closed her eyes and Grayson touched her cheek.

"Go ahead. Tell me your concerns. Tell me your worries. Tell me why we can't be together. You may be the FBI agent, but I'll shoot them all down."

"Concerns? Worries?" She brought his hands to her lips and kissed his knuckles, rough from his work on the docks. "I was just going to say I love you, too."

He slipped his hand behind her head and pressed his mouth against hers in a scorching kiss that incinerated all her doubts and promised everything.

* * * * *

TEXAS TARGET

BARB HAN

All my love to Brandon, Jacob and Tori,
the three great loves of my life.

To Babe, my hero, for being my greatest love
and my place to call home.

To my mom, you're almost there and you got this!

I love you all.

Chapter One

The sun blasted on what had turned into a pavement melting summer day in Austin. Texas was legendary for its August heat. This day was going to be one for the books. Despite the triple-digit temperatures, navigating Congress Avenue still felt like running through a horde. Summer Grayson didn't have time to care about the sweat literally pouring down the sides of her face and dripping onto her shirt. She didn't have time to register how dry her mouth already was or how great a drink of water would feel right then. All she could care about was breaking free from the men who were right behind her, gaining ground with every step as she darted through throngs of people.

There were two men behind her. Their eyes trained on her. *She* was their target. No matter how much she desperately wanted to escape, to live, those men had other plans. Were these the same men who'd made her sister disappear?

Summer should never have pretended to be her identical twin, Autumn. Rolling the dice and claiming to be Autumn was backfiring big-time. On a base level, she'd needed to know if there was any possibility her sister was still alive even though she knew in her heart it wasn't likely. Criminal investigations took months, sometimes years. In too many cases, the criminal was never found. After two months of her own investigation, she'd been no closer to finding answers than when she'd first started.

So, yeah, she'd decided to cut corners and step into her sister's shoes. Getting desperate for answers had caused Summer to make mistakes that put these jerks on her tail. Risking a glance behind her added another miscalculation to the growing list. It slowed her down enough for one of the men to gain more ground.

The closest guy was the shorter of the two. He had light blond hair, a tan and a swimmer's build. His long torso and shorter legs were clad head to toe in black. He was also the faster runner of the pair. He was quick and lean, his face set in a permanent scowl. Everything about him said he was scrappy. The other jerk was at least six inches taller and thick. Thick neck. Thick arms. Thick hands.

Summer picked up the pace and risked another glance behind her, tamping down the panic that had adrenaline bursts fueling her legs. Scrappy was gaining on her and his friend, Thick Guy, wasn't far behind. No matter how hard she pushed her legs she wouldn't be fast enough to get away from Scrappy. Repeating a protection prayer that she'd learned as a young child, she pushed harder against burning thighs. It would take a miracle to get away.

No such marvel came. He caught hold of her. His grasp nearly crushed her bones. Icy fingers gripped her spine at the thought she would never know what had happened to her sister. As his nails dug into her skin, fear slapped her into realizing she might just end up in the same position. Gone.

A little voice in the back of her head picked that time to remind her how strong she really was. Despite being born prematurely and a minute later than her stronger, more athletic sister, Summer had enough fight in her to keep going despite the odds. Determination reminded her she'd survived then and would now, dammit.

Pushing harder, her thighs burned and her lungs clawed for air. She kept her pace, doing her level best to jerk her arm free. Giving in to pain could land her in a grave beside her twin sister, and she was certain that Autumn was dead. That was the only explanation for her sister's sudden disappearance. Granted, her sister had distanced herself from everything and everyone in the small town where they'd grown up years ago. She'd moved away from the Austin suburb and never looked back. Until recently.

Shutting out the past had been Autumn's way of surviving it—a past she'd refused to talk about even with her twin. Summer understood her sister's need for silence on a basic level, except for the part about closing off their relationship. The bond between twins was supposed to be ironclad. But Autumn was a grown woman capable of making her own decisions and Summer had no choice but to respect them.

Even so, no matter how rough it got for Autumn or how much time had passed in between communication, she'd always returned a 9-1-1 text from Summer.

"How are you still alive?" Scrappy's voice came out in a growl as he tightened the vise around her upper arm.

Those words nearly gutted Summer. Her sister had been secretive for the past couple years and had only touched base a few precious times. There wasn't a scenario where Autumn was alive that included her going dark. Summer's gut instincts said her sister was gone but if there was a shred of hope that Autumn was out there, alive, there was no end to the lengths that Summer would go to find her. Hell would have to freeze over before she stopped looking.

And if her sister was dead, the same went for finding justice.

This jerk wasn't going to stop her from finding the truth no matter how tight his grip became. More of that Grayson resolve that had kept Summer alive through more situations than she could count kicked into high gear.

"Last time I checked hell hadn't frozen over." Summer jerked her arm as Scrappy caught her by the other elbow. She had about two seconds to react before he dug his bony fingers into her arms. All that came to mind was what she'd learned in second grade and it basically only applied to a fire, but it was all she had. Stop. Drop. And roll.

So that's exactly what she did. On her way down, it dawned on her that smacking the concrete at a dead run was going to hurt. There was no choice but to push through the pain. Give up now and thick hands would close around her this time. She'd be hauled backward, landing hard on her backside and at the mercy of these two jerks.

This way, she could trip them and create a scene.

Stabs of pain shot through her calves as she tripped over her own feet and prepared to hit concrete. At least this way she could control the fall. That was the little white lie she told herself. She'd gotten good at letting herself believe the little lies that her sister had told her. Ones like, *I'm fine.* And, *All I need is a little more time to clear up some bad karma in Austin.*

Summer should have forced her sister to talk. She should have cornered Autumn and not let her walk away until she came clean about everything that was and had been going on in her life. When her sister had emailed to say that she'd found a wonderful man and that they'd gotten married, Summer shouldn't have left it at that. She shouldn't have taken Autumn at her word that all of life was suddenly smooth. *Smooth* and *Autumn* didn't belong in the same sentence. Eventually her past would catch up with her.

Her sister had gushed about her new husband, saying how strong he was and how protected she felt. Looking back, Summer should've asked the question, *Protected from what?*

She could blame the fact that she'd been working two jobs to make ends meet. She could blame the fact that she was tired and not doing a heck of a great job managing her own life. She could blame her boss for keeping her late most nights. But the truth was that Autumn had always been a handful.

Until a year and a half ago when she'd announced the fact that she'd met *the one.* Learning that her sister had gotten married on a whim hadn't been the shock it should've been. Finding out she'd married into one of, if not *the* wealthiest cattle ranching families, had. Then again, Autumn had always managed to land on her feet.

Suspicion was second nature to Summer, who'd grown up watching over her shoulder for danger. And yet, her sister had sounded genuinely happy in her emails. That was something rare for a Grayson. And Summer had selfishly wanted a break from looking out for her sister. Autumn had a knack for placing herself straight-up in the middle of trouble. And trouble had a way of finding her. Like the time in high school when she'd made a pact with a star athlete on the soccer team to cheat off each other on a test. Adam Winston got caught and decided not to go down alone. He showed the principal his text exchange with Autumn. The funny thing was that Autumn had studied and could pass the test on her own merit. She'd played dumb because she thought he'd be more attracted to her.

As her shoulder hit the pavement, Summer unleashed a scream. She made the loudest noise that could come out of her mouth. The daytime crowd shuffled to get out of her way, like a sea parting. Summer realized the fall was going to be more than she expected, measured by the sheer number of gasps around her.

She did, however, elicit enough attention to make Scrappy think twice. In fact, his gnarly grip on her elbow released and he disappeared into the gathering crowd.

Summer's head smacked the ground harder than she'd anticipated. For a split second, she heard ringing in her ears. She could hop back up, but then what? The men would chase her again. This time, she might not be so lucky.

An authoritative female voice parted the crowd and a woman in uniform came into Summer's blurry vision.

"Ma'am, are you okay?" a female officer asked as she kneeled down.

"My name is Autumn Grayson and I need to confess to a crime."

The officer blinked shocked eyes at Summer. Those words seemed to grab her by the throat. "What was the offense, ma'am?"

The only thing that came to mind was the fire that had devastated a popular camping ground on the outskirts of Austin. It had been all over the news.

"Arson," she said.

"YOU'RE NOT GOING to believe who just confessed to arson." Dawson O'Connor's brother, Sheriff Colton

O'Connor, had been one hundred percent correct. Dawson couldn't believe that Autumn Grayson would confess to a crime there was no way she could've committed. Because he couldn't believe that his ex-wife could be capable of breaking the law. Not to mention the fact that she was scared to death of fire and would go nowhere near a campsite.

She'd been a city girl through and through. But then, he was still trying to believe that she'd served him divorce papers out of what felt like nowhere last year.

As far as he'd known, their marriage could have been saved. He wasn't the giving-up-when-times-got-tough kind. So, he'd been all kinds of surprised when he found out she hadn't taken their vows as seriously as he had. The note she'd left said she'd made a mistake, not to look for her, and he should forget he'd ever met her.

How was he supposed to do that? He'd been fool enough to spend time with her, marry her. And then he was supposed to…what? Forget any of that had ever happened? Far be it from him to dwell on unhappiness. Heaven knew he'd seen the effects of not being able to let go of a painful past firsthand in his own family. He had a wonderful mother who'd never really recovered from the night her firstborn child had been kidnapped in her own crib decades ago.

Dawson had had a sideline view to real tragedy. His mother had picked herself up and moved on best she could, always reminding her six O'Connor sons about the sister they never had the privilege to know.

Granted, getting a divorce was nowhere near the tragedy of losing a child and, worse yet, never knowing what had truly happened or if the child was alive. He chided himself for still hanging on to the pain of mistakenly falling for the wrong person. That was more a bad decision than a tragedy.

What was worse? He couldn't believe that he was sitting in the parking lot of the Travis County Jail with a handful of jewelry pieces in a box that his wife—correction *ex*-wife—had told him were family heirlooms. He'd had the sense from her that she hadn't grown up with much when it came to money or family. But then the subject of family had been off-limits. It should've been his first sign something was wrong.

He also shouldn't care about returning the pieces to her.

As a matter of principle, he didn't feel right holding on to them. Since she'd cut off all contact last year, he hadn't had an opportunity to hand them over. Call it cowboy code but he didn't like the thought of keeping someone else's belongings.

Engine idling. Hand on the gearshift. Foot on the brake. Time to make a decision. Drive away or go inside?

Dawson muttered a curse under his breath and shut off the engine. He made the trek into the jail and walked directly toward the officer at the counter.

"I'm here to see my wi—" He stopped himself right there. "Someone in your holding cell. Her name is Autumn Grayson." Since inmates in a holding tank weren't allowed visitors, Dawson pulled out his badge. Professional courtesy might get him through the steel doors. "My name is Marshal Dawson O'Connor."

The jailor perked up, his eyes widening for a split second. He extended his hand. "Nice to meet you, sir."

"The pleasure is all mine." He gave a small smile. "Is there any chance I can have a short visit with Ms. Grayson."

"Yes, sir." The cop examined the US Marshals badge

on the counter in front of him as Dawson pulled a coin from his pocket. It was a custom that started long ago to give out a department-stamped coin when visiting a cooperating agency.

"Are you picking her up? The crime she confessed to committing has already been solved."

"We'll see." He doubted she'd go with him voluntarily.

The jailor introduced himself and took the offering with a broad smile. The tall, thin man who wore a white Stetson nodded his approval. "I appreciate this." He tossed the coin in the air, caught it and then said, "You want to follow me?"

It was more statement than question and didn't require an answer. Dawson followed. He was led into a small room with a table, two chairs opposite each other and a pair of doors. There was one behind him and one in front of him.

"If you'll take a seat, sir, I'll bring Ms. Grayson." With a nod, the officer left the room.

Sitting in the interview room, it dawned on Dawson just how much trouble Autumn might be in. She had, after all, confessed to arson. The who, how and why remained to be seen. He would ask routine questions and try to determine why she would volunteer to be charged for a crime she didn't commit.

There had to be more to the story, and he intended to get to the bottom of it. His mind snapped to self-defense. She was a beautiful woman who might've gotten involved in a bad situation. It happened.

Nothing could prepare him for the shot he took to the heart at seeing her again. She had changed a lot in the past year. Her shiny wheat-colored hair fell well past her shoulders in waves. Even with her eyes cast down to the white tiled flooring, he could almost see their violet hue.

Her lips seemed fuller, pinker. Maybe it was the fact she had on no makeup and her hair looked natural, but this didn't seem like Autumn at all.

Maybe too much time had passed, and he wasn't remembering her very well. They'd had a whirlwind courtship before an even faster wedding.

She'd gained a few curves that made her even sexier. Hell, he didn't need to be thinking about those right now. He took in other differences, too. She no longer had bangs or wore designer clothing from head to toe.

Of course, those were cosmetic changes. He knew firsthand how a few little changes could make a person look completely different. He'd hidden enough witnesses in his day to know the value of a hat, scarf and pair of sunglasses.

Still, it struck him as odd that she wouldn't want to make eye contact with him. She had to know who was waiting in the room to talk to her. She would've been given the name of her visitor and even if she hadn't, that would give her even more reason to want to find out who would be sitting in the chair across the table from her.

Keeping her eyes cast down made her look guilty of something.

He cleared his throat and when she finally did glance up, the fear in her eyes was a second punch. What was she so afraid of? Him? Of his reaction to her walking out with no real explanation? He'd nursed a bruised ego longer than he cared to admit.

Dawson waited until the jailor instructed her to sit and then moved to the corner. Arms folded across his chest and feet apart in an athletic stance, he waited.

Autumn didn't sit. She stared at Dawson for a long moment and didn't speak, like they were playing a game and the person who spoke first lost. Her cheeks flushed, a telltale sign her body still reacted to him whether she wanted to admit it or not. Physical attraction had never been their problem. There was something different about the way she stood that he couldn't quite pinpoint. The oddities were racking up.

Even so, seeing her was a lightning strike in the center of the chest.

"Go away. You shouldn't be here." Hearing her voice again shouldn't send a shot of warmth through his heart.

"Really? Because I was about to say the same thing about you." He clasped his hands together on top of the table and leaned forward. "What's going on, Autumn?"

That question could go way back to their past but that wasn't what he was referring to right now.

"I don't know what you mean, and my life is none of your business." Her shoulders tensed and the lines on her forehead appeared like they did when she was concentrating. Her defensive posture spoke volumes about how she felt at seeing him again. He shouldn't have expected anything less. She'd been clear about her intentions when she'd walked out and then had divorce papers served.

Those violet eyes threw darts at him. "Why are you here?"

"I came to return a few things you left at the ranch and to see if I can help you get yourself out of this…" he glanced around "…mess."

"You don't care about me."

"That's where you're wrong, Autumn. I do care." He wanted to add that he wished like hell that he didn't. He'd known seeing her again was going to be hard on him. He just didn't know how bad it was going to get.

Chapter Two

"I'll sign whatever you need to let her go," Dawson said to the jailor who was standing quietly in the corner.

"You can't do that." Summer pushed off the desk and started pacing. Nothing prepared her for being in the same room with Dawson O'Connor. She'd recognized her sister's husband from the pictures Autumn had sent of their wedding day. There'd been two. One of the couple standing next to each other. Dawson's arm had been around the waist of his bride, who'd been dressed in all white. For some reason that one burned into Summer's memory. Could it have been the only time her sister had seemed remotely happy? And then there'd been one of Dawson that had been taken on the same day. His face was turned toward a wooded area. He didn't seem to care that a camera phone was aimed at him. He was strong, like the muscles-for-days type of body. But, it was his smile that struck her the most.

In the pictures, he'd been seriously good-looking. Tie loosened, top couple buttons on his shirt undone, he'd been leaning against a fence post looking all relaxed. Happy. Seeing him in person, she realized the snaps hadn't done him justice. There was a magnetism about him that drew her gaze and made it stick. His looks came through loud and clear on the digital files, but he was sinning-on-Sundays gorgeous in person.

"Like hell I can't. Just because we're divorced doesn't mean I can't help you."

Summer didn't bother to hide her shock. "Hold on. What did you just say?"

"I said I wanted to help—"

She waved her arms in the air, stopping him midsentence. "Not that part. We're divorced?"

A dark brow went up and she realized her mistake. Her sister never mentioned anything about a divorce.

Dawson O'Connor had that whole tall, dark and handsome bit nailed down. It was easy to see why Autumn would be attracted to a man like him. His rough, masculine voice traveled over Summer like warmth and sex appeal and temptation.

Summer folded her arms tightly across her chest. She turned toward the door. "I want to go back to my cell *now*."

"Go ahead and do that." There was something foreboding in Dawson's tone that stopped her in her tracks. "Call the cop over and have me kicked out of here. Then what? What's your next play?"

She didn't immediately answer, and he must've taken that as a sign she was hearing what he was saying and willing to keep listening.

He continued, "I sure hope you have a next move in mind because this one seems like an act of desperation."

She couldn't argue. She didn't have it in her to put up a fight. Plus, he was speaking the truth. In fact, no truer words had ever been spoken. She'd been desperate. Desperation caused her to pose as her sister. Desperation caused her to confess to a crime she didn't commit. The only reason she'd confessed was to escape the bad guys on her trail. And it was desperation that had her needing Dawson O'Connor to be as far away from her as possible.

And, no, she hadn't figured out her next move. Plus, she was starving. Her stomach growled, picking that time to remind her that she hadn't even figured out her next meal.

His tone softened when he said, "Allow me to get you out of here. We both know you didn't commit the crime you're confessing to and so do they. I don't know what you're up to and I don't know why this seemed like a good option." He waved his arms in the area. "Let's go somewhere we can talk and see if I can help you get back on your feet."

His unexpected kindness tapped into a long-forgotten place buried deep inside. A place that had no business seeing the light of day.

"I appreciate your willingness to help me after what I put you through." Summer had no personal knowledge of exactly what that meant but knowing her sister it was a lot. Based on the look in his eyes, it was far more than this man deserved. "I can't accept your help. We're divorced. What happens to me doesn't concern you anymore."

"Is that what you think? I'm the kind of person who could walk away from someone I cared about once? Because if that's true you clearly did us both a favor by walking out last year." He threw a hand up before she could answer. "Never mind. The past is the past. We both moved on. And now you find yourself here. You don't want my help. There's not a whole lot I can do about that. But let me ask you this. How long do you really think it's going to take for whomever you're running from to find you here?"

Those words were the equivalent of a bucket of ice water being dumped over her head. He was right. Hearing

him say those words as plainly as he had brought home
the fact that she wasn't safe anywhere anymore. The cops
were onto her about the lie and she figured they'd boot
her out soon anyway.

Autumn had gushed about life on the ranch. A remote
location far away from Austin sounded pretty good right
about now.

Summer took in a deep breath meant to fortify her
nerves and prepared to shock him. "Fine. I'll let you pay
my bail, but you have to take me home with you."

SUMMER WAS STILL surprised Dawson had agreed to her
terms as she walked into his home on an expansive ranch
property. Mental images of him sharing this place with
her sister slammed into her—images she didn't like for
reasons she didn't want to explore. An attraction was so
out of the question.

She glanced around the room and was initially shocked
to realize there were no photographs of the two of them.
Then, it dawned on her that her sister had filed for divorce
last year. Of course, any pictures that had been hanging
on the walls would've been taken down.

The place was decorated in a surprisingly masculine
style. Or, maybe it shouldn't be such a surprise. Again,
he might've redecorated. Thinking her sister had walked
in this very room not that long ago struck an emotional
chord.

Summer tucked her chin to her chest and blinked her
eyes, trying to clear away the tears threatening. For the
sake of Autumn's memory, Summer needed to hold it
together. For the sake of the investigation, she needed
to continue the lie even though after meeting Dawson it
was increasingly difficult to hold the line. For the sake

of her own sanity, she needed to keep her distance from him on both an emotional and physical level.

Getting too close to her sister's ex would only add to both of their heartbreak. Despite the tough exterior, one look in his eyes told her that his feelings had run deep for Autumn.

A sound in the next room caused her to jump over the back of the couch and drop to her knees. It took a second to register the fact that Dawson's eyes were on her, studying her. Analyzing her.

Of course, she should've realized her extreme reaction would draw his attention. She also shouldn't let it warm her heart that Dawson still cared enough about her sister to drive all the way to Austin to bail her out of jail.

"It's just Laurel. She's probably finishing up cleaning for the day." He didn't so much as blink.

"You have a housekeeper?" The raised eyebrow he gave her in response to her question told her she'd just made another mistake. She needed to keep the questions to a minimum. Lay low for a few hours until she could figure out her next move, grab a meal and definitely not talk to him more than she had to.

There was no way she would stick around and put Dawson or his family in danger. Was that the reason her sister had divorced him? Had she known trouble was coming and wanted to protect him? Cut all ties to save him from her fate? Had she married a US marshal thinking he could keep her safe?

"You know we did. I still do. Even though I've told Laurel a hundred times I don't need the help. She's stubborn that way. You remember that about her." From everything she could tell about the man so far, her sister was right. He was good-looking beyond a casual description. Carved-from-granite jawline. Check. Thick, dark hair—

the kind that her fingers itched to get lost in. Check. Serious brown eyes with a hint of sadness. Check. He was kind. It was the only explanation for him going out of his way to help her after being served papers. He didn't seem like the kind of person who took divorce lightly. In fact, he seemed like the type who put family above all else.

A middle-aged woman padded into the room. She had a kind face and a stout build. In one hand, she white-knuckled the handle of a pail. In the other, she gripped a white cleaning rag.

Summer scrambled to her feet. The woman—Laurel—gasped. Her chin practically dropped to her chest. Mouth agape, she released her grip on the bucket. It tumbled onto the tile, crashing against the flooring.

"I'm sorry." Summer glanced around, desperate to find something to help contain the spill. She ran toward the open-concept kitchen and made it to the counter with the paper towel roll at the same time as Dawson.

He gave her a small look of approval, like she remembered something because she was home. That look nearly cracked her heart into two pieces. Getting out of there and out of Katy Gulch just jumped up her priority scale. She hadn't found paper towels because this was her home. Their location had been intuitive. They'd been placed next to the kitchen sink—an obvious place. All she'd done was follow a line across the counter until she saw the paper towels.

It dawned on her that Dawson must've loved her sister and the divorce had to have been hard on him. Autumn had ended their marriage without explanation or ceremony.

This close, she could easily see the dark circles cradling his honey-brown eyes. She could almost feel the toll that caring for Autumn had taken on him, because the feeling was so familiar to her it was palpable. Caring for Autumn was hard. Draining at times. Still the question burned. What had Autumn gotten herself into?

Happiness had always been fleeting for a Grayson. It was beyond Summer's comprehension how her sister could've found it with this man and then walked away. She grabbed the paper towels off the counter and turned toward the mess. In all the commotion, Summer didn't notice the small black-and-white dog that had run behind Dawson.

She dropped to the floor and used half the roll of paper towels, trying to mop up the spill.

Laurel smiled nervously at her. She had kind eyes and what Summer was certain would be an equally kind heart.

Dawson joined them, the little dog by his side, which she could now see was a puppy. Since the dog was probably a safe topic, Summer decided to start there.

"Who is this little guy?"

"My shadow," Dawson said. "Hence, his name is Shadow."

"You should've seen this little guy when Dawson first found him." Laurel made a tsk-tsk noise. "It's impossible to imagine what kind of person could just dump a little guy like this all alone in the country, leaving him unable to fend for himself."

"What happened?"

"Nothing," Dawson said, looking embarrassed by the attention. "He got into a tangle with something—"

"Dawson's being modest. Shadow was attacked by a coyote. Dawson heard what was happening and hopped off Mabel—" she flashed eyes at Summer when no recognition dawned "—you remember his horse."

"Oh. Right. Mabel. Yes." Lying to this sweet woman

made Summer feel awful. There was no way she could keep up the charade. Telling Laurel, exposing the truth, might just put the woman in danger. Summer couldn't do that, either. This woman was all s'mores and camp-fires and the kind of person who probably baked cookies on a chilly day.

"So, Dawson here literally forced open the jowls of the coyote and ripped this little guy from its teeth." Laurel was clearly proud of him, not that Summer could blame the woman. "Never mind that the coyote's mouth then closed on Dawson's elbow. Tore him up pretty good before he managed to get free."

Summer didn't notice his left elbow until then. A pretty gnarly scar ran a solid four inches across his skin.

"Wild things are dangerous. It was really brave of you to take on the coyote." She tried to stifle the admiration in her voice. It was difficult. She also realized the statement covered more than just his coyote encounter.

"Laurel is making too big of a deal out of what happened. All I know is that helping this little guy out of trouble gave me a shadow I can't shake around the house." He nodded toward the black-and-white pup that had yet to grow into his oversize paws. The hint of annoyance in his tone seemed clearly just for show. Dawson scratched the dog behind his ears.

If the little guy had been a cat, he would've purred. She could think of worse problems than to have the ado-ration of an adorable puppy. And Summer figured little doggies weren't the only things willing to follow Daw-son O'Connor around, eyes filled with admiration. With sex appeal in buckets, she suspected half the women in town would do the same thing. The other half were ei-ther married or dead.

Summer also couldn't help but notice how Laurel kept

a tentative eye on her. The kind housekeeper looked like she'd seen a ghost. Based on her expression and reactions, the woman Laurel assumed was Autumn was the last person she expected to see. More proof that Summer's sister had left a mess in her wake. Autumn could be like a volcano. Mesmerizing to see and experience until she erupted. Then, it was pure devastation for anyone who got too close or landed in her path.

"The mess is all cleaned up now. Can I drop Shadow off at the barn on my way to the main house?" Laurel asked.

"He'd like that. Wouldn't you, little guy?" Dawson picked up the pup in one sweeping motion and brought him nose to nose.

"Having another dog to play with might be good for him." Summer could've sworn the puppy smiled.

"He loves playing with Apollo and it's good for him since he lost Daisy. Apollo has been moping around for weeks. The only time I've seen him perk up in the slightest is when Shadow comes around." Laurel walked over to Dawson, who handed over the sweet pup.

"Be nice to Apollo. No biting his ears with those sharp puppy teeth." Despite the warning, his voice was low and warm as he scratched the pup behind the ears. "Will you let me know when I need to pick him up?"

"I sure will." Laurel excused herself before gathering her supplies and making a quick exit.

Lying to the woman with kind eyes about Summer's identity was the equivalent of a physical stab. Perfection had never been her goal and heaven knew she got into her fair share of troubles growing up. Being her own parent from an early age had a way of teaching with a baptism by fire. No one would ever accuse Summer of being perfect. But she was not a liar.

Honesty rated highly in her book. Autumn, on the other hand, had always claimed that bending the truth never hurt anyone. It wasn't true. Summer knew from personal experience how her sister's tiny white lies left marks on the inside—marks that weren't visible to the naked eye.

So, she seemed to find herself between a rock and a hard place as she pushed to standing. Being in close proximity to Dawson, close enough to smell his warm, masculine scent, wasn't helping with the guilt racking her.

"You've been really kind, and I appreciate it. Especially after the way you were treated." There was something very primal in her that could not take the blame for her sister's actions. Maybe it was because standing in the light of Dawson's honey-gold eyes made her want to be honest with him. An important part of that was being authentic.

But honesty at this point in the game would have a price. It was easy to see that a man like Dawson wouldn't walk away easily from someone who needed a hand up. He would see it as his duty to help just as he'd seen it as his responsibility to get her out of jail and talk sense into her.

"Do you mean after the way *you* treated me?" He seemed to regret those words the minute they came out of his mouth. "Don't answer that. Whatever happened between us is water under the bridge. The reason I came to see you today wasn't as altruistic as you might think." He walked over to the counter where he'd placed his keys and picked up a small box. She'd noticed it in his hands earlier but with everything going on didn't think to ask about it.

She walked over to the kitchen counter and placed her hands on it to steady herself.

"These belong to you. You said they were important."
He set the box on the counter next to her and walked
away. "I'm about to make coffee. Do you want a cup?"

"No coffee for me. But, thanks." She had no plans to
stick around long enough to finish a cup.

Summer stared at the box like it was a bomb about to
detonate. Did she even want to know what was inside?
Sadness was a physical ache. Summer of all people knew
that even though her sister could be selfish and focused
on all the wrong things sometimes, Autumn had also
been her best friend and partner in crime growing up.
Autumn's faults could so easily have been Summer's
considering the childhood they'd shared.

Life had hardened them both at too young of an age.
Broken them? There'd been times when Summer wondered if her sister had been capable of caring for anyone
but herself. She'd asked the question countless times,
wondering if she was wasting her time and energy on
someone who would always be a taker.

"Your stomach growled earlier. You're here. You may
as well eat and have some coffee before you take off
again." She didn't want to hear the twinge of hurt in Dawson's voice. Especially since he did a fine job of covering it with a cough.

Trying to find out what had happened to her sister
was becoming an exercise in stupidity. So far, all she'd
done was attract the attention of very bad people. People
who wanted her dead. Maybe it was time to move on. It
would be easy enough to change her appearance and disappear off the grid for a little while. Could she, though?
Could she walk away without knowing what had happened to Autumn?

Summer tapped her finger on the lid of the small box.

She wrapped her fingers around it, still unsure if she wanted to see what was inside.

Her fist tightened around the top of the box as she opened it, memories assaulting her. These few pieces of jewelry were her sister's most prized possessions? It was all junk, worth nothing when it came to money. Memories were a different story.

Her fingers closed around a tarnished chain. The necklace that spelled out one word brought back a treasure trove of memories from the county fair.

This was considered one of her sister's most prized possessions? Because the name on the necklace read *Summer*.

Chapter Three

Dawson watched as his ex-wife stood in his kitchen, tracing the letters on the necklace using her index finger. Autumn had changed. A thought struck that maybe she'd been in an accident and suffered some type of head trauma. She pretended to know the house even though she never lived in it. In fact, he'd moved in three months ago after some tweaks to the original plan—a plan she'd helped him design.

The two of them had made big plans to move into the home that she was going to decorate. He'd even started contemplating the next logical step, a family. But those plans had never gotten off the ground.

After working with the contractor to make enough changes for the house to feel like *his* and not *theirs*, he'd moved in. It only took a few phone calls and clicks to cancel all the furniture and decorations she'd ordered. The custom pieces had been finished and donated to the House of Hope for abused women and their children.

With the addition of oversize leather couches and a large metal star hanging over the fireplace, the place had become home for the bachelor.

The twist of fate that brought Autumn into the space he never thought she'd see had him off-balance. He needed to stay focused. He poured a cup of coffee and took a couple of sips. It was time for answers.

"Why did you say you did it?" He started right in with one of the biggest.

She ducked her head, chin to chest. Her mannerisms were different from a year and a half ago. It was an odd sensation to be staring at a woman he'd known intimately and yet feel like he was staring at a total stranger now. Could the fact he was looking at his ex through a new lens be the impact of divorce?

"I was desperate." Well, now he felt like he was starting to get somewhere. He'd been beginning to think this wasn't Autumn at all, which was crazy because she looked exactly like her.

"Why?"

"Believe me when I say you really don't want to know." There was no conviction in those words. There was sadness in spades and a lost quality that caused a knot to form in his gut.

"Why not let me be the judge of that? I think I have a pretty good handle on what I do and do not want to know." That came out a little harsher than he'd intended. He tried to soften his tone when he said, "Believe it or not, I'd like to help."

"You can't. This is something I have to deal with on my own." Now her intention came out loud and clear. Hurt and stubbornness laced her tone.

"Will you at least tell me why you have to deal with this by yourself?"

She shook her head and didn't make eye contact.

"Does this have anything to do with why you walked out on our relationship?" His bruised ego needed to know because that darn thing still licked his wounds.

"I didn't give you a reason?" This time, she made eye

contact. Eyes wide with a look of disbelief caused more questions to form in his thoughts.

"No. But it's not too late. Tell me why. Your note didn't explain what went wrong. I thought we had a good thing going. Granted, looking back, it wasn't perfect, but we had a base to build on."

"I'm sorry. I can't do this with you right now." The hint of fear in her voice didn't get past him.

"Do what? Finally answer a question? Give me the real reason why you left our marriage after exchanging vows? In case you didn't notice, I took those seriously." He pushed even though he knew better. As a seasoned law enforcement officer, he had developed and honed instincts that told him he was doing nothing but backing her into a corner. Just like the coyote, she'd bite.

"I didn't deserve you." She broke eye contact and guilt stabbed at him. But guilt for what? Why was he suddenly feeling like a jerk for making her feel bad? She'd walked away from their marriage not the other way around. Losing the pregnancy had been even harder on her than it had on him, but he hadn't seen a need for a divorce despite that being the reason for the marriage in the first place.

Her admission struck a nerve. It was impossible, though, not to feel like he was forcing his help on her right now. She was in a desperate situation and he'd been pushing her to take his aid.

"It's not fair of me to put you in the position of explaining yourself. You didn't ask for me to show up today—"

"Which doesn't mean I'm not grateful you did." She had the necklace draped over her opened hand. Giving her back something that she so obviously cared about made him feel like maybe this day hadn't been a total mistake.

"It seems like you've gotten yourself into a situation

that maybe you're having a hard time figuring out how to get out of. We've all been there—"

She clucked her tongue. "Somehow I doubt that. I can't imagine a man like you would know anything about regret."

Dawson stood there for a long moment, taking in her body language. Shoulders tensed, her feet aimed toward the back door, everything about her said she was in for a quick exit. It was his fool pride wanting answers from someone who so clearly didn't care about the marriage as much as he did. *Hadn't cared.* Past tense.

"Okay, let me try this another way." He motioned toward the sets of keys. They hung on a key rack nailed to the side cabinet near the hallway that led to the garage. "There are several vehicles in the garage. I'm sure it won't be too hard to figure out which key belongs to what vehicle. Take whatever you want. No questions asked. You don't have to worry about returning anything. I'm not bringing in the law."

"You are the law. And didn't you just post bail for me? Won't you get into trouble if I disappear?"

"My lawyer can tie up the courts for years until they forget all about my connection to you and technically all I did was sign paperwork to get you released. We both know you're innocent, Autumn." A strange look passed behind her eyes when he said her name. He didn't go into the fact that he'd put his reputation on the line to help her. "Tell me an amount and I can pretty much have as much money as you need at your disposal." He checked the clock hanging over the cabinets in the kitchen. "Bank is about to close." Of course, he could call up his banker at any moment and have the bank reopened for him. A selfish part of him wanted to stall for time, maybe wanted a little bit more time with Autumn before she disappeared again.

She just stood there, a blank look on her face. "You would do all that for me?"

He waved her comment off like it was nothing.

"Seriously?" She started pacing. "That's pretty much the nicest thing anyone's ever volunteered to do for me." She glanced up at him nervously. "I mean, there are so many nice things you did when we were married but I walked out on you."

His ex didn't seem to remember much about their past. Had something happened? Trauma? Working the angle that she'd somehow lost her memory, he asked, "Really? You remember nice things I did for you? Name one."

"I-UH—" SUMMER DREW a blank. And then an obvious answer smacked her between the eyes. "You asked me to marry you."

His eyebrow shot up.

"And there were so many other things that it's hard to remember them all right now." She gripped her forehead, trying to stave off the massive headache forming in the backs of her eyes. Headaches were like that. They had a way of taking seed and then sprouting tentacles that seemed to wrap around her brain and squeeze.

"Did something happen to you, Autumn? Were you in some kind of accident?"

His questions registered. He thought she was suffering from some kind of brain trauma, which basically meant Autumn never told Dawson about her. It would be so easy to go along with that line, a quick escape out of an almost unbearable situation. But she couldn't go there. "No. I wasn't, Dawson."

"You've changed a lot in the past year and a half. More

than I expected. I mean, you look like my ex-wife. There's no debating that. But it feels like I'm talking to a complete stranger. On the outside, it's you but you don't act like her. Her mannerisms are totally different. And I just thought there had to be an easy explanation."

She wanted to give him one. She wanted to help him make sense of a marriage that had been cut short. She wanted to give him answers he seemed to crave in order to go on with his life. He seemed like the kind of person who deserved that and so much more. But how without adding fuel to an already blazing fire?

If she came clean with him right then and there, it would only lead to more questions. Worse yet, he might want to get involved and end up hurt or dead. That would be on her conscience for the rest of her life.

"Money would be a huge help, but only as a loan. You have to promise to let me pay it back." She could use a cash infusion to keep her off the grid. The investigation had to be put on the back burner until the situation cooled off. She'd riled someone up. Maybe she could rent a cabin in the woods until life chilled out again.

"Done. How much do you need?"

"A couple thousand dollars if you can spare it." She almost winced saying the number out loud.

"I can do a whole lot better than that. Twenty-five thousand—"

"I'd never be able to pay that much back." She blinked at him, a little bit dumbfounded. Her sister had said the man she'd married came from a wealthy family. Summer couldn't even fathom someone who could conjure up that kind of cash on a moment's notice.

"You don't have to. It's yours already. Remember? I put it in your account when we got married and you never used it."

"Now I know you're lying." Or testing her. The latter made more sense.

"The money is sitting in your account. What you do with it is your own business." There was a sadness to his tone she didn't want to pick up on. She couldn't afford to care about his feelings right now, not when there was so much at stake. The fact she was aware that he tried to cover with a sharp edge to his tone made everything so much worse.

"You said I could borrow a vehicle…"

"Take whatever you need. There are several in the garage to choose from. You didn't take your own when you left—"

She was already shaking her head before he finished his sentence. "I'd like to borrow one of yours. Preferably something I've never driven before."

He'd mentioned that the bank was almost closed. They needed to hurry if she was going to get out of there. "Is there any chance we can make it into town tonight?"

"It's too late to go through normal procedures." He glanced away from her when he spoke. What was he hiding?

Summer ran through possibilities in her mind. She could take twenty-five thousand dollars in cash and disappear for a while. Then what?

Keep on running the rest of her life? She'd been living a lie recently and it was coming back to bite her. Would she turn out exactly like her sister? Lying and then covering up the lies. Could she convince herself it was all for the best? That the only reason she lied was to help other people? Could she walk away from investigating her sister's disappearance? Because if she did that, she wouldn't recognize herself anymore.

Staring at a pair of honest honey-brown eyes standing

a few feet in front of her, she realized that she could never be the kind of person who could look into them and lie. That even little white lies meant to protect others ended up hurting them more than anything else.

Telling Dawson the truth was risky. It could put him in danger. Not telling him seemed like it could also put him in harm's way. Especially if he started digging around to figure out what was really going on.

Ignorance wasn't always bliss. Sometimes, it could kill.

She decided to clear up this whole mess by coming clean with him. He worked in law enforcement and he seemed to care about her sister. He would know how to protect himself if he was aware of a threat. When she really thought about it, he was a US marshal. Weren't they involved in witness protection? She personally had no idea.

"Dawson, I'm going to tell you something that you might not be ready to hear. You deserve to know the truth." Just saying those words caused her heart to hammer her rib cage.

He set his coffee cup down on the granite countertop and crossed his arms over his chest like he was bracing himself for the worst.

"I don't know much about your marriage except that I know you got married on the last day of January." She held her hand up to stop him from speaking before he could respond because she could already see the questions forming in his eyes. "I was honest before. I haven't been in an accident or had any kind of head trauma."

"Then, what?"

Speaking the words out loud was proving to be so much harder than saying them in her head. She was trying to think of a way to ease him into the news rather than blurt it out and completely shock him. "There's a really good reason why I don't know anything about this house or the life we shared together other than the fact that I know it was brief."

"Well then, you need to clue me in because I have no idea how you could forget the fact that you never lived in this house. You looked at Laurel like you've never seen her before and yet the two of you used to work side by side and talk for hours."

"I'm sorry. I'm seeing how difficult all of this is for you—"

"You can spare me your sympathy, Autumn. Just tell me the truth."

"Well then, let's start right there. My name is not Autumn." She held up the necklace and took a step toward him, noticing how the grooves in his forehead deepened. "My name is Summer."

"You lied to me?" He gripped the edge of the counter like he needed to ground himself.

"No, I didn't. I've never met you before in my life. You were married to my identical twin sister."

Chapter Four

Dawson studied the woman in front of him, trying to give his brain a minute to process what he'd just heard. He must've looked her up and down like she was crazy, because she put her hands up in the surrender position.

"I know how that must sound but it's true. I should probably be surprised that you don't know about me. In a normal family, we would. My sister kept secrets. We're identical twins and I absolutely know something happened to my sister. I tracked her to Austin where a pair of men found me. They said I wouldn't die and that they intended to finish the job." Those honest violet eyes blinked up at him and his heart stuttered. "If my sister was alive, I would've heard from her by now."

There were so many questions mounting. This one popped first. "I need to rewind for just a second. Your name is Summer, and I was married to your identical twin sister. You're here to find out what happened to your sister, who you believe is gone?"

She nodded. "I'm sorry to say this to you, because I know you lov—"

"Thing of the past." He cut her off right there. There was no use going down that road again.

"She is gone." Her chin quivered and she ducked her head to one side.

Summer's answer caused his chest to squeeze. He didn't have to have the same feelings for Autumn as he once did.

"How do you know?" Disbelief washed over him as he studied her for any signs she was lying. His brain couldn't process the news. More questions flooded him as his past unraveled. He narrowed his gaze and studied the woman in his kitchen. He'd noticed something different the second he saw her at county lockup.

"Hear me out. I've been living in Washington State where I work as a waitress. My sister and I always stay in touch."

"And yet I had no idea you existed," he said low and under his breath. Had she planned to leave all along?

"I'm sorry about that. I'm puzzled about that part as well because she told me about you. Granted, it was after you were married. We may go a while in between connecting but we always circle back. She'd been leaving cryptic messages lately about her past."

"A past you knew very little details about if I had to guess." A picture was emerging. Autumn would classify herself as a free spirit, forgetting all about the hurt and questions she left behind.

His comment seemed to offend Summer based on her deep frown lines. Hell, he hadn't meant to add to her hurt. It was obvious she cared about her sister or she wouldn't be here trying to find out the truth.

"My sister was far from perfect. No one knows that better than I do." She folded her arms across her chest and leaned back on her heels.

He was taking all this new information personally. How could he not? He'd met someone, had been told he was going to be a parent long before he was ready and with someone who he'd only known a handful of months.

Autumn had been good, though. When he'd popped the question, she said she had to think about it. Over the days that followed, she'd seemed genuinely anguished about the decision to rush their relationship and that had only made him want to protect her more.

How stupid was he?

Normally, liars gave themselves up. There were signs. The direction of their gaze when they responded to a question would tell him how truthful they were being. Or how fast a verbal response came. A liar paused in the wrong places. They were also good at hiding their eyes or mouth during questioning. There were other telltale signs like coughing or clearing their throat before answering.

A practiced liar could get around most of the signs. A pathological liar—someone who believed the lies—was the most difficult to detect.

Summer was a valuable witness and now that Pandora's box had been opened to his past, he needed answers. She was the fastest route and they both had the same goal.

"It'll take me a minute to get my head around this… situation. I don't take vows lightly and I'm currently in a tailspin, which doesn't mean I don't want to help. Please, continue."

Summer eyed him warily and his heart squeezed. Her pain was obvious. He wasn't the only one Autumn had hurt.

She took in a breath before her next words. "The last time I heard from her she said that she was going through something with an ex but not to worry. Everything was fine and she was happy with you."

He shot her a look but quickly apologized for it.

It was impossible to believe she ever cared about him, considering the fact she'd walked away without a backward glance. If she'd been in trouble, he couldn't think of a better person to help than a member of law enforcement. If she'd needed to hide, who better to ask than a US marshal? Relocating witnesses was one of his specialties.

"For what it's worth, I do think she loved you," Summer clarified.

Now he really shot her a look.

"What? You don't believe me?" she asked.

"No, I don't. How could anyone be happy who is living a lie? The woman I married told me she was an only child and that her parents were killed in a car crash on the interstate a few years after she went to college." He stopped right there because the woman's jaw looked like it was about to smack the floor. "Explain that."

"She doesn't like to talk about the past. It was hard for both of us. I think there was a year in California where we got passed around to four different foster homes and there was this point where I saw it break my sister. I think she shut down some critical emotions and never could get them back. She wasn't a bad person. She was just…" Her gaze shifted up and to the right like she was searching for the right word.

"Lost?" The way Summer, if he could believe that was her name, spoke about Autumn made him realize she *did* know her sister. As identical twins, it stood to reason the two would have known each other intimately. "Why would she suddenly move to Texas if she grew up in California?"

"You want my best guess?"

He nodded.

"We're originally from here. Our parents were together when we were really young, and we lived in Austin as a family. Our dad took off when we were still little. My mom had a cousin in California. She thought she could make a better life for us there. She was a very beautiful woman and she felt like maybe there was easy money out there in Los Angeles as a model."

"But there wasn't?"

"LA was harder than she expected, and she got depressed. Four of us lived in a one-bedroom apartment and her cousin wasn't happy Mom wasn't pulling her weight. There were some parties in our apartment complex, and I remember coming home from school to find her passed out on the couch. Her drinking got out of control and she couldn't keep it together."

Again, this was something Dawson came across in his line of work more than he cared to. Despite his frustration at the situation, he had sympathy for Summer and Autumn. No kid deserved a father who turned his back on the family or a mother who couldn't cope with the demands of bringing up children. There were resources out there for those who would use them but it was always the kids who suffered and they were the innocent ones in the equation.

"Someone called child protective services when my sister and I were locked out of our house. Our mom got in a really bad fight with her boyfriend, so he pushed us outside and locked the door while he broke her nose and her jaw. I think our neighbors were afraid of what might happen to us next, so they called the authorities."

His heart broke for their lost childhood. It was obvious that Summer was Autumn's identical sister. Put the two of them facing each other and it would be like one of them looking into a mirror. But they seemed like exact opposites in terms of personality despite growing up under the same conditions.

What he couldn't figure out was why his wife would lie to him. In fact, their entire life was built on lies. More of that anger and frustration built up inside of him.

"Autumn was in trouble based on the texts. What makes you think she's gone?" He couldn't imagine a scenario where this would be Autumn standing in front of him.

"She stopped all communication. She never would have done that." Summer seemed convinced on that point. Dawson couldn't say one way or the other. He should've known his wife better than that. Autumn had shown up in his life and tore through town, his heart, like a tornado.

"With all due respect, she married a man who never knew you existed," he countered.

"I see your point." She was rocking her head. "But I have known my sister for the past twenty-nine years. Even when she spirals, she answers my texts. And especially our emergency signal."

Well she obviously knew her sister a hell of a lot better than he'd known his wife. Had she been in real trouble? Was that the reason she'd taken off?

Dawson's mind was still spinning. He couldn't help but think he'd been taken for a fool. The unproductive thought wouldn't help matters.

He wasn't in love with her anymore. That ship had sailed. Lick his wounds? He'd done that. Being burned had a way of bruising the ego.

As weeks had turned into months with no word from Autumn after divorce papers had been signed, he realized his mistake had been marrying someone he barely knew.

There were other things that she told him and he now wondered if there was any truth to her words.

"Can I ask you a question?" Dawson wasn't exactly sure he wanted to know the answer.

She shrugged. "Why not?"

"Did she talk to you about me before the wedding?" He studied her, trying to decide if he could trust her.

"I didn't even know about you until after you were already married. She did send me a picture. Two actually."

"But did you communicate? Did you talk on the phone or whatever it is you guys did?" The question burning through him shouldn't matter. He wanted to know if she'd cared about him at all. Would he have been trying to build a life with someone who was callous? Or had there been something real between them? It might not have been that all-consuming something he thought he'd have with the woman he loved. He'd convinced himself that he could build a future with Autumn and their child.

"Nope, just the wedding pictures. I asked her if I could meet you and I never got a response. Whatever was going on with her back then was obviously big. It wasn't like her to go dark for too long. Although, to be perfectly honest, my sister could be unpredictable."

A shocked cough came out before he could stop it.

"Did she mention the baby?"

Now it was Summer's turn to be floored. Her violet eyes were huge and again her jaw seemed like it was about to hit the floor. "Are you saying what I think you are?"

"That your sister was pregnant? Yes. At least that's what she told me." Everything she'd told him was suspect now. Their entire relationship was tarnished with the latest information he was receiving.

"I'm so sorry." There was so much compassion in those eyes. "Did you ask for verification, like from a doctor?"

"She showed me a positive result on one of those stick tests. I didn't question much after that," he admitted.

"I'm sorry to tell you this." She glanced around like she was searching for the right words. The knot tightening in his gut that told him this was about to get a whole lot worse. "That would have been impossible. We were in a car crash with one of our fosters and my sister took an impact to her midsection. We were in the hospital for weeks. I got these scars." She rolled up her sleeve and showed him a four-inch scar running up her left arm. "My sister injured her abdomen. She had emergency surgery and the doctors had to remove most of her female parts including her fallopian tubes. There's no way my sister was pregnant."

The baby bombshell had been the reason Dawson had asked her to marry him. Looking back, he'd been a fool and he sure as hell felt like it right now. He'd been played in one of the worst possible ways. He muttered a few choice words under his breath, unable to suppress his frustration.

In his line of work, he spent the bulk of his time locking up people who lied, cheated and manipulated. How could he not have realized he was living with one of them?

The answer came quick. She'd been the best. He hadn't seen her deceptions coming. Most criminals were locked up because they weren't smart enough to pull off their crimes. Autumn had been intelligent and, if he was being honest, wounded. She'd brought out all his protective instincts by making him feel like she was alone in the world. He'd let his primal instincts take over, pushing logic out of the way in the process.

When he really thought about it, he deserved everything he was getting.

But, damn, he had to be suspicious of everyone he came across in his line of work. One of his favorite things about living in Katy Gulch and still being connected to his family's ranch was that he could leave work behind him and live a normal life.

In Katy Gulch, he let his guard down. He *could* let his guard down. Almost everyone in town knew each other. There were a few outliers who lived outside town and were very private about their business. They'd learned recently that a woman thought to be a little old lady turned out to be connected to an illegal baby adoption ring. Mrs. Hubert's case had brought up all kinds of questions about his sister's kidnapping decades ago.

Now he felt like he'd been duped in the place where he felt the most relaxed and himself.

"How long did you know my sister before the two of you got married?"

"Clearly not long enough."

Chapter Five

"I'm so sorry," Summer started but was stopped with a warning look from Dawson.

"You already apologized," he pointed out.

"Yes, but I—"

"Feel responsible?" he asked.

She nodded.

"Why? Did you know your sister lied about a pregnancy to get me to marry her?" His question came out more like he'd issued a challenge.

"No." Summer's heart sank. She shouldn't feel responsible for her sister's actions. "It doesn't make me hurt any less for what she put you through."

It was hard to look into his eyes with the admission, but she did anyway. He needed to know how badly she felt.

"I hate to break this news to you, but your sister is a grown woman capable of manipulating grown men. I'm not trying to brag but I'm good at my job. The fact that I lived with a con artist shows how good she was." He didn't add the fact she'd lied to a member of law enforcement and gotten away with it. Or that he must feel so burned right now even though the fact was written all over his face. "If you didn't know or weren't involved, it's not your fault."

Summer issued a sharp sigh. "How could I have not known how much trouble my sister was in?"

"I lived with her and didn't know. If what you're saying is true, and I believe it is, then she disappeared—" He put his hand up to stop her protest. "She tricked me into believing we were going to have a baby *and* a real marriage. Although, I was fool enough to volunteer for that last part to the point she had me thinking getting married because of a child was my idea."

No matter how hard or frustrating this had to be for Dawson, to his credit, he didn't raise his voice. Summer still flinched if there was conflict and especially the sound of a man yelling. Chin out, she could handle whatever came her way but those were hard-won skills.

Whatever had happened to the marriage was one thing, at least he'd cared about her sister.

"I have a lifelong habit of feeling responsible for my sister's actions. I can promise to try to do better and that's as far as I can go right now."

"That's all anyone can ask." He stopped as her stomach reminded both of them she hadn't eaten in a while. His gaze dropped to her midsection. "How about we grab some food and start searching for answers?"

"You'd still help me?" She couldn't hide her shock.

"I have a few days owed to me at work and no big cases pending. It won't hurt to request time off. Besides, there's a private family matter that has been needing my attention. Maybe we can kill two birds with one stone." He seemed to regret his word choice when he shot a look of apology.

She shook her head. He didn't mean to dredge up bad feelings and he didn't seem convinced that Autumn was gone anyway. With his help, she could get to the bottom of things quicker. If it was any other person besides

Dawson O'Connor, she would have doubts about taking his help. The man was a US marshal. He knew how to protect himself. Heck, the ranch had its own security if it wasn't enough that he worked in law enforcement.

"I probably have some leftovers in the fridge if you're not opposed—"

"Anything sounds fine as long as it's not too spicy. I don't do hot." She looked at him and her face flushed.

A ghost of a smile crossed his lips. "How does meatloaf sound?"

"I haven't had meatloaf in… I can't remember how long." Getting help breaking down the details of her sister's case gave Summer the first burst of hope in weeks.

"Meatloaf it is." He pulled out a container and dished food onto two plates. After pushing a couple of buttons on the microwave, the smell filled the kitchen.

"Can I help with anything?" she asked, not used to letting someone else wait on her.

"I'm almost done." He moved to the cabinet and located two glasses. The cotton of his shirt stretched and released over a strong back. Summer diverted her eyes. She had no business ogling Dawson O'Connor's backside.

Looking down at her hand, she realized she was gripping the necklace so tightly there were deep indentations in her left palm. She loosened her grip on the necklace and placed it on top of the small box of her sister's possessions.

"Water okay?" he asked.

"Perfect."

"I figure we can have coffee after we eat while you tell me what you know up to this point and we move on from there."

More of that dangerous hope blossomed. Summer wasn't kidding herself that her sister was out there somewhere still alive despite the fact her heart wanted it to be true. Scrappy and Thick Guy had made it abundantly clear about that. They seemed to have firsthand knowledge that Autumn was gone. It had been a long couple of weeks and more than anything else, she needed answers. Justice had been too much to hope for. Now? There was hope.

Since she'd learned early in life just how slippery a slope hope could be, she wouldn't get too comfortable.

Dawson set a plate down in front of her along with silverware and a glass of water. It was foreign allowing someone to do something for her. Even something so simple as serving food had been off-limits with anyone else.

Summer tried to convince herself that she was too tired to protest. A tiny voice in the back of her mind called her out. There was something easygoing and honest about Dawson that made her relax a little bit around him.

The food was beyond amazing. Before she knew it, she'd cleared her plate. "Did you make this?"

That ghost of a smile returned to his lips—lips she had no business staring at. She refocused.

"Not me. I'm not the best in the kitchen. Laurel cooks up a few meals so it's easy for me to heat something up after work. Other times, I eat at the main house with whoever shows," he said.

Summer wanted to know more about Dawson. She tried to convince herself it had to do with understanding the man who'd made her sister happy, even if it had been for the briefest amount of time.

Again, that voice called her out. She was curious about him for selfish reasons. Reasons she couldn't allow herself to go into now or ever.

"Does your family own this whole ranch?" she asked.

"We're fourth generation cattle ranchers," he said with a nod. She could've sworn his chest expanded with what looked a lot like pride. He finished the last bite of food and took a drink of water. He'd said those words like they were common knowledge. Maybe growing up here in Katy Gulch, it was. She was an outsider despite Dawson making her feel right at home.

It was easy to see why Autumn had fallen for him.

"A dynasty?" The question was meant to be a joke. One look at him stopped her from laughing.

"Something like that." He was serious.

"Okay, what does that even mean?"

"That we're comfortable." So basically, rich.

"Can I ask a question?" Trying to word this without being offensive proved tricky.

"Yeah." It didn't help matters that even when he spoke one word his masculine voice traveled all over her.

"If you own all this land and your family has all this money…why become a US marshal?" Her question caused a low rumble of laughter to escape his serious mouth.

"You said it."

She cocked her head to the side and her eyebrows pinched together.

"My family is wealthy. That gives me a roof over my head that I don't have to pay for and privileges that make life a whole lot easier, like Laurel. But it stops there. I may inherit money, but I have my own life. I live off my own paycheck and invest the money I would've spent on a mortgage. I know how fortunate I am, and I don't take it for granted. If my parents never left me a dime, I'd do just fine on my own. Better than fine."

"Your attitude is impressive. Most people would just ride their legacy out." Summer had even more respect for

Dawson now. Even though she'd barely met him didn't mean she didn't know him. He was one of the most down-to-earth people she'd ever met, despite growing up with all this and standing to inherit what must be one of the biggest fortunes in Texas.

He had honor beyond any man she'd ever known. The fact that he would bother to drive to Austin to bail out a woman who'd coldly left him, and to return a box of her prized possessions, struck her heart. He was showing incredible kindness to Summer, despite everything he'd been through. He was concerned about her having a decent meal when he could just try to pin her for answers—answers he deserved.

"Yeah? Seems like a waste of a life to me," he said, like his outlook toward life was no big deal.

"How many siblings do you have?" Getting to know him wasn't helping with her attraction.

"There are seven of us in total but my only sister was kidnapped when she was six months old. She was the firstborn and I doubt Mom would've survived the ordeal if she hadn't found out she was pregnant with my oldest brother a few weeks after."

Summer was stunned. "I can't even imagine what that would do to a mother, let alone being new parents." She studied him. He hadn't even been born at the time of the kidnapping and yet she picked up on something in his voice—a palpable sadness—when he mentioned his sister. "What happened? Did they find her?"

"The case was never solved." He shook his head before picking up the plates. "My father recently died."

"I'm so sorry." She stopped him with her hand on his arm. The sheer amount of electricity that pulsed through her fingertips startled her. She pulled her hand back and flexed her fingers.

She cleared her throat that had suddenly gone dry. "I can do those."

"Don't worry about it." His voice was trying to come off as casual but there was enough tension for her to realize he'd had the same reaction to physical contact.

"At least let me help."

He stopped for a second and the left corner of his mouth curled. She wondered if he even realized he'd done it. "How about this…you rinse these off and I'll make coffee?"

"Deal." It would give her something to do besides feel like she was betraying her sister with the strong attraction she felt toward Dawson.

Dishes done, fresh coffee in hand, Dawson motioned toward the sofa as she bit back a yawn. She caught him staring at her on the walk over, so he seemed to think it was a good idea to speak his mind when he asked, "When was the last time you slept?"

"It's been a couple of days." She suppressed another yawn. Now that she had a full belly, her body craved rest. Or, maybe it was being around Dawson that allowed her to let her guard down enough to think about dozing off. She'd been sleeping in thirty-minute intervals since arriving in Austin seven days ago.

Seven was the number of days it apparently took to show up in enough places to attract the interest of who she suspected were her sister's killers.

"Think you can sleep now?" He watched as she tried to bite back another yawn.

She took a sip of coffee. "This should help. I want to work on figuring out what happened to Autumn."

"First things first, I need to clear time off with my boss. I'll still have access to law enforcement resources and my guess is we'll need all the help we can get."

Summer didn't feel alone for the first time since this whole ordeal started. And maybe the first time in her whole life, but she didn't want to try to analyze that sentiment now. She sat up straighter and took another sip of coffee. The sofa was made to sink into. She blinked her eyes a couple of times. They'd gone dry on her.

"What do you need me to do?"

There was a laptop on the coffee table that he grabbed and then balanced on his thighs. "You believe your sister was murdered."

He was restating the obvious. "Yes."

"But you don't have proof?"

"No." Again, this was obvious. She wondered where he was going with all this.

"So, I'm looking for a Jane Doe in Austin."

Hearing those words were a hit to Summer's heart. It took a minute for her to be able to respond. "Yes."

A Jane Doe meant an unidentified body.

"She could be in a hospital somewhere." He seemed to be able to read her thoughts. Then again, he was a seasoned investigator. "She would be tagged as Jane Doe if she refused to give her name."

"Hospitals are a good place to start." Summer didn't have it inside her to hope after what the two men chasing her had said.

"And morgues." He was staring at the laptop screen when he seemed to realize how hearing that word might affect Summer. He glanced up and locked eyes. "I'm sorry. I've learned to distance myself from investigations. It's how we get through the rough ones. It doesn't mean that I don't care what happened to Autumn."

"That makes a lot of sense to me actually." Hadn't Summer been doing that on some level for most of her life? Tucking away her emotions. Forcing them somewhere down so deep she couldn't feel anymore. She and Dawson weren't so different.

"It can come off as uncaring but it's really all about focusing every ounce of energy and brain power on finding out the truth."

"And then what?"

"The really bad cases cause you to spend a lot of time at the gym trying to work off the frustration," he said honestly. It also explained why he was in amazing shape.

"Does your work cause you to have a lot of intense days?"

"Yeah," he said with another half smile. "It does. But there's a pretty big payoff when you take a criminal off the streets and give justice to a family that has been waiting. Everyone deserves that."

She thought about his sister and the fact that her case was never solved. It occurred to her that he brought justice to families when he'd never gotten it for himself or his family.

If she had to guess, he was in his early thirties, which meant the case was several decades old. That was a long time to go without knowing what had happened to a loved one. Her sister's lies to him about a pregnancy when he was the kind of person who wouldn't take that lightly made her angry.

"I'm sorry about your sister, Dawson."

"Thank you." He paused long enough to look at her, catching her gaze and holding on to it. "Now, let's find out what happened to yours."

Chapter Six

Dawson checked the last on his list of hospitals and came up empty. He and Summer had divided the names, working side by side and making call after call. In all, there'd been four Jane Does admitted in the last week to three major hospitals in Austin.

Patient privacy made it tricky to get information but Dawson had a few tricks up his sleeve. He was able to rule out all four Janes, which didn't mean Autumn wasn't in a bed somewhere under a false name.

So, that was a dead-end trail.

The morgue was easier to navigate. There'd been nine Jane Does this month, none of whom fit Autumn's description. If she was dead, her body hadn't shown up anywhere in Austin. There were plenty of places to dump a body in and around Austin. He gave his contact information to the coroner in the event a body showed up that might be a hit.

By eight o'clock, he'd filed a missing persons report and made sure she'd been entered into the database.

It was obvious to him that Summer was running on fumes, but she refused to go to bed. So, when he saw her slumped over on the couch with her eyes closed, he put a blanket over her and dimmed the lights.

Getting into the groove of treating this like any normal

investigation helped. He had a rhythm that went along with ticking boxes off a checklist. Routine was good in times like these.

When he'd made every call on Autumn's behalf that he could, he decided to do a little digging into her personal life. For instance, their marriage.

They'd had a small ceremony. She'd insisted on getting married in Austin and he was beginning to see that the city held a special place in her heart. Especially if that's where she went after she left him. He probably could've traced her, considering they were still legally married for a time. He'd been too busy licking his wounds.

But, now that he thought about it, a few of her actions seemed suspect. Like how she'd insisted on being the one to arrange everything. She'd said that she wanted to be married before they told his family about the pregnancy, insisting that it would lead to less embarrassment in the long run.

He hadn't cared one way or the other. He'd been busy with work and the ranch. So, he'd let her take the lead. She'd also insisted the wedding be just the two of them and Laurel. Again, he'd thought it was a little odd at the time but the most important thing to him had been to become a family so they could get ready for their baby.

The loss Dawson felt when she'd told him she'd lost the baby not long after the wedding still felt real. It had hollowed him out in unexpected ways. For one, he'd known that he wasn't ready to become a father, or a husband for that matter. He was still far too married to his work and kept way too busy on the ranch.

So, the devastation he'd felt when he'd learned about the miscarriage had caught him off guard. Don't get him wrong, he'd been scared as hell after first learning Autumn was pregnant. But he figured no person was ever truly ready for such a life-changing event.

And from firsthand experience he could tell anyone who asked that no one was ever truly ready for the loss, either. Looking back, Autumn had sure played the part. She'd seemed so broken after the news that he felt the need to protect her even more.

The fact she'd played him both ways still stung.

Dawson pulled up the copy of the divorce papers figuring he needed to interview anyone and everyone connected to Autumn. It had been so early in the pregnancy he hadn't been to a doctor's appointment yet. She'd said she had someone she trusted in Austin and had taken several daylong trips to tie up loose ends.

Katy Gulch had an incredible doctor that Dawson's mother had recommended. Autumn had burst into tears at the suggestion of changing doctors. At the time, Dawson's mother reassured him that pregnant women had all kinds of hormones and told him not to take it too personally.

Now he wished he'd asked for the name of her doctor in Austin. Of course, the pregnancy was a sham so she most likely would've made something up. He couldn't exactly count on anything she'd told him.

Which also made him wonder about the friend of hers, supposedly a minister who she'd insisted marry them. Dawson had asked for the marriage certificate so he could add her to his work benefits and she'd stalled big-time.

Had she backed herself into a corner?

The obvious reason someone would want to pin him down for marriage was money. But she hadn't asked for or taken a dime. Looking back, it was also the reason he'd signed the divorce papers so easily. She'd wanted nothing but her freedom. He'd been too hurt and angry to fight back. His pride had been wounded. He'd scribbled his name on the dotted line after reviewing the document and then mailed it back after making a copy for his records.

He wouldn't make the mistake of not fact-checking another relationship.

There'd been no need to cancel her insurance at work because he'd never officially added her to anything. Considering he'd never been married before, he took her word for everything. Why wouldn't he? She was his wife. Adding her to his insurance was a simple thing to him. She'd said something about being covered under a different policy that didn't run out until the end of the year.

In his personal life, he'd never been betrayed. Had that made him naive?

Dawson pulled up his divorce file and searched for the name of her attorney. Matt Charley Shank. There was no address on the letterhead, which was odd. He found it in the body of the second page.

Dawson typed in the name to get a phone number. He shouldn't be surprised at the search results. There was no Matt Charley Shank listed as an attorney in Austin.

He flexed and released his fingers a couple of times to work out some of the tension. He needed to hit the gym for a good workout but there was no time. He could, however, fire off a few push-ups. He had a set of weights in the garage for those times when he needed a quick workout.

This seemed like one of those times. But first, he checked the internet for the name of Autumn's minister friend, Grover Hart, to see what church he belonged to. Not a huge surprise at this point when Dawson learned Grover Hart's services could be bought and paid for. His big claim to fame? Weddings, no licenses required.

If the attorney was a sham and the minister was a sham, the marriage had to be a sham.

SUMMER STOOD IN the opened doorway leading into the garage. A heavy metal band played low in the background. It was the middle of the night. A shirtless Dawson pumped weights. Her gaze lingered a little too long on his muscled chest, mesmerized by the tiny beads of sweat.

She forced her gaze away and cleared her dry throat.

"Sorry to interrupt, is it okay if I use the restroom to freshen up?" she asked.

He didn't seem surprised that she'd been standing there and that made her cheeks burn with embarrassment. Getting caught staring at him didn't top her list of things to do when she woke up. She was still trying to figure out how she'd fallen asleep in the first place.

She'd woken to a dimly lit room with a blanket placed over her.

"Make yourself at home." He sat up and grabbed a towel.

Summer forced herself to look away as he toweled off his face. He stood up. He still had on jeans that hung low on lean hips. He had the kind of body she'd expect to see on a billboard somewhere. His abs were cut. His arms strong. His waist lean. Don't even get her started on how gorgeous he was.

Dawson O'Connor was the total package. Intelligent. Decent. Smokin' hot. And fierce. He had a look in his eyes that said he wouldn't hesitate to go all in to protect someone he cared about. He also had the kind of confidence that said he could back it up, too.

An attraction to her sister's ex-husband couldn't happen. The electricity she felt radiating from him was most likely residual desire that he felt for Autumn, not Summer. He had, in fact, loved her sister enough to marry her. Granted, Autumn had played a dirty trick to get him to ask. But his feelings for her sister must run deep.

"I can show you where everything is." He tossed the towel onto the weight bench and headed in her direction. She immediately took a few steps back to allow him room to pass by. She needed to put as much distance between them as humanly possible.

Dawson paused long enough to make eye contact as he walked by. There was something in his eyes she couldn't quite put her finger on. Was looking at her in the home they were supposed to share like seeing a ghost?

"I'm sorry. I must remind you of her," she said softly.

"You'd think that would be the case but I couldn't help noticing how different you both are. Beautiful without a doubt, but now that I've had a chance to get to know you, I was just thinking how different you look to me. Strange how personality affects looks once the initial impression wears off. You know?"

"Yeah." She did know. She couldn't count the number of times she met an attractive man only to get to know him and never see him in the same light again. That wasn't the case with Dawson. His personality enhanced already drop-dead gorgeous looks. The saying that beauty was only skin deep came to mind. It was so true. There was so much more to a person and she'd been turned off countless times by outwardly attractive, inwardly awful people.

Summer followed Dawson to the opposite side of the main living area and down a hallway. There were several opened doors revealing an office, a bedroom and a bathroom.

"This is the guest suite. Make yourself comfortable."

She had little more than the clothes on her back and her handbag. He looked her over and moved to the closet.

"Laurel's niece is probably about your size. Rachel is a grad student in Houston and has stayed here a few times. She left behind a jogging suit if you want to borrow it."

"Thanks. I'll take you up on that offer," she said.

"I can throw your clothes in the wash while you shower if you want." The thought of Dawson handling her undergarments had her shaking her head. That was a hard no. She didn't want the image of him touching any of her personal belongings anywhere in her thoughts. Fighting the attraction when he stood this close was difficult enough. She didn't need to add mental images to the equation.

"I'll take care of it when I'm out of the shower if you point me in the direction," she quickly said. Too quickly.

He studied her for a long moment before he spoke again.

"I didn't find a Jane Doe in any of the hospitals I called or at the morgue."

"Any hits on the missing persons report or is it too early?" she asked.

"Never too early to hope but no."

"I can draw them out again if—"

"Hell, no. I won't risk your safety."

"It might be the fastest way to find out who we're dealing with," she countered.

"I won't argue your point and it's easy to see that you care about your sister. Let me do this the right way and investigate in a way that keeps you safe in the process. Okay with you?" Those intense penetrating eyes swayed her away from running off half-cocked. Doing that so far had almost gotten her killed. She reminded herself that she wasn't alone in this. Dawson had resources she didn't. Plus, she couldn't bring justice for her sister if Summer was dead.

She took in a deep breath. "Okay."

"I'll let you know if anything comes in while you grab a shower."

Thanking Dawson didn't seem nearly enough to cover her gratitude. It was a starting point.

He nodded before stepping into the hallway. With his hand on the door, he said, "You have this whole wing to yourself. Do you want the door open or closed?"

"I'll close it." She did before getting her bearings in the oversize guest room. One door led to a walk-in closet and another led to a large bathroom. There were fresh towels hanging and, she noticed, a white bathrobe on the back of the door.

There were shampoos on hand as well as fresh toothbrushes and toothpaste. The place was stocked and ready for company. Mostly likely Laurel's doing. Summer doubted someone who kept a full-time job as a marshal while still working the family ranch had time to think about stocking a guest bath.

She was grateful for Laurel. Now that she really thought about it, she'd like to circle back to the woman and have a conversation. If she and Autumn used to talk, maybe there was some hint there as to what Autumn's life had been like.

Again, guilt struck that Summer hadn't been more in tune with her sister. To be fair, Autumn was complicated. She marched to her own drum and had a tendency to go all-in before going all-out. She could be charming. And, although she and Summer shared the same genes, Autumn knew how to make the most of their looks.

To Summer's thinking, her sister had always been the

prettier one of the two despite starting from the same blank canvas.

She showered in record time, thinking how great a cup of coffee would taste about now. She'd only managed a few sips of the other one before she'd conked out on the sofa. Like everything at Katy Bull Ranch, the coffee tasted better than anywhere else.

Autumn had found a sanctuary here. Why would she ever leave?

Had she gotten bored of the ranch? Best as she could remember about the timeline, Autumn and Dawson had only been together a few months before she'd played the pregnancy card. Summer was still mortified and embarrassed on her sister's behalf for that one.

And then what? How long had they been together before her sister had broken the news to him there was no baby? The web of lies was going to take some time and some untangling to find the truth. An honest man like Dawson would be frustrated by her sister's antics. Someone else might not handle the situation the same. Which begged the question, *was there someone else?*

Summer needed to sit down and develop a timeline. She always did her best thinking when she could see everything written on paper.

After meeting Dawson, even more questions simmered. One bubbled to the surface. Had Autumn come to Katy Gulch to hide and then found protection in Dawson O'Connor too good to pass up?

Chapter Seven

"Coffee smells amazing." Even the sound of Summer's voice was different from her sister's. He couldn't believe he'd ever thought she was his ex. And she looked even more beautiful after a few hours of sleep.

"I waited for you to get out of the bathroom to pour a cup." Dawson turned toward the voice and his chest tightened when he saw Summer standing at the kitchen doorway wearing the sweat suit on loan from Rachel. She had wadded up her clothes into a ball that she held.

There shouldn't be anything sexy about the clothes she had on. The material was standard cotton, and the top was tight at the waist. She had the zipper gripped so tight with her free hand there was no way the thing was moving.

He chalked up his reaction to her to simple biology. She was a beautiful woman, even more so as he got to know her. There was enough electricity pinging between them to light an entire house anytime the two stood close to each other.

Even at this distance, his body heated. And it was more than physical attraction. His heart fisted and he was in trouble. Then again, after the case was solved, she'd go back to living her life and he'd go back to his.

"Washer and dryer are down the other hallway." He

was pretty damn certain there was no annual Christmas card obligation to his ex-wife's sister. He hadn't even known about her until she'd dropped the bomb on him that she was Autumn's sister. He'd shot off an email to one of his buddies to verify what he already knew in his heart, she was being honest about her identity.

His need to verify every new person in his life sat hard on his chest. He was used to being suspicious in his job but had always surrounded himself with good people. With Autumn, he'd had a lapse in judgment.

Something else had been gnawing at the back of his mind. A pathological liar believed their own lies. It was what made them so good at delivering them. The fact that she was a pathological liar made him think twice about what he'd discovered from the internet last night as he poured a cup of coffee for Summer and tried to shake the fresh-from-the-shower image out of his thoughts.

Work started on a ranch at 4 a.m. sharp so waking up at this time wasn't uncommon. To a normal person, this was the middle of the night and Grover Hart would fall under the category of "normal" person when it came to sleep patterns. That was as much leeway as Dawson would give the man.

Again, Dawson was kicking himself for letting his guard down with the wrong person. Those mistakes felt the worst. Trusting someone when he should've known better made him kick himself twice as hard.

By the time Summer returned, he'd gotten hold of his frustration enough to hand over the mug he'd filled. Fresh-faced, her skin practically glowed. Thick, black lashes hooded violet eyes he could stare into for days.

She took a sip and he cleared his dry throat.

"Can you eat something?" he asked, trying to deflect much of his out-of-control reaction to her. Long, silky hair was still damp from the shower—a shower he didn't want to think much more about for obvious reasons.

"I couldn't eat another bite after filling up on that meatloaf a few hours ago. I'm still full." Her voice was a little too husky, a little too sexy. "It was heaven. Laurel must be a great cook."

Dawson had to fight every instinct he had not to lean in and kiss her. He imagined the horror on her face if he followed through with the impulse and that was a reality slap. Good. He needed to keep a clear mind.

"Did your sister ever mention any names to you in the past year or two?" he asked.

"Besides you? No. And she only gave me your first name in the beginning. I finally matched your picture to a news article." She took a sip of coffee and leaned her hip against the counter.

"How about Matt, Charley or Shank? Do any of those names sound familiar?" Following along the lines of Autumn being a pathological liar, she would use names that she wouldn't mix up easily. It was part of believing the lies.

Summer closed her eyes like she was reaching back as far as she could into her memory bank. "Seems like there was a Charley at some point."

Dawson retrieved a notepad and pen from the small built-in desk in the kitchen. He set them on top of the granite island and scribbled the names in those variations.

"You like to write stuff down?" she asked.

"Seems like everyone uses computers now. Call me old-fashioned but I like pen and paper," he admitted with a small smile.

"Same here. It's just easier for me to look at something when it's on paper for some crazy reason." She shook her head. "Go figure."

He didn't want to notice the similarities between him and Summer. He didn't want to notice how naturally beautiful she was or how a small line creased her forehead when she really concentrated. Or how sexy it was when it happened. He didn't want to notice how full her pink lips were or how sweet they would probably taste.

Dawson refocused on the piece of paper.

"What is it? Is there something on my face?" she asked.

"Nope. Your face is perfect." He caught his slip a few words too late. They were out there and he couldn't reel them back in now.

"Oh." The one word was all she said. He wished she'd said it with a little more shock or maybe even disgust. Instead, it was surprise and something that sounded a lot like hope.

Dawson's cell buzzed, a welcome break into the moment happening between them. He walked over to the sofa where he'd left it and then checked the screen.

"Hey, what did you find out?" he asked his buddy from work, Anderson Willis. Law enforcement worked round the clock and Anderson was one of the few people Dawson could call at this hour.

"I'm sorry to break the news to you, Dawson," came the familiar voice. "There's no record of you ever being married."

It was a double-edged sword. He shook off the shock and said, "I owe you one for tracking this answer down for me."

"You know I have your back."

"I appreciate it." Dawson ended the call and then looked to Summer. "Turns out, the wedding was a fake. I was never married to your sister."

"Why would she go through all that?" she asked.

"It explains a lot actually. She only wanted the two of us there for the ceremony with Laurel as a witness. Autumn insisted on handling all the details herself. I learned a few hours ago that the man who 'married' us was a for-hire and not a longtime family friend."

"But why trap you into marriage with a fake pregnancy story only to find out there'd never been a wedding in the first place?"

If he knew the answer to that question, he'd be so far ahead of the game. Investigations were like puzzles. Evidence often came one or a few pieces at a time. Sometimes the motive didn't make sense until all the pieces were in place.

This would most likely be one of those complicated cases.

"We'll start with the name Charley. It isn't much to go on but we'll know to pay special attention if his name comes up."

She moved over to the notepad, picked up the pen, wrote down the name.

"There was a coffee shop on Capital Avenue where my sister used to go. One of the workers did a double take when I showed up and it made me think he knew her. It could just be that she got coffee there when she was in town but the way he looked at me with…*surprise*… I guess is the right word…made me think there was something more to it."

"Capital Coffee?"

She nodded.

"I know that place," he said, trying to think of any politicians he knew with the first name of Charley. A political tie could explain her murder if she'd rubbed a politician the wrong way or if this was someone from her past. Austin was the capital. If she hung out at a coffee shop that was a known hangout for politicians, it could give them a direction.

"We need to look up any politician with the name Charley." That wouldn't be too difficult. Their names were public record.

"Or a political aid." She was right. And it made the list a whole lot longer and harder to track down.

"The only other people who frequent that coffee shop are UT professors. I doubt she'd have a run-in with one of those." Ideas started churning and they were making progress. Inching along at this point but he'd take what he could get. "How'd you find out about the coffee shop?"

"She sent me a picture from there a couple of times."

"It's a starting point. I don't like the idea of taking you back to Austin, though. Not while this situation is hot." He didn't doubt his skills in protecting a witness. One of the most important rules of the program was that the witness not return to the town from which they were relocated.

Technically, she wasn't the one being tracked. The men chasing her didn't seem to know that. If Autumn had hid her twin sister from her so-called husband, she probably didn't talk about her family member with any of the men she'd dated.

That might mean no one would ever go looking for Summer. She could be safe if she went back to her life in Washington. Even though he highly doubted she'd go for what he was about to pitch, he had to do it anyway.

"What do you think of letting me take over the investigation from here?" He'd barely finished his sentence before she started shaking her head.

"No way." The finality in those words told him not to argue.

"Would you at least think about stepping back?"

The look she shot him made words unnecessary.

"The only reason I bring it up is because I can protect you better if you go back to your normal life and let me lead the investigation into your sister's case." He had a moral obligation to make her aware of her options.

She didn't immediately respond. Her lips were set in a thin line. She'd made up her mind. Instead of overreacting, she seemed to take a minute to pick apart his reasoning. The small crease appeared on her forehead. "I think I understand what you really mean. I understand the risks I'm taking. Believe me. I barely got away and I know that was sheer dumb luck. I got even luckier that, despite what my sister did to you, you are a decent enough human being to actually want to help. So, I'm not taking it for granted."

He was impressed with how well she'd thought out her response.

"You have a big family, right?"

"Yes," he confirmed.

"You guys are all close based on what you've told me so far." Her argument was already being laid out for her the minute she brought his family into it.

"That's right."

"My sister is all I have in the world. She might not be perfect. Believe me when I say that I can count the ways in which she isn't. But we made a pact to have each other's backs. I told her that I'd always be there for her. I've let her down in the worst possible way. There's so much that I'd do differently now. I can't go back. I can't change what has happened. I can't bring her back. All I can do is nail the bastards who hurt her."

There were only two words appropriate as a response. "Fair enough."

THE WASHING MACHINE BUZZED. Summer forced her shoulders to relax. "I know where to go."

The washing machine was down the same hallway as the garage. The hallway was longer and there was a window at the end. She moved her clothes through to the dryer, pushing the sexy sweaty images of Dawson out of her thoughts. It was probably good that she would only know Dawson for a few more days before heading back to Washington and to her life there.

Not that she had much of one. She'd been saving tips to take a few computer classes so she could get a nine-to-five job. She wasn't particular about where she worked as long as it didn't involve hustling drinks or food. She'd done both. Often at the same time to make rent.

Summer and her sister had had a crazy dream when they were little of owning their own shop. When they were super little, the dream had been to open a toy store and then they'd wanted a small bookstore. At least, Summer had. Autumn had said she didn't care as long as there was a coffee shop attached for her to manage.

Then, her sister started drifting around and moved farther and farther away, not just physical distance. The calls had stopped coming. Autumn was later and later returning Summer's calls.

The reason Summer had been working in restaurants and bars was to save up enough to start their business. She'd been working every job from waitress to assistant manager trying to learn everything she could about running a business.

Everything came to an abrupt stop after Autumn sent news she got married. Her life was going to be with her husband and she said that Summer shouldn't worry about finances because Autumn had married well.

At first, Summer questioned whether or not her sister had married for a bank account. The look on her face in the wedding picture had given Summer hope that wasn't the case. Finding out her sister had forced Dawson's hand still didn't sit well. Now there was the fact she'd actually never truly been married in the first place.

But she'd wanted Summer to believe she was married, and still was married. She turned on the dryer and headed back to the kitchen. She walked over to the pen and wrote down the word *married*.

"My sister didn't tell me about the divorce." She flashed eyes at him. "Even though it was all fairy tale or smoke and mirrors, however you look at it."

"It wasn't real," he seemed quick to confirm.

"But she wanted me to believe it. I'm wondering if she wanted someone else to believe it, too."

"Possibly someone named Charley?" he asked.

"It's all I can think of," she said. "It worked with me. I really thought she was happy and I stopped worrying about her." The fact she'd rarely returned messages in the past year had barely registered with Summer. "I was busy coming up with a Plan B for my life after hers seemed settled."

"So, her wanting you to believe she was married was important," he agreed.

"It's also strange that she left this box here." She motioned toward the wooden box with what was supposed to be her sister's most prized possessions. "She knew she was leaving. Right?"

"I believe so."

"Then, why take off without something so personal? I'm guessing the way she left things with you that she never intended to come back," she said.

He rocked his head. "That's been my assumption this

whole time. The main reason someone leaves something of value behind is the person is in such a rush they forget it."

"I'm probably just wanting to see the best in my sister but I wonder if she left my necklace because she wanted to protect my identity." She picked up the pendant and let it rest on her flat palm.

"It's highly possible." He reached for the pen she'd set down and wrote "protect loved one."

"Have you considered that she might have been trying to protect you?" she asked him.

"It crossed my mind that she picked me for my ability to protect *her*." His response was honest, and she could give him that. There was far more hurt in his tone when he talked about Autumn now. He'd said before that he was in full-on investigator mode.

"That might be true. She seemed like she was hiding and making rash decisions. Some of it feels illogical."

"We have a lot of puzzle pieces missing," he agreed before glancing at the wall clock. "In a couple of hours, we leave for Austin."

His cell buzzed and this time it was still sitting on the granite island. He walked over to it. The look on his face when he checked the screen nearly stopped her heart.

Chapter Eight

"Thank you for letting me know."

Those six words were going to change Summer's life forever. She just knew it. Her legs gave and she smacked her hand on the island to stop herself from going down. All along, she'd known it. And yet confirmation of her sister's death nearly pulled her under.

Dawson was by her side in the next second, his strong hand steadying her, helping her stay upright.

"I'm sorry." Two words she hated more than anything in that moment.

He helped her to the couch and brought a fresh cup of coffee. For a long time, she couldn't speak as tears streamed. Dawson gave her space. He set his laptop up at the granite countertop and took a stool. He'd moved it to the side presumably so he could keep an eye on her.

Summer didn't want to know the details of what had happened just yet. She just sat there, suspended in time, unable to think or speak. Her brain refused to process. A fog descended, cloaking her with a heaviness that pressed so hard on her chest she could barely breathe.

Sipping coffee to try to jar herself out of the haze of grief, she hugged a pillow to her chest.

The dryer went off at some point. She didn't care. She heard Dawson move around without really registering what he was doing. The coffee in her cup had long since gone cold. She rolled the mug around in her palms.

Tears dried up at some point. She couldn't be certain when and didn't care. The sun came up and she cursed the fact. How could life go on when her heart had just been ripped out of her chest?

Come on, she finally tried to rally. She'd known this news was coming. She'd had time to deal with it. There was something extra devastating about that final blow, something extra cruel and final. She curled up on her side and pulled the blanket from last night over herself, suddenly feeling very cold.

The details could wait. In a few hours, she'd learn the condition of what would now be referred to as *the body*. She hoped like hell there was some evidence, a fingerprint or piece of DNA that could bring closure to the case and justice for her sister.

A small part of her didn't want this investigation to end. She didn't want to go back to the nonlife she'd had in Washington. The one where she had no real purpose anymore.

But then if wishes were being granted, she wanted her sister back. No matter how irresponsible Autumn had been or how lost, there had been something very good inside her that had been worth fighting for. At least Summer thought so.

Summer leaned forward and set the mug on the coffee table. A few seconds later, Dawson brought over a plate of food. She glanced at it, figuring there was no way that a breakfast sandwich was going down. It could go down but she highly doubted it would stay there for long.

The glass of water, on the other hand, she decided to try.

"Okay if I sit with you?" Dawson asked.

"I'd like that a lot." She meant it, too. The only light in this dark situation was the fact she hadn't been alone when she'd heard the news. Having been on her own for most of her life caused her to learn to depend on herself early. Being completely alone for the rest of her life was one of her worst fears. She'd been so afraid that if she lost her sister she would fade away, too.

She scooted over enough for him to sit next to her. It was unexpected for him to be her comfort. But she didn't hesitate for a second when he tugged her toward him.

Burying her face in his chest, she released the pent-up frustration that had been simmering for years.

DAWSON KNEW BETTER than to be Summer's comfort for too long. It was dangerous territory for him because it would be all too easy to get lost in her violet eyes. He couldn't argue how right she felt in his arms. Instead of giving in to what he wanted, he put up a wall.

His mind was still spinning from everything he'd learned in the past twenty-four hours. Autumn's lies stacked up from the fake pregnancy to the fact she never went to college or had a living relative. There was a lot to unpack and try to digest. Even though a year had passed, learning he'd been lied to and tricked caused all his old walls to shoot up. The thought of letting anyone else in seemed about as appealing as drinking motor oil.

Except, when it came to Summer, he found that he wanted to trust. There was a quiet strength and vulnerability in her that touched him in a deep place. Losing Autumn had hurt his pride. Losing Summer would break his heart.

Dawson's cell buzzed where he'd left it on the granite island. Summer tensed and then pulled back as though she realized the worst blow had already been delivered.

It had. He couldn't imagine losing one of his brothers out of the blue like that.

He pushed up to standing and got to his phone in time to answer after a glance at the screen. "Hey, Colton."

His older brother was sheriff but there was no need for formalities.

"I wish I had better news." The fact that Colton was getting right to the point sent an icy chill racing down Dawson's spine.

"What is it?" Dawson asked.

"It's Dad. A private investigator came forward and said he gave Dad information about possible known associations of Mrs. Hubert a few weeks before Dad's death. Someone might've come onto the property to stop him. And there's more."

"What else?" The question had to be asked.

"Someone used his credit card two days ago, so we're diving in to figure out who and how the person got it." Colton said.

"If Dad was following up on a lead and that's what got him killed, would the killer be crazy enough to use the credit card?" Dawson asked.

"It's a reasonable assumption. The fact that his credit card was used a few days ago could mean a lot of things. He might've dropped his wallet and someone found it before he was murdered."

"True." There was no need for them to go over all the possibilities since both worked in law enforcement and both had seen plenty in their time on the job.

"Where was his credit card used?" Dawson asked.

"Convenience store in Beckridge."

"That's not far. There'd be camera footage. Right?"

"The Mart doesn't keep the recordings. They wipe them

out every day. It would be impossible to know who used the credit card based on any footage," Colton explained.

"We could determine if the person was male or female, though. And the clerk might have a description. Let's see, the highway runs straight through there." Dawson was grasping at straws, hoping for a witness.

"The clerk couldn't remember who used the card. And, I talked to mother and she wanted to increase the size of the reward for information about Dad's murder. What do you think about that?" Colton asked.

"Ten thousand dollars is already a lot of money for someone to do the right thing."

"You won't get any arguments out of me there." At least he and his brother were on the same page.

"Did you tell her that might invite gold diggers into the party? The amount of false leads would go through the roof if we increased it five or ten thousand dollars?" Dawson asked.

"I sure did."

Dawson was preaching to the choir. His brother was a top-notch sheriff and would have already thought of all those things.

"For the record, I'm against the idea. I think it'll bring too many quacks out of the woodwork. You probably have your hands full as it is with a ten-thousand-dollar reward," Dawson said.

"All of us are in unison on that," Colton confirmed. He, no doubt, would have contacted their other siblings.

"Changing subjects. Are you doing okay with *everything*?" Colton asked. The emphasis he'd placed on the last word gave a strong hint that he was talking about Summer.

Dawson wasn't ready to discuss anything about the sisters with his brother just yet. Especially not where he was on a personal level with Summer and he knew that was the real question Colton was asking. Dawson paused for a minute and the pieces started clicking together. Given how many of his brothers worked in law enforcement, the news about Autumn's death would've traveled through the family by now. He'd intended to call his brothers once he got his mind around the news. For now, Summer had been and still was his priority.

"We have a lot going on over here. I'm planning a road trip to Austin in a couple of hours. There are a few people I want to interview over there," he said. "And if we can keep the news about Autumn as quiet as possible, I'd appreciate it. And that goes for everyone who knows, not just the family."

The news about Autumn had been hard but not because of any residual emotions. He'd turned those off a while ago and was down to a bruised ego. Any anger he had toward her dissipated the minute he heard she was in trouble. It explained a lot about the way she'd acted. He was down to being genuinely sorry for her and her family on a human level rather than as an ex-husband. Hell, their marriage had been too brief for him to put down roots in the relationship. She'd swept in and out of his life like a spring thunderstorm.

"It's true. What you heard about Autumn," he said to his brother.

"I saw Laurel yesterday. I was in the barn when she brought Shadow over."

"Then you've probably pieced together the fact that Autumn has an identical twin sister. She's here and I'm going to help her see this through." Dawson braced himself for the argument that was sure to come from his brother—a brother who would have Dawson's best interest at heart without a doubt.

"You know each and every one of us is here if you need *anything*." The way he emphasized that last word suggested the offer covered more than their brotherly bond. There was a hint of confusion in Colton's tone, which was understandable under the circumstances.

Dawson had no way to discuss something he didn't understand for himself. That "something" was his need to make this right for Summer.

"You say you're heading to Austin in a little while?" Colton brought the subject back to the investigation.

"That's right."

"You want any of us to tag along?" Colton asked.

"I got this. I appreciate the offer, though." Dawson figured he had enough contacts in Austin to get backup if anything went down. For now, he wanted to visit a coffee shop and a so-called minister. An internet search of Texas lawmakers didn't reveal anyone with the first name of Charles or Charley.

"You know I'm just a phone call and a couple of hours away if you need anything. I'm also pretty decent with the database, so if you need any help with research, I'm here for that, too," Colton offered.

"I appreciate you more than you know."

"It's what we do for each other. Right?" Colton said. It was true. Any one of them would drop what they were doing on a moment's notice for the other one.

Dawson thanked his brother before ending the call. He moved to the sink and filled a glass with water, and then polished it off. He'd pace if it would do any good. Frustration built when he thought about someone using his father's credit card like it was nothing, like they knew they wouldn't get caught. Finn O'Connor was strong and tough for any age. Under most conditions, he would have been able to hold his own. *Most* being the operative word.

Anyone could be taken down under the right conditions no matter how strong or well prepared. He needed to make a pit stop at the convenience store on the way to Austin. Shadow would be okay hanging out in the barn for a couple of days. He'd have to let the ranch foreman know, but that was easy enough. Shadow loved being at the barn so no reason to feel bad there. Apollo could certainly use the company.

From behind him, he heard the sound of Summer's bare feet on the wood floor. He could sense she was moving toward him. Her clean, fresh-flower smell filled his senses when he took in a breath meant to calm himself.

"Was that news about your father?" Summer's voice traveled over him, detonating in his heart.

"Yes. His credit card is in play a couple of towns over." He heard the hurt in his own voice when he spoke about his father—hurt he was usually so good at masking.

He set the glass down on the counter and released his hold on it for fear he might break it. He gripped the bull-nose edge of the granite countertop instead.

There were a whole lot of *should not*s rolling around in Dawson's thoughts. He should not turn around. He should not take a step toward Summer. He sure as hell should not kiss her. But that's exactly what he did.

Dawson dipped his head down and captured those sweet, full, pink lips. He exhaled against her mouth as her tongue darted out.

Now it was Summer's turn to take in a breath as he pressed his lips against hers harder and the two melded together. She pushed up on her tiptoes and brought her hands up, tunneling her fingers in his hair as she took the lead, deepening the kiss.

Electricity pulsed through his body, bringing him back to life. He looped his hands around her waist as she pressed her body flush with his. Through the cotton material of the robe, he could feel her full breasts against his stomach. She was perfection and fit him perfectly.

She parted her lips, which gave him better access, and he drove his tongue inside her mouth. She tasted like dark roast coffee and a little bit of peppermint from brushing her teeth earlier. Dark roast coffee mixed with peppermint was his new favorite flavor.

Dawson's pulse skyrocketed and his heart jackhammered his ribs. Summer molded against him. When she opened her eyes and pulled back just enough for him to see those incredible violet eyes of hers, his heart detonated.

She seemed to search his gaze and he knew what was coming next.

"Is this a good idea, Dawson?" she asked.

Looking into those eyes, he couldn't imagine doing anything with her would be a bad idea. Bad timing? Now that was a thing.

If he'd met her two years ago or a year and a half ago, it would be so much easier to get lost in her. Now timing was a problem. He couldn't go back and undo the past. Normally, he understood the value of life lessons and hard situations. He could appreciate how deep he had to reach and how much he had to grow when times were tough.

Selfishly, he wanted Summer. He wanted those bright violet eyes and sweet lips. He wanted to get lost and forget how complicated all of this was.

Dawson muttered a curse under his breath. Because timing.

"Probably not." It was difficult to say that, considering their kiss brought him to life in places that had been dead too long. No one had caused that kind of reaction from him with something so simple before Summer. Timing.

"Then, we should probably put a stop to this." The uncertainty in her voice made him want to convince her otherwise. It didn't seem like it would take a whole lot and it definitely wouldn't on his part.

Her body pressing against his wasn't making it any easier to think straight. She had the kind of curves that made her feel like a real woman. Long legs, soft round bottom, she was perfect, sexy...

Dawson stopped himself right there. His arms still looped around her waist, he dipped his head down and feathered a kiss on her bottom lip. "I want to do this. I sure as hell don't want to stop. But, the last thing I want to do is confuse the situation any more than we already have."

Those words were a bad idea. He heard how they sounded coming out of his mouth and the hurt in her eyes compounded it. The thing was, he could see himself going *there* with her. He could easily see himself doing the get-to-know-her-better thing. He wanted to know all those little details about her that made up a relationship. Could he?

Could she? Could she stick around long enough to see if there was anything deeper than spark between them? Could she stay in one place long enough to figure out if this could ignite into a flame? See if there was any substance to turn initial attraction into something so much more?

There was nothing inside Dawson that wanted to jump into another serious relationship. He would doubt his own judgment every step of the way because of Autumn. She'd burned him enough to back away from the stove the second time.

An annoying voice in the back of his head told him he was making up excuses. Was he?

Hell, maybe he was the one who needed some distance. Nothing in his body or mind or heart wanted to take a step back from Summer. And that was dangerous under the circumstances.

He could make all the arguments he wanted to. The truth was that while he was standing toe to toe with Summer, he couldn't force himself to be the one to step back. She would have to do it. And she did.

Which also told him she could.

If he was going to guard his heart, he was going to have to do a better job than that.

Turned out Summer Grayson was his weak spot. Dawson needed to get more control over his emotions. The phrase "get a grip" came to mind.

What he needed was to get a handle before this became a runaway train.

The first time he'd seen Summer opened up a sore wound. Although, to be honest, she had seemed different from Autumn from the moment he laid eyes on her. He'd noticed all those quirks that were uniquely hers. Her personality could not be more opposite her sister despite a likeness. And he stopped there at a resemblance.

Dawson couldn't think of Autumn and Summer as identical because they were so different. Summer had that fresh-from-the-shower face. She looked like she ran a brush through her hair and let it flow.

Autumn, on the other hand, spent quite a bit of time in the bathroom tinkering around with her looks. Being around her triggered his protective instincts, but that wasn't the same as love. She'd been helpless and he'd stepped in. To be fair, he'd always seen himself with an independent, spirited wife for the long haul. Someone who could challenge his thinking and yet be silly enough to laugh at herself because life was guaranteed to deliver some hard knocks.

Summer, on the other hand, was strong. Yes, vulnerable, too. There was a certain undeniable vulnerability about her, which wasn't the same as helplessness. Summer was the roll-up-her-sleeves type. If something needed doing, she was going to do it. She was far from a helpless victim.

Her personality couldn't have been more opposite from her sister's. Summer was quick-witted and resourceful. She was beyond intelligent. And, man, did she possess a strength about her, a dignity that he'd rarely ever witnessed.

He had to fight every instinct that had him wanting, no needing, to be as close to her as he physically could. Summer just had that way about her. She was like the sun. He wanted to tilt his face toward it and take in its warmth.

Dawson reminded himself once again that Summer lived in Washington and he lived in Texas. Those were a lot of miles to cover. And that was the easiest part about a relationship between the two of them.

"Where to first?" Again, her voice traveled over him, bringing to life those places that had been dormant far too long.

"I'd like to interview Grover Hart first. See if he knew your sister beyond her locating him on the internet. Maybe he can give us some insight into where she hung out and what she did while she was in Austin."

"It sounds like a good place to start." She paused for a few seconds and he could almost see the wheels spinning in her brain. "Is there some way we could change the way I look? Is there something here like a scarf or maybe a ball cap that I can wear?"

"I'm already a few steps ahead of you on that one. I do have to get witnesses to safety from time to time so I keep a duffel bag full of supplies in the closet. We'll be traveling during the day and it's sunny, so I have a variety of sunglasses for you to choose from. I definitely have scarves and a few other things I think you might find helpful," he said.

Dawson turned toward the front door and motioned to the closet. He also had to force his gaze away from her backside when she headed over to the closet.

Watching her walk away wasn't going to do good things to Dawson. He was still kicking himself for not having a better answer when the two of them had been close. And he probably would be for a very long time if he let her get away.

Chapter Nine

Summer didn't realize she was tapping her finger against the window on the passenger side of Dawson's truck until he glanced over at her. His look was one of concern, not annoyance. She realized her nervous tick was in full swing.

She'd like to say her thoughts were consumed with what they were about to face in interviewing Grover Hart, the internet minister, but that wouldn't exactly be true. Her thoughts kept winding back to the kiss she'd shared with Dawson in the kitchen and the way it held the kind of passion that had been missing in every kiss for her entire life.

Since that was about as productive as squeezing a turnip and expecting blood, she did her best to shove those thoughts aside.

Grover Hart lived far north of Austin in a small town called Bluff. His house sat on what looked like at least an acre of land, and mostly resembled a junkyard. There were tractor parts and what she assumed were truck parts littering the lawn. There was a couch that looked like an '80s relic sitting next to the front porch steps of the small bungalow.

Dawson parked and kept the engine idling. He glanced

over at Summer one more time, his gaze lingering a little
bit longer this time.

"This should be interesting," he said.

"I couldn't agree more."

On the east side of the house was a small white gazebo. There were fake flowers wound through the slats.
She imagined this was a place Grover performed quick
ceremonies. Her sister and Dawson had married on his
family's ranch. She shuddered, thinking about the kind
of person who would be on the outskirts of town needing a quickie wedding in basically a junkyard. She also
wondered how legal the nuptials would be. That was a
whole different issue altogether.

"Guess we better do this." Dawson shut off the engine
and exited the driver's seat. By the time he got around
to the passenger side, she'd let herself out. There was a
small look of disappointment in his eyes. Opening a door
was still considered chivalrous in Texas.

They hadn't made it more than a few steps when the
front door to the small green-siding bungalow popped
open. A man who looked to be in his late forties or early
fifties bounded out the door. He had on a variety of
brightly colored prints and a matching cloth headband
tied around his head. His hand was extended in front of
him. He had a tanned, weathered face and a gap-toothed
smile.

Grover had the whole Keep Austin Weird vibe down
pat. He also looked like a bona fide hippie and she half
expected him to offer them something besides the usual
water or alcohol fare.

"How can I help you?" He looked at Dawson and then
her. There was no hint of recognition.

Summer realized she had on a scarf, a ball cap and
sunglasses. Her hair was tucked inside the hat as best she

could. She removed a few articles and studied the man for any hint of recognition.

"Beautiful day," Dawson said, shaking Grover's hand. Dawson was stalling for time, waiting to see if Grover recognized her or him.

He looked from Summer to Dawson and back again before throwing his hands out to the side. "Would you like a tour of the wedding gazebo?"

The man looked confused when neither one of them answered.

"You married us a while back," Dawson began, and Grover really did seem caught off guard with the statement.

"Oh." He seemed to be searching his memory, trying to find a match to the couple standing in front of him. "I'm real sorry. I hope everything is okay with the—"

"It's all fine," Dawson reassured. "I was just hoping you could remember talking to my wife when you set up the arrangements."

Grover Hart seemed genuine enough, looking like he'd rather shoot the peace sign than anything else. He had flower child written all over him and she figured he was probably too high to remember much of anything most of the time.

"I could check my records if you'd like." He shrugged. His bushy eyebrows knitted together. "Was there something specific you were hoping I'd remember about the day?"

"No, I just thought you might recognize me. That's all," Summer said, figuring this was a dead end.

Dawson seemed to reach the same conclusion when he stuck out his hand and plastered on a smile. "Nothing to worry about here. We were driving by and thought we'd stop in and check with you. She lost her favorite earring on the day of the wedding and hoped you might remember seeing it. Since you don't, we'll be on our way."

Grover let out his breath like Dawson had just twisted a relief valve. She didn't think Grover was up to anything, but he did seem genuinely disappointed that he couldn't be of help.

"Thanks for trying," Summer said as she turned and headed toward the truck. Once inside, she said, "It's safe to say he didn't know my sister from Adam."

"I got the same impression." Dawson drove down the gravel lane, to the farm road leading to the highway. "Maybe we'll have better luck at the coffee shop."

She hoped.

The rest of the drive was quiet, save for the horns honking and general congestion of Austin where the term *rush hour* implied traffic actually let up at some point.

Using the map feature on her phone, it was easy to find Capital Coffee and not so easy to navigate downtown traffic, especially in a vehicle that took up much of the road.

By some miracle, Dawson found parking. The coffee shop was half a block away. It was midafternoon on a sunny day. Temperatures hovered around the midseventies.

He reached for her hand and laced their fingers together. His touch reassured her as she walked the downtown street with her glasses, hat and scarf. It was crazy to think Autumn had walked this same path countless times on her way to her favorite coffee shop.

It was reaching for another miracle that any of the employees would remember Autumn. Turnover in a coffee shop in a town with mostly college students had to be off the charts. Then again, maybe a good job with decent tips was hard to find.

For whatever reason, Autumn had come back to Austin after leaving Dawson. Summer could only think of one reason why her sister would do that…a man. Charley? Autumn was never the type to be alone and the divorce papers had Austin as the address of the 'lawyer.' She hated it and moved from relationship to relationship. Summer had hoped the marriage would stick, but now that she knew the details, she realized how naive she'd been to think her sister would've settled down.

Again, Summer was struck by how crazy her sister's actions had become over the past few years. She'd been straight-up crazy to leave Dawson. He was literally the perfect man.

Had she gotten herself into some kind of trouble? Autumn might have been lost and unpredictable but she'd never been one to break the law. Evidence would say otherwise, but Summer still knew her sister deep down. Autumn wasn't capable of doing much more than her little white lies.

A thought struck. How well could she say that she knew her sister? She was still scratching her head over Autumn leaving Dawson. Granted, her sister had built a mountain of lies—a mountain that she had to know would come tumbling down eventually.

She tugged at Dawson's hand for him to stop walking as she surveyed the street. "My sister had to know her lies would eventually catch up to her."

"It's possible they already were," he said, and she was already nodding. She'd been thinking the exact same thing.

Again, she couldn't for the life of her figure out what her sister had to lie about. "I've been thinking about what happens when people get married."

"Aside from the obvious part where they spend the rest of their lives together?" he asked.

"I'm thinking on a more practical level. The first thing people have to decide is whether or not to change their last names."

"Autumn was insistent on taking my name—"

He stopped cold.

"But she really wasn't. She only wanted people to *think* she was Autumn O'Connor."

Dawson was already nodding his head. "She wouldn't have to tell people her real last name if I believed we were really married."

"And we already know that the ranch is a safe haven. There's more security there than at the average bank." She didn't say Fort Knox even though she thought it.

"She never wanted to leave the property. A lot more makes sense about how squirrely she got when I tried to get her more involved in the plans to build. She kept saying that was my part. She only cared about the decorating."

"She might have been avoiding it because she had no plans to move into the house, after all."

"My thought exactly." There was no hint of regret in Dawson's voice. He spoke matter-of-factly about his past relationship with Autumn.

The realization gave her the sensation of a dozen butterflies releasing in her stomach.

"THIS EXPLAINS A LOT about her behavior." Dawson remembered how reluctant Autumn had been to commit to anything that had to do with the house or their future. At the time, he'd assumed her sadness about losing the baby was the cause. Now he realized she had been wriggling out of making those commitments possibly because she didn't want to stick him with her choices and her taste.

The strangest thing about the whole situation was that he would've done anything in his power to help her if she'd just asked. She didn't have to go through a fake pregnancy and a fake wedding to get him on her side. That was just how Dawson was made.

But it did make him think that she must not have felt like she had another choice. Her lies stacked on top of lies. He was one hundred percent certain that he wasn't the only person she'd been lying to. Or rather, in the other case, lying to get away from.

Signs pointed to her doing something against the law or…

Dawson had come across plenty of types of liars in the course of his career. Most of the time, people lied to save their own behinds. Other times, they did so in order to save someone else's behind. He had to wonder which way it went with Autumn.

"Who am I looking for once we get inside the coffee shop?" Dawson motioned a few storefronts ahead where the sign read Capital Coffee.

"The guy at the coffee shop is tall and skinny. He has long, brown wavy hair that is usually pulled up in a man bun. He looks more like a local than a student to me. He seems to always have a red bandana tucked in the back pocket of his jeans that I don't think he ever uses." Summer's grip around Dawson's hand tightened as she gave the description.

Dawson hoped like hell this would be a lead. Otherwise, they'd driven a heck of a long way for nothing. He scanned the crowded sidewalk to see if anyone looked twice at Summer. They were at a distinct disadvantage considering this had been Autumn's stomping ground.

Summer might not realize who she was looking at and she could be staring into the eyes of her sister's killer. The worst part was that someone could mistake Summer for Autumn, just like what had happened the other day.

It had only been a few days, but they didn't seem any closer to figuring out who killed Autumn. He didn't have to remind his brother or anyone in law enforcement to keep the news of Autumn's death quiet, but he'd done it anyway.

Summer took the first step toward the coffee shop and Dawson kept hold of her hand. He also realized he'd know immediately if she recognized one of the men from yesterday based on involuntary muscle spasms. Her grip would tighten on his hand. He would have a couple extra seconds of warning with physical contact that he wouldn't have had otherwise.

He opened the door for her and followed her inside. The coffee shop was at the end of the street and had a fairly large outdoor space from what he could see. The temperature inside was no different than out.

Several hipster-looking waiters and waitresses moved through the crowded space. The inside of the coffee shop was relatively small. There was a long bar-height counter with a couple of people working the register and another pair manning the machines.

There were roughly a dozen tables. Several of them had two or three chairs nestled around them. There was a long green velvet sofa along one wall with several small laptop-friendly tables in a line. There were outlets galore.

Outside was impressive. There were more tables than he could count and lots of trees in planters. They hid people's faces. It was harder to stand at the front door and get a straight-shot look at everyone.

He took note of the other little nooks and corners. A

couple of people in suits were hunkered over a table in one corner. There was pretty much every type of person in the coffee shop. The corporate types nestled around small tables and chatted. There had to be at least a couple of politicians, along with several political aids. At least one older gentleman had a hardback book the size of *War and Peace* in his hands as he sat with his legs stretched out and crossed at the ankles. His coffee mug sat on the table in front of him. He had that intellectual look with his sports coat and nylon slacks. He was most likely a professor at UT, which was a short walk from here.

Other than that, there were all manner of tattooed people milling about or at the chairs. Blue hair. Pink hair. Nose piercings. One lip piercing. Then, there was the usual crush of backpack-wearing students.

Dawson took it all in. He was used to sizing everyone up and evaluating all threat as a matter of habit. He knew where every exit door in the room was located.

Summer squeezed his hand. He glanced toward her and she nodded at a guy behind the counter. Man Bun was so busy manning the machines and frothing milk that he didn't bother to look up. He had an AirPod in one ear and seemed to be jamming out in a zone as he made orders and checked what looked like order ticker tape.

Time to see if Man Bun recognized Summer.

Chapter Ten

Dawson wanted to see Man Bun's unfiltered reaction to seeing Summer. He would be able to tell a lot about Man Bun's involvement or lack thereof in Autumn's death based on his initial reaction.

"I'm not sure how much I look like her like this. She never stepped out of the house without being all done up with full hair and makeup." Summer removed the glasses and ball cap. She fluffed her hair.

"In my opinion, the two of you don't look much alike. But there's enough of a resemblance to trick an acquaintance." He meant every one of those words. Autumn and Summer couldn't be more different as people. Summer had a warmth about her despite being very reserved. Autumn was more of an in-the-moment type. She had a bigger personality. The thought she'd been abused in her young life and that had caused her to become a bigger-than-life person on the outside with that same trapped little girl on the inside nearly gutted him.

Her defense mechanisms were well honed, and she'd had a lifetime to polish them. Knowing this helped ease the frustration he felt from being burned by her lies. Trauma could do that to a person. He'd seen it too often in his line of work where someone detached from society to protect themselves.

Those tendencies usually caused folks to fall into the trap of abusing drugs or alcohol, sometimes both. Based on what Summer had said so far, he believed Autumn had developed an alternate persona instead.

It was a shame she'd had to do that in order to survive their upbringing. He had even more respect for Summer as he got to know her. She embodied strength and probably a little bit of stubbornness, too.

Any survivor had to have a stubborn streak. Used the right way, it could be very helpful because they didn't give up once they set their mind to a goal. Sometimes, that goal was simply not to let the past break them.

It was a rare quality to have that kind of determination when it seemed the world was against a person. *She* was rare.

There was no arguing Summer Grayson was special.

She squeezed his hand before letting go, took in a breath and then closed the distance to the counter. Standing right in front of Man Bun, she cleared her throat.

Dawson stood back and to the side, pretending to study something on the screen of his cell phone.

"Can I help y—"

Man Bun looked up. A hint of recognition passed behind his eyes before he plastered on a smile. Fake? Or was it the kind that people gave when they couldn't remember someone who obviously knew them?

"Hi. Remember me?" Summer plowed ahead through the awkward gaze. He had to give it to her. The stubborn streak made her strong when she probably wanted to bolt. The streak in her also meant justice was coming for her sister because Summer had the kind of tenacity normally seen in a starving pit bull going after a slab of meat.

Man Bun cocked his head to the side and squinted at her. This looked like he was trying to figure out if they'd dated or not. He gave the impression that she looked familiar but he couldn't place her.

"Autumn Grayson," she persisted.

Dawson scanned the room for anyone within earshot who took notice of the name. Nothing there. He sure as hell hoped this trip would be more productive in the investigation than it was turning out to be. He was about to take Summer to identify her sister's body. He couldn't think of a more awful thing for someone to have to do.

The only bright spot about this trip was supposed to be coming home with a lead to bring them one step closer to justice.

Man Bun threw his head back and smiled, genuine this time.

Dawson took a step closer to the counter so he could more clearly hear what Man Bun had to say.

"You remember me?" Summer did her best to sound perky. *Perky* wasn't a word he'd use to describe her personality. She was playing the part well, offering a bright smile as she put her hands up on the counter.

Dawson had no idea if she realized what that meant with her body language. But it was a show of trust, instinct at its finest, showing the person she was connecting with that she wasn't carrying any weapons.

"I do now." Man Bun stepped to the side where the counter was lower and nodded for Summer to follow. She did. He leaned across the smaller table like he was about to tell her a secret.

Dawson leaned a little closer and for reasons he didn't want to examine, the green-eyed monster reared its ugly head. He didn't like Summer getting anywhere close to Man Bun. The guy would be considered attractive by most. He looked like one of those celebrity soccer players from Latin America who made millions for his ability on the playing field.

"Where have you been?" Man Bun seemed to recognize Summer now.

"Around. You know how it is." Summer shrugged her shoulder, playing nonchalant.

"I almost didn't recognize you. Did you get a haircut?"

"How long has it been since the last time I was in here?" She paused, playing the ditz. She reached up and twirled a long strand of her wheat-colored hair. "I know it hasn't been so long that you would actually forget me."

Dawson stepped forward interrupting their conversation. He reached into his pocket and pulled out his wallet, flipping it open so that Man Bun would get a glimpse of his badge.

"How well do you know this person?" He nodded toward Summer.

Man Bun's eyes darted over toward someone on the line who was wearing a slightly nicer shirt and Dawson assumed was in management.

"Is that your boss?" Dawson followed the man's gaze.

Man Bun nodded. "One more strike and I'm out of a job."

"I can speak to him. This is official business."

"Nah, man. I don't want to make him suspicious. Just ask me what you want so I can get back on the line."

"How do you know Ms. Grayson?" Dawson asked.

"She's a regular. Comes in here all the time. Vanilla latte with whipped. It took me a second to recognize her because she looks different today."

"You talk to her a lot when she comes in?" Dawson asked.

"Sure." He shrugged his shoulder casually. "You know,

when it's not busy. She's a good tipper and we like to treat our customers more like family."

Man Bun's eyes kept darting back toward his boss. Obviously, the guy was on his last strike and Dawson didn't want to be the reason he ended up without a job. The guy's answers were genuine and as much as Dawson wanted this to go somewhere, it wasn't going to.

"One last question. Did you ever see her come in here with anyone?" Dawson asked.

Man Bun looked at Summer as though she'd lost her mind. It was pretty obvious she was standing right there and his question was written all over his face, *Why not ask her?*

"She never really came in with anyone. Every once in a while, she would go outside, and I would lose track of her. People come in here all the time." He glanced around as though the crowded room was his proof. "As you can see, we're pretty busy."

He nervously glanced over at his boss and then the ticker tape machine that was kicking out orders. "If that's all, man, can I get back to work? My orders are stacking up."

"That's all I need for now. We'll be back in touch if we have more questions." Dawson produced a business card from his wallet. "If you think of anything else, I'd appreciate a call."

"Yes, sir." Man Bun's gaze bounced from Dawson to Summer and back. "Can I go now?"

Dawson nodded before reclaiming Summer's hand. He linked their fingers and turned to walk out the door.

Man Bun did an about-face. "Hey, now that I think about it there were a couple of dudes in here the other day asking around if anyone had seen her. I was thrown off a minute ago and forgot all about it."

"Can you describe what they looked like?" Dawson asked.

The descriptions fit the men Summer had encountered to a T.

"Have you ever seen them around before?" Dawson continued.

Man Bun shook his head.

"Thanks for the information."

Summer's hand tightened around Dawson's. She had a death grip on his fingers. The men who'd tried to attack her and who'd planned to kill her had come looking for Autumn in the coffee shop. The killer must not know Autumn was dead.

She didn't speak until they got outside, walked half a block and made sure no one was around to overhear their conversation. She'd already replaced the ball cap and sunglasses, and he could almost feel her heart racing through her fingertips.

"He was being honest, wasn't he?" she asked.

"I believe so. I didn't detect any deception in his behavior."

The disappointment on her face was a gut punch. He squeezed her hand for reassurance and his heart took another hit when she looked up at him with those big violet eyes.

"Then, we'll keep going until someone has information about her."

DEAD ENDS WERE EVERYWHERE.

Summer took in a deep breath as she and Dawson made their way back onto the highway and toward Katy Gulch. The body suspected to have belonged to Autumn Grayson had, in fact, belonged to her sister. Decisions had been made about her sister's arrangements, despite the thick fog that had settled over Summer. Dawson had been a rock and she couldn't imagine doing any of this without him. The fact that he knew her sister at least on some level provided comfort. He seemed to genuinely care about what had happened to Autumn, despite her lies. That was the thing, underneath all those lies was a terrified person. The lies were like a wall that Autumn had used to keep everyone at a distance.

All Summer felt since was a deep dread and a sense of being completely numb. At some point, her brain might get to the point it could process what it had seen. Not without justice. Not without making those bastards pay.

Summer realized she'd been gripping the seat belt strap across her chest. At least she wasn't tapping the window. As far as nervous ticks went, hers were on full tilt.

About halfway home, Dawson's cell phone rang. He fished it out of his pocket and handed it over to her. "Do you mind checking to see who that is?"

She checked the screen. "It's your brother Colton."

"Would you mind answering and putting it on speaker?" Dawson's grip on the steering wheel was as tight as hers had been on her seat belt moments ago.

Obviously, seeing Autumn at the coroner's office was affecting him. He'd cared about her sister once. He was a decent human being. And he was being incredibly understanding about Autumn's personality layers.

She pushed the button to put the call on the truck's speaker.

"Hey, Colton. You're on speaker and I'm in my truck with Summer Grayson."

"I look forward to meeting you at some point, Summer." There was not a hint of judgment in Colton's voice.

"Likewise," Summer said. She'd like to have the

chance to meet all of Dawson's siblings. If they were half as decent and kind as Dawson, she couldn't think of a better caliber of men to be acquainted with. It was a foreign feeling to have one person who had Summer's back for a change. She couldn't even fathom having an entire support system in the form of a big family.

She'd never given much thought to having kids of her own. She always figured she'd get to a point financially where she could take care of herself and her sister. Open that small business they'd dreamed about. Then, she could think about a husband and possibly children down the road.

"What's going on?" Dawson asked his brother.

"Are you heading home?" Colton asked.

"On our way now," Dawson confirmed.

"You might want to make a U-turn."

Dawson navigated into the right lane and took the next exit. "What did you find out?"

"Gert has been doing some digging. You know Gert. Once she's on a scent, there's no stopping her."

Dawson glanced toward Summer. "Gert is his secretary."

Gert sounded like Summer's kind of person.

"I'm guessing she found something." Dawson said to his brother. His grip on the steering wheel tightened.

"It might be nothing, but it's worth checking into and I know you'll want to follow up on this yourself." Colton paused. "I apologize in advance for being frank with—"

"Please, don't worry about me. All I care about is justice for my sister," Summer said.

"Okay. Here's what Gert found. There was another strangulation victim in the Austin area. The tool used was a violin string. There was no DNA evidence in the case. The victim was twenty-eight years old and she had violet eyes."

"Same MO," Dawson muttered under his breath as he flipped on his turn signal and then banked a U-turn under the bridge.

Chapter Eleven

"I'll send you the file so you can take a look at witness statements." Summer wiped a stray tear as Colton continued, "It's a cold case."

She turned her face toward the passenger window like she was listening intently. In truth, she was trying to hold it together.

"How old is the case?" Dawson tapped his flat palm against the wheel.

"The murder happened two and a half years ago." The timeline could mean this guy moved on to Autumn. She might've gotten away and relocated to Katy Gulch to hide out where she met the one man who she believed could protect her. That would explain her wanting to stay on a secluded ranch and all the lies.

"What was her name?" Summer asked. She couldn't help herself. People in law enforcement would refer to her sister now as *the victim.* Summer wanted to know the young woman's name.

"Cheryl Tanning," Colton supplied.

Cheryl Tanning. She didn't deserve what happened to her, either.

"There were several suspects."

"Which one do you like?" Dawson asked.

"She used to frequent a coffee shop called Capital Coffee. Didn't you say you were visiting a place downtown that Autumn used to go to?" Colton asked.

Summer put her hand over her mouth to cover her gasp.

"We were just there," Dawson admitted.

In Summer's mind, the coffee shop would be a great place to scout a target for someone with an agenda. It was busy. All types of people came in and out. So much so, that people hardly noticed each other.

"So, it's the same place," Colton confirmed. "Okay."

"Is there mention of any other spots Cheryl used to hang out?" Dawson asked.

"That was the main place. There was a guy in her life, but her friends said she was very protective of him. No one knew who he was. A few names came up in the investigation. You'll see those in the file notes."

"I'll grab a place to stay. We might want to settle in for the night," Dawson said on a sigh. "I appreciate the information and tell Gert she did good work."

"She'll be tickled," Colton said before saying goodbye and ending the call.

The signs for Round Rock, a large suburb north of Austin, showed they were close to Austin again.

"Thought we might grab a place here for the night. We can take a look at the files and then follow up on any discoveries. There's every kind of food imaginable, which I can pick up. I'd rather you be seen as little as possible while we investigate." There was so much warmth and compassion in his voice. "And now it looks like we need to circle back and visit the coffee shop again."

She couldn't agree more with what he said. There was no reason for her to be exposed more than necessary.

His cell phone buzzed and she assumed that meant the file was coming through.

"I have a laptop and an overnight bag in the backseat."

She quirked a brow.

"Don't always get a ton of notice when I have to head out. I keep most everything in the trunk of my sedan. The bag here is just for backup," he explained.

Her mind was still churning over what they'd just learned but she nodded. She was interested in hearing the details of his job. Staying focused when her mind was reeling proved harder than expected.

A serial killer? That couldn't be. How would she explain the two men chasing her yesterday if Autumn was killed by a serial killer? Hit men weren't serial killers and they usually didn't have henchmen.

Oh, Autumn. More of those fresh tears sprang to her eyes. She blinked them back. At least she felt something besides numb. Had her sister been in a relationship with a murderer and not realized it until it was too late? What kind of person seduced his intended victims?

Dawson pulled off the highway and into a big chain hotel. She straightened her baseball cap.

"I'll check us in and be right back." Dawson left the truck idling and headed inside the lobby. He was back a few minutes later, card keys in hand. He slipped into the driver's seat and then pulled ahead to a parking spot.

Summer kept her chin to her chest as she exited the truck and waited for Dawson. He quickly grabbed his emergency bag from the backseat before locking up the truck and joining her.

He put his arm around her, shielding her from other eyes. To onlookers, the move might seem intimate. A husband and wife stopping off at a roadside hotel on their way somewhere else.

She knew he was covering as much of her as was humanly possible. She was able to hide more of her body and face.

Their room was on the fifth floor, number 510. Dawson opened the door to the small suite. There was a microwave and a mini fridge in the entryway along with a coffee maker and an assortment of coffees and teas. The bathroom was larger than the one in her Washington apartment. The shower was travertine tile and the vanity area was large enough for half a cosmetic store.

The main room had a work desk, a small table with four chairs and a seating area. A flat screen TV took up half the wall in the living room. There was a comfortable if slightly worn sofa and two armchairs along with a marble coffee table.

This place was larger than her apartment back home. *Home.* Where was that anymore? Home was a foreign word to her now. Thinking about a future without Autumn was like walking forever in the dark, knowing light was out there in the distance but too far for her to see it.

Until she looked at Dawson and saw a glimmer of hope. Hope that she might somehow find her way through this darkness and toward the sun again. Hope that she might not want to spend the rest of her life alone. Hope she could have things she'd long ago dreamed about but never believed would be.

Anger seeded because she didn't want to think about a future that didn't involve her sister. Where did she even start?

"There's only one bed in the suite. It's yours. I can make myself comfortable here on the couch," Dawson said by way of explanation.

"That won't be a problem. I trust you. You can sleep

in the same bed. I don't want to put you out." She was rewarded with a smile.

"It's no trouble." Dawson set his bag down, unzipped it and pulled out his laptop. He positioned it on the marble coffee table.

Summer moved next to him on the sofa and curled her left leg underneath her bottom.

"I want you to be prepared for the fact there are going to be graphic pictures. There's nothing wrong with skipping that part if you—"

She was already shaking her head. "I need to look at them. There might be something about her that reminds me of my sister. Something you wouldn't catch that I would."

Nothing in Summer wanted the images of a murdered Cheryl Tanning imprinted in her mind. But this was important. She would do whatever it took to find justice for her sister. This was the best way to see if there were any similarities.

He looked into her eyes like he was searching for confirmation it was okay to move forward. She gave him a slight nod before he fixed his gaze on the screen and opened a protected link.

There were two files in the one marked, Tanning Murder. The picture file contained two folders: evidence and victim. He clicked on the one marked Victim, and the screen was filled with thumbnails. He pulled up the first.

Cheryl Tanning's lifeless violet eyes fixed on a point above her. Her eyes were striking. Summer was always told that she and her sister had very rare-colored eyes. There was something haunting about the pair she was looking at.

Other than that, Cheryl Tanning was a beautiful young woman. She had pale skin and ruby-red lips. She had slightly darker hair than Summer and Autumn, and blunt-cut bangs. She was stunning. There was no question about that.

Dawson clicked on another photo and it was a full-body shot at the crime scene. Based on the photo, she looked to be about the same size as Autumn. Similar figures.

"This bastard likes a certain type." Dawson muttered a few more choice words under his breath.

She'd picked up on the similarities, too.

Her heart battered her rib cage as a weight dropped down around her arms. There was what looked like a wire wrapped around Cheryl's neck. They now knew it was a string from a violin.

What were the odds that Autumn would be killed by a similar method, two and a half years later? They had to be slim.

An icy chill gripped Summer's spine as she looked through the crime scene photos one by one. Dawson opened the case file next. A short description of the murder outlined that Cheryl Tanning had been found in an old dried up well on the back of someone's land. A group of teens who routinely rode dirt bikes on the property had stopped because of what they described as a smell that made them physically sick.

When they investigated, expecting to find an animal carcass, they received the shock of a lifetime when they found a body instead. All of the teens had been traumatized by the finding and during the course of the investigation had been cleared of any involvement.

There'd been a mystery man, who Cheryl's friends confirmed she'd been very secretive about.

"Do you think he was married?" Summer asked as she pointed to the screen.

"It's possible. A married man could have a lot to lose if word got out that he was having an affair." Dawson confirmed.

"It's Austin, so my mind snaps to a married politician," she admitted.

"Can't be ruled out. But those aren't the only powerful men in the capital or men with something to lose if word of an affair got out. There are three things we look for in a murder investigation: means, motive and opportunity," he stated.

"Opportunity wouldn't be difficult in a secret affair. The person would be used to meeting one-on-one in possibly secluded locations," she reasoned.

"True. Affairs are sticky. She was hiding his identity and was protective of him, which gives me the impression he was the power broker in the relationship."

"Someone older than her? Someone smarter or more cunning? Someone used to getting exactly what he wants from people?" she asked.

"That's along the lines of what I'm thinking," he confirmed. "I'd add to that someone who stands to lose a lot, be it money, prestige or social standing if an affair is uncovered."

"A murder conviction would rock his world." She caught herself tapping her finger on the marble coffee table as her brain started working overtime.

"Attorneys, bankers, anyone with a professional license would be in jeopardy."

"Look here." Summer pointed to the screen. "It says at least one of her friends thought she was getting depressed. He blames the affair."

"The jerk could've been manipulating her, asking her to do things she didn't want to. She might've complied for fear of losing him."

Autumn could be a manipulator. But the shoe could easily have been on the other foot. She wasn't strong mentally, and when it came down to it, a person could exercise power over her.

CHERYL TANNING HAD no visible signs of molestation. There was no DNA left on her body or found on the scene. Nothing under her fingernails. No sign that she'd fought back.

She'd been secretly dating someone. There was nothing in her cell phone record that would indicate she'd been seeing someone. Her credit cards showed no unusual activity. At least one of her friends regretted teasing her about being a call girl, saying she started having a lot more cash than usual. The response had been that Cheryl stopped returning calls and texts for a while.

The strangulation came from behind. The method of killing was personal. The killer would have to have been literally standing right behind Cheryl. She didn't fight back, so maybe she thought her lover was playing a joke or trying to arouse her.

There were several bruises on Cheryl's body in varying stages of healing. She worked as a waitress and took night school classes. A waitressing job could explain the bruises on her thighs and arms. But so could sexual exploration.

A defense attorney might argue Cheryl Tanning liked it rough in the bedroom. Or, at the very least, participated. Even if her lover had been identified, he wasn't necessarily guilty. Although, this kind of killing was personal. Staring at the evidence and the summary, Dawson was convinced the murderer was someone inside her circle despite the way the body had been dumped down the well.

The killer might have panicked. The police officer's report stated there'd been leaves tossed into the well after her body. Covering her up? Or covering her? As strange as it sounded, the sicko might have been covering her so she wouldn't get cold.

Dawson had seen enough deranged and sadistic people to last a lifetime. So, the leaves could actually be a sign of caring in a twisted way. Or a type of burial depending on religious affiliation. Even some cold-blooded killers believed they were spiritual. Hell, some killed out of ritual.

In this case, though, this bastard seemed well on his way to becoming a serial killer. The rule of thumb was three murders spread out over time.

If this killer believed that Autumn had lived, he would stop at nothing to silence her. There were all kinds of questions racing around in Dawson's mind.

"She didn't have a family, either," Summer noted.

"But Autumn did have a family. She had you."

"He didn't know that. Think about it, she hid me from you, too. I barely knew about you and the two of you were married." She made a good point. "Except that you weren't really."

"True." He rocked his head. "Then, that's part of his MO."

"Maybe he thinks no one will notice that they've gone missing and it'll give him more time to cover his tracks."

"I was thinking the same thing." Dawson pulled out the notepad and pen that he'd tucked into his emergency bag. He jotted down the fact the perp isolated his victims.

"Why did he decide to kill her, though?" she asked. "Like when did he know? The minute he started the affair?"

"It's possible. If Cheryl is his first victim, and so far Gert hasn't found any other that match this MO, he might have started the affair not knowing how it would end. At some point, he knew he was going to kill her."

"When he was done with her?"

"It's likely." He feared those words were like a physical blow. Of course, Summer would take them personally considering her sister was involved.

"My sister must've been scared of him. She might have felt backed into a corner with no way out," she continued.

It explained a lot about how she'd acted when he'd first met her and her actions after the fact. More of those puzzle pieces were clicking together.

"Do you think she figured out what happened to his former girlfriend?" she asked.

"It's highly possible."

"I just don't understand why she didn't go to law enforcement and explain her situation or tell me."

"Abusive men are master manipulators. He could've made her feel like he'd find her no matter where she went—"

"She could've come to me. I would've helped her find a way out of this."

"And she might think she would be bringing him right to your doorstep," he countered.

"The necklace. My name. You said it was one of her most prized possessions." Puzzle pieces were clicking together in her mind, too.

She tapped on the words they'd written on the notepad earlier. *Protect loved one.*

Chapter Twelve

A picture was emerging. Autumn had gotten into an unhealthy relationship that possibly even turned abusive. She didn't want Summer to know and so a couple of years ago, she withdrew.

The relationship became more than Autumn could handle. Luckily, she must not have told the guy about Summer. She'd kept her sister's identity safe and the necklace bearing her name locked in a box that she'd most likely kept hidden.

One day, Autumn decided enough was enough, or maybe things got heated between them and she began to fear for her life. Rather than go to Summer, and bring that blaze along with her, Autumn found a small town to hide in. Maybe she wanted to lay low.

Then, she met Dawson. He was honest and kind. It probably didn't hurt matters that he was smokin' hot. Maybe she even fell for him, fast and hard. He was everything she didn't have with the other guy.

There were perks to living with Dawson. He lived on a remote property and worked in law enforcement. As did several of his brothers. Autumn couldn't have asked for more or better protection. Her conscience got the best of her and she couldn't commit Dawson to an actual marriage, so she made up a pregnancy story, insisted on a low-key affair and then hired an internet guy who didn't care if proper papers were filed or not. It was a lot but sounded just like her sister to do something like this.

Summer relayed her theory to Dawson. It was met with nods of approval and that meant she was on the right path.

"The divorce makes no sense to me, though," she confessed.

"It was possible that he'd found her, or that she thought he would. She wasn't acting right in those last few weeks we were together. At the time, I chalked it up to her losing the baby. I tried to give her time and space to heal. I figured she would talk when she was ready but she just closed up. She stopped leaving the property and slept a lot of the time."

"Your logic sounds reasonable. Except that we both know there was no baby. So, he must've gotten to her somehow." How? was the question of the day. There was another bigger question…who?

"There were three suspects at the top of a short list in Cheryl's murder," Dawson said, pointing to the screen. "Sean Menendez, a creepy janitor, Jasper Holden, coffee shop worker and Drake Yarnell, ex-boyfriend."

"Okay. Where do we even start?" Something had been gnawing at the back of Summer's mind. She stared at the notebook page rather than the screen. Why was the name Charley bugging Summer?

"Is this exactly how my sister spelled the name, Charley? Just like it's written?" she asked Dawson.

"Yes. Why?"

She picked up the pen and wrote Cheryl next to Charley. "Does anything about this strike you as odd?"

"If I rearrange the letters and add an *a* the names are alike?" He rocked his head. "Look at that."

"She knew about Cheryl." That was the reason her sister was afraid. She knew about the murder.

"It's possible. She might have stumbled on a name and went to investigate. I can't imagine why she'd go back to Austin under the circumstances." Dawson tapped his finger on the screen. "We can start by interviewing Menendez, Holden and Yarnell."

More of those puzzle pieces Dawson had talked about before were being discovered. Finding where they fit and how they fit together was another story. Summer would take the progress. "I'm wondering why my sister went to the same coffee shop as Cheryl. Autumn didn't seem afraid to make her face known."

"It's possible she found evidence linking the murderer to the crime. If the perp found her in Katy Gulch, she had to know he would find her anywhere."

"Maybe he didn't know she'd found him out," Summer reasoned. "He could've convinced her to come back to Austin. Possibly even set her up in an apartment. Wine and dine her. She technically got away once. If this guy is a master manipulator, he might have convinced my sister that he loved her. He might have brought her back under his control."

Dawson nodded some more.

"He wasn't able to finish the job before. He wouldn't be able to let it go if he intended to kill her all along."

"What a sick bastard," Summer said.

"Agreed." The muscle in Dawson's jaw clenched.

"Then we're thinking that he lured her back in town." Summer hated the thought her sister could be manipulated. If the jerk said the right things, though, she could see her sister going back to him unless she knew he'd killed his other lover.

Autumn had had a knack for picking up guys who obsessed over her. At least until she'd met Dawson. He was the most levelheaded and down-to-earth person she'd ever met.

Summer hated all the secrets her sister held inside and all the lies. She hated that her sister couldn't just live a normal life and follow through on the dream of opening their own business. And she hated that she hadn't been able to protect her sister.

There was no use looking back now. A tidal wave of emotion was building inside Summer behind the wall that had kept her safe. There were cracks—cracks that threatened to pull her under and toss her around until she didn't know up from down anymore.

"You know, she wasn't always like this," she said on a sharp sigh.

"Tell me about it." Dawson clasped his hands together and rested his elbows on his thighs.

"The two of us were inseparable growing up. Our parents used to fight. I don't remember the details because we were so young when my father left. But I do recall feeling a sense of relief once he was gone."

"Kids pick up on so much. I've noticed it with my niece and nephew and they're only a year old. It's like a Record button has been hit in the back of their minds and someday, when they're much older, an invisible finger will hit Play. They won't even know why they're acting a certain way—it's just programming," he said.

"That's a really good point actually." Autumn had definitely recorded a lot of sadness. She seemed to take it more personally. "I can't say my sister even had good taste in the opposite sex." She flashed eyes at him, realizing how that would sound to him.

He feigned heartbreak before chuckling. "You really know how to hurt a guy's pride."

"Except for you," she quickly added.

"Right. Of course." Now he really laughed.

"No, seriously, I mean it. Don't take this the wrong way but I'm surprised you two were ever in a relationship. And what I mean by that is you're not normally her type. She always seemed to date guys who were edgy, you know, a little rough around the edges. Looking back, she always dated complicated people—a musician down on his luck or a guy in between jobs who needed her help. I used to always worry about her taste in men and told her she deserved better. Maybe that was part of the reason she came and found you. To protect her and show me that she was capable of finding someone who was amazing." She made the mistake of looking into his eyes as she said the last word.

DAWSON'S CHEST FISTED at the compliment. He couldn't afford to keep looking into those violet eyes without falling deeper into the well.

So, he coughed to clear his throat and asked, "What made you decide to work as a waitress?"

"I wanted to get experience in food service. I guess I saw it as my duty to take care of my sister and so we... *I...*dreamed of opening a small coffee shop together. Looking back, I did all the planning and talking about the coffee shop. She went along with it." There was a wistful quality to her eyes now. "She might not have wanted to hurt my feelings by saying she didn't want to open a business together."

"It sounds like you were trying to give her something to look forward to."

"True. I was. Now I'm wondering if I ran her off because I steamrolled over her."

"Don't do that to yourself. None of this is your fault."

"Oh, I doubt that. I should've done some—"

"I'm going to stop you right there. You didn't ask for this. You didn't contribute to this. As much as you might have felt responsible for your sister, you didn't do anything wrong. She had the will and the right to do whatever she wanted, and the person I knew did exactly that."

Summer paused and he hoped like hell she was letting his words sink in. This wasn't the first time she'd blamed herself for her sister's actions and if he could do anything else, he wanted to leave the impression with her that she didn't have to feel responsible. Adults were capable of making their own choices and did. Not all of those choices were good, and Autumn certainly made bad ones, but down deep, he didn't believe she was a bad person. Mixed up? Hell, yes. Confused? Absolutely. Bad? Not in his opinion.

"I hear what you're saying, and I know that in my mind. My heart is another story." She ducked her chin to her chest and turned her face away, a move he'd noticed she did to hide when she was getting emotional.

"It's okay to be upset. It's easy to see how much you love your sister. That's not going away and nothing will change that." He offered more words of comfort and when she turned to look at him, his heart took a dive.

She sat there, gazing at him, exposing her vulnerability to him. All he could offer by way of reassurance was a few words and his arms. He looped his arms around her, and she buried her face in his chest.

They stayed in that position for a long time. When she was ready to pull back, he feathered a kiss on her forehead. Being together with Summer like that, vulnerabilities exposed, was the most intimate moment in Dawson's life.

"Thank you." Her voice was shaky despite her chin jutting out.

"I'm here anytime. I mean that, Summer." He did. He meant long after this case was behind them and the grief settled in. Long after they were gone from this hotel room, from Austin and back into their normal everyday lives. He wanted to be there for her.

Summer and her sister didn't seem to have had a whole lot of breaks in life. He regretted that he'd missed so many signs with Autumn, but he would be there for Summer anytime she needed a friend.

"You can't know how much I appreciate it, Dawson." He could tell by the way she said those words she had no plans to take him up on his offer.

Why did that sting so much?

"So, Charley could possibly mean Cheryl." Summer brought the conversation back on track. "Which meant my sister either knew about Cheryl or heard the name."

Dawson nodded. "We're missing the connection, if there is one. Since you don't know much about your sister's daily habits, it's difficult to figure out where her and Cheryl's lives might have overlapped."

"That's true. It's interesting to note that Cheryl doesn't have any relatives who she was close to." Summer frowned and he immediately realized why. "So, they have that similarity. And we know that they both visited the same coffee shop. Maybe they lived near each other. Maybe that's another link. So, the perp lives or works in the area of the coffee shop."

Dawson wrote the question down on the pad of paper: "Did they live near each other or possibly know each other?"

"We know they looked alike and spent time in the

same area of town. They might have had a few other touch points."

"Your sister left the money I gave her in the bank. She never touched it. I still can't figure out why. She must've needed it," he said.

"Unless she went somewhere she didn't, which would mean she left you to go back to the perp."

"Why?"

Good question. One he intended to find an answer to.

Dawson didn't realize how late it was getting and neither one of them had really slept last night. He'd be fine running on a few minutes of sleep here and there but Summer looked absolutely wrung out. She needed food and rest.

"What do you think about taking a break and grabbing some dinner?" he asked.

"I seriously doubt I could eat anything," she countered.

"Would you be willing to try?" It was important and she might surprise herself like she had with the meatloaf.

"I probably should but I don't want to be alone right now." Her violet eyes pleaded.

Taking her with him carried risks. One could argue leaving her alone in a hotel room also left her vulnerable. The mental debate going on in his head was a force to be reckoned with and yet he knew in his heart he couldn't leave her there alone.

He thought about ordering food and staying in. That could draw unwanted attention and expose them should someone be watching the room. It was dark so the sunglasses wouldn't work. That, too, would draw attention. Granted, Autumn had always been done-up with full makeup and her hair done to the nines, and Summer went with an all-natural look. It was possible the perp could recognize her.

"You could wrap the scarf around your hair," he said.

She was on her feet faster than he could say, "Boo."

Her violet eyes were red rimmed. He wanted her to know how brave she was. Most would buckle under the circumstances and yet she kept pushing forward, searching for answers for her sister.

When she was finished covering her hair, he linked their fingers and walked with her outside. Glancing around, the hair on the back of his neck stood on end. Not exactly a warm and fuzzy feeling, but he was on high alert.

The feeling persisted during the entire walk to the truck. Again, he put his arm around her to shield her as much as possible from view. Being this close to Summer, breathing in her clean and flowery scent, filled his thoughts with the kisses they'd shared.

Under different circumstances, she was exactly the kind of person he'd want to spend time getting to know better. Now?

It was complicated. His feelings were complicated. And despite their off-the-charts attraction, acting on it any further would make things between them even more complicated.

And the crazy thing was that a very huge part of him didn't want to care about the consequences.

Chapter Thirteen

The restaurant was one of those taco chain spots found in every major Texas city. Loud music was playing when they entered and, unlike everyone else, she didn't love tacos. They were okay. Edible.

Summer pointed toward the booth in the corner where she and Dawson could continue talking about the case. The images of Cheryl Tanning would haunt Summer for a very long time. Erasing those wouldn't be easy.

And her mind drew the parallels to her own sister's case. Obviously, the bastard had killed Autumn in a similar way. It was impossible not to imagine Autumn's face instead of Cheryl's.

She'd tucked the notebook and pen under her arm before leaving the hotel room, just in case they wanted to jot down more notes. She placed the items on the table and scooted them toward the wall in case a server brought their order.

One word jumped out at her. *Suspects*. Below the word, there were three names. Dawson had explained that law enforcement officers had interviewed everyone they could find. Cheryl Tanning might not have had a family to stand up for her but she'd had a voice in the detective who had taken the case.

"Drake Yarnell, what do you think of him?" she quietly asked Dawson.

"He was an ex-boyfriend who was in a biker club. He had a jealous streak and I didn't like that at first. But the timeline of their relationship ending? They'd broken up almost a year prior. I doubt he still had the kind of feelings or possessiveness required to circle back and murder his ex-girlfriend."

"Even though their neighbors overheard him threaten to kill her if she walked out the door when they lived together?" she asked.

"He was a hothead. I can't see him waiting almost a year to act on his threat. It was idle, said in the heat of the moment. I still want to talk to him but he isn't sending up any red flags to me so far."

"Okay. How about Sean Menendez?"

"He was the creepy maintenance worker in her apartment complex." Dawson tilted his head toward her and then looked down at the pad of paper.

"Right."

"It's possible he had a thing for her and even more possible he was stalking her. Going down that path, she rebuffed him and that's the reason the detective thought he was a good suspect." Dawson made a face.

"You don't think so."

"Not really. Why would anyone cover the body with the leaves? And what's the connection to the violin strings?" he asked.

"This detective believed he might've found the strings in one of the trash bins," she stated.

"Which makes sense and would be possible. But then, what about your sister? How is she connected to the apartments and this guy? Did she live there? He's a creep, don't get me wrong. If I was a beat cop, I'd be keeping an eye on him. But, I can't connect him to Autumn and we're banking everything on these two cases being connected." His lips formed a thin line.

The waiter brought their taco baskets, so they tabled the discussion for the moment. The minute he left, they started up again.

"So, Jasper Holden? What are your thoughts about him?" she asked.

"He was a server at the coffee shop and that meant he would know both of the victims. He might not *know* them but he was acquainted with them both. Or at least, we think he was. He would've seen both of them coming and going, except that they might not have been there at the same time," he said. "He was a biochemistry major, which meant he was smart."

"Did he graduate by now?" she asked. It might be harder to track him down if he'd moved on. People came from all over Texas and beyond to attend UT in Austin. It wasn't an easy school to get into and a major like biochemistry would be even harder. Jasper would've had to have been pretty brilliant to pull that off. She wondered if he'd played in his high school band.

"I can't remember off the top of my head if he was a junior or senior at the time of Cheryl's murder. Could rule him out if he'd graduated and moved away at the time of Autumn's murder."

"There's another thing that's been bothering me about my sister. How did she have money for things like coffee? As far as we know she didn't have a job. And she didn't touch the money you put in the account for her." The fact he'd done that despite how her sister had treated him was above and beyond honorable.

"It's possible she had a job. The coroner's office had very few of her personal belongings. No purse, no wallet and no cell phone. It's a big part of the reason he was having trouble identifying her."

"And also unheard of not to carry those items around everywhere. I can't live without my cell." She nodded toward her purse.

"We could talk to the detective in the Tanning case. She might be able to give us insight into Jasper's current whereabouts."

"That seems like a good idea," she agreed.

"She also seemed especially thorough in Cheryl's investigation. It signals to me that she didn't want to give up on the case."

"What do you think happened?" Summer must've been hungrier than she realized because she finished off the beans and rice that came on her plate alongside her pair of tacos.

"Austin's a fairly large city with higher crime rates than what we see in smaller towns. These things generally come down to available resources. Detective Libby was most likely pulled from the case when she stopped making progress. She might've worked it on her lunch breaks or after hours but eventually leads dry up."

Summer shivered. An icy chill ran down her spine. The thought that Cheryl Tanning had died alone nearly broke Summer's heart. Their lives were not so different now. It wasn't like there was anyone at home waiting for Summer. No life that extended much beyond a small group of coworkers at the diner who she spent hours on end with but barely knew on a personal level.

Actually, that wasn't entirely true. She knew about Marta's boyfriend who revved his motorcycle engine out front to signal he was ready to pick her up after her shift was over. She knew that Dane, one of the cooks, had tattoos running up both arms. He used to joke that he'd gotten them so no one would try to chat him up in line to get his morning coffee. He was the biggest teddy bear once she got to know him.

Summer, on the other hand, shared very little about her private life with her coworkers. She'd always seen the diner as a temporary stop, a place she shouldn't get too comfortable. She'd always played her cards close to her chest, sitting quietly in the breakroom while the others talked about weekend plans or bills due.

She'd gotten so good at keeping everyone at a distance, not unlike Cheryl or Autumn. Cheryl probably had goals. She was probably working toward something when her life had been cut short. Everyone had a dream. Didn't they? Everyone deserved to live out their potential.

Seeing two lives cut so drastically short sent a hot, angry fireball through her veins. Her eyes were too dried up to cry. She let those tears flow earlier in sweet release.

The anger motivated her to find answers. If Sean Menendez wasn't the killer, or Jasper Holden, or Drake Yarnell, Summer wouldn't stop until she figured out who was. The small amount of money she'd socked away for the business would be enough to get by. She'd been afraid to turn up at the bank after the jerks had chased her.

An idea struck.

"I could draw him out, Dawson."

"We talked about this before. This bastard isn't getting within five feet of you."

"Think about it. I could hang out at the coffee shop. My sister used to go there and so did Cheryl. That means this jerk might go there, too," she countered.

"Yeah? What if that's true. Do you really want to walk right into his hands?"

"I could dress up like my sister—"

"I think the words you're looking for are *a sting op-*

eration and it would be way too risky. No responsible law enforcement officer would use you as bait to bring out a deranged killer and I might not be able to cover you from every angle. He knows what you look like, which puts us at a huge disadvantage."

"You're right." She needed to do something. Sitting here, doing nothing, would drive her insane.

"We have to be patient."

IMPATIENCE ROLLED OFF Summer in waves. Dawson understood. They were still studying the facts of the case and it wouldn't feel like they were making any progress to her. The way she was twisting her fingers together, picking up her food just to put it down before eventually taking a bite told him that her nerves were on edge.

It was easy to feel like they were spinning their wheels at this stage of the investigation. They were making progress, though. Slow, steady progress. Inch by inch but he'd take it. They had a similar and linked case to work with. It was a lot more to work with than what they'd had twelve hours ago.

Getting a strong lead with no real break was frustrating. Dawson had been involved in enough investigations over the years to know not every case was solved. As sad and frustrating as it was, there were times when the trail went so cold there was nothing left to follow.

And yet, he couldn't let himself think they wouldn't find the truth. Besides, they had a secret weapon. They had Colton and Gert back in Katy Gulch. Once Gert latched on to a case, her nickname quickly became Pit Bull.

The name responsible for Cheryl's and Autumn's murders were not in that file. Dawson was almost one hundred percent positive, which didn't mean he wouldn't retrace Detective Libby's tracks. He had every intention of interviewing Jasper Holden, Drake Yarnelle and Sean Menendez. Dawson never knew when a seemingly insignificant piece of evidence or interview might blow the case wide-open.

When he glanced over at Summer and realized she'd cleaned her plate and was studying the paper that contained their notes like it was the night before a final exam, he knew it was time to go. Her finger tapped double time on the wood table, a sign her stress levels were hitting the roof again.

The waiter stopped by the table and asked if they needed anything else.

"Just the bill," Dawson said, noticing how much the good-looking waiter kept staring at Summer.

She was beautiful, and he'd noticed most men checked her out when she walked into a room. Not exactly easy to keep her on the down low. Dawson tried to convince himself that was the reason their stares burned him up and not because a piece of him—a growing piece at that—wanted them to stake a claim on each other.

The waiter disappeared, returning a minute later with the bill. Dawson always carried cash. He never knew when he would need it on the road or in a small town, so he'd learned to keep a small stash with him at all times. This was one of the times he was grateful for the habit because he was ready to get her back to the hotel and out of plain view.

He wrapped his arm around her as they headed out the door, again noticing how right she felt in his arms. Again, ignoring the part of him that wanted this to be permanent.

It was dark outside and would be easier to move around at night without risking her. Most of the time, his witnesses were moved under the cover of night. Of course, it all depended on where he was going. Night in a big city still bustled with activity and no one really paid much attention to each other after a quick, primal is-this-person-a-threat-to-my-safety check.

Clean-cut couples barely hit the radar. That was always a good thing in Dawson's line of work and generally the goal. Colton had been in touch with Detective Liddy to let her know about the connection to Autumn and what they were now investigating. Dawson had to follow the right channels.

"I want to make a pit stop before heading back to the hotel." He'd scratched down Drake Yarnell's address on the notepad.

"Oh, yeah?" Summer's face lit up and he wondered if she realized how much danger she was in, *still* in, despite being with a US marshal.

"Yarnell lives in downtown, on the southwest side of Austin. I'd like to swing by his last known address. Detective Libby wrote down that he'd taken over the family home once his mother passed away five years ago. I'm thinking it's a safe bet he still lives there if the house is paid for. Holden and Menendez could be more mobile, especially Holden." They already knew one was a college student and the other worked at the apartment complex where Cheryl lived. A few years after the fact, he might've moved on. It was a safe bet he would stay in the same line of work but that didn't mean he would be at the same place of employment.

She nodded quietly and he wondered what was going through her mind. It took him a second to register that she would be wondering if she was about to come face-to-face with her sister's killer.

He walked her to the passenger side of the truck, and opened the door. Not because he didn't think she was capable of doing it for herself, but it was part of that cowboy code that required putting others first. It was a tradition well rooted in a Texan and one he hoped would never die.

Aside from being ingrained in him, it was protection for Summer. The less she was visible, the better.

He ignored the fact that he liked being in constant physical contact with her.

Chapter Fourteen

The southeast area of Austin's downtown was a row of bungalow-style houses in various states of disrepair. Rentals to university students—the kind who used lawn furniture inside the house and might have a keg on tap at all times but no food in the fridge—ensured the area was prone to crime.

As always, there were a few residents who'd decided to stick it out and whose social security checks or pensions weren't enough to cover new sod when needed or paint.

It was an interesting mix on Fourth. There was a steady wail of sirens in the background and, despite being what most might consider a rough area, an almost constant stream of foot traffic regardless of the late hour.

He pulled the truck up to the house across the street from Yarnell's place and pointed. "His is that one."

The porch light wasn't much more than a bulb hanging from a wire, and it kept blinking. Not exactly a good sign for stable electricity. He reminded himself to ask Yarnell to step outside. Getting fried by electrical current wasn't high on his list of favorite things.

Lights were on inside the house. Didn't necessarily mean Yarnell himself was home but someone had to be. One of the lights in the front window turned off. Proof someone was moving around.

The front door opened, and a big burly guy stepped out.

"Wait here," Dawson requested as he hopped out of the driver's seat. The person's back was to him. The guy wore a black leather jacket with a massive orange logo covering the entire back. It explained the motorcycle parked in the front yard and they already knew Yarnell was a biker from Cheryl's case file.

Dawson crossed the street and made it to the metal fencing with overgrown scrub brush winding through the slats.

"Excuse me," he said.

Motorcycle Guy turned his head to one side but didn't look at Dawson. "Can I help you?"

"I hope so. I'm looking for Drake Yarnell." This guy fit the physical description of five feet eleven with a stocky build. His arms were covered by the jacket so Dawson couldn't tell if there were tattoos. But then, tattoos in Austin were commonplace so they didn't exactly stand out necessarily as an identifier. According to the files, Yarnell had a snake winding up his left arm, the tail of which stopped at the middle finger on his left hand. Now that was distinctive.

Dawson's question got the guy's attention. He slowly turned, looking ready for a fight. Dawson noticed his right hand fisted around his key. There was no reason to poke the bear.

"You found him."

Yarnell had grown a beard and mustache since the photos of him were taken two years ago. He looked like he'd aged more than two years but hard living could do that and, based on the condition of his home, it looked like he was doing just that. There were empty beer cans littering the yard. Dawson wasn't sure he wanted to know what else was.

"I'm a friend of Detective Libby's. My name is US Marshal Dawson O'Connor." He pulled out his wallet and produced his badge.

Yarnell's dull blue eyes widened. His skin was sun-worn, his hair a little too long, and it looked like he'd just gotten off tour with a heavy metal band with a red bandana keeping his hair out of his eyes.

"I told the detective I wasn't involved then and nothing's changed, man." Yarnell put his hands in the air, palms out, in the universal sign of surrender. "But I hate that Cheryl's gone and hate the bastard that killed her."

"Good. Because I'm here in the hopes you can help us find him and lock him away forever."

"I'd like to help out but I'm late for work. You know how it is." If Yarnell was waiting for Dawson to ask him to schedule an appointment and give another statement he had another think coming.

"All I need is a couple minutes of your time," Dawson said.

Yarnell glanced at his watch before glaring at Dawson. "I'll do it for Cheryl. But, damn, I thought this whole thing would go away by now."

There was a weariness in Yarnell's voice that said he'd been put through the ringer. He'd been the prime suspect for a while according to the file. His shoulders deflated and it looked like the wind was knocked out of him.

"Not until her killer is behind bars," Dawson said, matching Yarnell's intensity.

"Fair enough." Yarnell relaxed his hand by his side. "What do you want to ask me that can't be found in my statement or in the files?"

"There's been another murder." Dawson figured coming out with the truth was the best way to gain Yarnell's cooperation.

"Who?" Yarnell asked.

"Autumn Grayson. Do you know her?"

Yarnell shook his head. His response was instant, which made Dawson believe the man was telling the truth.

"Do you think I did it?"

"No. But, to be honest, I would've interviewed you, too. Possibly more than once. Because Cheryl deserves justice and in talking to you, I might have found a clue." Using her first name would bring this conversation onto a personal level. It was personal, too. Any time a life was taken, it was personal for Dawson.

Yarnell's gaze traveled over Dawson like he was sizing him up for a fight.

"Good," he finally said. "Because she didn't deserve what happened to her."

"How did you first hear about the murder?" Dawson asked.

"When four cops showed up at my house with a battering ram," he stated matter-of-factly. "No one seemed to care that we'd been broken up for a while. I'd thought she was cheating on me and I said some things I shouldn't have. An older couple used to live next door and they were always calling the law on me. I guess my shouting at her gave them ammunition."

Dawson already knew Yarnell didn't retaliate against the neighbors. No additional reports had been filed against him despite the fact he'd been watched like a hawk.

"I'm a day late and a dollar short but I care about your history with Cheryl. When the two of you broke up, did you have any proof she was seeing someone else?"

"Nah, just a suspicion. She started acting weird. Secretive. She would disappear for a morning and get offended if I asked where she'd gone." He tucked his hands in his pockets. "Hell, I was just curious at first but after a while I started to think something was up. She would tell me she had to work an extra shift at the hospital where she checked patients in and then I'd show up to surprise her with dinner but her coworkers said she wasn't on the schedule. She got real upset about me going to her job."

"Did you stop?"

"Yeah." He shrugged. "I'm not going to lie. I waited out in the parking lot for her a few times with my lights off. I got caught by the night guard once and he threatened to turn me in if I did it again."

"Was that the end of it?"

Yarnell shrugged. "I'm not proud of the fact now but I used to drink and I waited for her more than once across the street from the hospital. She always parked in the south lot. I'd cruise through with a friend to see if her car was there."

"Was it?"

"Sometimes. Others not so much. She would make up some lame excuse about having to leave early. I guess she got tired of all the questions and moved out."

"She lived with you here?"

"For a few months. She didn't have enough saved up for her own place. She needed first and last month's rent, which was pretty steep. So, she stayed here and cooked instead of pitching in for rent. My roommates weren't crazy about it at first but they got over it. It's my house."

Dawson nodded. The report never said she'd lived with Yarnell. The detective must not have thought the fact was important. He couldn't say he would agree with the assessment and it also indicated a sloppier investigation than he would've liked to see.

"Over the course of your relationship, were you ever

physically violent with Cheryl? While you were drinking?" He added that last part after catching the look of disappointment in Yarnell's eyes. He seemed like the kind of guy who'd partied a little too hard and became something he wasn't proud of. The report said he couldn't hold down a job and Dawson wondered if the drinking was a big part of that.

"I left marks on her arms a couple of times from grabbing her too hard. If you're asking if I roughed her up, the answer is no. She did come home with bruises sometimes. It got worse after she moved out. Suddenly, she had enough money to pay the deposit on her apartment. I stayed over once or twice and there was cash in her nightstand—"

Again, Yarnell put his hands in the surrender position.

"Hey, I was just looking for a condom. I wasn't rooting through her stuff like some crazed stalker."

"When was the last time you saw Cheryl?"

"Alive or dead?" He was goading now, understandably angry at having to dredge up what must've been a painful past.

Dawson didn't respond. There were times when it was a good idea to shut someone down and remind them to be respectful and there were times when the law had chewed someone up and spit them out on the other side. Yarnell would pull it together if given a minute to regain his composure. His stress level was through the roof and he looked like he was about to blow. He needed a release valve. In this case, a few minutes to blow out a sharp breath and reset was all it took.

He covered his mouth with his hand, a move someone did right before they were about to lie. In this case, though, he seemed like he didn't want to say the words he had to say next.

"I saw dead pictures of her. The detective, the blonde... what was her name again?"

"Libby."

"Right." He blew out another breath and looked up to the stars. "The Big Dipper."

"Excuse me? I'm not following."

"It was Cheryl's favorite. She pointed it out every time we went outside at night. She would stop in the middle of the street and search for it." He hung his head. "I can't count the number of times I had to pull her out of the road before she got hit by a car."

Dawson had seen this before in investigations. The person interviewed needed to remember something good about the deceased. The memories just bubbled up and it was like they had to come out. Remembering was a good thing. It connected Yarnell to Cheryl's memory. It would rekindle his anger that her life had been cut short.

"I can't say that I remember anymore. Whatever I said in the report is right. It had been months since I'd seen or heard from Cheryl, but I lost track of how many." He glanced down at an empty beer can with a deep longing. Like he needed one of those but couldn't because of work.

"The report says she called you a week before her murder. The call lasted forty seconds," Dawson pointed out.

"My girl answered when she saw my ex's name. She said a few choice words and Cheryl never tried to call back. Detective Libby brought that up a lot before. She swore I was lying but it's the truth. I never spoke to Cheryl before..." His voice broke on that last word and he turned his face away before clearing his throat and regaining his stiff composure. "I never got a chance to say goodbye."

Drake Yarnell's suffering could be seen in his weary eyes. "What if she was calling for help or to get back together. If she'd come back to me, I could've taken care of her."

It was easy to see Yarnell cared for Cheryl and that he'd been racked with guilt ever since her death.

Dawson brought his hand up to Yarnell's shoulder in a show of comfort. "You didn't know what was about to happen. There's no way to go back and undo the past. Try to make peace with it if you can."

"I appreciate that, bro." Yarnell seemed genuine and his honesty touched Dawson. One of the bright spots in his job was being the one to help someone see a tragedy wasn't their fault or helping a family find answers or justice.

He was frustrated that he hadn't been able to do that for Summer, or for Autumn for that matter.

"If you ever need to talk." Dawson pulled a business card out of his wallet. "I'm around."

Yarnell looked Dawson in the eye like he couldn't believe his ears.

"That's cool, bro. Uh, thanks."

What was the point of his job if he couldn't help people? He was usually picking up some lowlife with a felony warrant who'd evaded law enforcement and was considered dangerous. Yarnell had made mistakes in his past and Dawson would never condone being physical with the opposite sex.

He did, however, believe in second chances if any person was serious about cleaning up his or her act.

"I'm serious. Use it."

"I will." Yarnell took the offering. Those dull blue eyes held a momentary spark of hope—hope that he might get some relief from the hell he'd been living in since the dark day Cheryl was murdered.

This was the hell of investigations. A suspect who was innocent. The toll it took on a person's life.

"I'll let you get to work on time."

Yarnell nodded and tucked the business card in the inside pocket of his leather jacket. As Dawson left the yard, he accidentally stepped on a beer can, crushing it with his boot. He kicked the can aside before making his way back to Summer.

"He's innocent. There's nothing more to get out of him," Dawson said as he reclaimed his seat. He'd left the keys in the ignition in case Summer had needed to make a quick getaway.

"I'm wondering if the coffee shop is still open. Maybe we could stop by there and ask around for Holden."

He glanced at the clock as he navigated down the small residential street. There was barely enough room to get through with cars parked on the street and being in his truck wasn't helping. This part of Austin had the most narrow streets. He was used to it, having been here countless times to apprehend a criminal. But it was making Summer nervous based on her expression as he squeezed through.

As he turned on his blinker and pulled up to the light of a busy intersection, Summer gasped.

She pointed her finger at a guy who was walking behind a young woman. She seemed to be alone. Earbuds in, she didn't seem to be paying attention to her surroundings.

"That's him. That's one of the guys who was chasing me the other day," Summer said.

Chapter Fifteen

Summer's pulse raced as adrenaline pumped through her veins. She flexed her fingers a few times, trying to release some of the pent-up nerves as she sat ramrod straight in her seat. The guy who'd almost grabbed her stared at the back of the head of the woman walking ahead of him.

Thick Guy's arms extended, his focus laser-like, about to grab the unaware young woman. An icy chill raced through Summer and an involuntary reflex caused her to shout. No one would hear her inside the truck with the windows rolled up.

Dawson cut over to the other side of the street, and then pulled alongside the curb. He was out of the truck before Summer had a chance to take her seat belt off. The burst of adrenaline that put her body on high alert also caused her hands to shake.

She fumbled with the clasp but finally got the thing off. It pulled back with a snap against the door, but she was already shoving her shoulder into the door to open it.

Summer was out of the vehicle and gunning toward the young woman in seconds. She stumbled over the curb and nearly face planted. Taking a few steps to right herself, she glanced up in time to see a sneer on Thick Guy's face. Another chill raced down her back.

Thick Guy's gaze bounced to Dawson. A look of shock and then anger crossed his features before he turned and bolted in the opposite direction. For a sturdy guy, he had a superfast gait. Dawson turned up the gas and was right behind the perp.

The young woman glanced around and seemed to realize what had been about to go down. Her mouth fell open, her eyes widened and her skin paled. She tapped the white bud in her ear and started crying.

"You're okay," Summer soothed as she wrapped the young woman in an embrace. "Nothing happened. You're fine."

The young woman bawled in her arms. Summer was keenly aware that Thick Guy had had an accomplice last time. She scanned the area, searching for Scrappy. She also keenly realized she and the young woman were alone. Dawson had disappeared down the dark street.

"What's your name?" Summer asked, trying to get the young woman to focus on something besides what had almost just happened.

"Harper."

"Here's what we're going to do, Harper. We're going to go into my friend's truck and wait for him. Don't be scared. He works in law enforcement," she said as calmly and evenly as she could.

"Okay," came out through sobs.

Harper looked to be no older than nineteen. Summer walked the young woman over to the truck and locked them both inside.

"Do you live around here, Harper?" Summer asked.

"No." Harper shook her head. "I was walking to the UT shuttle after a study group meeting a few blocks away from here."

There were bus stops all over the city for UT students.

Right about then, Summer caught sight of Thick Guy walking toward them. Head down, hands behind his back, he looked to be in handcuffs. He heaved for air.

Dawson shoved him across the hood of the truck and wiped blood from his busted lip. Panic washed over Summer at the thought anything could happen to him. She reminded herself that he was standing right there, on his phone, most likely calling in what he'd seen so Thick Guy would be taken in.

Face down, Summer couldn't see Thick Guy's face. But she knew it was him. He had the same height and build. The same black hair. He turned his head to the side and tried to look through the windshield. She caught a glimpse of those same dark eyes.

"Is that him?" Harper asked even though the answer was obvious. She was practically hyperventilating.

"Yes. He's handcuffed and going to jail." If not for what he was about to do to Harper, then what he'd almost done to Summer.

Was hers a random attack? There was no way. She distinctly remembered him and his friend talking about Autumn. What had they said? *She just won't die.*

Summer couldn't imagine her sister getting involved with Thick Guy or Scrappy. Were they for hire? Had Thick Guy seen a pretty young coed walking down the street and decided to take one for himself?

She shivered and her skin crawled at what could have just happened to Harper.

"I need to call my roommate and let her know that I'm going to be late." Harper's voice sounded small and scared.

"Okay. Where's your phone?" Summer asked when Harper didn't immediately make a move.

"My backpack." Harper shrugged the floral-patterned

quilt-like material backpack off her shoulder. She unzipped it as tears streamed down her face.

"Hey, he didn't get to you. You're going to be all right. You're safe." Summer looked into Harper's eyes, willing her to be strong. She looked even younger with red, puffy eyes.

"Thank you for stopping. I didn't even hear him over my music, and he must have been right behind me."

"He's done this before. He didn't want to be heard," Summer said.

"I don't know what I would've done if you hadn't shown up when you did."

Summer didn't want to think about it. Thick Guy seemed strong. Harper probably didn't weigh more than a hundred pounds wet. She was five feet two inches in heels.

"Call your roommate so she doesn't worry. We'll give you a ride home," Summer said. She doubted Dawson would mind that she'd made the offer.

Harper made the call and got through it with a few more sobs. Her roommate promised to be home and to wait up for her. Summer was relieved the young woman wouldn't be alone. She would be experiencing the effects of that trauma for a long time to come if Summer had to guess.

"Is it okay if I call my mom?" Harper asked.

"Of course, it is. Where are you from?" Summer wanted to calm Harper down before she worried her parents.

"San Antonio," Harper said, gripping her phone like it was a grenade.

"Is this your freshman year?"

Harper nodded. Her eyes were still saucers and she was probably still in a little bit of shock.

Lights with sirens filled the air. A patrol car pulled up alongside the curb. An officer got out and within a few minutes, Thick Guy was seated in the back of a squad car. The officer took statements, and then thanked them.

Dawson introduced himself to Harper once the dust had settled.

"I said we'd take her home," Summer said.

There was no hesitation in Dawson's voice as he agreed. Within twenty minutes, he reached the address on campus and deposited Harper at her dorm. He returned to the truck and asked, "How are you doing with all this?"

"Fine. It's crazy to run into him."

"I'm sure as hell glad we did. He invoked his right to remain silent," Dawson said as he navigated them back onto the freeway that, even at this time of night, was stacked with vehicles.

"He's obviously been in this situation before."

"Wouldn't surprise me if he had a rap sheet longer than my arm," Dawson admitted.

"The officer said he'd see us at the station. Does that mean we're headed there now?" she asked.

"No. He won't talk and there's nothing we can do about it. You already gave your statement. We'll swing by tomorrow morning when the detective who worked Cheryl's case is in. I have a few questions I'd like to ask her."

"You don't like how she handled the investigation, do you?" It wasn't really a question.

"Not really. I think she tried to pin the whole thing on Yarnell. He was a little too easy to try to nail. But the guy didn't do it. An experienced detective would've seen it right away. I'd like to know what I'm dealing with when it comes to Detective Libby and that's best done in a face-to-face meeting."

Despite cars as far as she could see on either side of

her, in front of her and behind her, they were still moving. The progress was slow but she'd take it.

Forty minutes later in a drive that should've taken fifteen, Dawson pulled in front of the hotel and then around to the side of the building to park.

"I hope Harper called her mom." It was a strange thought to have now. Summer wondered what is was like to have that. She'd known that her mother had loved her children in her own way. She'd just been so broken that she kept herself too medicated to show it.

If Summer ever became a mother, she'd be the kind a child wanted to call in an emergency. Someone a child could lean on during tough times. She'd want to be part of her child's life like she imagined Dawson would be. His entire family was a support system for each other. What was that even like?

If she had a child, and she'd never really given it much thought, she'd want to have one with a man like Dawson. He'd be an amazing father.

Summer gave herself a mental slap to root herself back in reality.

Where did all that come from? She'd never once thought about what it would be like to have children. Now she couldn't help but wonder if it was because she'd never been around a man she trusted enough to try.

DAWSON WALKED SIDE by side with Summer through the hotel lobby. At this hour, there were very few folks downstairs. The only group he saw was a family of four with their luggage being wheeled to the check-in desk.

He and Summer made it to the room without anyone giving them a second look.

"Do you think it's an odd coincidence that the guy

who was after me was in Drake Yarnell's neighborhood?" she asked.

"His name is Jesse Lynch." Dawson couldn't say he was surprised. "It's one of the worst neighborhoods in Austin. We got lucky running into Lynch when we did but I can't say I'm surprised we saw him in that general area."

"Do you think he was behind the murders?" she asked.

"Not Lynch. I do believe he's for hire and someone used him to get to your sister and possibly Cheryl. A violin string might be his MO."

"Autumn and Cheryl didn't know each other as far as we can tell." Summer kicked off her shoes and reclaimed her seat on the sofa.

Dawson joined her, opening the laptop and entering the password to bring the screen to life.

"They were connected by the killer," she continued. "That's obvious. But it was someone they'd both dated."

"There's the coffee shop," he added.

"I can't help but think we need to park it there tomorrow and watch everyone who comes through those doors." The lines in Summer's forehead deepened as she concentrated. Her lips pursed and her unfocused gaze stared at the screen even though she wasn't really looking at it. "If he walks in, he's bound to have some kind of reaction to seeing me alive."

"It will also alert him to the fact you exist. Your sister seemed to go to great lengths to keep you hidden and I'm certain it was for good reason."

"What about the necklace, though?" she asked. "She had to know you'd go through her stuff eventually even if it was just to toss it in the trash."

"It's possible she wanted me to figure out the connection with you." It was all speculation but that was all they had at the moment.

"What about Sean Menendez?" she asked.

"We can stop by the apartment complex on our way in town," he said. He also made a mental note to check with Detective Libby about the name Matt Shank, the fake lawyer name that Autumn had put on the divorce papers.

Summer glanced at the clock on the wall and bit back a yawn. "What time do you want to head downtown tomorrow?"

"We could get a jump on traffic. Say, six o'clock in the morning. If the apartment complex doesn't net any leads we could stop for breakfast before heading to the station." He wanted to stay up and peruse the files to get a better handle on all the statements and evidence.

Summer excused herself to the bathroom, returning twenty minutes later wearing a hotel bathrobe. She had the waist cinched up tightly. She stopped at the doorway to the bedroom. She bit her bottom lip and shifted her weight from side to side. Was she nervous?

"Will you lie down with me until I fall asleep?" she asked. "Every time I close my eyes, I see those pictures in my head." She motioned toward the laptop and he immediately knew she was talking about Cheryl.

"Yeah, sure." He said the words casually like lying down next to Summer in bed would be no big deal. His pulse kicked up thinking about being in such close proximity to her. Since he no longer ran on hormones and caffeine like in his younger days, he told himself he could handle it. And he could. There was no way he'd cross a boundary with Summer that she didn't want.

The problem was that when he stood up, he saw desire in her eyes. Desire for comfort. Desire to get lost in someone. Desire to shut out the world for just a few hours.

Dawson took her by the hand and linked their fingers, ignoring all the electrical impulses firing through him as best he could. It wasn't easy. Being this close to Summer wasn't easy. But the easy road was underrated.

He lifted the covers for her, and she climbed into bed. He knew better than to follow, so he toed off his boots and propped up a couple of pillows. He sat on top of the comforter and even then his heart detonated when she curled her body around his.

Dawson watched as she fell into a deep sleep beside him. He closed his eyes, telling himself a catnap would do him some good.

The next sound he heard was the snick of a lock.

Chapter Sixteen

"Housekeeping." The small voice along with a knock on the door caused Dawson to shoot straight up to standing.

The sun was already up and he realized he'd fallen asleep. He couldn't remember the last time that had happened when he'd intended to stay awake. He missed the feel of Summer's warm body the minute he stood up.

A cursory look said he hadn't peeled his shirt off in the middle of the night and his jeans were still snapped. He was decent enough to face the person coming into their room. He cursed himself for not putting the Do Not Disturb sign on the door handle.

He moved to the doorway, trying not to wake Summer as he glanced at the clock. Seven a.m.

"Sorry," he said to the short, middle-aged woman standing at the door. She couldn't be much taller than five feet. "My wife is still asleep. Do you mind coming back in about an hour?"

"No problem, sir." The round woman with the graying hair and kind eyes waved as she took a backward step in the opened door. "I'll come back."

"Thank you." Dawson followed her to the door and put the sign out. When he returned, Summer was sitting up and rubbing her eyes. Seeing that honey-wheat hair spill down the pillow he'd been sleeping on moments ago didn't do good things to his heart this early. He made a beeline for the coffee machine and raked his hand through his hair.

As the coffee brewed in his cup, he made a quick pit stop to the bathroom to wash his face and brush his teeth. Splashing cold water on his face helped shake him out of the fog that had him going down a path of real feelings for Summer.

She was in trouble and he was helping her out. That was all. She needed answers to what happened to her sister. That was all. He was going to nail the bastard who killed Autumn and then walk away from the Grayson family. That was all.

Too bad his mantra wasn't working. There were so many cracks in the casing around his heart there was no threat he'd use it instead of his Kevlar vest for protection.

As he exited the bathroom, Summer stood on the other side of the door. She squeezed past him as soon as he opened it.

"Coffee?" he asked.

"Yes, please." The door closed and he heard the water running as he moved into the next room. He didn't need to stick around the door and think about the fact she was naked underneath that robe any more than he needed the image of her waking up next to him etched in his brain.

Because it felt more right than anything had in longer than he cared to remember.

A couple of sips of fresh brew should shake his brain out of the fog and keep it on track. He brought both cups over to the coffee table and retrieved his cell phone. He called the station and identified himself. He was immediately transferred to a supervisor, which he'd expected.

"This is Sergeant Wexler. How may I be of assistance?" Wexler had one of those voices that made him sound like he'd been on the job longer than he cared to and had seen just about everything. He was the two *C*s: curt and courteous.

"My name is Marshal O'Connor and I'm calling to check on a suspect by the name of Jesse Lynch."

"Right." There was an ominous quality to Wexler's tone. "I'm sorry to be the one to tell you but Lynch hung himself last night."

This news was the first indication this case was bigger than Dawson realized. He'd been thinking the perp was someone small-time who'd dated Cheryl and then Autumn. He got a taste of what it was like to kill with Cheryl. It had possibly even been an accident or an argument that had gone too far. By the time he got to Autumn, he'd developed a taste for it. The guy was someone who had access to a violin string, an unlikely murder weapon. A musician or music teacher? It also made a statement because strangulation was a very personal method for murder.

"I'm sorry to hear the news." Dawson had no doubt in his mind that Jesse Lynch was not the type to hang himself in his cell, especially considering they'd caught him before he'd done anything to the young coed. The case against him wouldn't stick if he had a decent lawyer.

Summer was a different story altogether. But then all he'd done was chase her. He hadn't actually caught her. All the evidence against him was hearsay.

"It's a shame," Wexler said in a tsk-tsk tone. "Young people today have a lot of emotional problems. A university kid was sitting on the side of the road the other day with a flat tire. He was bawling and pacing. I calmed him down and told him I'd help him. I was tired. On my way home from a long day but if it was my kid, I'd want someone to stop. So, I'm working on the tire and he stops crying but instead of jumping in to help, do you know what he does?"

Wexler paused.

"Can't say that I do," Dawson supplied.

"He gets on his cell and starts snap-ticking a friend... or whatever that social media site is. The one where the kids send messages to their friends instead of calling."

Dawson wished Wexler would get to the point.

"I had to tell him, no-no. Get the hell off that thing and get over here. You're going to learn how to change a tire." He finished his sentence in ta-da fashion.

"Next time he'll know how to do it himself." Dawson had no idea how to respond or how this story was linked to Jesse Lynch's hanging.

"Yeah, that's what I was thinking. I can do it for him and he'll never learn or I can tell him to put the damn phone away and pay attention. These kids are lazy and the minute anything goes wrong, they fall apart." Wexler might believe that about Jesse Lynch but Dawson didn't.

Based on what he knew so far, Lynch was street-smart. He got by working the streets and taking what he wanted. He was from the wrong side of the tracks though. Not a kid who got busted for a dime bag of weed and thought his parents would never speak to him again.

This kid knew how to survive.

"Was he alone in his cell all night?" Dawson asked.

"According to the night watch, he was."

Dawson didn't like the sound of that. It could mean the killer was someone on the inside or had connections. The violin string bothered him, though.

"Thank you for letting me know about Lynch. That's unfortunate," Dawson said.

"Such a waste," Wexler said.

"Can you do me a favor?" Dawson asked.

"Sure, anything."

"Transfer me to Detective Libby." The quiet on the line sent another warning flare.

"She isn't around."

Dawson wasn't so sure what that meant but it sounded like a sore subject.

"When will she be back?" he asked.

"She's not with the department anymore," Wexler supplied.

"What happened?" Dawson asked.

"She left the department about two years ago."

"Do you have a forwarding address?"

"I can transfer you to personnel," Wexler offered.

Now Dawson needed to decide if the sergeant was involved or just complacent. His instincts said the latter was true.

"I'll call back another time." Dawson wanted to give the impression he didn't care all that much, so he added, "It's not that important."

Wexler seemed satisfied with that answer. "You take care."

"Will do." He ended the call. When he glanced up, he saw Summer studying him.

"What happened to Jesse Lynch?" Her forehead was creased with concern that their first lead had just dried up.

"He was murdered in his cell last night, but the department is calling it a suicide."

Stunned, Summer took a couple of steps backward until she sat in a chair at the small table. She seemed to pick up on the implication.

"I checked all the names of the politicians in Austin and didn't find a single Charles, Charlie, Charley or Matthew and no relation to the last name of Shank." Dawson reviewed his findings or lack thereof with her.

"So, Lynch is gone." She paused like she needed a minute for the news to sink in. Like saying it out loud made it that much more real and scary. "What about the detective on the case?"

"She quit the department six months after Cheryl's murder." The timing of her resignation was suspect as hell. The whole situation reeked of foul play.

"And this is the same department that is going to investigate my sister's murder?" Summer brought her hand up to her face.

"They gave Cheryl's case to a young detective. I'm guessing they didn't expect her to do a very good job being so green," he stated.

"Except that she stayed with it. We thought she was pulled off the case and it was marked cold, when it turns out she left the department. What would make her do that?"

"I'll ask Colton to look into it and see if he can dig up some information. He has a trusted contact at Austin PD and that might be our best route. I can call human resources but they won't be able to give out personal information about the detective." Her exit must have been the reason the investigation stalled.

"What would make her up and leave like that?"

"Bribery. Threats. Your guess is as good as mine. If we can figure out where she landed after leaving and how she's living now, we'll have a better idea of the reason."

And just who the department was trying to protect.

THIS NEWS WAS BIG. It screamed cover-up. And if the same person killed Autumn, there'd be no justice for her. If the person was so big or connected that he could make a detective leave her job and a witness be killed in jail and marked as a suicide, how could they bring him down? Who would listen?

"I got away," she said under her breath. "He must've had eyes on the jail in case one of his minions got picked up."

"Or Lynch used his one phone call to the wrong person."

"Why not just kill him before?" she asked.

"He wasn't done with the job, for one. Plus, the body count was racking up."

"There were two guys chasing me." She wondered what had happened to the second one.

"It's possible he's still out there. Once word gets out in their circles that Lynch is dead, the others will likely go underground for a few months. Maybe even hop over the border." He referred to Mexico. "There are plenty of little towns to get lost in."

She'd read about Americans living in both countries. It was easy to move back and forth with US citizenship. She'd also read about young people going over to party and never coming back. Many border towns were dangerous. But then, Scrappy wasn't exactly a college coed and he wasn't exactly innocent.

"I doubt Sean Menendez has the kind of connections necessary to pull off a jail murder." Dawson was right about that.

"Agreed." She didn't care how creepy the maintenance man was, he'd be hard-pressed to find the resources it took to kill someone while in a jail cell. "Do you think we can stop by and talk to him or the property manager anyway? Maybe I can get some information about my sister from the staff."

"It doesn't hurt to stop by for an interview. I also need

to let my brother know what's going on." Dawson paused and stared at his phone. "No one at Austin P.D. knew your sister had been murdered."

"The coroner must be honest," she observed.

"I've known him a long time. He's always been one of the good guys."

"If you ever needed proof the coroner reported the death but it was covered up by Austin P.D, I think you just got it." She picked up her coffee cup and took a sip. The burn felt good on her throat. "You said Yarnell has been living in hell ever since Cheryl's murder. I can't imagine what he must've gone through with a department bent on hanging a crime on him."

"The guy was in pain learning about his ex. She'd tried to call him and his new girlfriend picked up. She said a few choice words to Cheryl and that was it. She never tried to contact him again and then she shows up dead." Dawson studied his cell phone screen. It started going off in his hand like crazy.

He immediately stood up and started pacing. A feeling deep in the pit of her stomach caused her to be nauseous because the look on his face said it was bad news—news about his beloved family.

"Sorry, I need to—"

"Don't apologize, Dawson. Your family is just as important as mine."

He stopped and looked at her, a bit shell-shocked. And then he nodded, smiled and made a call.

Summer was confused by his look of surprise. His family was important to him, and to her. He was becoming important to her. There was something about living in fear of her life for the past few weeks that made the grand scheme of things crystal clear. Family came first.

And maybe clarity had to do with the fact that she'd

lost hers. Summer had always believed in family. She'd just never really had more than her sister.

She couldn't help but overhear Dawson's conversation despite the fact he'd gone into the bedroom for privacy. There was news about his father's case. An address came up for a possible suspect.

Dawson ended the call before walking into the room, a look of despair darkened his eyes.

"I overheard bits and pieces of your conversation. I'm sorry—"

He shook his head before raking a finger through his thick curls. A couple laps around the room later, and he seemed to calm down enough to tell her what was going on.

"Do you need to go investigate?" She didn't expect Dawson to stay with her under the circumstances.

"One extra person would just be in the way. My brothers are all over it and I'm needed here." The look on his face said he wanted to be with his siblings.

"You don't have to do this, Dawson. Your family needs you and I wouldn't want you to have any regrets about—"

He wheeled around on her so fast, she stopped mid-sentence.

"Last time I checked, you were family, too." His voice was sharp, and his eyes shot daggers. "But if you don't want me here then say the word."

Her entire body stiffened as she geared up for a fight. Before she could open her mouth to argue Dawson shot her a look of apology. He put a hand up and took another couple of laps.

Summer drew in a few breaths meant to calm her but all she ended up doing was breathing in more of his spicy and clean scent. She tried to form words but none came.

All she wanted was to stand up and put her hand on

his chest to stop him and get him to breathe. So, that's exactly what she did. Summer stood up and then stepped in front of him, forcing him to stop. Hand to his chest, she locked gazes with him.

He started to speak and clamped down, compressing his lips instead.

She could feel the moment the air changed from anger and frustration to awareness. Awareness of their hearts pounding against their rib cages. Awareness of the chemistry that had been sizzling between them since the moment they'd met. Awareness of their raspy breathing.

Call her wrong, but one look in his eyes made her think he wanted to reach out to her as much as she needed to feel him. She ran her fingers along the muscled ridges of his chest. There was only a thin layer of cotton preventing her from skin-to-skin contact.

Dawson brought his hands up to cup her face. He looked at her with a longing so deep it robbed her breath.

The need to feel his lips move against hers was a physical ache. She tilted her face toward his and he brought his lips down on hers.

Summer brought her hands up to his shoulders to brace herself, digging her nails in when he deepened the kiss. His hands dropped and his arms looped around her waist, bringing her body flush with his. She could kiss this man all day. She *wanted* to kiss this man all day.

She couldn't.

Reality lurked and they'd come to their senses in a minute. But for right then, Summer didn't care about his past or hers. Nothing mattered except this moment happening between them, a moment they both wanted so badly they could hardly breathe.

She felt that kiss from her crown to her toes and when his tongue dipped inside her mouth, heat spread through her. She ignored the fact he was the best kisser in her life and the other obvious fact that he'd be mind-numbingly amazing in bed.

The other facts, she couldn't ignore so easily.

They didn't have a lot of time to waste. Kissing him had been a luxury. And she needed to pull back while she still could.

Easier said than done.

With a deep breath, she managed to break away from those full lips of his—lips too soft for a face of such hard angles.

One look in his eyes said they were playing with fire.

Chapter Seventeen

Dawson pressed his forehead to Summer's while he took a minute to catch his breath. Being with her was doing things to his heart that he never knew possible. Rather than get inside his head about what that meant, how that changed things for him, he refocused on just breathing with her.

He knew one thing was certain. He'd had great sex in his life before and none of it would compare to what he would have with Summer. He meant that on every level. She had that rare kind of beauty that started on the inside.

Her smile, rare as it might be, was so genuine she radiated. She smiled from her soul, if that made any sense. Hell, he'd never been the poetic type, but she made him want to put his attraction to her into words. He just needed to find the right ones first.

There hadn't been much to laugh about lately but when she did he could swear it was the most beautiful sound. There wasn't a musical instrument in existence that compared to her, and hearing it did things to his heart that he'd tried to shut down long ago. It made him think of foreign things like forever—something he'd thought would never be possible after the way his marriage ended.

He'd cared about Autumn and had been determined to make things work because of the child he thought she was carrying. There was no forcing his feelings when it came to Summer.

Her face was blue skies and sunshine after a storm. Her mind kept him on his toes. And the fire burning inside her made him think life with her would never be dull.

But that wasn't on the table. He wasn't sure he could go down that road again with anyone. If he did…he'd want it to be with Summer.

After feathering a kiss to her lips, he cleared his throat and took a step back, hoping for a little clarity. Looking into her eyes only muddied the waters for him even more.

Damn.

He needed more coffee to wake him up because he wasn't thinking clearly. He'd promised himself that he wouldn't let things get out of hand with Summer and he had every intention of keeping that commitment to himself.

Besides, with his personal life in upheaval, this was the worst possible time to add more confusion into the mix. Summer didn't deserve that, either. She needed a strong shoulder to lean on while she got her bearings. The woman was fully capable of handling herself and yet he wanted to be her comfort in a storm.

Best not to confuse the sentiment with emotions. He'd keep himself in check better than he had been. For Summer's sake.

THE APARTMENT COMPLEX downtown wasn't exactly the kind Summer could see her sister living in. It was most likely what she could afford, and that broke Summer's heart even more. Why hadn't Autumn reached out for help? Why did she live like this? Was this place better than being with Summer?

She reached inside her purse where she kept the "Summer" necklace and rolled it around in her fingers. In a strange way, touching this piece of junk jewelry made her feel more connected to a sister who she admittedly didn't know very well.

This was the last place she would've looked for Autumn. Maybe that was part of the reason her sister rented an apartment here.

Dawson parked the truck and they both got out. The office was a small brick building with double glass doors. The sign said it was open. She took a deep breath and started toward the entrance.

For the life of her she couldn't figure out why her sister would've left twenty-five thousand dollars sitting in a bank account in her name without touching it. The money had been a gift from Dawson. It was free and clear with no expectation of payback.

Had Autumn regretted getting him involved in her life? Had she walked away and tried to minimize the damage?

If she didn't take anything from him, did she think she could convince herself the lies she'd told him were for his protection? It was possible she convinced herself that her disappearing act was harmless.

Did she leave Dawson to go back to the secret boyfriend she'd been involved with in the past? All signs pointed to just that. She remembered what Dawson said about women in abusive relationships. She just wished she'd known what her sister was going through. She could've been there for Autumn. Her sister wasn't alone.

A rogue tear escaped thinking about Autumn.

Summer wiped it away and stepped inside the glass doors. A little bell rang when Dawson opened the one on the right. Inside there was a tiled foyer. Beyond that was a great room overlooking a small pool. There was a kitchenette and two offices.

An overeager youngish woman dressed in a pantsuit bounded into the room. She had Shirley Temple curls and wore too much makeup to pull off the innocent look.

"Hello, I'm Marcy." She stuck out her hand toward Dawson.

Her gaze lingered a little too long on his face and Summer wanted to snap her fingers at the woman to get her attention.

"Dawson, and this is my wife—"

"Sandy." She nodded like she'd just answered the last question correctly on a game show. "I know."

Summer reined in her confused look because she realized this person might know her sister.

"I just didn't realize you were married." Marcy had one of those voices that grated. Fingernails on a chalkboard sounded like a relief after hearing her speak.

"Oh, right. I forgot to mention it because we've been separated. You know, trying to figure things out."

Marcy looked from Dawson to Summer and laughed. "You've been busy."

She flexed and released her fingers as she felt Dawson's hand clasp hers. He gave a little squeeze and it grounded her. They had a purpose and the ever-annoying Marcy didn't get to detract from that. Besides, she didn't seem very bright, which was a potential gold mine of information for them if they played it right.

"Your things have been boxed up. Headquarters makes us hold on to them for ninety days after eviction." Marcy shrugged.

"Oh. Right. I guess I forgot to keep my rent payments up once I got back together with my husband," Summer said by way of explanation, ignoring the fact that calling Dawson her husband had just rolled right off her tongue like it was truth. Not being honest hit her at her core but couldn't be helped if she wanted access to Autumn's things.

"I almost didn't recognize you at first. You look so… different." Marcy made a show of looking Summer up and down.

"Well, it's me." She had to tamp down the urge to come back with a snarky remark. This wasn't the right time for pride. "Is it possible to see my belongings?"

Marcy blew out a sharp breath and gave Summer a death stare.

"It's against policy when there's an overdue rent situation," she huffed, making her disgust with anyone who was late on rent clear as if the glaring eyes hadn't done it already.

"Do you take a credit card?" Dawson stepped up immediately. "I didn't bring a check with me today."

The annoying woman perked up at the sound of payment.

"We add 3 percent to the outstanding balance," she warned like that might be a tipping point that caused them to turn around and walk out the door.

Summer almost laughed out loud. Dawson O'Connor could cover 3 percent and so much more. He could keep the twenty-five thousand dollars in Autumn's bank account, and Summer would figure out a payment plan to cover her sister's expenses.

"Just give me a total." Dawson smiled and Marcy practically beamed back at him. It was enough to make Summer hold his hand a little tighter. And, yes, she was being territorial.

Dawson's smile was meant to disarm Marcy. Summer figured that part out on her own and yet a streak of jealousy still crept in. Keeping a safe distance from her emotions had always been a matter of survival for Summer.

Despite the magnetic pull toward Dawson and the absolute fire in every kiss that promised so much more than great sex, breaking down her walls would take time and patience. She didn't even know if it was possible anymore. In every past relationship she'd been afraid of heights and there'd been a cliff in the distance.

Before Dawson, she wouldn't consider getting anywhere near the edge. Now? She was starting to think that maybe it could happen. The problem wasn't the relationship. She knew being with a person as intelligent, kind and respectful as Dawson would set the bar for every future date. When the shine wore off and it ended, she would be shattered.

Because she wouldn't be able to keep Dawson at a distance. He was the sun, drawing everything that got near into his orbit, spinning faster and making her forget that if she stepped out, she'd spiral out of control.

"Let me check with my property manager," Marcy chirped. Suddenly, fingernails on a chalkboard didn't seem so bad to Summer.

Dawson thanked her before tugging Summer a little bit closer and dipping his head to press a kiss on her lips.

Marcy exited quickly and it made Summer smirk. The move from Dawson was most likely meant to sell the marriage story but damned if it didn't feel like the most natural thing for him to kiss her. Summer was in his orbit all right. Pulling away from him when this came to a close might be more difficult than she'd anticipated.

Still, walking away would be the right thing to do, she reasoned. There was no other choice when she really thought about it. This case would end. She needed to get used to a new normal and a life without Autumn.

Her sister had been preparing Summer for this in many ways over the past few years.

Autumn had been difficult to get ahold of and she'd disappeared for long periods. She'd been putting more and more emotional distance between them. The notion of looking through her sister's last possessions hit her so hard it nearly knocked her breath away. So many thoughts raced through Summer's mind about what her sister had held on to. How had her sister lived in those final months? What had been important to her?

Irritating chirp lady walked back into the lobby.

"You owe three months' rent at one thousand five hundred and fifty dollars a month. Plus, four hundred and fifty dollars in late fees and a thousand dollars for us to release your belongings. The total comes to six thousand, one hundred dollars." She produced an invoice.

Dawson pulled his wallet out of his back pocket. "Do you have a preference when it comes to plastic?"

"We'll take whatever you have available as long as the charge is approved." Marcy beamed at Dawson but when her gaze shifted to Summer, her forehead creased with disapproval.

He didn't hesitate to hand over his card.

"I'll be right back as soon as I run this," Marcy said before bebopping out of the room.

"I'd like to pay you back," Summer said in a whisper.

"You don't have to worry about that. It's the least I can do," he said and there was regret in his voice.

"What do you mean?" she asked.

"I let your sister down. She came to me for sanctuary and I couldn't protect her." His serious tone said he meant every word. Here, Summer had been so focused on the fact she'd let her sister down she hadn't once stopped to think Dawson might be in the same boat.

"You didn't know her. She walked out. You believed her. You did nothing but trust her and she betrayed that. Don't get me wrong, I love Autumn with all my heart. That doesn't mean I'm naive to the fact she made a lot of bad decisions in her life. But believe me when I say that you're the last person on earth who should feel responsible for her."

"Your card is good," Marcy interrupted the conversation.

Logic said Summer should be able to forgive herself for not being there when Autumn needed her. The advice she'd given to Dawson seconds ago was true for him and somewhere down deep she could acknowledge it was true for her, too.

Dawson took the card Marcy held between them. He tucked it back inside his wallet at the same time Marcy seemed to catch sight of the badge. She looked up at Dawson and studied his face.

Summer couldn't tell what the woman was thinking but the badge seemed to make her stand up a little straighter.

"Where do you keep eviction belongings?" Dawson asked. It was the question on Summer's mind.

"You'll have to wait thirty days and then you can buy them back from us." Marcy sounded a little less certain of herself and a lot less bubbly than she had a few minutes ago.

"We paid up my rent with late fees plus the thousand dollars to release those belongings. There's no reason to keep my stuff." Summer tensed up, ready for a fight.

Dawson squeezed her hand.

"How much to buy all of her belongings?" he asked.

Marcy glanced around. "I'm not really supposed to—"

"I don't trust that you've taken care of my stuff. I'd

like to check on it to make sure everything's there." Summer was grasping at straws here but there might be something in her sister's personal items that could give a hint of who she'd been seeing. Leaving empty-handed wasn't an option.

"We have the right to dispose of your items. We sent out a notice of our intentions—"

"Which technically I never received."

"Your…" Marcy's gaze bounced from Summer to Dawson and back "…*boyfriend* stopped by a couple of months ago and emptied out your storage. There isn't much left but some makeup and toiletries. There are a few towels and some clothing. I don't think my boss would be too mad if I showed you what was left."

The wheels were already turning in Summer's mind as to how to tactfully ask what her "boyfriend" looked like.

"That would be great if it's not too much trouble." Summer softened her tone, reminding herself she'd get more out of Marcy with honey than vinegar.

"Stay right here and I'll get my keys." Marcy disappeared long enough for Summer to make eyes at Dawson.

He seemed to read her apprehension even though he didn't speak. How had he become so important in such a short time? She'd tell herself the desperate life-and-death situation she'd been in would cause her emotions to be all over the place. But that wouldn't be fair to her feelings for Dawson.

Marcy returned and motioned for them to follow her. She led them to a golf cart parked out front. Summer climbed inside and looked around. The person who'd killed her sister had walked around on these same paths. Cheryl's killer had been here.

No way to bring up Summer's "boyfriend" came to her tactfully. So, Summer took the front seat and leaned over when Marcy claimed the driver's side and popped the key in the ignition.

"I don't want my husband to hear this but can you tell me which one of my boyfriends stopped by. I dated around a lot after my husband and I separated. We got married straight out of high school and needed to find ourselves as people." She was overexplaining, adding details to convince Marcy of the untruth.

Marcy mouthed an *Oh*.

The woman winked and smiled, looking a little too happy that "Sandy" seemed to be a little loose.

Chapter Eighteen

"He introduced himself as Matt…um, hmm. That's weird. I'm not sure he ever told me his last name. If he did, I sure don't remember it. He was gorgeous, though." She glanced back at Dawson, who was making a show of checking his cell phone.

Luckily, the backseat faced the opposite direction so they couldn't see his face. It gave the illusion he couldn't hear.

Marcy backed out of the parking spot. The beep, beep, beep of the golf cart masked their conversation.

"If you ask me, this one's the best. Hands down." Marcy blushed as she nodded back toward Dawson. "But then I've always been partial to tall, muscled men. Matt looked like he stepped out of one of those Abercrombie and Fitch ads if there was one for middle-aged men. You know?"

"Yeah." Summer didn't have a clue. She'd gotten a first name, though. Matt. The name of the so-called attorney who'd handled the fake divorce had been Matt Charley Shank. The first two names were clues. What did Shank mean?

For some reason, Summer doubted it was his actual last name. In fact, she was certain that Dawson would have checked every Matt or Matthew Shank in Texas. She tabled that thought, figuring Marcy was feeling chatty.

"I never liked his hair, though," Summer said.

"Too curly?"

"Exactly. And the color—"

"Black never bothered me. It was a little long for a guy who wore a suit, though," Marcy stated.

Summer committed the details to memory. Matt, last name unknown, who looked like he'd walked off an Abercrombie and Fitch ad for middle-aged men, had curly black hair.

"His eyes were nice, though," Marcy continued in a hushed tone as she whipped around a corner and toward the back side of the complex. They passed a row of mailboxes before Marcy made another turn. "I don't normally like blue eyes on a man but his were so light. They looked good on him. And he had just enough gray at the temples to be sexy."

She added the extra details, repeating his description to seal it into her brain. Matt, last name unknown, who looked like he'd walked off an Abercrombie and Fitch ad for middle-aged men, had curly black hair. He also had light blue eyes and wore a suit. And he had just enough gray at the temples to be sexy.

A picture was emerging.

"He turned out to be a creep." Summer fished for any signs there'd been fighting between her sister and Matt. Marcy seemed like the nosy type who would know if a couple had problems.

"Really?" Marcy seemed shocked. She took a minute to think about it and then said, "You know, that explains all the flowers."

"His way of apologizing," Summer continued.

"My mom always said never trust a man when he

sends flowers out of the blue. It means he's doing something wrong." Marcy looked at Summer in a show of solidarity.

Summer noticed there was no ring on Marcy's left hand.

"Dating is hard," Summer continued.

"It's the worst." Marcy smacked her palm on the steering wheel. "Right?"

"There are so many jerks out there," Summer agreed.

"And they take all shapes and forms." Marcy was really into the conversation now. Good, Summer had gotten good information out of the woman so far. And Summer was getting used to her nasal tone of voice. Fingernails on a chalkboard still had a better sound but Marcy was growing on her.

Summer repeated her new mantra. Matt, last name unknown, who looked like he'd walked off an Abercrombie and Fitch ad for middle-aged men, had curly black hair that was a little too long. He also had light blue eyes and wore a suit. And he had just enough gray at the temples to be sexy.

"You think you can trust a guy in a suit and then he turns out to be more of a jerk than you could ever have imagined." Summer kept pouring it on. She was always so careful when she met a new person and was always guarded if someone tried to interact with her for the first time online. She'd been too busy working extra shifts and socking away money to have much free time. When she did have a day off, she usually spent it at the library researching how to start her own business or under the covers trying to catch up on her sleep.

Marcy rocked her head as she pulled into a parking spot. Dawson, who'd been quiet up until now, was off the cart first. He clasped hands with Summer the second she exited.

"Right this way." Marcy took them to a storage building with five large doors. Keys clanked as she searched for the right one. "Hold on just a minute. Where'd you go?" She was talking to herself as she checked keys, one by one, and occasionally glanced over at Summer with an awkward smile.

At least Marcy was focusing on Summer now instead of Dawson. He moved behind Summer and looped his arms around her. The feel of his masculine chest against her back sent sensual shivers racing through her.

In the move, he also slipped his cell phone into her hands and swiped so that the screen came to life.

"Are you from Texas, Marcy?"

Summer could feel his chest vibrate when he spoke. More of those inappropriate shivers raced down her back.

"San Angelo originally." She beamed at him before refocusing on the keys. She slid one in and said, "Finally."

When her back was turned, Summer glanced at the screen of Dawson's phone. He'd written down the description of Matt, which was basically the same as the mantra she'd repeated a couple of times since getting off the cart.

He ran his thumb inside the palm of her hand, and it sent a trail of warmth.

"And, we're in," Marcy said after wrestling with the door. "Be careful. We don't usually let people back here, so it's a mess. Maintenance is supposed to clean up but Jared has been calling in sick lately and it's all we can do to keep residents happy."

"What happened to Sean?" Summer took the opportunity to ask another question that had been on both her and Dawson's minds.

"We had to let him go," Marcy said with a frown. "He made a few of our female residents uncomfortable, so he wasn't working out." She paused. "I didn't realize you liked him all that much."

"Can't say that I knew him very well." She shrugged. "Now that you mention it, he was a little creepy."

"That's the same word a few other residents used to describe interactions with him," she admitted. Those few minutes in the golf cart had won over Marcy's trust.

Steeling her nerves, Summer followed Marcy into the space. She flipped on a light, which was one of those basic builder installs hanging from the ceiling. The walls inside weren't finished. There were only boards and posts.

The storage shed was large and there was enough dust on the flooring to cover half the state. People's belongings were stacked in piles, some were wrapped in what looked like oversize pieces of Saran wrap.

Marcy navigated around a few of the piles until she located Autumn's belongings.

"Here's your stuff," she said to Summer.

The stack consisted of a pile of clothing on top of shoes. There was makeup, like Marcy had mentioned before. There wasn't a whole lot else. A couple of purses, some blankets and toiletries.

"I'll go get the truck," Dawson said as an icy chill raced down Summer's spine. All of her sister's belongings could easily fit in the back.

Summer didn't have much, but she'd worked for her small apartment and filled it with things she loved. Her neighbor was looking after Summer's plants. She had a wall of bookshelves with her favorite paperbacks. There were a few shells from the beach along with art she'd bought on the street. She'd made a few pieces herself, nothing fancy, just pottery she'd painted and fired. She had the most comfortable bed and her blanket was the softest thing she'd ever felt.

Again, nothing extravagant but everything in her home meant something to her. She still had a white starfish blown from glass that she'd picked up in Seattle at the Pike Place Market. Clothes weren't her big thing and neither were purses and shoes. She carried a handbag, of course, but back home she usually just stuck her wallet inside her backpack and moved on. It was easier to carry and keep track of that way.

Nothing really stood out in her sister's personal effects but she wanted to take them home with her anyway. This was all she had left of Autumn.

She glanced up in time to see Marcy studying her.

"If you don't mind my saying so, I like the natural look on you much better than what you did before."

"I'll take all the compliments I can get." Summer realized if there was anything important, Matt would have picked it up when he came and got Autumn's stuff. He must've been worried something might link her back to him.

"Don't take it the wrong way. You were always beautiful, but you never really talked much."

"I was going through a lot while deciding if we were going to give our marriage another shot." Summer felt defensive of her sister, which was silly. Marcy didn't mean anything by it and she didn't come across as the most sensitive person.

"There are earrings in the makeup holder that I had my eye on to buy," she admitted and then seemed to catch herself. "Before I realized you were coming back for your stuff, of course. Most people never do. Once they skip out on rent, we don't see them again. Their stuff ends up in here and we eventually sell it. My boss takes forever to get rid of this stuff."

All Summer could figure was that was Marcy's way of offering an apology.

"Which earrings did you like?" Summer knelt down beside the makeup container and then opened it, kicking up a small storm of dust.

Summer coughed.

"Sorry about the dust. No one has run a broom through here in forever." Marcy waved her hand in front of her wrinkled nose.

The makeup container had pockets like a tackle box. Summer unfolded it and in the bottom were several pairs of earrings.

"Those are beautiful." Marcy pointed to an art deco throwback. The pair she was talking about were like chandeliers. They had more sparkle than a craft store's glitter aisle.

Summer picked them up, figuring she could buy a little more good will. "They're yours if you want them."

"Are you serious right now?" Marcy was ecstatic. If a pair of cheap free earrings could do that for her, so be it.

"Definitely." Summer picked them up and held them out.

"I'm not sure I should. I mean, I want to…but… I don't know what the company policy is."

"How about this? They belong to me. I don't want them anymore since I wore them on a date with my ex-boyfriend. I don't think my husband would appreciate me bringing them into our home and I don't want the reminder of a horrible relationship. So, you'd be doing me a favor if you took them off my hands." Summer could tell she was winning Marcy over with her logic.

"Well, if I was doing you a favor…"

"You would be." Summer meant it, too. They were not her style one bit and she'd rather they bring someone else joy than end up at a garage sale. She wouldn't even begin to know what to charge for them.

Marcy took the offering and splayed them out on her flat palm. "They're so gorgeous."

"They'll look better on you than they would on me." Summer caught her slipup, but Marcy was too busy admiring her new earrings to notice.

The door opened and Summer's heart dropped. She stood up a little too fast and scared Marcy.

"Is that you, Dawson?" she asked as she heard boots shuffling across the dusty floor.

"It's me. Pickup is outside. We can gather up your things and head home." He must've noticed the panic in her voice because he was a study in calm when he got to them.

She flashed her eyes at him and he walked straight over to her and kissed her. It was another couple move and probably for show but being with him and especially when he made contact in any way made her feel like she'd found home.

"Truck is backed up as close as I could get it." Dawson realized his mistake in leaving Summer alone the minute he looked into her eyes. He wouldn't do that to her again. He'd jogged back to the front parking lot and gotten back as fast as he could.

A bad feeling caused the hair on the back of his neck to prick. He'd scoped the area without seeing any cause for alarm and yet that uneasy feeling wouldn't let up.

He was keenly aware that he had Summer at a known hangout of her sister's. The killer was powerful and had connections. He might have eyes everywhere and especially his old haunts.

Dawson was ready to get Summer out of there.

With three of them, loading the truck only took three trips. Marcy had warmed up to Summer, who she believed was Autumn. He noticed Marcy had a pair of earrings tucked into her shirt pocket. They seemed like prize possessions considering she patted her pocket after every load to make sure they didn't fall out somewhere along the way.

When they'd tucked in the last load, he thanked her for her help.

"No problem." She patted her pocket again and looked straight at Summer. "Thank you for these."

Summer smiled one of those genuine, ice-melting smiles that was unique to her at the exact time the crack of a bullet split the air.

Chapter Nineteen

Before Summer had a chance to process what she'd heard, Dawson's arm wrapped around her and he was taking her and Marcy down. He covered them with his heft and the next thing she knew she was on all fours being ushered around the side of the truck.

The sight of blood normally made her sick to her stomach. This time, it sent panic rocketing through her. In the crush of the three of them, she couldn't tell which one of them was bleeding.

Everything started happening fast after that.

"Stay down." Dawson had drawn his weapon and was on his feet in a heartbeat. He made eye contact with Summer. "You got this."

And then he seemed to see the blood, too. He clenched his back teeth and took in a sharp breath.

A bullet whizzed by over his head. In another second, he'd held up his index finger to indicate he'd be right back and then moved toward the driver's side of the truck.

Head low, weapon leading the way, he glanced over the hood of the truck, fixated on someone and then fired.

Despite originally being from Texas, Summer didn't know much about guns. She couldn't tell what kind Dawson had except that it fired real bullets, one at a time.

She scanned her own body looking for signs of a bullet wound but when she looked at Marcy, her stomach sank.

Marcy had that shocked expression that Summer had only seen in movies—a look that said she realized she'd been shot but the news hadn't quite been absorbed yet. Eyes wide, mouth open, she grabbed at her side.

There was a lot of blood. Too much.

Summer jumped into action, sitting on her back haunches and lifting Marcy's blouse on her left hip to assess the damage. The minute she saw the wound area, she knew she needed to stem the bleeding.

She dropped her shoulder, letting her purse fall onto the pavement.

"I need you to do something for me, Marcy," Summer whispered. When that didn't work, she brought her hand up to Marcy's chin and forced her gaze to meet her own. "Find my phone in my purse. I have to put pressure on your wound to stem the bleeding."

Dammit. She wasn't getting through to Marcy.

Oh, well, she didn't have time to waste. She glanced around looking for something she could use. The answer came to her. The scarf. She quickly untied it and then wadded it up into a ball.

"This might hurt but I need you to stay with me, Marcy." Summer had no idea if the woman understood a word, but she had to try to explain. This must be what shock looked like.

The minute Summer put pressure on the wound, Marcy let out a scream and tried to slap away her hand.

"I'm so sorry." Summer had to fight to keep the scarf in place. She took a hard slap to the face. Ringing noises sounded in her ears, but she spun around to her side instead of giving up. She realized Marcy wasn't rational.

With one hand keeping pressure on the wound and

the other trying to keep Marcy from digging her fingernails into Summer's shoulder, it was all she could do to
contain the situation. And then, out of nowhere, Marcy
seemed to snap.

"It's okay," she said.

"Yes. You're going to be okay," Summer confirmed
firmly. Marcy needed to hear that Summer believed those
words one hundred percent. No question about it. No
hesitation.

"Sorry," Marcy said.

There was no time to worry about being polite. Summer didn't fault Marcy one bit for her panic.

"Can you grab my phone out of my purse and call 9-1-
1?" Someone in the apartment complex might have already done it by now but Summer had no plans to chance
it. She needed to get back up on the way for Dawson.

"Yes. Where?" Marcy glanced around and her eyes
landed on the purse. "Oh. Here."

"Just reach in and feel around for it," Summer instructed.

"Got it." Marcy came up with the phone. Her skin was
pale but her eyes were bright. She held out the phone.
Summer put her thumb on the pad to get through the security feature because it was easier than explaining the
step wasn't necessary for emergency calls. The screen
came to life and Marcy called for help.

With Marcy's cooperation, Summer could risk a
glance toward Dawson. Most of his head and body would
be covered by the truck and yet she still panicked that exposed sliver of him could be hit. Realistically, the shooter
would have to be an excellent marksman.

He'd missed his mark, Summer. Despite the fact he'd
shot Marcy, he clearly wasn't accurate. Summer would
have been his target.

Dawson identified himself as a law enforcement officer as Marcy relayed what was happing to the dispatcher
on the call.

"Tell them you need an ambulance," Summer urged.

Marcy complied. Now that she'd snapped out of the
temporary shock, she seemed to be rational again. Good.
They would need all the help they could get.

"She wants to know how bad it is," Marcy said to
Summer, glancing down at her wound.

"You're going to be okay. I've stopped the bleeding
for now but we're in a situation that could blow up any
second. Tell them we don't have any more time."

She did.

"Do they have an ETA?" Summer asked.

Marcy nodded. "An officer is en route. He's five minutes out."

"And the ambulance?" she asked.

"Oh, right." Marcy asked the dispatcher. "Right behind him. They might get here first."

"Okay. We need to get you to a safer spot." Summer
glanced around. The storage shed?

No. That wouldn't work. They could be shot while
on the move. There was enough furniture inside to hide,
though, and it would provide much-needed mass between
them and bullets.

Whatever gun this shooter was using seemed to fire
one at a time. That was a saving grace that could turn at
any second if he had accomplices on the way.

And the storage shed could also trap her and Marcy.
What about inside the truck?

It seemed dangerous but offered a getaway.

"Put your hands where I can see them," Dawson commanded.

The response came in the form of a shot being fired.

And then she heard the glorious sound of sirens wailing in the distance. Backup would be there in a matter of minutes.

The sounds of tires squealing from across the parking lot sent an icy chill racing down her spine. The shooter was going to get away.

Dawson hopped into action. He was by her side in a second and pressing a small handgun into the flat of her palm.

"This is the safety and how you take it off. Use the gun if you have to. Go inside the storage shed and find a hiding spot until help arrives." His voice was a study in calm, but his words sent another chill down her back.

Dawson was going after the shooter.

He pressed a kiss to her lips and then he was gone. He climbed into the driver's seat as she helped Marcy to standing.

Summer glanced around as the truck pulled away. Relief washed over her when no one was standing on the opposite side of the parking lot like she'd half feared. The respite was a temporary feeling at best. And it was shattered when she heard another shot ring out.

Marcy flinched.

"We need to tell dispatch where we're going," she said to Marcy, who had a death grip on the cell phone. Within a few seconds, Marcy and Summer were back inside the shed. Marcy mumbled into the phone and, best as Summer could tell, she provided a good update.

At least Marcy knew her way around the storage. Summer flipped off the light and they felt their way around, kicking up enough dust for both of them to cough.

Summer's nose and throat burned but she figured they had more pressing problems at the moment.

DAWSON GUNNED THE ENGINE. He had dispatch on the line. He'd given them a quick rundown of the situation. A uniformed officer was being sent to Summer and Marcy's location along with an ambulance.

He was currently giving chase to a late model SUV, all black with blacked-out windows. The SUV was heading toward the highway where it could get lost in all the traffic. There were temporary plates on the vehicle that, up close, looked like homemade jobs.

The SUV was already onto a road that led to the highway. Dawson cursed under his breath because it had sped up and navigated through enough traffic that he was having difficulty keeping pace. The engine must have been modified.

"I'm losing him," he said to dispatch. And then he saw something he didn't expect. The SUV made a U-turn over the median despite traffic and honking horns. Most people had the sense to get out of the way, but the vehicle was heading right toward him. "Scratch that. He did an about-face."

Dawson ducked low as the driver fired at him. The bullet pinged the top of his truck missing the windshield but nailing the metal roof.

"Are those shots fired?" dispatch asked.

"Yes, they are." He filled her in on the SUV's new direction. "Heading southbound."

"Copy that."

The sound of a chopper roaring toward them clued Dawson in on the change in direction. The SUV weaved in and out of traffic before popping a curb and nearly wiping out a sidewalk full of people.

Folks scattered as the SUV came to an abrupt stop. From this angle, Dawson had to make a U-turn to see the driver's side but he'd bet money on the fact the guy just took off.

"I'm going on foot." He glanced up and then provided the street name before parking. He jumped out of his vehicle, caught sight of a guy full-on running, and gave chase.

Runner was fast. The man was in good shape. He also had a weapon and wasn't afraid to turn and shoot, which he did.

The bullet took a small chunk of brick out of one of the buildings they were cutting in between. It was a wild shot, far off the mark.

Weapon drawn, Dawson wouldn't risk injuring an innocent person. But he sure as hell wasn't letting Runner get away when he was this close.

This was the first mistake and real break in the case.

Staying back far enough for Runner not to be able to get off a good shot was key. Dawson could keep running for a long time without a break. He hoped Runner's stamina was weak.

Runner spun around and fired. Dawson flattened his back against the wall. He'd gotten a little too close for comfort that time, the bullet pinging a couple feet away. He muttered a curse and froze when he realized Runner had stopped.

This time, the man slowed down enough to take aim when he fired. Except nothing happened. Nothing but a click noise came out of the gun.

Dawson made his move. He charged toward Runner and dove at him, tackling him at the knees as he tried to turn and run. Pavement bit hard. Pain shot up Dawson's elbow where he took the brunt of the fall. That was going to leave a mark, he thought wryly.

The weapon in Runner's hand went flying. It was no

good to him anyway unless he wanted to use the butt of it as a hammer against Dawson's skull. The thought probably occurred to Runner as his gaze seemed to search for something to use.

And because everything that could go wrong usually did, Dawson's weapon flew out of his hand, too.

His target spun like an alligator with prey in his mouth. Runner might be middle-aged, but he was in great shape. Dawson could almost hear the crack as his head slammed into the concrete alley. A raging headache would spoil the rest of his day. He tried to shake off the ringing noise in his ears as Runner's hands wrapped around Dawson's neck.

Oh. Hell. No.

Curling up in a ball, despite Runner's best efforts to stop him, Dawson launched the heel of his boot at Runner's chest like it was on a spring. Impact knocked Runner back.

Hard contact loosened the man's grip on Dawson's throat. He sucked in a burst of air just in time to stave off the dizziness threatening. He coughed the minute air hit his lungs. His throat burned. But he couldn't focus on that right now. Runner was scrambling to his feet and reaching for Dawson's Glock.

Chapter Twenty

Summer kept pressure on the wound as she and Marcy crouched down behind a dresser. Marcy had led them to the middle of the room and to a spot where there was heavy furniture.

The door opened when they'd barely had time to squat down. Since she didn't hear sirens right outside, she feared someone had been left behind to deal with her and Marcy.

Fear tried to clasp its icy talons around her chest and squeeze her lungs. She forced herself to breathe and prayed Marcy would stay quiet.

Whoever was in the shed was stealth. There was no sound and Summer couldn't tell if the person had just opened the door to see if anyone was inside.

The light flipped on and Marcy gasped. Their location had been compromised. Summer scrambled to move them to a new location. She needed to get them out of there. Being locked in the small space with a killer wasn't going to end well.

Marcy's wound started bleeding again and Summer was certain they were going to leave a trail of blood. Could she secure Marcy somewhere, maybe in an empty cabinet? Summer could draw attention to herself and then run out the door.

It was risky. There wasn't enough time to go through all the reasons this was a very bad idea. Or, map out all the ways in which this plan could backfire.

All she knew for certain was that if they stayed together, they would most likely die. Trying to move the both of them as a unit might be certain death. Marcy was getting weaker, slower. Her panic was setting in.

Then again, emergency workers would be there in a matter of minutes. A thought struck. Had the driver left the scene to throw law enforcement off the track?

Summer was grateful for Dawson as she helped Marcy move toward the far right corner of the building. He wouldn't be easily tricked and yet he had no idea what was going down.

Inside the small space that seemed to shrink by the minute, she'd never felt more trapped. She scanned the area, looking for any kind of hiding space for Marcy. She could give her the small handgun Dawson had left with Summer.

Summer's hands were shaky as it was. Marcy might be the steadier shooter.

Another wave of panic engulfed Summer when the light flipped off. Whoever was inside the shed seemed to have gotten his bearings and decided moving in pitch-black was his best option.

More of those icy chills raced down Summer's back at the implication. It would also make identifying him that much more difficult should Summer and Marcy survive.

Another thought struck and it lit a fire deep in her belly. This could be the bastard who'd murdered her sister. At the very least, he was involved.

More of that white-hot anger licked through her as she placed the gun in Marcy's shaking hand in case things didn't go the way Summer planned. She felt around for a cubby space that she could tuck Marcy inside.

Waiting it out for emergency personnel who might show too late was not an option. Not when this guy was inside the building. Besides, EMTs could be shot on arrival.

Summer had no idea how it all worked or who would show up. She wasn't willing to risk her or Marcy's life to find out. With a deep breath, she helped Marcy into a small space before crawling away. She made sure to swipe her hands on the floor to mess up the dirt trail just in case this guy decided to use a light. Every cell phone had a flashlight app.

This guy might find them, and he might kill them, but she didn't have to serve both of them up on a silver platter.

Winding through the tall stacks of furniture, she ran her hand along the plastic wrapping. Moving from bundle to bundle, she tried to get her bearings. It didn't take long to realize she was completely turned around. She stopped and listened for signs of him breathing.

She couldn't see her own hand if she held it out in front of her face. Hope that she could find the exit fizzled.

And then Marcy screamed and fired a shot.

Summer's bearings came real quick after that. She oriented herself and immediately beat feet, backtracking to Marcy. She could only hope Marcy's aim was on point.

Then again, she might have panicked and gotten off a wild shot.

"Sandy!" Marcy screamed.

Adrenaline spiked. It wasn't good that Marcy just let the creep know there was another person in the room. Now he would expect her to show.

It didn't matter, because she heard the sounds of a

struggle and more screaming came from Marcy. Summer had no choice but to get back to the corner as fast as she could.

Glorious sirens sounded right outside the shed, close enough to know that help was so near she could almost reach out and touch it. Marcy might not have any more time. Summer might be too late. But she had to try.

So, she kept moving toward the scuffle.

The door opened. Light peeked in and she saw Scrappy three feet in front of her. He'd pinned Marcy to the ground and was running his hand along the floor, no doubt trying to find the gun.

Summer launched herself on top of him, screamed at the top of her lungs for help, and dug her fingernails into his eyes.

The light flipped on as Summer continued to scream for help.

"Everyone step outside, hands up." An authoritative female voice made the demand.

"There's a gun. He's…he killed my sister…"

This wasn't the movies. No cop would risk their own life by running in blind.

Time was the enemy.

Scrappy refocused all his attention on Summer. He twisted around, his height and weight giving him an advantage. After a grunt, he knocked her flat on her back, but Summer kept digging her fingernails in his face anyway. She clawed at his cheeks when her hands slipped from his eyes.

Even if he killed her and got away, she'd have enough DNA underneath her fingernails for police to nail him. Justice would be served.

He drew back his fist and before he could get off a jab,

she bucked and rolled. He regrouped a little too quickly as Marcy started kicking.

It gave Summer the advantage she needed to knock him off balance and roll away from him. Something hard dug into her left arm. She moved away enough to check. It was the gun. Her hands were no longer shaky when she thought about her sister's senseless murder.

Scrappy's hand gripped her shoulder and when he spun her around this time, he met the barrel of a gun. Using her thumb, she clicked off the safety.

"You better back up right now or they'll be scraping your brains off the ceiling," Summer said through clenched teeth.

His gray eyes widened in shock but he listened.

"Put your hands in the air," she demanded. That part of all cop shows rang true.

Scrappy's eyes darted from left to right, no doubt looking for an escape route.

"Don't even think about it. I'll shoot."

He seemed to debate that for a split second.

"Give me a reason," she said, not backing down an inch.

A female officer poked her head around one of the heavy chests.

"Drop your weapon," she demanded.

Summer had no plans to argue. She moved slowly so the officer would be clear on her intent, lowering the gun to the floor. "Can I move it away from him?"

"Slide it toward me," the officer said, her weapon trained on Scrappy.

Summer complied. "My friend was shot. She's bleeding pretty badly. Is there an ambulance? She needs medical attention right now."

Another officer rounded the other side of the stack of

furniture. He didn't speak but his weapon was trained on Scrappy.

The door opened.

"My friend took off. He's a US marshal. Is he okay?" Summer was desperate for information about Dawson.

The first cop shook her head.

"Lace your fingers on top of your head," she said to Scrappy. He placed his hands up and shot a go-to-hell look at Summer.

Officer number two moved in and took Scrappy down. In a half second, he was face down chugging dust through his nose and out his mouth.

"I'm certain this guy was involved in my sister's murder." Summer realized that her nose was bleeding. "And he hurt my friend."

Marcy was sitting up, hands in the air.

"She needs medical attention," Summer repeated just as EMTs arrived on the scene.

The female officer patted down Summer and then Marcy. She signaled for waiting emergency workers to go ahead and treat the patient.

Within minutes, Marcy's bleeding had stemmed and she was being carried out of the building. Summer followed outside to the waiting ambulance.

"I'll come to the hospital as soon as I can," Summer said, praying she wouldn't be visiting two people in there.

Marcy grabbed hold of Summer's hand.

"You've got this. You're going to be okay. This is just a speed bump," Summer reassured.

Marcy squeezed Summer's hand and smiled through the oxygen mask.

"Sorry, ma'am. We've gotta roll," one of the EMTs said.

"I'll see you soon," she said to Marcy, who nodded.

Summer took a step back and watched as Marcy was loaded into the ambulance, the doors closed and one of the men in uniform bolted around to the driver's side. Lights on, the ambulance took off.

She reminded herself that Marcy was in good hands then turned to the female officer to give her statement.

"Is there a way you can check on my friend the marshal?" she pleaded with the officer, who was beginning to realize Summer wasn't a threat.

The officer nodded and spoke low into her radio, and then she listened. "Ten-four. Thank you."

"What is it?" Whatever was going on didn't sound good.

"Marshal O'Connor was involved in a vehicle chase. The suspect abandoned his vehicle and Marshal O'Connor pursued him on foot. Witnesses near the scene reported shots being fired. The whereabouts of the suspect and Marshal O'Connor are unknown at this time."

Summer's legs turned to rubber and she had to take a step back until she found the golf cart to keep herself upright. She leaned against the solid vehicle with the feeling that it was the only thing connecting her to Dawson.

"I'm sorry, ma'am." The officer was short, five feet three inches if Summer had to guess. Her long black hair was in a braid that ran halfway down her back.

Although she might be tiny, Summer had no doubt the woman could take care of herself.

"I'll need to take your statement if you want to help the marshal." The officer was sympathetic. "I'm Officer Williams."

She stuck out her hand.

"Summer Grayson." She took the offering.

Officer Williams looked Summer up and down, focusing on the bloodstain on her pale blue shirt. "Do you need medical care?"

"It's Marcy's blood, not mine. Other than a bloody nose, I'm not hurt." Summer scanned her body just to be sure. There were going to be a few bruises but nothing that a warm bath and some antibiotic ointment couldn't handle.

"Okay. Start from the beginning and tell me everything that happened." Officer Williams pulled a notepad out of her pocket along with a small pen.

Summer relayed everything that had happened since they showed up at the apartment complex. "Dawson." She flashed eyes at the officer. "Marshal O'Connor wrote down the description Marcy provided. Matt visited my sister's things and most likely took evidence if my sister had any against him."

Officer Williams nodded as she jotted down key words along with the description.

Minutes ticked by with no word on Dawson or the guy he'd abandoned his truck to chase. Summer could barely breathe.

DAWSON TIGHTENED HIMSELF into a ball and rolled back onto his shoulders. Lifting his lower back off the ground, he sprang to his feet in a martial arts kip-up maneuver. He didn't have time to thank his training when he landed on his feet and in ready position. Runner's hand was within inches of the Glock.

He plowed into Runner, closed his arms around the guy's midsection like a vise, and rolled forward, bringing Runner with him. Dawson dug his fingers into the man's ribs before tucking and rolling.

Runner practically howled in pain.

Unwilling to let up or give the man an inch, Dawson

rolled them both onto their sides and wrapped powerful legs around his target in a scissor leg lock. Runner squirmed and tried to break free from Dawson's grip.

Not this time.

Runner twisted and turned, and Dawson squeezed harder, waiting him out. The saying, patience won wars, was as true in hand-to-hand combat as it was in any battle.

Adrenaline would fade and, at this pace, Runner would deplete his energy. Both were already heaving for air. Dawson made a point to slow his breathing so he could control his racing pulse.

The struggle started to ease, and Dawson tightened his grip even more. This was where his endurance training would kick in and he damn sure needed it.

Dawson managed to wrangle one arm around Runner's elbow, locking it into place. The man was lying on his other arm, rendering it useless. There was still a loaded gun in the vicinity and Dawson couldn't risk Runner getting to it first.

Reaching back, Dawson felt around for his Glock. He knew it was close behind him. He just didn't know how close.

Arching his back, he reached a little farther. Unfortunately, the move gave Runner enough room to break his elbow free. He jabbed it into Dawson's chest, knocking the air from his lungs.

Well, that just angered him even more.

Dawson bucked as his hand landed on the butt of his weapon. The cold metal felt good in his right hand. He spun around onto his back, bringing Runner with him. The move freed his right hand to bring the Glock up to Runner's temple.

"Go ahead. Make another move. Flinch the wrong way

and this is all over. I'll put a bullet through your skull."
The last thing Dawson wanted was to give this guy the
easy way out with death.

"Don't do that." Runner grunted, his muscles stiffen-
ing. "I can explain this whole mix-up."

Mix-up? Dawson grunted.

Runner, whoever the hell he was, needed to serve his
time and spend the rest of his freakin' life locked behind
bars. It was the only way to bring justice to Cheryl, Autumn and their families.

Despite what Summer had said, Autumn had family.
She'd had her sister and no O'Connor would've turned
their back on her. She'd become part of the family, a rare
club that took care of its own. Her legacy was complicated, but that didn't mean she didn't have family.

Tying this bastard to the crimes was another story
altogether. A slick guy like this would lawyer up. Running away from a crime scene wasn't exactly the same
as murder.

"Roll over onto your stomach and keep your hands
where I can see them at all times," Dawson instructed.

Runner did.

"Hands behind your back." Gun trained to Runner's
temple, Dawson rolled onto his side and then he sat up
on his knees.

He was winded, but that didn't stop him from pulling
zip cuffs from his back pocket and tying up Runner's
hands. He patted the man down next and felt in his pocket
for a wallet or some form of ID. There were no other
weapons. All Runner had on him was a money clip with
close to a thousand dollars in mostly hundred-dollar bills.

It figured there'd be no ID. If Dawson had to guess
there wouldn't be anything tying the SUV back to this

guy, either. He was smooth. This had been well thought out. And it might've worked against a civilian.

"What's your name, sir?" Dawson knew to dot every i and cross every t when it came to this guy. There was no way he was making a mistake that could cost the case.

When Runner didn't answer, Dawson identified himself one more time as law enforcement before Mirandizing him.

Chapter Twenty-One

Backup arrived.

Dawson had never been so happy to see fellow law enforcement officers. And they came running. A pair who looked opposite in every way possible came bolting toward him and Runner.

"Marshal O'Connor, sir, I'd be honored to help you with this suspect," the first one said. He was on the short side. Dawson would guess him to be in his early twenties. What he lacked in height he made up for in brawn. He had the body of a world-class gymnast. His nameplate read Smith.

"Be my guest." Dawson moved back enough to lean the back of his head on the nearest building to try to catch his breath. Every place he'd been kicked, punched or jabbed was waking up, making its presence known, bringing all kinds of pain to the forefront. He couldn't focus on any of that right now. "I had to leave behind my…" Words failed him on exactly how to describe his relationship to Summer. He decided on, "Girlfriend and an office worker at an apartment complex. One of them was shot and I don't know how bad the injury is. Do you—"

The second officer, Jenkins, was tall with dark skin and a mustache. He was nodding his head. "We've been following along on the radio. One of the victims was taken to the hospital by ambulance, the GSW. The other is giving her statement to a colleague, Officer Williams."

"Is there a way I can talk to her?" Dawson needed to hear Summer's voice. For reasons he couldn't explain, he needed to know she was all right. *Hells bells, O'Connor.* The reason was obvious. He loved her. He wanted to know she was all right because the thought of losing her knocked him in the chest so hard he couldn't breathe.

"I can call Officer Williams," Jenkins offered.

Dawson nodded.

"What's your name, sir?" Officer Smith asked Runner.

Apparently, the guy was invoking his right to remain silent.

"He didn't talk for me, either," Dawson said as he watched Jenkins make the call.

When the officer turned the phone over, Dawson immediately listened for Summer's voice.

"Dawson, are you there?" Her voice was like velvet.

"I'm here." He took a second to breathe as relief flooded him. Hearing her voice set things right inside him that he didn't realize had been broken. "I heard Marcy's on her way to the hospital."

"She looked pretty bad, Dawson. There was so much blood and then the skinny guy from—"

"Hold on a second. What skinny guy?" All his internal alarm bells sounded. The thought he'd left them alone and vulnerable tightened the knot in his gut. And then it dawned on him who she was talking about. The two guys who'd chased her were nicknamed Scrappy and Thick Guy. "The one from a few days ago?"

"Yes—"

"Are you hurt?" Fire raged through him at the thought.

"No. I'm okay. A couple of bumps and bruises, a

bloody nose… I'm just worried about Marcy. She lost a lot of blood."

"I'll pick you up as soon as I'm cleared here. Did they say which hospital she was going to?" he asked.

"No. I forgot to ask. The EMTs got going with her really fast. She was so pale," she said, and he heard the worry in her voice.

"I can find out. I'm on my way to my vehicle right now." He pushed up to standing. "I'll see if an officer can stay with you until I get there."

"Okay." There was hesitation in her voice. This wasn't the right time to tell her how he felt about her. Not while Marcy was in a hospital fighting for her life. "Dawson…"

"Yeah?"

"I—uh…never mind. I guess I'll see you in a few minutes," she said. He needed to ask what that was all about but everything could wait until they got a status update on Marcy.

Plus, he needed to get to her. He needed to hold her in his arms. He needed to be her comfort.

And he hoped like hell she needed the same from him.

"I'll be there as fast as I can." Dawson had caught his breath and his truck was in good shape. He could jog back to his ride and get to her inside of fifteen to twenty minutes if the roads were clear.

"I'll see you soon." Summer ended the call.

Dawson turned to Officers Jenkins and Smith. "Can you guys handle this from here? I need to pick up my… *someone* and get her to the hospital to check on our friend. I'll be there for a little while if you want to swing by for my statement. Or, I can come down to the station."

Jenkins was already shaking his head.

"No, sir. You go take care of your *friend*. We got this suspect from here."

"Thank you." He'd never meant those pair of words more. He took off back toward his truck and started feeling the effects of the fight with Runner.

This guy refused to identify himself. He carried no ID. One look at him said he had plenty of money to smooth over any bumps in the road.

The fact the evidence against him was all circumstantial burned Dawson's gut. A sympathetic jury pool would acquit in a heartbeat. If the runner was powerful enough to have a detective leave her job and someone killed in county lockup, he could find a way out of this.

Dawson made it to his vehicle, thankfully right where he left it. He fished keys out of his pocket and slid into the driver's seat. He navigated back onto the road and backtracked using his GPS.

His pulse galloped the entire ride back to the apartment complex. He pulled up to the scene where a female officer stood outside her squad car, arms folded as she talked to Summer.

The second Summer locked gazes with him, she started toward him. He didn't bother parking, he just stopped in the middle of the lot. He wasn't concerned about turning off his truck, either.

All he wanted was to feel Summer in his arms where she belonged. Dawson had never felt home in another person before Summer.

And the world righted itself for just a moment when she buried her face in his chest. He looped his arms around her and she pressed her body flush with his.

This was what love was supposed to be. Not obligation. It was supposed to feel like this, like he didn't want to spend another day without her in his arms.

Even though she'd ran straight to him and held on to

him like there would be no tomorrow, he had no idea if she needed a friend or if she needed him. Big difference.

Dawson would take whatever she was willing to give. But first, they had to get to the hospital and check on Marcy.

Officer Williams walked over and introduced herself. Dawson thanked her for staying with Summer.

"You're welcome, sir. It's a pleasure to meet you." Officer Williams had stars in her eyes when she looked at him. Other departments gave him a healthy amount of respect and he appreciated them for it. His division prided themselves on cooperating with other agencies and it had bought them a helluva lot of good will over the years.

"Take care," he said as he walked with Summer to the truck. She climbed in on the driver's side and scooted to the middle of the bench seat. She seemed to need physical contact as much as he did. He hoped that was a good sign.

He also had bad news to deliver but that could wait until they checked on Marcy.

THE HOSPITAL WAS a ten-minute drive that took twenty in traffic. Summer sat scooted up against Dawson, thigh to thigh. Her heart had fisted when she'd seen his face and then relief flooded her that they were both alive.

"I just realized something. We don't even know Marcy's last name," she said to Dawson.

He gripped the steering wheel as he navigated through the heavy traffic. "I can get us past the lobby with my badge. I'm guessing there aren't a whole lot of GSWs in the middle of the day at the hospital."

"GSW?" She had no clue what that meant.

"Gunshot wound." His reply was low and reverent.

"Oh." Those weren't exactly her favorite words to hear right now. Seeing the scared look on Marcy's face would haunt Summer long after this ordeal was over. She leaned into Dawson, drawing as much strength from him as she could. Her body started shaking and she imagined it was because her adrenaline finally wore off.

Exhaustion hit like a motorcycle going a hundred miles an hour and then slamming into a wall.

Dawson pulled into the ER bay and parked. He threw his shoulder into the door to open it and grunted. She realized he must've taken a few blows. His face was perfect unlike hers. Officer Williams had given Summer a few wipes while they waited for Dawson.

Summer was able to wipe off the blood, but her busted lip couldn't be cleaned so easily. That was sticking around.

He opened the door before helping her step out of the truck. As soon as her shoes hit concrete, he blew out a breath and then kissed her. His lips were gentle on hers but that didn't mean there wasn't a sizzle below the surface.

He locked gazes, holding for just a few seconds before linking their fingers together and heading inside the ER.

With his free hand, he pulled out his wallet and flashed his badge. "You had a GSW come in during the last hour via ambulance."

The nurse at the intake station was already nodding her head. "There's a waiting room through those doors, all the way down the hall and to the left. I'll update the file to let the doctor know you're waiting."

"Thank you," was all Dawson said before heading down the hall.

The waiting room was small. There were only about a dozen chairs. Everything was blue. The chairs, the carpet, the curtains. The wallpaper had hints of blue. None of which mattered because all she cared about was Marcy being well cared for.

There was coffee. She and Dawson seemed to notice it at the same time because they both made a move in that direction.

He poured two cups and handed one over. She took a few sips, welcoming the burn on her throat.

"Do you want to sit or stand?" he asked.

"I'm not sure my legs can hold me up much longer." She wasn't kidding. The past few days had caught up to her and she could barely stand. She also glanced down at her shirt and realized she must be a sight.

A nurse stepped inside the room and identified herself as Ramona. She was late thirties, with kind eyes and a round face.

"I brought you something to change into if you'd like," she said to Summer, holding out a shirt that looked like scrubs.

"Thank you." Summer took the offering and hit the bathroom. She washed off more of the blood and splashed cold water on her face.

"She's in surgery but the outlook is good," Dawson said as soon as Summer returned. Ramona had already left.

"That's great news." Summer reclaimed her seat and took another sip of coffee, anything to wake her up.

He nodded. Then said, "There's not so good news about the case."

Dawson's serious expression sent a wave of panic rippling through her.

"What is it?" Bad news only got worse with age.

He explained the situation with the guy he called Runner, and her heart literally sank.

"Marcy can ID him. He came to the apartment complex to go through my sister's personal belongings," she said.

"Won't make a difference. It's all circumstantial evidence. We don't have anything directly linking this guy to the murders. Our Runner did try to kill a US marshal and that should be enough to jail him for a long time. And Scrappy tried to kill Marcy and Summer. The police officers in the shed are witnesses, as well." There was so much frustration in his voice. "With a good lawyer, he could get out of jail in a few hours."

"Even though he shot at a US marshal?"

"Trust me, an expensive lawyer could create doubt." Dawson issued a sharp sigh. "That's how the legal system works."

"Well, that's messed up."

"At times, it is. Most of the time, though, it works. That's why I still do this job," he explained.

"We need proof that he's tied to my sister or Cheryl." She sat up straighter and took another sip of coffee. It was strong and black.

"I'd hoped we would find something in your sister's personal effects."

"But he got there first." Of course, he had. The bastard.

Chapter Twenty-Two

Summer felt around in her handbag, needing to feel the necklace in her fingers and some connection to Autumn. A thought came to her. “My sister would’ve known him well enough to realize he’d go through her stuff at the apartment complex.”

She pulled out the necklace and stared at it for a long moment.

Dawson’s cell buzzed. He fished it out of his pocket and stood up. “This is Dawson O’Connor.”

He paused for a long moment before saying a few uh-huhs into the phone. He thanked the caller and then ended the call. “The runner’s name is Mateus Hank.”

“Sounds a lot like Matt Shank.” The wheels started spinning in Summer’s head. “She left clues, Dawson. She wanted us to figure this out.”

The cold metal warmed in her hand and she traced the letters with her index finger. Holding the necklace in her hand gave her an idea.

“What if she wasn’t protecting me? What if my sister tucked this inside the box as a clue?” There was no need for coffee now with the way her mind clicked through theories.

"It's possible." He nodded. "But where does the clue lead?"

"I don't know yet. My first thought is the place where we bought these. The fairgrounds." She flattened out her palm and looked at the dull piece of metal. "I can't let that bastard walk away scot-free."

"Agreed."

The door to the waiting room opened and a man in scrubs walked inside. He was average height with a runner's build and a full head of gray hair. "Good afternoon, my name is Dr. Warner."

Dawson stood and Summer followed suit. Each shook the doctor's hand.

"Your witness is doing well. She's out of surgery now and did great." He went through the procedure using medical jargon that Summer couldn't understand if she'd tried. But she got the gist of what he was saying.

"We gave her a transfusion because she lost a lot of blood. All in all, we're expecting a full recovery. She'll be resting for a little while. We're keeping a close eye on her. No visitors for the next few hours until she gets out of ICU." He put a hand up to reassure them. "Out of an abundance of caution."

Dawson thanked the doctor. He reassured them, once again, that Marcy was expected to make a full recovery.

"I wish she had family here waiting for her," Summer said after he left.

"Her parents are being notified. I'm sure they'll be here soon." He walked over to where they'd been seated and drained his coffee cup. "We have a couple of hours. Are you ready to hit the fairgrounds?"

"I'm ready to find evidence that will nail that bastard to the wall."

"That's my girl." Dawson seemed to catch himself on

those last words. Her heart performed a little flip at the term of endearment.

She walked over to him and pressed up on her tiptoes. He met her halfway and their lips touched so gently it robbed her breath.

This time, she linked their fingers.

WALKING ONTO THE empty fairgrounds brought on a rush of memories. The smell of funnel cake. Livestock. The bright lights and all those carnival rides.

Autumn's favorite had been the Tilt-A-Whirl. Nothing said the fair like strapping themselves into a ride that spun so fast and hard they almost tossed up their candy apples.

Cotton candy. Autumn couldn't get enough of it. She was terrible at games but never passed one she didn't think she could win anyway. Her seven-year losing streak was always on the verge of being over, according to Autumn.

The fair was the one place they'd gone every year without fail. They laughed and played. They would feed llamas and pet baby pigs. For that one day, they weren't poor or hungry.

Tears welled at the memories.

Walking hand in hand, she led him to where she remembered the necklace booth to have been. There wasn't much there now but a patch of grass. She looked around for a hiding place.

There was a light pole with a metal plate screwed onto the base. "Maybe in there, Dawson."

He'd brought a pair of gloves and a paper bag that he'd explained was used for collecting evidence. He'd grabbed a few other items that he explained were useful. Things like tongs.

Dawson moved over to the light pole and took a knee. He examined the plate. "There's a screw missing."

Her heart leaped in her throat at the possibility of this hunch panning out.

"It's loose." He jiggled the plate.

Chill bumps ran the length of her arms. Experience had taught her not to get too excited before she had something concrete but this was promising.

Somewhere deep in her gut, she knew that if her twin hid something anywhere that it would be here. She prayed someone else hadn't gotten to the evidence first.

Dawson snapped a few pictures of the plate from different angles. He pulled a screwdriver from his pack and went to work loosening the screws. He set the plate down carefully and shone a light inside the six-by-four-inch opening.

A small smile crept across his lips. Summer knew. There was something inside.

Using the tongs, he pulled out a freezer bag through the opening. He set it down and then checked for more. A second freezer bag came and then a third.

One of the bags contained what looked like a journal. It was labeled My Story.

The second bag was labeled Cheryl. It contained some type of bloody clothing along with pictures that had been taken of her after she'd been strangled.

In the final bag, there were pictures with labels on the backs.

Dawson flipped over the bag with the journal in it. There was a folded-up sheet of paper tucked in the back with Summer's name on it. He opened the bag carefully and, using the tongs, pulled out the note.

He set it down on the grass and smoothed it out for her to read.

Summer,

this is bad. I've gotten myself involved with a bad person and I don't know how to get out without him hurting the people I love. He's powerful and rich. And I just found evidence that he killed his last girlfriend, Cheryl. I put it in the bag with her name on it. I think he knows I've figured him out. He's been threatening to dig into my past and find all the dirt if the cops show. He's been to parties at the governor's house. He took me as his date. He can cover up anything he wants. His name is Mateus Hank and he's the CEO of some bank. Anyway, I think he has politicians in his pocket.

I can't risk him finding you. So, I have to figure something else out. I wish I could tell you about all this. But, knowing you, you'd just come here and get yourself in the same hot water I'm in.

I tried to get out with Dawson O'Connor. I thought he could keep me safe and I cared about him. No one can hide from Mateus for long. He knows too many people and I saw one of his friends at the O'Connor ranch. I knew then I had to get away from there or risk him getting hurt.

I have a lot of regrets, sis. I thought I could come back to Austin and handle Mateus. He says he loves me but it's not the good kind. Anyway, I have to go. Love you more than words.

Tears streamed down Summer's face as she read the note from her sister.

"Now we know. She said it herself. She collected evidence against him and probably threatened him. He knew she had something but he didn't know where," Summer surmised.

"He kills her and then you show up. He knows you are trouble for him so he hires thugs to take care of you," Dawson said. He glanced at the plastic bags. "These are proof. This is all we need to link him to the murders."

Summer took the necklace out of her purse and held on to it. Her sister had been protecting her all along.

AN HOUR HAD passed by the time the last officer had left the fairground. Summer looked up at Dawson as he walked over to her and pulled her into an embrace.

"Where do we go from here?" She realized this was the end of the road for them. There would be justice for Autumn and Cheryl. Her sister was gone. There was no reason to stick around Texas, except that she'd never felt more at home than since she'd been back.

"Look into corruption at Austin P.D. for one," he said. "Make sure the evidence is handled properly and justice is served."

"Agreed."

"I don't make rash decisions." Dawson looked into her eyes and her heart fluttered like a dozen butterflies were trapped inside her chest.

"Good. Neither do I."

"So, I've given this a lot of thought. Over the past few days, we've had a crash course in getting to know each other. I feel like we skipped over all the formalities and dove straight in with both feet. I got to know the *real* you."

She nodded. About the only thing she was certain of was that she didn't want to walk away.

"I have to caution you right there, Dawson. This is my heart we're talking about and I don't normally *do* trust. But the thought of things ending right here—"

"Who said anything about ending what we have?"

"Weren't you about to?" Her heart really worked overtime now.

"No. I was about to ask you to stay. I haven't done a great job of expressing it but I'm in love with you, Summer Grayson. I've never been in love with anyone before you and I promise to love you for the rest of my life if you'll have me." He got down on one knee. "So, I'm asking you to stay. I'm asking you to consider making what we have permanent and official because I don't want to spend another day without you in my life."

Happy tears rolled down her cheeks now.

"I love you, Dawson O'Connor. You're my family and the only home I've ever known. Of course, I'll stay. And I'll spend every day of the rest of my life loving you."

Summer pressed a kiss to Dawson's lips, tender but with the promise of passion. He pulled back enough to smile at her and her heart took another hit. She could look into those eyes forever.

"My beautiful Summer," he said against her mouth. "Let's check on Marcy and then go home."

Summer couldn't think of a better plan. She'd found home. And she was ready to get started on forever.

* * * * *

COMING SOON!

We really hope you enjoyed reading this book. If you're looking for more romance, be sure to head to the shops when new books are available on

Thursday 12th November

To see which titles are coming soon, please visit

millsandboon.co.uk/nextmonth

MILLS & BOON

LET'S TALK
Romance

For exclusive extracts, competitions
and special offers, find us online:

f facebook.com/millsandboon

🐦 @MillsandBoon

📷 @MillsandBoonUK

Get in touch on 01413 063232

For all the latest titles coming soon, visit
millsandboon.co.uk/nextmonth

MILLS & BOON
A ROMANCE FOR EVERY READER

- **FREE** delivery direct to your door

- **EXCLUSIVE** offers every month

- **SAVE** up to 25% on pre-paid subscriptions

SUBSCRIBE AND SAVE

millsandboon.co.uk/Subscribe

JOIN US ON SOCIAL MEDIA!

Stay up to date with our latest releases, author news and gossip, special offers and discounts, and all the behind-the-scenes action from Mills & Boon...

 millsandboon

 millsandboonuk

 millsandboon

It might just be true love...

MILLS & BOON

HISTORICAL

Awaken the romance of the past

Escape with historical heroes from time gone by. Whether your passion is for wicked Regency Rakes, muscled Viking warriors or rugged Highlanders, indulge your fantasies and awaken the romance of the past.

Six Historical stories published every month, find them all at

millsandboon.co.uk/Historical

MILLS & BOON
MODERN
Power and Passion

Prepare to be swept off your feet by sophisticated, sexy and seductive heroes, in some of the world's most glamourous and romantic locations, where power and passion collide.

Sensual love stories featuring smart, sassy heroines you'd want as a best friend, and compelling intense heroes who are worthy of them.

MILLS & BOON
True Love

Romance from the Heart

Celebrate true love with tender stories of
heartfelt romance, from the rush of falling
in love to the joy a new baby can bring,
and a focus on the emotional
heart of a relationship.

MILLS & BOON
MEDICAL
Pulse-Racing Passion

Set your pulse racing with dedicated, delectable doctors in the high-pressure world of medicine, where emotions run high and passion, comfort and love are the best medicine.